PACK UP
THE MOON

Also by Kristan Higgins and available from Center Point Large Print:

On Second Thought
Now That You Mention It
Good Luck with That
Life and Other Inconveniences
Always the Last to Know

**This Large Print Book carries the
Seal of Approval of N.A.V.H.**

PACK UP THE MOON

a novel

KRISTAN HIGGINS

CENTER POINT LARGE PRINT
THORNDIKE, MAINE

This book is dedicated to
Charlene Marshall.
Warrior. Educator. Badass.

ACKNOWLEDGMENTS

I could not have written this book without the grace, humor and generosity of Charlene Marshall, who shared her IPF journey with me. Thank you, Char. Even though we haven't met in person yet, we're already friends.

My team at Berkley is the very, very best, and wicked fun, too. Thanks to Claire Zion, my funny, wonderful editor, for being my teammate in shaping this book (and for crying when I told you my idea, which let me know I was on the right track). To Craig Burke, Jeanne-Marie Hudson, Erin Galloway, Danielle Keir, Bridget O'Toole, Jin Yu, Anthony Ramundo, and all the folks in editorial, sales, art and marketing who do such a fantastic job getting my books out into the world . . . thank you. It is an absolute joy to work with all of you.

My agent, Maria Carvainis, and her unwavering team—Elizabeth Copps, Martha Guzman and Rose Friel—are the very best in the business, always there to guide and support me.

As always, I made ample use of information available through the Mayo Clinic, the Pulmonary Fibrosis Foundation, the American Lung Association and hundreds of articles on this complex disease. To Peter, Sophie and Richard, thank you for sharing your stories of neurodiversity and autism spectrum disorder, and thanks as well to Autism Speaks for the heaps of information they offer. Any mistakes are mine.

Personal thanks to Jen, who cheered me on, and to Joss, Stacia, Karen and Huntley. Kwana Jackson, Sonali Dev, Susan Elizabeth Phillips, Robyn Carr, Jamie Beck, Xio Axelrod, Kennedy Ryan, Deeanne Gist, Nana Malone, Nancy Robards Thompson, Marie Bostwick . . . the list goes on and on, and my goodness, I am well and truly blessed. Special thanks to LaQuette R. Holmes, M.A. for her brilliant class, The Critical Lens.

To Hilary Higgins Murray, my dearest friend and the absolute best person to be with during a zombie apocalypse or pandemic, thank you for being the perfect sister.

Thanks to my husband, Terence Keenan, for . . . well, for everything, really. To my funny, intelligent, gorgeous children, you are my favorite people on earth. Sitting on the front porch with all of you (including you, Mike-o!) is all I can ever ask for.

Thanks to my sweet dog Willow, who was at my side these past ten years, keeping me company as I wrote, making me smile every single day. See you at the Rainbow Bridge, sweet girl.

Finally, thanks to you, readers. Thank you for the gift and honor of your time.

1

Lauren

*Eight days left
February 14*

Dear Dad,
I'm dying, my husband is going to be a widower, and this has been the most wonderful year of my life.

How's that for surprising?

These past few weeks . . . months . . . I've been feeling things changing. Remember the time we all flew to California and drove home? I think I was ten. I remember being able to feel us getting closer to the East Coast, all those miles behind us, home getting closer, even when we still had hundreds of miles to go. You could feel it. You could tell you were getting close.

That's where I am these days.

But I'm too busy living to dwell on that fact. Like Red says in *The Shawshank Redemption*, get busy living, or get busy dying. I'm going with the first one.

People carry a terminal diagnosis

differently. I wanted to ride on its back like it was a racehorse, Dad. I think I have. I can't say that being sick is the greatest thing that ever happened to me, because I'm not an idiot. But it's an undeniably huge part of my life . . . and I love my life. More than ever.

Writing to you has been a way to keep you in my life after you died, Dad. You've been gone for eight years, but I've always felt you with me. That's what I want to do for Josh. I've been working on my plan, and today, I finished. Kind of fitting that it's our anniversary. Three years. I want to make today great for Josh, make him laugh, make him feel loved to the moon and back, because I don't think we're going to make it to our fourth.

We're so, so lucky. No matter what's coming, no matter how soon.

It's easy to cry and even panic over this stuff. But then I look around and see everything I have, and all that joy . . . it pushes everything else away. It truly does. I've never been so happy in my life.

Thanks for everything, Daddy. I'll see you soon.

Lauren

2

Joshua

February 14

On their third wedding anniversary, Joshua Park came home to Providence, Rhode Island, from a meeting in Boston with a medical device company. They'd bought his design, and he was glad to be done being around people, and very, very glad to go back home to his wife.

He stopped at the florist and picked up the three dozen white roses he'd ordered. This was in addition to the chocolates he'd bought from his wife's favorite place, which he'd hidden carefully; the leather watch; a pair of blue silk pajamas; and two cards, one sappy, one funny. He did not take anniversaries lightly, no sir.

Joshua unlocked the apartment door and found the place dark except for a trail of candles leading down the hall. Pink rose petals had been scattered on the floor. Well, well, well. Guess he wasn't the only one who'd gone to the florist. Pebbles, their dog, was asleep on her back on the sofa.

"Is this your work?" he asked Pebbles. Pebbles wagged her tail but didn't open her eyes.

He took off his shoes and shrugged off his coat,

which was wet from melting sleet. Cradling the huge bouquet, he walked slowly down the hall to the master bedroom, savoring the moment, banishing the worry over knowing she'd gone out in this raw weather. Anticipation fizzed through his veins. The bedroom door was open a crack, and the room flickered with more candlelight. He pushed the door open, a smile spreading slowly across his face.

His wife lay on the bed on her stomach, wearing nothing but a red ribbon around her waist, tied in a bow on the small of her back. Her chin was propped on her hands, her knees bent so that her heels almost touched her very lovely ass.

"Happy Valentine's Day," she said, her voice husky.

"Happy anniversary." He leaned in the doorway and just took in the sight—his wife (the word still gave him a thrill)—her dark red hair loose around her shoulders, her creamy skin glowing in the candlelight.

"Guess what I got you," she said.

"I have no idea."

"It starts with 'sexy' and ends with 'time.'"

"Just what I wanted." He loosened his tie. "You're not too tired?" he asked.

"Do I look tired? Or do I look like someone who's about to get shagged silly?"

He laughed. "Definitely the latter." He went to their bed, knelt down and kissed her with all the love, gratitude, lust and happiness in his heart.

"You taste like chocolate," he said, pulling back a little. "Shame on you."

"Is it my fault you left me alone in the house with Fran's salted caramels?" she asked. "I think we both knew what would happen."

"Those were hidden."

"Not very well. In a shoebox in a suitcase on the top shelf of the closet? Please. You're such an amateur."

"You have a nose like a bloodhound."

"Yes, yes, talk dirty to me," she said, laughing. "Come on. Unwrap your present and make love to your wife."

"Yes, ma'am," he said, and he did, sliding his hands over her silky skin. God, he loved being married. He loved Lauren, loved this room and this bed and the fact that she'd go to the effort of lighting candles and scattering rose petals and undressing and finding a red ribbon. Her skin smelled like almonds and oranges from her shower gel. She'd painted her toenails red. All for him.

"I'm the luckiest guy in the world," he whispered against her neck.

"Ditto. Except woman," she said, and she started laughing, and when they kissed again, they were both smiling.

In love wasn't a phrase. It was how they lived, wrapped in the warm, soft blanket of mutual adoration, and in this moment, on this evening, nothing else mattered. They were untouchable, golden, immortal. He would love her the rest of his life, and he knew, with absolute certainty, that she would love him the rest of hers.

However long or short a time that would be.

3

Joshua

Twelve days later
February 26

Was it weird to look for your wife at her funeral?

But he was. He kept glancing around for Lauren, waiting for her to come in and tell him what to say to all these people, what to do during this service. Where to put his hands. How to hug back.

She would know. That was the problem. She *knew* all about these things—people, for example. How to act out in the world. At her wake last night, she would've told him what to say as her friends cried and held on to his hand and hugged him, making him uncomfortable and stiff and sweaty. Classic spectrum problem. He didn't like crowds. Didn't want to hug anyone except his wife. Who was dead.

She would've told him what to wear today. As it was, he was wearing the one suit he owned. The same one he'd worn to propose to her, the same one he wore to their wedding three years ago. Was it a horrible thing to wear your wedding suit to your wife's funeral? Should he have gone with a different tie? Was this suit bringing shit up for her mother and sister?

This pew was hard as granite. He hated wooden chairs. Pews. Whatever.

Donna, Lauren's mother, sobbed. The sound echoed through the church. Same church where Josh and Lauren had gotten married. If they'd had kids, would they have baptized them here? Josh was pretty much an atheist, but if Lauren had wanted church as a part of their life, he'd go along with it.

Except she was dead.

It had been four days. One hundred and twelve hours and twenty-three minutes since Lauren died, give or take some seconds. The longest time of his life, and also like five seconds ago.

Lauren's sister, Jen, was giving the eulogy. It was probably a good eulogy, because people laughed here, cried there. Josh himself couldn't quite make out the words. He stared at his hands. When Lauren had put his wedding ring on his finger at their wedding, he couldn't stop looking at it. His hand looked complete with that ring on. Just a plain gold band, but it said something about him. Something good and substantial. He wasn't just a man . . . he was a husband.

Rather, he *had been* a husband. Now he was a widower. Utterly useless.

16

So much for being a biomedical engineer with numerous degrees and a reputation in health-care technology. He'd had two years and one month to find a cure for idiopathic pulmonary fibrosis, a disease that slowly filled the lungs with scar tissue, choking off the healthy parts for breathing. He had failed. Not that a cure was easy, or someone would've done it before. The only devices on the market were designed to push air into lungs, work chest muscles or clear mucus, and those weren't Lauren's problems.

He hadn't figured it out. He hadn't created something or found a drug trial that would kill off those fucking fibers and scars. Since the day of her diagnosis, he'd devoted himself to finding something that would save his wife. Not just slow the disease down—they had those meds, she'd been on them, plus two experimental drugs, plus the Chinese herbs and traditional medicine, plus an organic diet with no red meat.

No. Josh's job had been to find—or make—something that would *cure* her. Restore her. Keep her.

He had not done so.

A large picture of her was placed on the altar. It had been taken on their trip to Paris just before Christmas that first year they were married. Before they knew. Her red hair blew back from her face, and her smile was so full of fun and love and joy. He stared at that picture now, still stunned that he got to marry her. She was way out of his league.

The first time they'd met, he'd insulted her.

Thank *God* he'd gotten another chance. Not that God existed. Otherwise, she'd still be alive. Who the hell took someone like her at age twenty-eight? A merciful God? Fuck that.

It didn't seem possible that she was gone forever. No. It seemed like Lauren, who had enjoyed childlike tricks such as hiding in the shower and jumping out at him as he brushed his teeth, could pull off the biggest trick of all—jump out from behind the altar and say, "Boo! Just kidding, babe!" then laugh and hug him and tell him she was just testing him these past few years. She'd never been sick at all.

Then again, she'd already been cremated.

Apparently, Jen was done, because she came down from the altar of the church and stood before him.

"Thank you, Jen," he said woodenly. His mother, sitting beside him, gave him a nudge, and he stood up and hugged his sister-in-law. Former sister-in-law? That didn't seem fair. He *liked* being related to Jen and her husband, Darius, not to mention their two kids. He even almost liked Donna, his mother-in-law, who, after a shitty start, had been great at the end there. When Lauren was actively dying.

Now, his wife was ashes inside a baggie in a

metal container. He was waiting for the special urn to arrive from California, at which point he would mix her with an organic soil mix. He'd plant a tree in the bamboo urn, and Lauren would become a dogwood tree. Cemeteries were unsustainable, if beautiful, she'd said. "Besides, who wouldn't want to be a tree? Better than compost."

He could almost hear her voice.

Everyone began filing out of the church. Josh waited, being at the front of the church. His mom slid her arm through his. "Hang in there, honey," she whispered. He nodded. They both watched as Ben and Sumi Kim, his mother's best friends and next-door neighbors, went to the altar and stood in front of Lauren's picture. Ben bowed from the waist, then knelt on the floor and pressed his forehead to it, then rose and bowed again while Sumi sobbed gently.

Josh had to cover his eyes for a minute at the reverence, the heartache in that gesture. Lauren had loved the Kims, who were essentially Josh's second parents. Ben was the closest thing to a father he'd ever had. Of course Lauren loved them. She loved most people, and they all loved her right back.

The Kims came over, hugged him. Josh stood there with the three adults who'd raised him, all helpless now in the face of his loss.

No one could help him.

"You'll get through this, son," Ben said,

looking him in the eye. "I know it seems like you won't, but you will."

Josh nodded. Ben wasn't the type to lie. Ben gripped his shoulders and nodded back. "You're not alone in this, Josh."

Well. That was a nice thought, but of course he was alone. His wife was dead.

"Shall we head out, then?" the older man asked. Like his mother, Ben was good at giving Josh the cues he often needed in social situations. Not as good as Lauren, though.

Panic flashed painfully through his joints. What was he going to do without her?

"Let's go, honey," his mom said.

Right. He hadn't answered. "Okay," he said. It felt wrong, somehow, leaving the church. Ending the funeral.

There was a lunch after the service. So many flowers, despite Lauren's wish that in lieu of, there'd be donations for the Hope Center, her favorite place in Providence, her hometown. Her workmates from Pearl Churchwell Harris, the architectural firm where she'd worked as a public space designer, were all here—Bruce, who'd been such a great boss to Lauren, crying as if he'd lost his own child. Santino and Louise, who'd gone on walks with Lauren to keep her lung capacity up. That shitty Lori Cantore, who'd asked if she could have Lauren's office *two years ago*. Such a vulture, coming to the funeral when she'd been a pill in real life. He imagined grabbing her scrawny arm and dragging her out, but he didn't want to make her the center of attention. This was Lauren's funeral, after all.

And there were so many of Lauren's friends—Asmaa from the community center; Sarah, her best friend from childhood; Mara from Rhode Island School of Design; Creepy Charlotte, the single woman who lived on the first floor of their building, and, Josh was almost sure, had been making a play for him since they'd met, wife or no wife. People from Lauren's childhood, high school and college, teachers, classmates, the principal of Lauren's grammar school.

Some people even came for Josh, having read Lauren's obituary. Not exactly his friends . . . he didn't have many of those. Lauren had been his friend. His best friend. Her family had welcomed him, but he was really just a phantom limb at this point. An amputation without her.

A short, stout woman with steel-gray curls came up to him. "I'm sorry for your loss," she said. Her voice was familiar. He glanced at his mother, who gave a small shrug.

"Uh . . . how did you know Lauren?" he asked.

"I don't. I work for you. I'm Cookie Goldberg. Your virtual assistant."

"Oh! Hi. Uh . . . right." Cookie lived in New York. Long Island. They'd never met face-to-face, though he'd seen her on Zoom and Skype often enough.

"Yeah, well, I'm . . . shit. I'm so sorry for you, Joshua. My heart is breaking for you." Her raspy voice cracked, and she looked a little shocked at her own words. "Okay. I got a long drive home. Call me if you need anything."

She turned and left.

"She works for you, but you didn't recognize her? You only have one employee, Josh," his mother chided gently.

"She's out of context," he said, sitting back down.

He didn't eat, or maybe he did. Darius, Jen's husband, got him a glass of wine, forgetting that Josh didn't drink. Eventually, Josh got to hold Octavia. Was she still his niece? He was her dead aunt's widowed husband. Did he still get to claim her and Sebastian? Was he still Uncle Josh?

Sebastian, age four, wailed, inconsolable despite Darius's best efforts. The kid was just old enough to understand Auntie Lauren was never coming back. Josh envied him. No stiff upper lip there. He was crying the way Josh wanted to: unfettered, anguished, horrified.

"Call if you need anything," said Creepy Charlotte, her pale blue eyes eerie. She handed him a piece of paper. Her phone number, he assumed. As she moved in to hug him, Josh stuck out his hand at the same time. Awkward. Lauren would've fixed it so it would've been funny, but it stayed awkward. Charlotte lifted an eyebrow, but Josh wasn't sure how to interpret that. He took the paper and put it in his pocket, then sat back down, but the paper rankled. It felt like betrayal, so he wadded it up and tossed it under the table with a silent apology to the cleaning staff. *Those people,* he pictured them saying. *Throwing trash on the ground like animals.*

He bent over and looked for it. "What are you doing?" his mother hissed.

"Stephanie," he heard a woman say. "I'm *so* sorry! She was a lovely girl. Um . . . where's Joshua?"

The wad was just out of reach. He stretched, heard his chair fall over behind him, grabbed the paper and stood up. Righted the chair. "Hi," he said to his mother's friend.

"Joshua, you remember Nina, right? From the lab?"

His mother had worked at Rhode Island Hospital's lab for thirty years. He didn't remember this woman. "Yes," he lied, shaking her hand.

She pulled him in for a hug, and he winced. "So sorry for your loss, honey," she said.

"Thank you." He stood there another minute, then turned and went to the bathroom to throw out the paper. He didn't want Creepy Charlotte's number, or anyone's number. He just wanted his wife not to be dead.

The face in the mirror was nearly unrecognizable. He lifted his hand to make sure he was really there. This had to be a dream, right? Groping under a table for a piece of paper, all these people he didn't quite know . . . next thing would be he wouldn't have any clothes on, and then he'd wake up next to his wife. He'd hold her close and breathe in the smell of her hair and she'd smile without opening her eyes.

But he was still in the bathroom, looking at the face in the mirror.

Sarah, Lauren's best friend, was waiting for him when he came out. "You okay?"

"No."

"Me neither." Her eyes were wet. She took his hand and squeezed it. "This is a fucking nightmare."

"Yep."

"Did you eat anything?"

"Yes," he said, though he couldn't remember.

Sarah walked him back to his table. People spoke to him. Some of them cried.

Josh stared at the table. He may have responded to the people who talked to him. It didn't really matter, though, did it?

Sometime later, Darius drove him home to the old mill building turned condos. "Want me to come in, buddy?" he asked in the parking lot.

"No, no. I . . . I think I want to be alone."

"Got it. Listen, Josh, I'm here for you, okay?

24

Anytime, night or day. We married sisters. We're family forever. Brothers."

Josh nodded. Darius was very tall and had rich brown skin, so Josh doubted anyone would mistake them for brothers, but it was a nice thought. "Thanks, Darius."

"This really sucks, man." His voice broke. "I'm so sorry. She was . . . she was a peach."

"Yes."

"I'll text you tomorrow. Try to get some sleep, okay?"

"Yes. Thank you."

He went up the stairs, his legs heavy. For the past six days, he'd been staying at his mom's house, glad for the familiar comfort of his childhood home, the smells and furniture. Lauren, whose own mother was a bit of a drama queen, had welcomed his mother's calm ways, understood her devotion to her only child, admired Stephanie for raising him alone. Lauren was more than a daughter-in-law to his mom; she was the daughter Stephanie never had.

Had been. She had been.

Jesus. He had to change tenses now. He unlocked the apartment door and went inside. He hadn't been here since Lauren was hospitalized . . . when was that? Six days ago? Eight? A lifetime.

The island lights shone gently, and the lamp by the reading chair was on low. Someone had been here. The place was immaculate. The pillows were plumped on the couch, pillows Lauren had bought. A bouquet of yellow tulips sat on the kitchen island, smack in the middle, obscenely cheerful. The blankets that Lauren had used, since she was always cold, were folded, one draped over the back of the couch.

It was so quiet.

Pebbles, their goofy Australian shepherd mutt, had been staying with Jen since Lauren's hospitalization; Josh had forgotten to ask for her back. Well. Another day wouldn't matter.

Josh went into the bedroom. Lauren's medical stuff—her at-home oxygen, her percussion vest—was gone. Josh had agreed to that, he remembered vaguely. Donate the stuff to someone in need or something. The pill bottles that had sat on her night table, the Vicks VapoRub . . . those were gone, too.

Idiopathic pulmonary fibrosis. Twelve syllables of doom. A disease for which there was no cure. A disease that usually hit older people but, occasionally, chose a young person to invade. A disease that had a life expectancy of three to five years.

Lauren had gotten the shorter end of that.

Their bed was made perfectly, same as Lauren used to make it, before the small task took too much out of her. He always tried to make it as precisely as she did and never quite managed, something that made her smile. The cute, useless little flowered pillows were in place.

It was as if she'd just been here.

Josh grabbed some jeans and an MIT sweatshirt and changed into them. In the kitchen, he pulled the tulips out of their vase and threw them in the trash, then dumped the water and tossed the vase in the recycling bin. He gathered up his suit, shirt, socks, even his boxers, and carried them up to the rooftop garden that had come with this apartment. For once, he didn't think about how much he hated heights. The bite of cold, damp air was welcome.

A seagull sat on one of the posts of the iron railing that encircled the garden, watching him, its feathers ruffling in the breeze.

He turned on the gas grill, all burners, as high as they'd go.

Then he burned the clothes he'd worn to his wife's funeral, and stood there long after they were ash and the snow began to fall.

4

Lauren

Three months left
November 20

Dear Dad,
How's it going in the Great Beyond? Please tell me you can fly. I'm going to be very disappointed if I can't fly. Also, I'd like to be able to save people. You know those reports where someone says, "I don't know how that truck missed me! I thought I was a goner!"? I'm hoping that's what we get to do, because how cool would that be?

We're back from the Cape, more or less. It gets really quiet up there in the off-season, and I was getting a little melancholy and cold. Walking on the beach isn't as fun if the wind knocks you backward, you know? I mean, it's thrilling, but it's exhausting, too.

Sebastian turned four, Dad! Josh and I gave him the biggest Tonka truck we could find, one that made lots of beeping and grinding noises, and he LOVED it.

Octavia is six months old and has two tiny teeth, sharper than razor blades, but so cute. The drool that spills out of that kid's mouth should be gathered to end drought in small countries. Honestly. I had no idea a human could produce that much drool.

Mom's doing fine. You know. She's wicked sad and doesn't understand the philosophy of "keep on the sunny side." Still, you'll be happy to know I have dinner with her every Tuesday night, just the two of us, because . . . well, because Mom is going to need these times to look back on.

After this summer on the Cape, I took a turn for the worse. It's not awful, but . . . well, the IPF is really undeniable now. I'm on oxygen almost all the time, and I shamelessly nap at work almost every afternoon in the office Bruce set up for me. I work from home a lot, too. To my own credit, I'm not slacking off. I'm leaving my mark, Dad, just like you told me to. But a cold laid me low for two weeks, and I was in the hospital for five days with another lung collapse and mild pneumonia. At least I didn't need intubation this time. Listen. You and Mom shouldn't have skimped on my lungs. You should've sprung for the Usain

Bolt model. These are bargain-basement lungs.

When I was in the hospital, Dr. Bennett mentioned a lung transplant, and I thought Josh might have a heart attack. He had to leave the room and couldn't talk for about an hour once he came back . . . he shuts down when the news isn't great.

The thing is, Dad, once you get a lung transplant, another clock starts ticking. A lung transplant is like . . . well, it's like the three hundred Spartans holding off the Greeks. They're glorious and brave, and you really believe they're gonna win, until they don't. For some reason, lungs don't take as well as other organs. It's not exactly a cure. The Mayo Clinic, whose website is my go-to medical source online, said, "Although some people have lived ten years or more after a lung transplant, only about half the people who undergo the procedure are still alive after five years."

So. I have a 50 percent chance of living five years if I get new lungs. Not great. Scary to think that could be my best option.

These days, I can feel the difference. Josh understands the numbers—spirometry flow, lung volume, pulse oximetry, lung diffusion. He can see when I'm tired, and he takes such good care of me, but I can't say, "How was that phone call to Singapore, hon? By the way, I can't breathe as well today." I know why Josh is obsessed with finding a cure—it seems like there's something that could fix this. I picture the "fibrotic material," as Dr. Bennett calls it, as a tangle of feathery yarn. Pink yarn. Pepto-Bismol pink. Where's the tiny excavator that can get in there and shovel them out and give me my lungs back? A microscopic flamethrower that can burn it out without damaging the good stuff?

I'm so glad I had this spring and summer. I felt better on the Cape, and I got to spend so much time with friends and just looking out at the ocean. There's something about being near the ocean that puts your life in perspective. It's reassuring, that's what it is.

I don't want to focus on being sick, and yet it's a part of every day. I have some tricks up my sleeve, courtesy of pulmonary therapy—hold the air in my lungs, puff it out, repeat. Lots of good visualizations of healthy pink air pockets expanding and contracting. But little things are getting harder, Daddy.

Showering can be exhausting. My lunch-time walks with Santino and Louise at work are getting shorter and shorter. It's embarrassing, which I know is a dumb thing to say. But I'm twenty-eight, and walking around the block wears me out.

I have to have an energy plan for most days—if I shower and shave my legs, I'll need a twenty-minute rest. If I want to see Sebastian and Octavia, I need to take a nap first, and a nap after, and I'll probably be out of commission the next day, too. At work, I plan my bathroom breaks; it's about thirty steps, and if I wait too long and have to hustle, it takes ten minutes to get my breathing back to normal.

It's harder to hold Octavia, and my arms tremble, but I just can't give her up. When I read to Sebastian, I have to look at the words on the page and plan when to breathe, because he gets upset if I run out of air . . . he's too smart, Daddy. He knows I'm sick, and he's scared, and it's awful when he cries, my sweet boy. So I try my best around him. Oh, Dad, you would love him so much! He's an angel. Well, a little demon sometimes, but mostly an angel. I can't resist him. I'm smitten by them both.

So life is changing, and I know it won't be changing back. That's the bastard of IPF—every time I lose a little lung function to the scars and fibers, it's permanent. It sucks, but I don't have time to waste feeling bitter. God! That's the last thing I want to feel. Whenever I get scared, I just look at Josh, or think about how lucky I am that we found each other. Sappy, isn't it? And you know what he thinks, Dad? He thinks he's the lucky one. He really does. He adores me. He loves, honors and cherishes me, just like he promised on our wedding day.

Well, I should go. I love you, Dad. Watch over me, okay? I'm glad you're there. It's not that I didn't love Gangy and Pop-Pop and Grammy and Gramps (please tell them hello from me). It's just that you're my dad, and I know you'll be there for me when the time comes.

Love,
Lauren

Pebbles had learned to fetch the remote, the genius. If Lauren was on the couch, Pebbles was there, too, a ball of silken brown-and-white fur curled up right on Lauren's perpetually cold feet. "What did we do before we had this dog?" Lauren asked Josh.

"You mean back when *I* was the love of your life," he said, grinning as he cooked.

"Were you, though? Or was I just waiting for Pebbles?" she said, and he laughed. Getting him to laugh was akin to medaling in the Olympics, Lauren thought as she stroked Pebbles's head. His kind of intellect didn't have a lot of room for humor, so his laughter . . . the occasional joke, it meant the world. "Right, Pebbles?" she whispered. "You'll need to brush up on your wisecracking, missy."

"Before we eat," he said, turning off the stove, "I got you a present."

"Hooray! Is it a horse?"

"Um . . . no. But it's really fun, and actually, you *can* ride it."

She waited as he went into his study. A second later, he came out, pushing a . . .

A mobility scooter.

Her throat immediately clamped shut. *Don't cry, don't cry, don't cry,* she told herself, but her fists were clenched. She wasn't supposed to need that! She wasn't even thirty! He should've gotten her a damn horse. Or a motorcycle.

He was smiling, but she could see the echo of sadness in his dark eyes. He knew it was an awful present.

And he knew she needed it.

It was fine. It was smart. They could do more because of it.

So she flashed Josh a big smile, and after a second, it became genuine. "That is one damn sexy scooter," she said.

"Please tell me you'll wear leather when you use it."

"Of course! Red leather, I think." She got off the couch and walked around it. Unsurprisingly, it was top of the line and, for a mobility scooter, as sleek as it could be, looking almost like a motorcycle from the front. Which Josh would know would help with the indignity aspect. A surge of love for her husband brought tears to her eyes—and these tears, she would allow. She kissed Josh's neck, then hugged him. "I love it. I'm calling it Godzilla. Every bike needs a name. Come on, let's break it in."

She climbed on it, hit the forward button, then laughed as it lurched. Pebbles leaped and barked, and Lauren turned in a tight circle. "Whee! This is fun, honey! Come on, you try it."

He did. He went down the hall, tried to do a K-turn, got stuck, and the two of them laughed till it hurt.

From then on, it *was* a little easier to take walks and be outside. The reality of needing a scooter was outweighed by the ease of getting around. Sarah came over one night and bedazzled the back of the seat with hearts and gave her an air horn to scare the bejesus out of inconsiderate pedestrians.

Lauren and Josh combed through Providence for places with good paths—Blackstone Boulevard's gravel paths, the Botanical Center at Roger Williams Park, India Point Park, or Providence College's pretty campus. Being outside made Lauren feel less like an invalid, even if she was sucking oxygen and riding a scooter. She'd always loved the cold air (which was also easier to breathe). Godzilla let her spend more time outside, so it was a win. She loved going as fast as possible, then circling back to herd Josh or Jen and the kids, telling them to hurry up. Sebastian loved riding on her lap, and really, why had Lauren ever thought a scooter was an admission of defeat? Godzilla let her be even cooler in the eyes of her nephew, and that was everything.

One evening, with Lauren bundled in a pink wool coat, scarf, hat and mittens, they walked/rolled down Blackstone Boulevard, admiring the gorgeous houses and Christmas decorations. A familiar figure came running at them, blond ponytail swinging. "Sarah!" Lauren cried. "Hey, you!"

"Hey!" Sarah stopped. "How's it going?"

"Great! You look very fit!" Sarah looked like Catwoman, dressed in tight all-black running clothes.

Sarah smiled. "How's Godzilla?"

"Awesome. Want a turn?"

"Yes!"

Lauren climbed off and took her portable oxygen out of Godzilla's basket. "Go for it. I'd love to walk for a little while."

"See you later, losers!" Sarah said, and she waved and went full speed ahead. "This is awesome!" she yelled over her shoulder.

"Now we can walk like normal people," Lauren said, taking Josh's hand.

"Normal people are overrated," he said. "But this is great."

It had been a while since they'd held hands and meandered for no reason. The loveliness of the fall evening settled around them, the smell of wood smoke and crisp leaves, a hint of cold in the air.

"I love this house," Josh said, stopping in front of a sprawling Victorian. The lights were on inside, and the yard was tastefully decorated for the holidays, strands of white fairy lights meticulously twined around a few trees. It looked like a Christmas card, so cozy and posh and welcoming. Lauren suspected her husband had stopped to give her a rest, and she was grateful. *Slow and easy, slow and easy, fill those lungs as much as you can.*

"What kind of house should we get?" she asked.

"Something like this would be nice."

"In the city, though?"

"Wherever you want, honey."

The thought that she wouldn't live long enough to pick out a house flitted through her mind, as fast as a hummingbird, here and gone. "I do like this one," she said. "Or the brick one up here. Very impressive, as my genius husband deserves."

"That's big, all right. We could have ten kids in that house."

"Ten, huh? Spoken like a man. We might have to adopt a few."

"That's fine by me." He kissed her then, and she hugged him close, his mouth so perfect against hers.

"Break it up, lovebirds," came Sarah's voice. "Are you trying to make me jealous?"

"Why don't we have dinner together?" Lauren said. "Us three. And get off Godzilla. He misses me, and if you break him, I'll kill you." The fatigue was heavy tonight, but she didn't want to go home just yet.

They switched places and headed for Declan's, an Irish bar on Hope Street. As they walked ahead of her in the deepening dark, Lauren had a thought. That someday, maybe, Sarah would be holding Josh's hand. That she would be his wife. It would be good to know that Josh had a lovely, caring, smart woman as his second wife . . . someone who had known her and would understand that he

38

would always love Lauren just a teeny bit more.

She rolled her eyes at herself and bumped Godzilla up a little faster. *Not today, Satan. Not today.*

5

Joshua

Three (or four?) weeks after Lauren's funeral
March

For a stream of unmarked days after his wife's funeral, Joshua Park, BFA in industrial engineering (summa cum laude), MS in biomedical design (ditto), and PhD in mechanical engineering, watched TV. Not his usual shows—*The Great British Bake Off* and *Star Trek*, the original series—but cooking shows that involved frantic dashes to the grocery store and making a dish out of rattlesnake and watermelon. Those docudramas about ancient battles. Alaskans looking for gold. People who cleaned hoarders' homes.

He was fine. It was fine. The shows all put him to sleep, which was the point. Numbness settled in around him, and he welcomed it.

He ate. Or he didn't eat. It was one extreme or the other—an entire pizza in one sitting, resulting in his feeling sick for the next twelve hours, or blurry days without food, marked by his phone; he'd set an alarm to feed Pebbles so she wouldn't starve to death. His own intake seemed irrelevant. Back before he'd dated Lauren, and when they were first dating, he'd been like this—unstructured, eating to survive, not to enjoy. It had driven Lauren crazy. By their third date, she was organizing his life.

Let her do it again. Let her come back and get right to work.

He looked around the apartment and was horrified at the mess. Lauren would hate it. She was—had been—a very tidy person, and she would hate seeing their place like this. He was forty-five minutes into cleaning before he realized he was cleaning up for her. In case she came home.

When people called, he said he was doing okay. Getting through it. Hanging in there. But he kept looking at the door, same as Pebbles did. The poor dog did not understand that her owner wasn't coming back. Pebbles used to sleep with them, but Josh couldn't bear the thought of sleeping in the bed he'd shared with his wife. Pebbles and he now slept in the guest room at the end of the hallway.

He didn't want to work. He didn't care what was happening in the world or nation. He powered off his computers and set an automatic response for emails, saying he was taking some time off after a death in the family.

Jen, Darius and the kids had come over the day after the funeral to return Pebbles. Little

Sebastian had run around the apartment, opening doors, looking under the couch, in the cabinets. "Where's Auntie?" he demanded. "Is she hiding? She's *not* dead! She's not! She's hiding!" A screaming tantrum had followed. Josh knew exactly how he felt. Darius had left with both kids, apologizing.

Grieving together, Josh found, was worse than grieving alone. His own searing pain was shocking—physically agonizing, causing him to bend in two, his hands over his head as if warding off a blow.

But seeing Jen sobbing into a towel in the bathroom, or sniffing the sweater Lauren had worn so often, ripped his heart out and ground it up with shards of broken glass. The sight of Donna, his mother-in-law, stroking a picture of Lauren, her mouth trembling, suddenly looking twenty years older, gutted him. His own mom, her face swollen from crying, trying to hide her tears by scrubbing his counters. Ben, squeezing his shoulder, wordless, his eyes wet as he looked away from a photo of Lauren on her wedding day. Ben had served as best man that day.

Yeah. Solo was definitely the way to go. Without his family, or hers, it didn't feel so real. Sitting alone on the couch with the dog in the evening, all the lights off, he and Pebbles could both pretend Lauren was just about to walk in the door.

It was exhausting. It was like swimming in hot black tar. He worried about Donna and Jen, already having suffered the loss of Dave, Lauren's beloved father. He worried about his mother, who had worried that Josh would never find someone and had been so glad when he did, and now had a thirty-year-old son who was a widower. He worried that Pebbles would die of a broken heart. He worried that he would die, and there would be nothing, no Great Beyond, no afterlife, no reunion, and then he wondered if that would be a chance worth taking.

In a nutshell, life was ruined.

He'd jerk awake at night to check her, reaching for her side of the bed, worried about her breathing, then realize, nope, she was dead. He got up in the morning and put the kettle on for her tea. One night, he called down the hall for her before remembering. Sometimes he woke up and wondered if he'd dreamed their entire marriage.

Dead. The word sounded exactly like what it was. Hard. Flat. Ugly and cold.

Since her diagnosis, taking care of her had been his job. Oh, he'd finished one medical device design and sold it to Johnson & Johnson, but mostly, he'd been trying to save her. He'd read every scholarly article about IPF he could find. He spoke to doctors, foundations, patients and pharmaceutical researchers, and the desperate search for a better outcome had eaten up hours of his day.

Then there was her actual care. Cooking for her, doing the regular household chores, getting her prescriptions filled, taking her to the myriad doctor's appointments, arguing with the insurance company. Taking walks with her, doing her respiratory therapy, monitoring her O2 sats. Getting her to the bathroom when the medication gave her such bad diarrhea, he had to hold her on the toilet because she'd been too weak to stay there on her own. The past six months, he'd helped her shower almost every day. He'd had to make sure she took her meds at the appointed times. Make sure she had enough oxygen. Make sure she was eating enough. Make sure she was sleeping enough, happy enough, entertained enough, loved enough.

He missed every second of it. He'd cut off his arm to go back to that time.

He was lost. Utterly and completely lost. The Josh who was Lauren's husband no longer existed, and all that was left was . . . this.

Pebbles was the only reason he left the apartment. Sometimes, he was too tired to face the outside world, so he took her up to the roof and let her shit up there. He wasn't too proud of that, watching his dog crap where he and Lauren had had so many nice evenings—her sitting near the edge, him solidly in the center, since he didn't like heights—but he couldn't guilt himself into doing more. The seagull who had watched him burn his funeral clothes seemed to hang out there, judging him. Too bad. It was winter and cold as hell. Or maybe it was spring. He didn't know. It didn't matter.

Her "living urn" came—the soil, the supplements, the seedling. He couldn't remember ordering them, but he must have. She'd bookmarked the page on his laptop. Joshua stood there at the counter, looking at the kit, his wife's ashes, and got to work.

Lauren had loved plants. She'd grown herbs and flowers in pots on the rooftop and had bought hanging baskets for their rented house on the Cape. Their apartment was filled with plants, which reminded him they probably needed watering. He glanced around. Nope. Too late. They all looked dead.

As he followed the instructions, mixing his wife with the additive and soil provided by the living urn company, he was almost cheerful. He could picture her coming in. "What are you doing, hon?"

"I'm planting your tree."

"Oh! Cool! Make sure those roots aren't too squished."

"You got it, babe," he said aloud. Pebbles lifted her head to look at him.

This plant would not die. If it did, he'd kill

himself. In a sudden panic, he booted up his laptop and ordered a gauge that monitored the soil's moisture, pH, sun exposure, nitrogen, phosphorus and potassium. He read about what kind of exposure dogwood trees favored. The best room in their apartment would be their bedroom.

He'd have to go in there, then.

He did, spending not a second more than he had to, then fell asleep on the couch, hoping to dream of her.

Since her death, he'd dreamed of her often. In one, he came home, and she was tidying up the kitchen. "I came back just for a little while," she said. "God, what a mess!" Or she was in her mother's house, and he came in just as she was about to go into the attic. "Lauren!" he said, and she ran into his arms and hugged him, laughing.

The worst dream was almost an exact replica of her final hours in the hospital, a memory that Josh, when awake, had forbidden himself to think about. In the dream, though, she sat up at the end and said, "I feel better! How are *you?*"

The cruelty of waking from that made Josh feel like he'd been hit in the chest with a baseball bat. Why would God give him that dream? Josh was raised as a Christian—Lutheran—though it didn't really take. But these days, it was hard not to blame someone. To want to kick God in the nuts. *Thanks for nothing. I* knew *you didn't exist.*

Jen texted every day. She was the only one Josh could tolerate, and only because Lauren had loved her so much. Darius checked in every fourth day, asking if he wanted company or to get out of the apartment. Donna would call, leaving tearful messages on his voice mail, and he'd call her back dutifully. Jen finally told her to give him some space, which Donna took very personally, and Josh just didn't have the energy to care.

One day, when his hair felt sticky, he took a shower, standing under the spray, unable to tell if it was too hot or too cold. Why was he in here again? Oh, yes, hygiene. Lauren's shampoo and shower gel were still on the shelf. He took the cap off, inhaled, then found himself lying on the shower floor, racked with the pain of losing her, the sounds coming from his mouth terrifying and unstoppable. He eventually fell asleep there, exhausted and wrung out, and woke up only when the water had turned frigid. Lauren would've been horrified to find him passed out like that. Let her be. Let her come in and say, "Jesus, Josh, what are you *doing?* Don't be such a loser, hon!" She loved saying that to him, her voice always playful and full of love.

He found himself studying the framed pictures of them that Lauren had put throughout the apartment. Their wedding day. Hawaii. New Year's Eve, when they'd hosted an actual party here, Josh's first time ever doing so. Lauren giving

Sebastian a piggyback ride. With his mother on her birthday. With her family at the wedding. The two of them in Paris. The two of them in the Caribbean. The day they got Pebbles. Holding Octavia in the hospital.

Knowing he couldn't stop her illness and believing it were two different things. Wasn't he the golden son of Rhode Island School of Design? Of Brown University? Didn't he have a fucking PhD from Massachusetts Institute of Technology? Hadn't he sold nine medical device patents in the past decade with five devices already on the market? He was a certified genius, and his purpose in life had been to be her husband, to protect her, and he'd failed. He'd failed.

He should eat something, he thought, tearing his eyes off the photo. Instead, he lay on the couch and fell asleep.

Lauren was walking on the beach way, way ahead of him. They were on Cape Cod, but the spinner dolphins they'd seen in Hawaii were leaping out of the ocean, and Lauren was running ahead to get a better look, and he couldn't reach her, because he kept stumbling on the sand. The rocks at the shore's edge knocked together, clacking rhythmically, and Lauren's long pink summer dress was just a dot now, and the clacking was louder now, banging, knocking, barking—

He woke up in a lurch. Pebbles was barking, and someone was knocking on the door. "Quiet," he said sharply to the dog, and she obeyed, making him feel cruel and hard.

The knocking stopped. "Josh? It's Sarah."

Shit. He did not want to see anyone. Especially Sarah, who was all too healthy. Why couldn't she have been the one who—

"Josh? It's important."

He hauled himself to his feet, the blanket tangling in his legs. "Um, it's not a great time," he said, moving closer to the door so she could hear him. His voice was strange to his own ears.

"I know. Open the door anyway."

"Can you come back, um . . . next week?"

"No."

He leaned against the door and ran his hand over his face.

"Joshua. Open the door or I'm calling 911 for a wellness check."

She worked in social services, so he imagined she meant it.

"Josh. I've called you every other day, and you haven't answered once. Please open the door. You're not the only one who's been grieving this past month."

Jesus. A *month* since his wife died? It seemed like a decade. It seemed like thirty seconds ago.

He opened the door, and Sarah flinched, then

hugged him. He patted her shoulder, wishing she would stop.

"You smell horrible," she said, hugging him tighter.

"Sorry," he said, stepping back.

She came inside and bent down to pet Pebbles. "Hi, honey! I missed you!" Pebbles wagged joyfully, and Josh felt a stab of resentment. That was *Lauren's* dog. Lauren should be the one petting her, calling her honey.

Which was stupid, he knew.

Sarah straightened, wiped her eyes and looked around the place. "Oh, boy."

He'd drawn the shades against the view, the sun. Cartons of food were in various places, some full, some empty. He noticed a pizza box under the coffee table, the corner chewed off. Pebbles must've swiped it. He hoped it wasn't because she was hungry.

"Well." Sarah put her hands on her hips. "Um . . . why don't you take a shower, and I'll clean up a little? Open the windows, get some fresh air?"

"I was just going to take a nap."

"Go shower, Josh." He opened his mouth to argue and then, lacking the energy, trudged down the hall to the bathroom.

He hadn't liked Sarah that much when he'd first been introduced. The two women had been friends since elementary school, but Josh wondered if they would have been friends if they met as adults. Sarah had an edge to her, a subtle resentment toward Lauren, glittering like a piece of glass in the sand. He saw it immediately, and kept seeing it every time they got together, during their engagement, even at the wedding. She went through the motions required, but it was clear she envied Lauren.

Then again, who wouldn't? His wife had always been the brightest star in the sky.

But after the diagnosis, Sarah had been a rock. A perfect friend to Lauren. A helper for him, even.

He took a shower, listlessly rubbed soap over himself, then got dressed in not-filthy clothes and went into the living room. Sarah had opened the shades and windows, and had thrown out a lot of food cartons and pizza boxes. Made herself right at home, he saw. She was now using that weird little mop that picked up dog hair. Swiffer, that was it. It irked him that Sarah knew where everything was.

That being said, there *was* a lot of dog hair on the Swiffer cloth. Sarah took it off, tossed it in the trash and replaced it efficiently.

He sat down on the couch. "What's so important, Sarah?" Oh. She was wiping her eyes. Right. She'd lost her best friend, and he could be a little nicer. Lauren would want him to. "It's good to see you," he lied.

She took a deep breath and let it out, then sank into the chair opposite him. Pebbles sat next to her, whining a little, making Josh feel guilty.

"First of all, this dog is getting a little chunky," she said.

"Yeah, I . . . I might be overfeeding her."

"Maybe she needs to get out more."

He nodded, looking at the floor. Pebbles deserved better, it was true.

"This is tough, being here without her." Sarah's voice shook.

"Yes." He searched his brain for something to say. "How have you been?"

"Shitty. Lonely. Heartbroken. You know."

"Right."

Sarah scooped her long hair around her neck to one side. Blond hair. It seemed like blond women valued their hair above all else, always calling attention to it. It was pretty enough, he supposed. Lauren's hair had been deep, dark red, and so shiny. He didn't know the word for hair the color of Lauren's. Chestnut? Burgundy? Irish setter? So much more interesting than blond. To him, anyway.

Sarah pressed her fingertips under her eyes, wiping away more tears. He passed her a box of Kleenex from the coffee table.

"Thanks," she said. She blotted her eyes and blew her nose, then stuffed the tissue in her bag.

"Here's the thing, Josh," she said. "Lauren asked me to do something for you."

What? Clean his house? Become his best friend? No, thanks. He didn't want anything from Sarah. God help him if she thought she should move in or . . . or cook for him or, oh, God, offer to have his child. Jesus Christ, what was it?

Sarah reached into her bag and pulled out an envelope, and suddenly, Josh's heart was convulsing, because he could see his wife's handwriting.

Josh, #1

"It's from her, obviously. So I'm just gonna leave this here and go, okay? I don't know what's in it, but she said she'd explain. I'm just the delivery person." She wiped her eyes again. "I'll . . . I'll see you soon."

"Okay. Sure. Thank you." He couldn't take his eyes off the envelope. His hands were shaking.

"Take Pebbles out more," she said, and then she was gone, the door closing behind her, her heels clicking down the stairs.

He didn't want to open it right now, he thought as he ripped it open. He should save it. He was hyperventilating a little.

Slow down, slow down, this is the last thing you'll ever get from her, take your time.

Good advice. He should listen to himself. He took a focused breath, like Lauren used to, then blew it out in puffs. Pebbles jumped up next to him, and he took a second to pet her head, feel her silky ears.

Was now the time to read it? Should he save it? He couldn't. He needed to hear her in his head. Tears were already burning his eyes.

Okay. He would read it. Now. If he could get his hands to stop shaking. He unfolded the paper, and the sight of her handwriting sliced him open.

Dear Josh,
Hi, honey! Are you doing okay? I'm wicked, wicked sorry I died. Oh, Joshua, I am. But I think you know that already. I hope it was a good ending. I hope I didn't die on the toilet.

I love you. Did I say that yet? I do. I love you so much.

So, honey, here's the thing. I've been feeling like I might not last that long. Hopefully I'm wrong, and you're reading this at age ninety-seven, but I kind of doubt it. Please know that I stayed as long as I could, because I loved every day with you. Every single day.

I couldn't bear the thought of you trying to get through this first year without me to help you. I'm bossy, as we both know. So I wrote up some letters for you, one for each month of this first year, each with a thing for you to do. You know how I love making lists. Sarah will bring the letters to you.

Josh closed his eyes. *Oh, thank you. Thank you, Lauren. Thank you.* He would still hear from her. She would still be with him. She *was* still here, in a way. He pressed the letter against his chest and bowed his head for a second. Then he wiped his eyes on his sleeve and continued reading.

I hope it won't mess with your head, Josh. You don't have to read them. Maybe this is really morbid.

"It's not," he said. "It's not."

You can throw them all away, or tell Sarah to burn them or whatever. But I think you won't. I think—I hope—it might help, honey. The truth is, I've never been able to stop feeling guilty for being sick. This is as much for me as it is for you. The past few months, as I've written these letters, it's made me feel like I can still take care of you in the only way I can now. And that makes me happy, because I love you so much.

So in every letter, I'm going to give you a job to do, and you have to do it, because (ahem) I'm tragically dead and also watching you from the GB.

55

The GB. The Great Beyond. Their joke. He smiled. He damn well hoped she was watching. It made him feel less alone.

Just so you know, I'm writing from the patio of our gorgeous hotel in Turks and Caicos, and you're sleeping in the bedroom. I can hear you snoring. Even your snoring is hot. I don't know how you pull it off, but you do. You are definitely getting a little some-some in about fifteen minutes. This vacation is the BEST. Thank you, honey, for filling my life with so many beautiful moments.

Okay, back to the present time, or your present time, I guess.

Since this is the first month, I'm going easy on you, because I imagine you're still wrecked. If you have a new wife already, I don't want to hear about it. But I'm picturing you in a filthy apartment, unshowered, unshaved, looking like a pathetic ninth grader trying to grow a beard.

"You're not wrong," he said.

Are you ready? You are? Super!
Go to the grocery store!!!
Are you so excited? Listen. If I know

you, there are dead veggies in the bottom drawer turning into green ooze. The milk is the consistency of cottage cheese. There are moldy leftovers and cold cuts that smell like feet. There's plenty of food, but you're not eating. You've barely left the house since I died. So go on! Take a shower! Shave. Brush your teeth. Go to the grocery store and stop eating food from cartons over the sink. Don't be a loser!

I love you. I love you. I love you.

You can do this. You sort of have to. As the great Morgan Freeman once said, get busy living, or get busy dying.

Love,
Lauren

"Don't you Shawshank me," he said, and he laughed, the sound rough and foreign.

Suddenly elated, he jumped from the couch. His wife had given him a chore, and he was going to do it. What was the weather like? Warm, right—Sarah had opened the windows. Was it Saturday? Could he go to the farmers' market with Pebbles? Where was his phone so he could see the date?

First things first, clean out the fridge. Milk, lumpy and disgusting. In fact, all dairy products, see ya. Gross turkey slices—God, the smell. She was right. Some of the food he'd ordered and stuck in the fridge, some Tupperware containers of food from Sumi Kim, all of it way too old or mysterious. He filled the trash bag in record time.

Lauren was right about the vegetables. Those had been bought when she was still alive. When eating leafy greens was supposed to boost her immune system. "Fuck you," he told the slimy spinach and liquefied zucchini. He opened the cupboard and saw the giant container of turmeric, supposedly so good for health. The vitamins and Chinese supplements. The lies, the hope.

None of this had saved her, so he jammed it all into the trash. Liars. False prophets. Snake oil. His mood plummeted back to the tar pits.

No. No. Lauren had written him a letter, had given him a task, and there were more to come, a dozen of them, and that was so *amazing,* so great, such a gift, he wasn't going to ruin it by thinking about how dead she was.

With this letter, she was still here.

Ten minutes later, he had Pebbles on a leash. It wasn't Saturday . . . it was Tuesday, so no farmers' market, but that was okay, because he could drive to the Stop & Shop, which had been Lauren's favorite grocery store. She hated Whole Foods and was mystified by Aldi. He'd take Pebbles for a walk first, because she did deserve some exercise, and then they'd get in the car so she could go for a ride, her favorite thing on earth.

Pebbles trotted joyfully next to him as he

walked down the street, then into the park. It was mild out, in the midfifties, and the sun was bright and strong. People were all around, and maybe they recognized him as the guy with the brown-and-white dog, the guy with the wife on oxygen. Maybe they called out and said hello, but he was too buzzed with excitement to notice.

Get busy living, or get busy dying. Ha. Their joke.

He walked back to the apartment building's parking lot. "You wanna go for a ride?" he asked their dog. "A ride?"

Pebbles answered with a nearly human string of sounds, her feathery tail swishing, those cute triangular ears at high alert.

"Let's go, then." He opened the door and she leaped in. He started the car, rolled down the windows enough so she could stick her head out, but not enough that she could jump out. It was a *beautiful* day. Very mild and sunny. The trees were turning faintly red with buds. That's right. It was now officially spring.

At Stop & Shop, he parked, raised the windows enough so Pebbles could have fresh air but not lick passersby. He grabbed a cart and went inside and began zooming down the aisles. Arugula, broccoli, cabbage, tomatoes, peapods, red peppers, yellow peppers, oranges, ginger, garlic. Cheerios, sort of nutritious. Peanut butter, great on everything. Pasta, why not? Bread.

Salmon, so healthy, plus Lauren loved it. Chicken breasts. Paper towels, the extra-soft tissues Lauren liked. Clorox Clean-Up, because they always had to make sure any contagious germs were . . .

Oh. Right. The germs were a moot point. And there was no *they* anymore. He wasn't shopping for *them* anymore. Ever.

It was just him. The knowledge made him light-headed.

"Excuse me. Excuse me. Sir? Can you move?"

Josh blinked. Someone was trying to get around him, because apparently he'd stopped in the middle of the aisle.

"Yes. Sorry." It was a mother, a toddler in the front of the cart and an older kid, maybe five, sitting among the groceries.

For the first time, it hit him that he'd never be a father. Not to Lauren's kids. He'd always hoped that her IPF could be stopped, that she'd live decades more, and he wouldn't give up on the idea of kids. Anything was possible. She'd only been twenty-eight. There was still time for the wonder cure that would put her IPF into permanent suspension, or even cure it.

But time had run out. There would be no kids. No genetic memory of her, no seeing her smile on a child's face, no hearing a laugh that was just like hers.

The smaller child looked at him and started to cry.

"Sorry," he said, and this time, he actually moved the cart.

Why was he here? He had to get home. He somehow had to figure out how to get these groceries put into bags, pay for them, get into the car—he had driven, right?—and get home.

"Hey, Josh," came a mellow voice. It was Yolanda, their favorite manager here, who always wore earrings proclaiming her name. Lauren used to chat with her about Yolanda's kids, knowing which grades they were in, what sports they played. How did she *do* that? How did she know Yolanda had kids? People just *talked* to Lauren. They trusted her. He was nothing compared to her. He was a piece of plywood, and she had been a rose. It was even her middle name. Lauren Rose Carlisle Park.

Yolanda tilted her head, her eponymous earring brushing her shoulder. "You okay?"

"She died," he said.

"Oh, baby," Yolanda said, and she opened her arms, and suddenly Josh had his head on her shoulder, his body stiff, his face aching with the effort of not crying. "I'm so sorry, honey. She was the sweetest thing."

He straightened up before he broke. Nodded.

"Let me check you out, hon. Come on." Yolanda led the way, opened a register and started ringing him up.

He hadn't brought the grocery bags. They were

in the back of the car, but going to get them seemed akin to running a marathon. He stood, staring at the floor, as Yolanda bagged. "That's $159.23, hon."

"Sorry?"

"You need to pay, hon. Did you bring your wallet?"

He didn't know. He felt for his back pocket. "Uh . . . no. I don't think so." He could feel himself shutting down, powering off.

Yolanda smiled sadly. "Okay. I got you this time. Just pay me back when you come in again. Take care, Josh. Take care of yourself."

"Thank you," he whispered.

When he got home, he shoved all the bags in the fridge, gave Pebbles some water and went into the guest room. He got into bed fully clothed, pulled the covers up and prayed that he'd dream of his wife once more.

6

Lauren

Eight months left
June 5

Dear Dad,
A lot has happened since the last time I wrote.

When Josh and I came back from the Caribbean in March, and just after Octavia was born in April, I got pneumonia again. I don't know how. Everyone cleans everything these days, Josh and I still swab down everything with good old Clorox wipes. Nevertheless, two days after we got back, I had a fever and chills. My O2 sat was crap, so we called Dr. Bennett, and she said to head for the hospital.

I had to be intubated. That is no fun, Father. I hate it, because I'm sedated, you know? It steals time. Plus it worries Josh and Jen and everyone else. I lost four days, but we beat the pneumonia, at least.

I'm on Ofev, which is one of the only medicines that seems to slow IPF down. I've been eating organic food only for two years, and I take those Chinese herbs and exercise, and still, Dr. Bennett said my lung function tests were "lower than we'd like," which sounded ominous. Also, I've lost weight, courtesy of a side effect of the meds . . . diarrhea like Old Testament wrath, Dad. Not that you want to hear this, but who else can I tell? Dr. Bennett added another medication, which stopped the weight loss, but it makes me a little dizzy. The steroid inhalers make it a little easier to breathe, but also give me insomnia.

And every time I lose a little lung function, it's gone forever. IPF is a greedy bastard.

Stephanie, who is the world's best mother-in-law, got me a Himalayan salt lamp, which is supposed to help with breathing. Let no stone go unturned, right? She's also big on the healing wonders of Vicks VapoRub, which, let's be honest, is a miracle drug. I love the smell. She said to rub it on my feet at night. Mrs. Kim agreed, so it must work, because she had four kids and is a nurse, and therefore knows everything.

Sometimes, I have to sleep in the recliner, because being flat isn't great for me, but I hate to be away from Josh. He (of course) found a special wedge pillow so I could be more comfortable in bed.

I love him, Dad. He is everything a husband should be. Protective, funny, kind, thoughtful, gorgeous (not necessary but it does NOT hurt that he has cheekbones like a Nordic god and a smile that curls up in the corners and makes my ovaries ache. Sorry, sorry, TMI, I know that). But I want you to know how he is. That I couldn't be in better hands or with a better person.

Work is great. I started designing the interior of the children's library wing, and what could be more fun than that? Everyone at work is so nice; Santino and Louise and I go for slow walks at lunch, and Bruce is incredibly flexible with my hours. Oh, you'll love this— Lori Cantore, the only mean girl of the firm, asked Bruce for my office "down the line." Second time she's asked! Can you believe that? I said, "I'm right here, Lori. Still alive, sorry to tell you." Bruce sent her home for the day and told her to cut the shit or find another job. Best boss ever! Still, I hate her. Before I got sick, I'd try to look for some redeeming qualities, but now, forget it. She's a bitch, and she deserves nothing from me. I may have taken one of her Diet Coke cans and dribbled the remains on the floor by her desk the other night. You can never really clean that kind of stickiness.

Anyway, the thing about getting sick was that Dr. Bennett, Bossy Pulmonologist, told me she didn't think I should be tackling airports and hotels for a while.

Which is a big bucket of suckiness, Dad. Traveling is one of the things that almost lets me forget I'm sick. And it lets Josh forget, too, at least for a little while. He's obsessed with finding a cure. I don't blame him. If he was the one who was sick, I'd do the same thing. But—and this is a big one—I need him to take breaks from that, because otherwise, I'm just a sick person who needs to be fixed. I'd rather be his wife.

So when we travel, he can forget about trying to invent a microscopic fiber-eater that can go into my lungs, or calling every research hospital in the world to talk about drug trials. When we travel, we get to be a happily married couple with a few health considerations. We'd been talking about going to as many of the national parks as we could—Zion and Yellowstone, maybe Denali, in case the pure, cold air would help my lungs.

Dr. Bennett advised against it. For now, she said.

So guess what my husband did, Dad? He rented a crazy-beautiful house on Cape Cod for the entire year! It has five bedrooms so we could have Jen, Darius and the kids whenever we want! There's a chef's kitchen, a screened-in porch and three decks, and it's right on a cliff overlooking the ocean. One serious winter storm could take it out, but hey, for our purposes, it's perfect. A house on the ocean. Who knew I'd ever be that lucky? We're going up next week, and I can't wait.

So your son-in-law is doing his job beautifully, Dad. Just wanted you to know.

Love,
Lauren

That Cape house made Lauren fall in love, not just with the gorgeousness of the place but with her husband all over again . . . and also, with how they could *be* here.

They went up the first weekend in June and sat on the deck, staring at the ocean, holding hands. Pebbles jumped up next to her, unaware that she wasn't a tiny puppy anymore. The day was sunny and clear, so peaceful and so full . . .

the gentle roar of the waves, the wind that gusted erratically, the birds twittering and chattering in the trees. The air smelled like lilacs and salt and pine needles, and if it could be bottled, no one would need antidepressants ever again.

"I feel more like us," she said.

Josh looked at her, the sun glinting off his black hair. He would tan in minutes with that olive skin of his, courtesy of his mysterious father. "What do you mean?"

"Well . . . we don't have doctor's appointments here. No mail cluttering up the counters—"

"Clutter, Mrs. Park?"

"Dr. Park, you're a slob."

"I'm reformed. That shock collar worked great."

She snorted and squeezed his hand. "You know what I mean. It's not regular life with appointments and obligations. It's just us and Pebbles. No schedule to keep." She leaned over and kissed him softly. "Thank you. I love it."

"I know not being able to travel hit you hard."

"Well. This is just as good. Better, even." Though she felt a pang at the idea of possibly never traveling again, it was definitely muted by this view, the deep blue of the Atlantic, the perfect sky above. "I don't want to waste time feeling bad about what I don't have when what I do have is all this. You. Jen, the kids, Miss Pebblety-Pie."

"Get busy living, or get busy dying."

She laughed again. "Don't you Shawshank me."

"You sure you'll be okay?" he asked over dinner that night. He had to fly to Sacramento for a meeting tomorrow, and Lauren was a little glad. They'd barely been apart since getting married, aside from his three-day medical device conference each fall, and a weekend trip to Vermont she'd taken with Jen. She wanted to be alone here, so close to the sea, in this beautiful house where the sunrise woke her, and she could sip coffee and study the clouds, Pebbles by her side. "I'd feel a lot better if Jen was with you. Or your mom."

Lauren pulled a face. "Jen just had a baby, and Mom would look at me and cry and tell me how hard this is for her? No, thanks. I'll be fine, babe. I already called the fire department to let them know exactly where this house is in case of emergency. Sarah's coming up on Wednesday, and you'll be back Friday. Relax."

"I don't do relaxed."

She smiled at him, then got up from her chair. "Come to bed, handsome. I'll relax you. *And* I'll clean the kitchen afterward."

"Winning on all fronts today." He stood up and wrapped her in his arms, and Lauren felt, as she always did, that this was the best place in the world. Right against his neck, smelling his nice Josh smell, slipping her hands up his lean

69

back, feeling the slide of his muscles. When he kissed her, it was slow and warm, and she felt everything in her rise and lean into him, from the hairs on the back of her neck to the tugging deep in her stomach.

They still had this. Desire, attraction, affection, lust . . . and love, that golden light that seemed to wrap around the two of them, shielding them from the outside world.

When he left the next day, Lauren savored the house, wandering from room to room, looking out at the ocean in a state of wonder. Pebbles, who took her Australian shepherding heritage seriously, stuck to her heels. Around three, they took a nap, and when Lauren woke up, she checked her O2 sat and found it was on the low side. She put in the cannula and turned on her oxygen, then sat on the deck with a blanket around her shoulders and sipped some wine as she listened to the ocean.

It had been a year and a half since her diagnosis. It seemed longer. In hindsight, she could see that the IPF had been there for *years* before Dr. Bennett gave it a name. So, assuming it had started around age twenty-three, the first time she could definitively remember feeling short of breath for no reason, she'd been living with this for almost five years.

The life expectancy of most IPF patients was

three to five years. But she was young and otherwise healthy, and she was a damn good patient, complying with everything and then some—yoga, meditation, exercise, healthy foods, Chinese herbs, respiratory therapy. So there was plenty of reason to think she'd live *years* longer. That she and Josh could come back to this house every summer for a few weeks. That they could celebrate her thirtieth birthday here, *and* her fortieth. She'd made friends with Charlene, another young woman on the IPF forum, and Char had just gone to Australia and swum with dolphins off the Great Barrier Reef. So there.

A seagull drifted down from an air current and landed on the deck post. Pebbles cocked her head but didn't bark.

Seagulls were lovely. Lauren had never understood why people called them rats of the sky (pigeons held that title, in her opinion). No, seagulls were impressive, flying like no other, diving, fishing, bobbing on the water. Calm and fearless. If she had to pick a Patronus, seagull would be in the running. Maybe part of her experience in the Great Beyond could be seagull-for-a-day.

She didn't realize she was crying till a tear plopped onto Pebbles's head. Her fortieth birthday? Who was she kidding?

But maybe . . . maybe she could make it till thirty.

• • •

She started working remotely more often. And while Lauren had always loved her job, she loved it even more now. She currently had two projects: one, an easy but satisfying job of creating a lookout in a tiny patch of land the City of Providence had just acquired on College Hill. Though it was a circle of only about thirty feet in diameter, it overlooked the beautiful dome of the capitol building and the rooftops of a few blocks of historic homes. She planned on incorporating a couple of benches, a circular contemplation maze that would encourage people to spend time in the small park, and a raised stone structure in the center. The other project was a new wing in the downtown library, which was a bit more complicated. Bruce the Mighty and Beneficent had just given her that one, and she was waiting on a use study that would guide her design.

She wanted to leave her mark. That was the advice Dad had given her when she was seventeen and wondering what to do as an adult. "Whatever you choose, do with all your heart, and leave your mark," he said, covering her hand with his. "If you're going to be a bartender, be the bartender everyone loves to talk to, who invents the best drinks and makes you feel right at home. If you're going to be a hairdresser, make every customer feel good about themselves."

"If I'm going to be a fashion designer, make clothes that make people feel happy and confident," she said.

"Exactly, punkin. Exactly."

He'd never know how she'd changed majors after his death, wanting something different, something that would benefit the community, not just customers. He'd never see an area she designed.

But they existed, and she had more to do. "Miles to go before I sleep," she said to Pebbles, who wagged. "And I do mean miles." Attitude was everything, after all.

The summer spooled out like yards and yards of silk, beautiful and gentle, one day sliding into the next. Like Lauren, Josh could work from anywhere, so he was always here unless she ordered him to go back to Providence for a night. He needed his space, whether he wanted it or not. He needed his punching bag and to see Ben Kim, who understood him like no one else. Lauren knew that, even if Josh wouldn't admit it.

In July, Jen took a leave from work for two months and brought the kids up for days at a time, much to Lauren's delight. Josh would give them piggyback rides and take them in the surf while the sisters sat on the beach. When Darius came up, they'd eat late—after Sebastian and Octavia were in bed—laughing and telling stories. Lauren's mom came sometimes, too, though she had to be cajoled into making the trip. "I don't want to intrude," she'd say, or "You girls don't want me there."

Whatever. Lauren lacked the energy to convince her mother to come. Not everyone was the type to rise to an occasion, and Lauren just didn't have the time to beg her mom to . . . mother. Donna had never really been the type who nurtured. That was her dad's area of expertise, and unfortunately, he was dead.

Sarah and Stephanie came often, too. The Kims spent a week in July and promised to visit again. There was plenty of space, after all. Her sickness had become part of their lives, too, which made things easier. "Grab me another tank while you're up," Lauren might say, and Sarah would get the oxygen and attach the hose like a pro. Stephanie, who had once planned on going to medical school, would hand her the Ventolin inhaler before Lauren realized she needed it.

One day, when she and her mother-in-law were alone, opting not to go to Poit's for mini-golf, Stephanie mentioned that once again, someone had asked her if she'd adopted Josh. "He looks like *both* his parents," Steph said. "You just have to look harder to see me in there."

"Did you love him, Steph?" Lauren asked. "Josh's father?"

"That bum? No." She looked at Lauren with beautiful Nordic-blue eyes. "Nope. It was a fling."

"Did you ever look for him, or tell him about Josh?"

Steph was quiet for a minute. "I tried," she said. "We were both students. He left for a summer program, said he'd be back before the baby came, and I never heard from him again. I emailed him; his address was defunct." Steph sipped her water. Like her son, she didn't drink alcohol. "After Josh was born, I stopped trying to contact him. He had my email. We weren't hard to find."

Lauren tried to imagine anyone turning his back on his pregnant girlfriend and just . . . vanishing. "Sounds like he was a spineless toddler."

"There you go. We're better off without him."

"Do you think Josh ever wonders about him?" Lauren asked.

"He used to ask," Stephanie said. "And I didn't know exactly how to put it, so I just said, 'Families come in all shapes and sizes,' that kind of thing. We had Ben and Sumi. Ben did all those father-son things for school."

"I love that guy," Lauren said.

"Yeah. I think Josh liked people asking him if he was Korean when they saw him and Ben together."

"What was the bio-dad's background?" Josh could fall into any category—Latino, Asian, Middle Eastern, Roma . . .

"I honestly don't think we ever talked about it. Like I said, it was maybe a five-week thing. He was from the Midwest. That's all I remember." If she knew more, she wasn't saying.

"It left a mark, of course," Stephanie continued. "The facts are the facts. Joshua's father deserted him before he was even born. It's part of his identity, same as being a high-functioning super-genius with Asperger's, or autism spectrum disorder, or neurodiversity, or whatever we're calling it these days. Those terms change so fast. Anyway, are you hungry? I'm starving. Want a grilled cheese? It's my specialty, after all."

The conversation was over, clearly. "Thanks, Steph. I'd love one." Her mother-in-law did make the best grilled cheese sandwiches, using at least three types of cheese. Otherwise, she wasn't much of a cook. Steph patted her shoulder as she went in the kitchen, and Lauren opened her notebook.

Almost every day, she and Josh drove to the bay side to watch the sunset and let Pebbles splash and swim and sniff (and roll in) the carcasses of fish or birds or crabs. The house had a very convenient and huge bathroom on the ground floor, and they'd designated it for Pebbles's baths. Josh would hose her down and shampoo her, then blow her dry (spoiled beastie), so Pebbles would be silky smooth and gorgeous and able to sleep on their bed.

Lauren took to waking up early at the Cape

house and tiptoeing to the windows to watch the sunrise by herself, letting Josh sleep. She always started the coffee, because it had been her job even in childhood, when she'd get up early and measure out the grounds. Daddy would come in and act so pleased every time. "Who was so thoughtful? Lauren, sweetheart, thank you! Aren't you the best girl ever!"

She missed her dad with a constant ache. She missed the reassurance, the comfort a good father brings a daughter. She found herself wondering about the moment of his death, if he'd had any warning, any final thoughts. She hoped it wasn't "Oh shit, that hurts."

Note to self: Say something profound for your last words.

Her dad felt closer these days. They had more in common now; she would die young, too. She was glad she knew. Sure, sure, a rogue bus could take her out at any moment, but being someone who liked to have a plan, she'd take a diagnosis like IPF over her father's type of death any day.

Meanwhile, it was impossible not to love life even more on Cape Cod. Was it just the thrill of the ocean, or was her IPF on hold for a bit? She felt good. Stronger. Maybe it *was* the salt air. Every day, she did gentle yoga on the deck, filling her lungs, visualizing the air having plenty of room, pushing aside the fibers, filling in every available space. Some nights, she didn't need her oxygen. She knew there was no cure for pulmonary fibrosis, but maybe . . . just maybe . . . it had slowed down.

The occasional thunderstorm made her giddy with joy, and with every flash of lightning she'd say, "Did you *see* that?" even though Josh was right beside her. The stars were fierce and bright on clear nights, and they could hear coyotes sometimes, or a fox yipping.

This would be a good place to die, Lauren couldn't help thinking. *This would be such a beautiful last thing to see.*

One weekend in late August, Lauren sent Josh home again so she could have a proper girls' weekend. Asmaa from the Hope Center, Mara from RISD, Louise from work, Sarah and Jen all came up to the Cape, fighting the monstrous traffic on Route 6, and stayed for five days. She had convinced Josh to stay in Providence, saying she needed some time with her girlies, assuring him that Jen would call him if she had a flare-up. They dressed up and put on makeup, then drove to Provincetown and had dinner overlooking the bay, eating lazy-man lobster, drinking fancy martinis, telling embarrassing stories about past loves and bad dates. Afterward, they saw a drag show and laughed so hard Lauren had to up her oxygen flow. Totally worth it.

It was lovely, she thought, looking around at them. They were wonderful friends. She'd miss them. Or not. The Great Beyond probably had contingency plans for spirits who wanted to check in on their friends.

Besides, she reminded herself, she could have years more. Years!

"I could get hit by a bus tomorrow," people were fond of saying, their way of trying to be sympathetic when they heard about her disease. No one knew what the future held. And hey. Unlucky bus drivers aside, it was true. Staying in the moment was better than wringing hands about the future. She wasn't going to waste this glorious summer thinking about how sick she was.

7

Lauren

Ten months left
April

Dear Daddy,
You have a granddaughter! Her name is Octavia Lauren, and she is the most beautiful thing in the entire universe, as you probably know because I swear you were there.

Holding her before she was ten minutes old, Daddy . . . the smell of her, her little sounds, grunting and squeaking. I said, "I love you, sweetheart," and, Dad, she opened her eyes. She looked right at me, and it was like staring into all the mysteries of the universe, like this tiny baby (well, she was eight pounds, five ounces, so not tiny for Jen . . .) was telling me that no matter what, everything will be okay. We just looked and looked at each other, and I have never felt more perfect or known in my life.

Eventually, I had to give her back to

Jen, who was a champion. She is amazing, Dad. Amazing.

Then Josh came in with Sebastian, because he was in the waiting room with the little guy. Sebastian ran in with a stuffed bunny and said, "My sister! Hi, my sister! You're so cute!" Then he started crying with love. He kissed her forehead and said, "I love you, my sister!" and everyone was bawling.

When Mom came in, for once she didn't make it about how sad she was that you weren't there. She was just beaming, and when Jen told her the name, Mom said, "Oh, how beautiful! What a perfect name!" and hugged me.

There was so much love in that room, Dad. I know you felt it, too.

Josh and I took Sebastian home with us later that day so Jen could rest, and he slept over. Pebbles slept on his bed, which he thought was so funny. And you know Jen; she was up and about in two days, oversharing about her bleeding and how much it stings to pee.

I'm so happy, Dad. Seeing Octavia being born . . . it was a miracle. I know, I know, it happens every day. It's still a miracle.

Congratulations, Daddy! Take good

care of your little granddaughter and her big brother. Love you!

Lauren

"Don't think this is because you're sick," Jen said two weeks later. "I was always going to have a daughter with Lauren for a middle name."

Lauren was babysitting; Jen needed a nap and a shower. Darius had taken Sebastian to the library with plans to visit Newport Creamery for lunch, and so Lauren was summoned.

She did not mind in the least.

Little Octavia fussed and cried and pooped (would Lauren ever look at pumpkin pie the same way?). Lauren put her in the baby carriage and took her for a walk to get her fresh air and vitamin D. The baby didn't mind how slowly she walked; Octavia just made little snorting and grunting sounds, like a tiny and very adorable piglet.

"Congratulations," said one lady from a park bench.

"Thank you," Lauren said, smiling. "She's my niece."

Back home, she gave the baby a bottle, changed her diaper yet again. Lauren sat in the recliner and put her feet up, bending her knees so Octavia rested against her legs. They stared at each other. The baby's eyes were so . . . special. Giant and wise, like she knew everything.

When Octavia yawned, Lauren couldn't help grinning in delight like a good auntie. Then Octavia started to fuss, so Lauren shifted her to her shoulder and patted her back, making little humming noises. After about five minutes, the baby grew quiet, and Lauren shifted her to the crook of her arm for more staring, drinking in the baby's sweet lashes, silky little eyebrows, pale brown skin, almost exactly the same shade as Sebastian's. Her hair was fine and brown, and she had the sweetest mouth.

And then, a tear dropped on her chin. Lauren's tear, because apparently, she was crying. Silently, but a lot.

This, she knew with an aching certainty, was as close to having a baby as she'd get. She knew. She *knew*. She would never be a mother. Never go through what Jen and Darius had shared in the labor and delivery room, never look at a baby and see Joshua's eyes or her own ears.

The tears wouldn't stop falling, and Lauren's chest was jerking. She cough-sobbed, then got up with some effort, not wanting to wake the baby. She put her in the little bassinet and went into the kitchen to cry into a dishtowel. She wouldn't have children, and she was going to die too soon, and Sebastian and Octavia might not even remember her. She was going to miss so much. She would leave Jen, her beloved sister, and these perfect, beautiful kids and her mom and Josh, oh,

God, Josh, and it was like all her skin was gone and she was raw and terrified and wailing into the void of despair because, goddamnit, she was going to die.

Then Jen was there, hugging her, and Lauren lost it. She clung to her sister and wailed, and Jen was sobbing, too, because they knew. They knew. They held on to each other and cried and cried and cried until there was nothing left.

The baby slept through the whole meltdown.

They looked at each other, eyes red and noses stuffed, skin blotchy, and Lauren gave a half laugh. "Come on, sit down," Jen said, wiping her eyes on her sleeve. "I'll make you some witch's brew." She went back to the kitchen and made some tea out of the Chinese herbs she kept on hand for Lauren . . . astragalus root and raw schisandra berries, because she was a great sister.

Lauren was still hiccuping when her sister came back. "Sorry," she said.

"Oh, go fuck yourself," Jen said, squeezing her hand.

They sat there in silence, listening to Octavia breathe. After a while, Jen said, "Let's go to the movies one night soon, okay?"

When Lauren was a dorky adolescent, wearing overalls and a cropped T-shirt and too-short bangs with a beret, Jen had generously overlooked her fashion choices and would take her to the movies. Alone or with Jen's cool friends, and she never skimped on popcorn and Reese's Pieces.

"Okay," Lauren said, her voice cracking.

"I don't know what I'll do without you," Jen said, putting her hand over her mouth.

"I'm glad I'm dying first, so I don't have to live without you," she answered. "Hand to God, I'm glad."

"I could get hit by a bus. You never know." And then they started laughing, that wonderful, ridiculous, unstoppable laugh, sitting there, holding hands, drinking weird-tasting tea. When Sebastian and Darius came in, Sebastian ran to Lauren and gave her a slobbery kiss, and everything was good again.

But they knew. Lauren would die young. Maybe she'd see Sebastian's first day of school, but she wouldn't see him get his driver's license. She wouldn't take Octavia shopping for bras and listen to her talk about friends. She wouldn't see them for prom pictures or talk to them about college.

But hopefully, she'd see all those things from the Great Beyond, with her father. *Please let that be true, that we'll be together, Daddy. Surely we deserve that. Also, being a dolphin for a day. Do not fail me, Great Beyond.*

She held Octavia again before she left the house, breathed in the smell of her head, kissed her impossibly soft cheek. "I love you," she whispered.

Octavia answered by puking breast milk into her hair. It was, oddly enough, just what Lauren needed. *Snap out of it, Auntie.*

So she did. When you're living with a ticking clock, you can't be a loser. You can't think about what you won't get to see, what you'll never have. Ain't no one got time for that.

8

Joshua

Month two
April

Dear Joshua,

I love writing your name. Full swoony geek disclosure: I practiced writing it after our first date. In calligraphy. How dorky is that?

Are you doing all right, honey? I hope you're sleeping okay. I know how you get when you're stressed. Listen to one of those relaxation apps at bedtime. Try some CBD gummies—they helped me—or a Benadryl if you need to. I worry about you.

Me, I bet I'm sleeping great . . . not in the sleeps-with-the-fishes way, but maybe in the sleeps-with-the-dolphins way. Wouldn't that be amazing? I could be on a raft on a gentle azure ocean where there are no sharks or bitey things. I'm dozing and rocking while baby dolphins leap over me. Maybe I am one of those dolphins. At any rate, you don't have to worry about me. The Great Beyond is (I'm 99.999 percent sure) fantastic.

Are you getting outside enough? Taking Pebbles for a walk or run? Keep her healthy. Don't overfeed her. Please tell her I love her, okay? Tell her I'm sorry I had to go away, and she was the best dog ever. IS the best dog ever. (She's sitting next to me on the bed as I write this, and when I cry, she sits right on my lap, puts her paws on my shoulders and licks my tears. I want to think she's comforting me, but I think she just wants the salty deliciousness.)

I hope the grocery shopping task went well. Tell Yolanda hi from me. Actually, that would be weird, wouldn't it? "My dead wife sends her best!" Better skip that.

This month, honey, I want you to have some people over for dinner. I know you'll hate that idea, but I think you need to eat with humans once in a while, not just Pebbles. Bring some life into the apartment. Maybe have a few laughs, even.

Invite my sister and Darius, Mom (or not), your mom, maybe Sarah. Cook for them. Let them hug you. Go ahead and talk about me and cry if you need to. But let them come into our home and be part of your life, honey. Don't shut them out. They love you. Or just invite people who don't know you that well but seem nice. Your patent attorney whose name I can't remember right now. She was nice. One of your old professors from RISD. Creepy Charlotte from the first floor, who eye-fucks you every time she sees you. (Just kidding! Do not invite that woman to my house!)

It really doesn't matter who. I'm so sorry that I put you in this place, Josh. I'm with you, though. I live in your heart, and there's no better place I could be.

I hope you're doing a little better, showering and eating and maybe working some, too. Getting some sunshine. I don't know what time of year I died, but get sunshine even if it's winter.

I love you so, so much. With all my heart, liver, pancreas, stomach, kidneys, and even with my crappy lungs.

Now make some calls. Don't be a loser.

I love you.

Lauren

She was right. He hated the idea.

But God, he *loved* hearing from her. He'd read the first letter so many times he had it memorized.

Knowing he was going to have twelve of them, he'd ordered a museum-quality, pH-neutral box, handmade by a craftsman in Louisiana. Tiger maple exterior, lined in special cloth so the letters wouldn't age.

He read the letter again. He could hear her voice, which had gotten raspier throughout her illness from intubations and coughing, but which he loved just the same. He could almost smell her skin . . . the faint floral scent of her shower gel, the citrusy perfume she loved, the hint of menthol from the Vicks VapoRub she swore helped her breathe.

He closed his eyes, summoning her. *Be with me,* he thought. He might not believe in God, but he did believe in Lauren. *Come to me, honey.* The sunshine on her dark red hair, illuminating a dozen different colors of brown, red, gold. Her pink lips and dark lashes. Eyes the color of whiskey. Her big laugh, bellowing out of her.

That laugh made her cough relentlessly in the last few months. How malicious, how *evil,* that laughter made her wince in pain.

With a sigh, he opened his eyes. He was still alone, but he had a little piece of her in his hands. Her words. Her sense of humor. Her love, shining from the letter.

He *had* been trying to do better, per her instructions. Shaved when he saw that he needed to. Set his phone to go off so he'd remember to shower.

For the past month, he'd taken Pebbles for long walks in Swan Point Cemetery or drove her to Colt State Park in Bristol, where the two of them would run and hopefully not see anyone he knew. He'd been better about throwing trash away. He tried not to nap for more than an hour. He set the alarm so he'd wake up in the morning and tried to remember to eat.

He was trying to show her he could do this.

It was as if, by doing what she said, he'd pass a test, and the reward would be Lauren, alive again. He knew the letters fed that idea. He'd catch himself thinking, *When I talk to Lauren in April . . .* Once, he thought, *I can't wait to tell Lauren about her letter.*

Grief was a heavy, dark blanket, weighing him down, making the smallest things difficult. Before Lauren, he'd been a loner, sure, but it had been by choice. Now, it felt like the sun had fallen out of the sky, and the world was a wasteland of gray. He had to turn away from couples in the park or on the street. When his phone showed 183 texts, and his email inbox held 624 unread messages, he didn't bother looking at them. None of them was from the one person he wanted.

As if on cue, his phone buzzed with an incoming call. Donna. "No," he snapped, abruptly furious at the intrusion. He declined the call, then tossed his phone onto the chair opposite. "Talk to someone else."

While his mother-in-law had gotten her shit together that last week—that last day, especially, the one he couldn't bear to remember—she'd been an ass pain for most of Lauren's illness, wringing her hands, worrying about how *she,* Donna, would deal with this, how sad she was, how she couldn't sleep, eat, laugh. Two wasted years of self-pity when she could've been helpful, strong, a comfort to her daughter. He knew it wasn't possible to judge the level or means of grief when a parent loses a child, but Jesus, Donna had a gift for making it all about her. And right now, he wanted to think about Lauren's letter.

So. A dinner party. His wife wanted him to throw one, and he would comply with her wishes. He'd go with people he knew well—Jen and Darius. And Sarah, he supposed.

He retrieved his phone and texted them. They were all in, which was good.

Josh was aware that he wasn't close to many people. He'd had a couple of friends from college who'd had the same major—Peter from RISD, who was out in California, doing research at Stanford. Keung from MIT, who worked for a medical device company in London. Both had been groomsmen in his and Lauren's wedding. He had seen Peter a couple of years ago when he was in San Francisco at a conference, before Lauren had been diagnosed.

His closest childhood friend, Tim, had moved when Josh and Tim were juniors in high school. They'd seen each other only a handful of times since then. Tim had met Lauren but wasn't able to come to the wedding.

All three had left messages and sent cards after her death. But they weren't *here.* They didn't know the details of Lauren's sickness. They hadn't seen her weaken and grow smaller, hadn't seen her skin get white and then faintly blue when her sats were low. In a way, he was glad the last memory they had of her was when she was so happy, so vital. They got to remember her that way. They got to remember *him* as a happy man.

Darius, his brother-in-law, was trying to be his friend, but he was so different from Josh himself. Darius was a good-natured, easygoing executive in a big advertising firm, a former football player for the University of North Carolina. He was suave and well dressed and seemed to know something about everything, never at a loss for words. Pretty much the opposite of Josh, who still couldn't recognize a Kardashian and whose mind shuttered at most social events.

Except when he was with Lauren. She had thought he was the most interesting person on earth, and because of that, he had been. In her eyes, at any rate, and that was the only thing that mattered.

The four of them had had some great times,

the two sisters, their husbands. There'd been lots of laughter before her diagnosis, and quite a bit after, too. Dinners together. Cape Cod. The holidays.

But it was different now. That was back when he was half of Lauren-and-Josh, when he didn't feel like his skin hurt and his brain was an empty shoebox, his body sinking in tar.

Oh, fuck. A thought occurred to him. If there were four of them at dinner, it might seem a little . . . couple-ish. Jen and Darius, Sarah and Josh. And that was a firm no.

He didn't want to give the appearance in any way, shape or form that he was interested in Sarah. Not that anyone would think that, but still, the two-plus-two of it made his stomach hurt.

Sarah dated often, but no one ever stuck. Lauren used to say she had bad taste in men because her father had been a jerk. Whatever the cause, Sarah had commented more than once that Lauren had set the bar unfairly high with husbands. And if she thought that . . . if he gave any indication . . .

He didn't *really* think Sarah would assume dinner was a date, but just in case. He wasn't great at reading social cues and vibes and body language. Lauren had always helped him along there.

He grabbed his phone and texted Sarah.

Why don't you bring someone Saturday night? A friend, a date, Asmaa, whatever.

That would do the trick, wouldn't it?

His phone chimed almost immediately.

You sure? It might be weird.

No, not weird at all. It will be fine.

Okay. What can I bring?

Just your date. Friend. Whatever.

There was a bit of a pause, the three dots waving.

Yeah, okay, I'll ask a guy I'm dating. Ken. This will be our second date. If we can call it a date. That doesn't sound 100% right. Our second meeting, know what I mean?

No, he didn't, and he didn't want to. He typed a quick response.

Sure. 7:00. See you then.

He clicked off the phone and tossed it beside him, earning a bark from Pebbles. "We have to find something to cook, puppy," he said. She wagged her tail. Something he'd made before, something that wouldn't take too much effort. That dish Mrs. Kim made, maybe—crispy fried chicken with a spicy red sauce. Mrs. Kim had taught him to cook during those two years when he was too old for after-school daycare and too young to stay on his own. The dish was pretty easy. He'd cook some rice, roast some vegetables, all easy enough.

Lauren had loved it. In fact, Josh had made

it for her when they were dating, hoping to impress her. It had worked. "Dakgangjeong it is, Pebbles," he said. "Because you asked so nicely."

He went grocery shopping Saturday morning, leaving an envelope of money for Yolanda, since he hadn't been back to the grocery store since his meltdown. This time, he put in earbuds so he wouldn't have to hear anyone and tried not to make eye contact. Got the chicken, grabbed Korean red pepper and gochujang, since he couldn't remember if there was any in the pantry. Should've checked before he left the house. In the produce aisle, he grabbed a knot of fresh ginger and a head of garlic.

Cooking for Lauren, going all-organic and unprocessed, had honed his kitchen skills. As a single guy, he'd been content to order food, eat on the fly or avail himself of his mother or Mrs. Kim for home-cooked meals. But as a married man, he upped his game, and after her diagnosis, he got even better. Lauren was easy—she loved food, loved to cook when she had the energy, and ate everything except veal or lamb. "Who wants to eat a baby?" she said. "Would you want some other species eating our kids, Joshua?"

Their kids. Except there'd be no kids.

His heart spasmed, and he rubbed his chest. *Don't go there,* his brain warned. *Focus.* When he was a kid and his mood threatened to shatter, his mother had given him a sentence to repeat over and over, to think about and distract him. *The quick brown fox jumps over the lazy dog.* Every letter in the alphabet in that sentence. He'd chant it out loud, thinking about the letters, making order in his mind to head off the emotional storm.

Sometimes, it worked.

The quick brown fox jumps over the lazy dog. The quick brown fox jumps over the lazy dog.

It was helping. Spicy chicken would require rice. Did he have rice? Did he have chicken? He'd buy more. Broccoli for a vegetable. How many heads would he need? Four? Ten? How many people were coming? Didn't broccoli shrink when you cooked it? He got eight heads.

He paused at the floral section. Lauren had always bought fresh flowers when they had people over. No. This was not a celebration or a party. This was seeing his wife's sister, brother-in-law and best friend. It was part of mourning. They were all trying to deal with grief, to move on.

Except he didn't want to move on.

That black tarry pull began at his feet, and Josh turned up the volume on his podcast and forced himself to the self-checkout, so he wouldn't have to talk to anyone. But once he got home, Creepy Charlotte pounced the second he walked into the lobby.

"Oh! Groceries! You cooking tonight? Want

company?" she said. She was very short, not more than five feet, and fast, blocking Josh's path to the stairs.

"Yes and no. Thank you."

"You've got to come down for a glass of wine, Josh. We can talk. People tell me I'm a very good listener."

"I don't drink."

"Even so." She leaned in the doorway, scanning him up and down. "You need a friend."

"I have a dog. Excuse me."

He got past her, unloaded the groceries and took Pebbles for a run (using the back door to avoid Charlotte). When he returned home, he showered and started food prep, blasting Prince to make it seem less lonely. *Don't think. Just cook.*

When Lauren was alive, a night like this had been fun, the air charged with energy and anticipation, the room filled with laughter and instructions—*Honey, grab that vase. Honey, would you unload the dishwasher? Josh, do you mind cutting the chicken?* When she was alive, he was more relaxed, more competent, more present and funnier. When she was alive, he wasn't dead inside.

For a minute, he stopped chopping broccoli and stared at the counter.

If he was very still, he could picture this as a different scene. His wife was down the hall, taking a shower. She'd take forever drying her hair and change at least twice. She'd put on makeup, because she loved makeup. He could almost hear her rustling around, singing under her breath.

"Honey?" he called. Just in case.

Obviously, there was no answer. He resumed chopping, hard. If he sliced off a fingertip, he could get out of this evening.

But Lauren had asked him to do this, so he would muscle through it.

It might be time to take up drinking.

Right at seven, the doorbell rang, and he opened the door. All four of them were together—Jen, Darius, Sarah, her friend. Their faces were somber.

"Hi," he said.

Jen burst into tears.

Pebbles pushed past him and went right to her, and Jen knelt down, hugged the dog and sobbed.

No one said anything for a second.

"Um . . . do you want to come in?" Josh said.

"Good idea. Hey, brother, how are you?" Darius said, giving him a hug. "We brought wine." He put his hand on his wife's shoulder.

Shit. He didn't have any. "Good," he said. "Thanks."

"We did, too," Sarah said. "Ken, this is Joshua Park. Josh, Ken Beekman." Ken was tall—taller than Darius, even. And thin. White guy, pale yellow hair, looked a bit like a heron, friendly-enough face. He had a messenger bag slung across his torso, and he whipped it off and put it on the floor, offered his hand and shook Joshua's firmly with both of his. "Joshua. So sorry about your wife. Thanks for letting me come. You have a beautiful home."

"Nice . . . nice to meet you. Hey, Sarah." She looked nicer than usual, a dress, makeup and red lipstick.

Jen stood up, then hugged him hard. "Sorry," she whispered.

"It's okay. Really." He hugged her back, one of the few people he could hug and have it feel normal.

"Babe, I'm getting you some wine," Darius said, and so they all moved into the living room area, sort of shuffling as one. Darius made himself useful, opening a few drawers to find a corkscrew. It hadn't been used since . . . well. Valentine's Day. Their anniversary.

That was just nine weeks ago. Nine weeks and two days. How could she be dead now, when, on February 14, they'd made love in a room lit by candles? How could life have changed so much?

"It smells wicked awesome in here," Ken said. "What is it?"

Josh blinked. "Um . . . It's a spicy Korean chicken dish. Flavored by my actual tears." No one laughed, unsure if he was joking. Poor taste, he guessed.

"Do you like cooking?" Ken asked.

"Uh . . . yes. Yes, I do. I like cooking. Have a seat." He should've made snacks or something. Cheese and crackers at the very least. Did he have cheese? He didn't think so. Sarah was wiping her eyes.

The five of them stood there, not looking at each other. "Why don't I put some music on?" Darius said.

"Sure. Great idea." He should've thought of that.

"Can I, um . . . wander around?" Jen asked, her voice cracking.

"Of course," Josh said. "Of course you can." He seemed to be repeating himself, parrot-like, since he had nothing else to say.

"Josh, do you want me to rustle up some appetizers or something?" Sarah asked.

"Yes. That would be great. Thanks."

"On it," she said. "Ken, give me a hand, okay?"

"Abso-tively!" Ken said, the only cheerful one among them.

"Come with me," Jen whispered to Josh. It was only her second time here since Lauren died, and Josh could feel a burning at the back of his eyes. She took his hand, and they went into his office, which was off the living room.

There were half a dozen framed photos of Lauren, on the desk, on the wall. Her face surrounded them, reminding them of all they had lost. All that love. All that happiness.

"How are you?" Jen asked.

"I'm horrible."

"Me, too. Josh, she left me a letter." Jen's eyes filled, and Josh was struck with guilt that he hadn't taken better care of her. After all, Jen was lost, too. "It was perfect, you know? I had it framed." Her face scrunched up.

He hugged her again. "I miss her so much," Jen whispered. "I keep starting to call her. I can't bear to delete her number from my phone, you know?"

"I do."

"Of course you do. I'm sorry." Jen sighed, grabbed a tissue from the box on the desk and blew her nose loudly.

"How's your mom?" he asked.

"Oh, you haven't heard? She's doing great," Jen said bitterly. "I mean, she's wrecked, but suddenly this is her new identity. She goes to a grief group every day. It's like her new religion. And get this, Josh. She met someone. A man. They had coffee last week."

"Wow."

"Right?"

"That's . . . good, I guess." Lauren had always urged her mother to make new friends or date after her father's death. Donna had always rejected the idea of doing anything new, but . . . well, now she was. Maybe Donna was doing it for Lauren. If so, that was kind of nice. "Are you okay with it?"

"Whatever brings her peace. Or a distraction. At least she doesn't call me seven times a day like she did when Lauren was . . ." She took a shaky breath. "I don't mean to judge. I look at my kids and think of one of them . . . being sick, and I just fall apart. So whatever helps keep Mom together, go for it, right?"

"Right."

She wiped her eyes again. "You're such a good guy, Josh."

Was he, though? He had no idea anymore.

Jen swallowed hard, audibly. "Can I see the . . . tree?"

"Yes. Absolutely." They left his office, walked through the living room and down the hall to the bedroom, Pebbles padding behind them. Josh stopped in front of their bedroom door, and after a second or two, opened the door.

He came in here to check the tree every third day. That lasted about thirty-five, forty seconds. Fewer, if possible.

But looking at the pristine, empty bedroom now, he remembered the many days when Jen came over and lay on the bed with her little sister, spooning against her. How they always laughed together. How Jen would paint Lauren's toenails sometimes.

Jen went to the tree in front of the window and gently stroked a leaf. "Oh, Lauren," she said, her breath hitching. Her tears began again. Josh went over and put his arm around her shoulders. They both looked at the tree. Soil. Soil and a scrawny tree that looked like a stick with seven leaves. That was all they had left of her.

Say something. Tell her something nice, for God's sake. "You were her hero, Jen," he said, and it was the right thing, miraculously. Jen hugged him tight, shaking with tears.

"There's no word for me anymore," she said. "I've been a sister since I was five. Now my sister's gone. What does that even make me?" She started bawling in earnest.

Would the grief ever lift? Would they—any of them who had loved Lauren—ever be happy again? It didn't seem possible.

Darius popped his head in. "Oh, sweetie," he said, and Josh sort of transferred Jen to her husband. Should he leave? He should. Even if it was his bedroom. Pebbles was on the bed, but what the hell. Josh had to get out of the room before he broke.

He went into the half bath and took a couple of breaths. He'd never have to relive this night again. *Just get through it,* he told himself, but his composure, thin as it was, was cracking.

Try to be normal, loser. Lauren's voice.

He nodded. Splashed water on his face. Looked at himself in the mirror.

It was a lonely face if ever there was one. Lauren had always told him he was a handsome guy, and yes, women had always sought him out or looked at him twice (see Exhibit A, Creepy Charlotte). He could see traces of his mother—strong bones and wide-set eyes. But his mother's eyes were blue, and his were brown. Like the man who fathered him, Josh supposed. Whoever that was.

Back to the kitchen. Sarah was cutting up carrots and celery and had found some hummus. Not exactly glamorous, but not bad, either. Ken was leaning on the counter, arranging the vegetables on a plate.

Fuck. Josh would have to make conversation, wouldn't he?

"So, Ken," he said. "What do you do for work?"

"I'm in sales for a nutrition company."

"Cool. Uh, how did you meet Sarah?"

"Online, right, babe?"

"It's a little early for *babe,* isn't it?" Sarah asked mildly.

"Sorry!" Ken said. "I'm jumping the gun a little. Because she's great, isn't she? Josh, do you mind if I ask how much this place cost you? I'm looking for a new apartment myself."

Josh *hated* talking about money. "Uh, well, it was a few years ago, so the market was different."

"I hear you, Josh, I hear you. Half a mil, maybe?"

"Sounds about right."

"Any more places available in this building?"

Oh, Jesus. Don't move in here. He didn't want to have to talk to anyone. Creepy Charlotte was bad enough. "Most are one- or two-bedroom units. We got the only three-bedroom, though, because, uh, I work from home, so one bedroom is my office." The study, Lauren insisted on calling it. It was classier, she'd said.

They'd had sex in that study. More than once. Had they really been as happy as he remembered? As it seemed? Could any couple be that perfect together?

"Sorry, what?" He realized he'd missed out on some conversation.

"No problem, Josh, no problem. You're still grieving. I understand, man. It's not easy. Takes time." Ken took a swig of wine.

"Did you lose someone, too?" Sarah asked, looking up from the chopping. Josh was wondering the same thing.

"No. Nope. I've been lucky so far. I'm just . . . well, people say I'm very compassionate. In fact, one of the reasons I liked Sarah so much was because she told me a lot about Lauren, and I could see how much of a bond they had. It was very . . . affecting."

They smiled at each other, and then Ken turned back to him. "What do you do for work, Josh?"

"I'm a medical device engineer," he said. Sarah was bustling around the kitchen, opening a drawer, pulling out a serving spoon. She knew where everything was, quite at home. It irked him a little, even if she knew their kitchen because of all the time she'd spent helping out. But it wasn't *fair.* Why did Lauren have to die? Why was it Lauren? He'd stab Sarah through the heart right this minute if it could make his wife come back.

"Cool," said Ken, and Josh didn't know what he was commenting on.

"He's selling himself short," Sarah said, smiling. "Josh is kind of a big deal. He's sold . . . what, twelve patents? Five that are already on the market?"

"Nine. Nine patents, five on the market."

"So it's a pretty lucrative field for you, Josh?"

Was it him, or was Ken using his name an awful lot? Maybe that was what normal people did, a method to remember names. "Sure. I mean, so far, yes. Um . . . I should finish cooking here."

It would be *hours* before he was alone again in the apartment. An eternity. He got a pan out for the rice and started boiling water.

This is hard, Lauren, he thought. *I'd like to call you later and tell you what a failure it was, but you were incredibly rude and died.* His throat tightened at the memory of her last hours. No. Absolutely not. He would not revisit that time. Ever.

The thought made him relax the tiniest bit. He

could put that day away. It would be best that way. Far better to think of her smile, her laugh, her freckles, her eyes.

I miss you. I miss you. I miss you.

Darius and Jen returned from the bedroom, thank God, and sat with Ken in the living room. Ken asked Darius about his profession, how much he traveled, where they lived. It was so weird to have a stranger here, but the conversation was like white noise, and Josh was grateful that no one was asking him anything at the moment. Sarah set the table while Jen sat on the couch with Pebbles and stared out the window, wiping away tears from time to time.

Josh fried the chicken, set it to dry and reheated the glaze he'd made earlier. Shit. He'd been planning to grill the broccoli on the roof. Nah. Too much effort, and plus he wasn't sure how clean that grill was . . . the last time he'd used it, he'd burned his clothes. Steaming the broccoli would be fine. Darius came into the kitchen, opened another bottle of wine—everyone was having some except Josh—and went back to the living room.

"It's funny that you don't drink at all," Lauren had said once. "Most people have at least tried alcohol."

"I don't see a reason to," he said. This was on their second date. She stared at him like he was an interesting riddle, her brows drawn, a faint smile on her lips, and he smiled back, his stomach thrumming with attraction and the strangest feeling . . . that he *belonged* with her. That they were meant to be together. That the flirty college girl cliché he'd first met a few years earlier had grown into something . . . more. Deeper. Wiser.

And maybe he'd gotten out of his own way, finally. He hadn't allowed himself to have much fun in college, so focused on work, on making a difference, on being someone who mattered despite having a father who had never bothered to even learn his name. He had no room for anything else.

But that night, looking at her face, her pretty eyes the color of cognac or brandy, feeling like he belonged to her already, Josh decided he had plenty of room after all.

A sharp smell pierced his memories.

Fuck. The glaze was burning. He yanked the pan off the burner and flapped a dishtowel in the air so the smoke detector wouldn't go off. Sarah leaped up from the couch to help, but it went off anyway, bleating his failure. Darius and Ken opened the windows, and Jen opened the door, and Pebbles whirled in circles, barking at the painful noise.

After an eternity, it stopped. Josh's ears were ringing. The glaze was charred but still liquid.

"It'll be fine," Sarah said. "I mean, who doesn't

like a little scorching? Seriously, it smells even better."

She really was a good person. "Thanks, Sarah."

She lowered her voice. "Hang in there, buddy. We won't stay long."

He looked at her, surprised that she'd read his mind. "That obvious?"

"Yeah."

"Sorry. Ken's nice, by the way."

"He is. Very . . . energetic. Not *that* way. Well, maybe he is. I don't know. We haven't . . . I'll stop talking."

He nearly smiled. "Why don't you herd everyone to the table?" he asked, and she did. He put the chicken on the rice, drizzled the blackened sauce over it. He'd made too much, and some slopped over the edge. He added sesame seeds. Lauren had loved this dish.

Crap. The broccoli was on the stove. He turned to check it, finding it way overcooked, a dull, ugly green. He tested it with a fork; it disintegrated into mush.

Then came a clatter and the crash of something breaking.

"Pebbles!" Jen said, and yep, the dog was eating the dakgangjeong off the floor. Wolfing it down without pausing to chew.

"Pebbles! No!" Josh said, but she just wagged her tail and kept going for it.

"Bad dog," said Darius, his deep voice

scaring her. She glanced at him, took a final bite, then ran down the hall, clots of rice and sauce in her wake, her muzzle and paws coated in dark red sauce, as if she'd just eaten a baby antelope.

That shit was sticky. Was their bedroom door open? Yes, it was. God*damn* it. The dog would mess up Lauren's room, and it was his own fault. He ran down the hall. The spice had caught up with Pebbles, and she was rubbing her muzzle on the fluffy white rug Lauren had loved. Reddish-black paw prints already marred the pure white comforter. The room looked like a crime scene. "Pebbles!" he shouted, his voice way too loud. "You're very bad!"

She bowed her head, and it hit him in the heart. This was Lauren's dog. Lauren's friend.

"I'm sorry," he said, closing the door so she couldn't trash the rest of the house. "You're very beautiful. You're a good girl." She wagged her tail, then threw up. "Oh, honey. I'm sorry."

She came to his knee, and he patted her sticky head. Went into the master bathroom, grabbed some towels, cleaned her up as best he could and closed her in the guest room. He'd deal with the mess when everyone left.

With a sigh, he went back to the kitchen. Sarah was wiping up the stream of burnt sauce that had sloshed on the side of the island. "Ken, grab me the Windex from under the sink," she said.

Darius was on his phone, and Jen was leaning on the counter, watching.

The platter that broke had been a wedding gift from Lauren's boss. It was from Italy, Josh thought.

"We can probably still eat this food," Ken said, looking at the mess, the broken platter. "There's a lot left."

"No, we can't," Jen said, her wineglass in her hand. "The *dog* just ate it, there are shards of broken porcelain in there, and it's on the *floor,* where all our shoes have been. So . . . we're not eating it, Ken."

"Yeah, no," Ken said. "I just . . . it's a shame, that's all. Josh. Nice try, man."

"Maybe we should go," Jen said.

Yes, go, he thought. But then he'd have to do this again some other night, if he wanted to follow Lauren's instructions. She thought he should do this; do this, he would.

"Please stay," Josh said. "I'll order something. Don't go yet." He looked at Sarah, who nodded. He hadn't told her about Lauren's letters. Maybe Lauren had told her. Regardless, they were all here, he was going to stick with the plan, damn it.

"I'm on it," Darius said, taking his phone out. "Everyone okay with pizza?"

"The faster the better," Jen said.

Forty minutes later, after he'd cleaned up the

kitchen mess and tried unsuccessfully to make conversation, and Ken had given up on gluing the platter back together, the pizza arrived. Josh sat down, exhausted. Took a sip of water.

They ate. The pizza was awful, and they chewed grimly. Jen scratched her arm. Her face was flushed, but she kept drinking wine. Who could blame her? Sarah had offered to make a salad, but he didn't have lettuce, and she'd used up his remaining vegetables for the appetizer. He served the flaccid broccoli, noticing Darius shudder as he took a bite.

Someone mentioned that baseball had started up again, and the Sox had lost two-thirds of their games so far. Typical.

"Funny story," Ken said, and Josh jumped a little. "My real name is Kenobi. My parents are total *Star Wars* geeks."

"Well, that's a fucking curse, isn't it?" Jen said, and Darius subtly moved her wineglass a few inches away from her. "Is your brother named Darth Vader?"

"No, but my sister is Leia."

"Shouldn't you be Luke, then?" Jen asked.

"Our dog is Luke. Was. He died a long time ago."

There was an awkward silence. "*Star Wars* is a great movie," Josh offered.

" 'Help me, Obi-Wan Kenobi,' " Sarah supplied. " 'You're my only hope.' "

Ken(obi) grinned. "I *will* help you," he said. "I will totally help you, Sarah. And all of you. Jen. Darius. Josh. In fact, now that we're all pretty much done with dinner, I have something I want to show you guys."

"You do?" Sarah asked.

"I do! Come on, let's go in the living room." He got up, went to his messenger bag by the front door and pulled out a laptop.

"We should go," Jen said. "We have children. Who are *not* named after *Star Wars* characters. But maybe next time, huh, D? Little Lando Calrissian? Baby Kylo Ren?"

"Okay, hon, tone it down," Darius said, trying to hide his laugh. "We can stay a little longer."

"Right," Jen whispered loudly. "We can't leave Josh all by himself with this weirdo."

Josh was grateful.

"This will only take a second," Obi-Wan Kenobi said. "I promise, you'll love it."

Was he going to show cat videos? What . . . Josh looked at Sarah, who shrugged and grimaced.

"So you're probably thinking, 'Ken, what can *you* do for *me?*' "

"Teach us to use the Force?" Jen asked, then snort-laughed.

Ken was undeterred. "And I get that, I do. So here's the deal. Darius, my brother—"

"Nope. Not your brother," Darius interrupted.

"Sure! No worries! Darius, you look like a guy who works out a lot. Right? Football at UNC, you said. Awesome team, my broth—uh, man! But are you feeling a little tired these days?"

"No," said Darius. "Can't say that I am."

"Ken, maybe this isn't the time," Sarah said. "Actually, it's *definitely* not the time. For whatever it is you're about to do."

"Like I said, it's five minutes that will change your life." Ken touched the keyboard. A logo floated onto the screen. *VitaKetoMaxo* in pulsing letters, along with images of very fit people working out behind it. Bicycling, lifting weights, running, leaping through the air.

"VitaKetoMaxo is more than a protein shake," Ken went on, his voice rhythmic.

"Stop," said Sarah, her teeth gritted. She was mad, Josh deduced. Kind of interesting, her face getting blotchy that way.

"It's a way of life," Ken said. He clicked, and more fit people appeared on-screen, now all drinking from green bottles.

"Jesus Christ, are you trying to *sell* us something?" Jen asked, a little late to the party. She scratched her arm vigorously. "Dude. Fuck off." She grabbed her wineglass, polished off the last bit and handed it to Darius. "Hon, could you get me a tad more?"

"You've had enough, haven't you, babe?"

"No. Babe."

"In that case, yes, my queen." Darius got up and got the bottle.

"You might *think* I'm trying to sell you something," Ken went on. "But I'm not. I'm trying to *give* you something. A new way to look at the world."

"Like, from the deck of the Death Star?" Jen said. "Obi-Wan, are you going to blow up our planet?"

"Just for the record, the *real* Obi-Wan Kenobi would never do that," Josh said. *Star Wars* had been very important to him during his adolescence, and loyalty was important in these matters.

"Oh, God, Ken," Sarah said. "You're trying to sell us a nutrition drink, aren't you?"

Ken was lit with a zealous passion, his pasty skin turning pink. "Oh, my gosh, babe, it's so much more than that!"

"I thought we agreed not to use *babe* just yet."

"Do you know why we're all here, Obi-Wan?" Jen asked. "Because my *sister* died. Joshua's *wife*. We're in fucking mourning, okay?"

To be honest, Josh was kind of enjoying the show. It was better than thinking about loneliness. On the computer screen, people were doing cartwheels across a meadow. "Tell us more, Ken," he said, earning a dismayed look from Sarah.

"Thanks, Joshua, man! It's about lifestyle. It's the chance you've been waiting for. The opportunity to build a new life filled with riches."

"I'm itchy," Jen said. "Is anyone else itchy?"

"Maybe we *should* go," Darius said. "You're kind of flushed."

"I already *told* you, we can't leave Josh here alone with this freak!" Jen barked. "You know he's way too polite to kick this asshole out. Sarah, I'm sorry, but collect your date."

Sarah tried to push the laptop closed, but Ken jerked it away. "Ken," she said firmly, "you're embarrassing me. Well, you're embarrassing yourself, but also me."

"Babe! Just listen. Some people say VitaKeto-Maxo is a pyramid scheme, but it's actually very differently structured." Another click showed a diagram of a pyramid scheme. "See, I'd be your distributor, and you'd sell . . . well, really, *give* your friends the chance for a better life. Some of that money *would* flow back up to me to reinvest—"

"You know what, babe?" Jen said. "I think you're right." She stuck out her arms. "Are these hives?" Sure enough, blotches of red marred her skin. "Shit. I might be having an allergic reaction. What was on the pizza?"

"Nothing you haven't eaten a thousand times," Darius said.

"Where was it from?"

"The sketchy place down the block."

Jen let her head flop back on the couch. Darius

glanced at Josh. "You have an Epi-Pen, right? Just in case?"

Josh nodded. "Benadryl, too." Lauren had been on so many medications that the doctor had prescribed an Epi-Pen preemptively, in case of an allergic reaction, since a compromised airway was not something they needed.

Ken saw this as a great segue. "Interesting that you bring up food allergies, Jen—Jenny, if I may?"

"You may not."

Josh felt the stir of laughter in his stomach.

"So, Jen, if you drank VitaKetoMaxo, hives would *never* be a problem. Ever. Food allergies would never be a problem. VitaKetoMaxo is known to cure all food allergies *and* eliminate the need for vaccines."

"Oh, my Jesus," Sarah said, closing her eyes.

"Can I have the scientific data on that?" Josh asked. "Three reputable sources, please."

Ken didn't pause. "It's a proven fact that VitaKetoMaxo users live longer and healthier." He turned to Josh, his blue eyes wide and earnest. "In fact, I'm guessing that if your wife had used VitaKetoMaxo, she never would have—"

And then Josh must've moved from the couch, because he had Obi-Wan Kenobi by his bony, long throat and was dragging him to the door and everything was going red. "Get the fuck out of my house," he said, opening the door and shoving him out. Josh went back, shoved the laptop into Ken's computer bag, threw them out into the hallway, then slammed the door.

The quick brown fox. The quick brown fox. The quick brown fox jumps over the lazy dog.

The red began to evaporate. Josh's heart was thudding.

The other three were silent.

"I'm very, very sorry," Sarah said eventually. "I had no idea."

"I definitely have hives," Jen said.

"Probably too much red wine, baby," Darius said.

"Benadryl is in the bathroom," Josh said. He looked around. "But aside from the dog eating our dinner, and your hives, Jen, and the shitty pizza and the sales pitch, how's everyone doing?"

Darius started laughing, and then so did Jen, and then Sarah.

Josh felt himself almost smiling. He'd forgotten he could make people laugh from time to time. In another minute, he managed a smile. After a second, he even laughed, the sound rusty from neglect.

The first time he'd laughed since Lauren had died.

9

Lauren

Eleven months left
March 13

Dear Dad,
I was in the hospital again. Ugh. Right before my second anniversary, too. Just for three days this time, but I definitely know the staff by now. I had pneumonia, which is not good.

Here's an insider secret: Being sick is really boring. Boring to live, boring to discuss, boring to hear about, and yet everyone asks. Everyone. "You look too pretty to be in here!" said the guy taking me to a chest X-ray. "What's the matter with you, honey?"

So I told him, like I tell everyone. I'm a walking advocate for idiopathic pulmonary fibrosis research, education and treatment. I can recite facts in my sleep. Then there are the other sick people I see. Most of them are older, and I think I make them feel good about themselves. "At least I'm eighty! That poor girl over there isn't even thirty!"

The worst thing is to see the sick kids. If I could donate the time I have left to them, I'd do it, Dad. I'd do it in a heartbeat.

Sorry to be a downer today. I seem to have the blues.

Miss you, Pop.

Lauren

"We should take a vacation," Lauren said. She was itchy and scratchy, still irritable that she'd had to go to the hospital again. "Maybe somewhere tropical and warm, since we didn't do anything for our anniversary."

"We could go back to Hawaii," he suggested. "Rent the same house."

It seemed *so* long ago, their honeymoon. That carefree time when she thought an inhaler could cure her, when they talked about baby names and learning to scuba dive and how they'd come back to Kauai for their twenty-fifth anniversary to renew their vows.

She didn't want to taint that beautiful place with her sickness.

"Let's go somewhere different," she said brightly. "The Caribbean, maybe? I've never been. And the flight's a lot shorter."

"Whatever you want, honey." He squeezed her hand, and she squeezed back. Lucky. She was damn lucky.

That's my girl, she could almost hear her father say. *That's my girl.*

The difference between the trip to Hawaii and the trip to Turks and Caicos was the oxygen. In Hawaii, they had been a gorgeous couple on their honeymoon; here, they were That Tragic Couple. Oh, the looks, or overly kind faces, and yes, even tears her mere appearance brought on! So young! So attractive! The horror, the horror, etc.

Josh had chosen a spectacular resort filled with stone pathways and tropical gardens, a spa and five-star restaurants. The sky was impossibly blue, and the turquoise water so clear they could see a turtle from fifty feet away. Their villa had a living room, covered porch, and a bedroom with an enormous bed. First things first—put that bed to good use, and Lauren wasn't talking about a nap.

They walked slowly down the beach afterward, her long pink summery dress blowing, a big straw hat on her head—redheads were cursed when it came to the sun. Her oxygen was in her leather bag, and if you didn't look closely, you might not notice the cannula in her nose.

For a little while, she wouldn't notice it, either. She'd notice the soft sand and hot sun, her husband's hand in hers, the brush of her dangly earrings on her shoulders. She'd listen

122

to the birds and figure out how to go snorkeling tomorrow.

That evening, they chose one of the restaurants on the resort property. There was a huge terrace scattered with tables, candles and flowers everywhere. They got a table overlooking the garden and the ocean beyond, and ignored the pitying yet encouraging looks that said, *Good for you, eating even though you're sick! Aren't you brave!*

Sigh.

They'd made their way through their appetizers when a server approached. "Another couple would like to pay for your dinners," he murmured. She and Josh exchanged puzzled looks.

Ah. Over there, an older couple waved discreetly.

"No," Josh said.

"It's very kind, but no thanks," Lauren said.

"They insist."

"It's so sweet, but no," Lauren said. She looked at the couple and shook her head, smiling firmly.

The waiter grimaced. "They said not to take no for an answer."

"Tell them to donate to a veteran's group or Save the Children instead," Lauren suggested.

"They said you were very brave—"

"No!" Josh said, leaping to his feet. "I can pay for my wife's dinner, goddamnit!" He turned to face the couple, whose expressions had morphed into abrupt shock. "Take your pity and shove it up your ass!"

"Honey!" she said, standing.

"No. Mind your own fucking business!" he yelled, his voice hard. "We don't need your money. We're not the Make-A-Wish Foundation!"

"Sir," the waiter said. "Please, I'm so sorry."

"It's not you," Lauren said, putting her hand on Josh's arm. "Joshua. Sit down, honey."

"No! We're not animals in a zoo, okay? We came here for dinner and to be left the fuck alone!"

His anger . . . it was so rare, so unlike him, her heart was thudding sickly, and if she wasn't really careful, she'd cry, which wouldn't help anything. Everyone was staring. "Can we cancel the rest of our order?" she asked, and the waiter nodded and scurried away. "Josh. Come on. We're leaving."

Rigid with fury, he let her take his arm, and they walked back toward their suite. His strides were long, and she was out of breath before they'd made it ten yards. "Okay, enough," she said sharply. "I can't keep up. Can you slow down, please?"

He jerked to a stop. "They had no fucking business—"

"Josh! Knock it off! They were trying to do something nice, that's all."

"I don't care."

He wasn't mad at the offer. He was angry because . . . because she was sick. Because life wasn't fair. And Josh wasn't good with anger. It flummoxed him, confused him, ate at him.

"Sweetheart, go for long walk or run, okay? I know you're upset. Just . . . burn it off. I'm gonna go to the bar and eat and read, and I'll see you when you're . . . over this."

"Fine." He strode off, and Lauren went back to the restaurant, apologized to the waiter, left him a big tip and went to the bar, collapsing into a booth, winded and distressed, trying not to cry.

She wasn't mad at him. She was *heartbroken* for him. Those people had touched a nerve by singling them out, and all Josh wanted was for them to be a normal couple, in love, enjoying each other.

Not a couple with a clock ticking. Not a couple where one would be left alone.

How could she do this to him? How could she help him, her beautiful loner husband? What would happen to him? He had told her she was his first love. "My one and only," he'd said. But in a year or three or ten, he'd be a widower. Being alone by choice was one thing. Her death . . . it could ruin him. She could ruin the person she loved best in the world.

She went back to the empty suite and got ready for bed. She missed Pebbles. She missed Josh. She missed her sister. The skylight above their bed showed the vast, starlit sky, and tears trickled out of her eyes and into the pillow.

But sleep wasn't a choice as much as a necessity, and the bed was huge and white and cool, and within minutes, she was asleep.

Sometime later, she woke up to Josh getting into bed. He wrapped her in his arms and kissed her forehead. "I'm sorry," he whispered.

"It's okay."

"I sent flowers to that couple," he said. "And a gift certificate to the spa."

She smiled against his chest. "Did you apologize?"

"I did. In a note."

She kissed him. "You're a good guy, Joshua Park."

"I'm an idiot."

"No. You get to be upset."

"I love you." His voice was rough.

"I know, honey. I know."

The stars burned in the sky, so bright on this moonless night it felt like a message. She kissed him again, more intently, suddenly aching for him, and tugged at his T-shirt. Her beautiful Josh. He cradled her face in his hands and kissed her back, and tonight, they were more in love than ever before, desperate for each other, complete only with each other, hearts thumping, mouths seeking and finding, their bodies joined in the shelter of the bed.

He fell asleep after, exhausted from his rare anger, from their lovemaking.

She suddenly knew what to do. How to look after Josh when she was gone. As quietly as she could, she slipped out of bed and found her notebook.

There were a few things she wanted to do on this little trip. Snorkel and swim in the clear water. Take a horseback ride. Sleep in the hammock that was strung between two trees. Watch a porno. Hey! "Adult Selections" was part of the cable package that came with their suite, and she'd never seen one before. *Clitty Clitty Bang Bang* looked promising, even if it did ruin her childhood with its title alone.

Josh arranged everything. He had a hammock set up in the little garden that led to the beach. Shade, an arrangement of tropical flowers in a vase, a bottle of champagne. "My queen," he said. "A nap on the beach awaits you."

"Oh! How fabulous! A dream come true," she said.

She climbed into the hammock, and Josh set her oxygen next to her and adjusted the cannula. He covered her with a soft blanket, because even though it was eighty degrees, she got cold easily. Then he sat on the lawn beside her, looking out at the gentle azure ocean. She reached out and stroked his hair, which gleamed in the sun. "I never knew anyone could ever love me as much as you do," she said.

He looked at the grass, then back up at her, and those dark-lit eyes were shiny with tears. "Same here," he whispered. "Same here. And you never know. I could die first. Get hit by a bus."

"Look both ways, loser. The world needs you. Besides, when you're a widower, maybe Beyoncé will be free."

"I'd rather have one hour with you than a million days with Beyoncé."

"Oh, please. You're lying. *I'd* take Beyoncé in a heartbeat." She traced his adorable ear with one finger. "You're married to a woman with a terminal illness. Our life is a catastrophe."

"Now that you bring it up, you are kind of a loser."

She snorted. "Ah, well. What was on that card from Mean Debi? 'It's not about counting the days; it's about making each day count.' "

"I just threw up in my mouth."

"I hear you. Let's stop talking about death. It's a beautiful day. I'm sorry I'm so maudlin today. I don't know what's wrong with me."

"You have a grave lung condition," he intoned.

"Right, right, I forgot."

He turned to look at her, and his eyes were full of tears. "I love you with all my heart, Lauren Park."

"I love you with all my pancreas."

"I love you with both kidneys," he said, smiling just a little.

"I love you with all my liver. And the liver is very important, as you know."

"Go to sleep, wife. I have plans for you later involving a certain magical car that can somehow induce orgasm."

"Oh, my God." She fell asleep, still smiling.

She slept. And when she woke up, they went inside to the big bed and got naked and turned on the porno. A UPS man appeared on the screen, knocking on the door of a woman wearing a red thong and sparkly pasties, holding a broom.

"What?" Lauren exclaimed. "That's what I wear when doing housework, too!"

"What is it about UPS?" Josh asked. "Do they know what their drivers are doing all day? And where is the magical car? I was promised a magical car."

They lasted four more minutes into the film before their laughter made watching it impossible. It served its purpose, though . . . they made love afterward, and it was gentle and filled with laughter and smiles.

On their second-to-last night there, they sat on the patio sofa, her back against his chest, his arms around her, and they watched the sun sink into the cream-and-orange clouds. When the sun slid behind the ocean, the water turned cobalt, and the clouds faded to purples and pinks, then gray. Herons, sandpipers and pelicans gabbled as the waves shushed against the shore, and the stars came out, one by one, growing brighter as the sky turned indigo.

If she could choose where to die, she'd pick here. Just one gentle last breath, then nothing.

Unfortunately, the odds were against her in that respect. She'd Googled the videos. She'd seen the documentaries. Dying of oxygen deprivation was not pretty.

She sat up and wrapped the blanket more snugly around her shoulders. "Josh, we need to talk about something."

His face locked. "What?" he asked, but she knew he knew.

"Stuff." She stifled a cough and swallowed. "End-of-life stuff."

Josh bent his head. "It's too early to think like that."

"Well, honey, it's obviously on your mind, or you wouldn't have gotten so mad the other night. And it's on mine. This is the perfect time to talk, because then we can put it away and have fun tomorrow. I want to go swimming again." Tears were thickening the back of her throat. She coughed to clear it. The last thing she needed was mucous gunk choking her. A nice yoga breath, a conscious relaxing of her neck and throat muscles. But her eyes stung nonetheless. "Please, Josh. Let's get it out of the way."

He looked away. A night bird trilled, then fell silent. "Okay," Josh said, and his voice was flat and expressionless. "Go ahead."

Her heart hurt. It *hurt* like a dull knife was pushing through it, a centimeter at a time. "So I've been thinking about it a little, here and there. And I know it's probably a long way off, but just in case . . ." Her voice choked off as she swallowed a sob.

He took her hands and studied them, the diamonds of her engagement ring winking like a star.

That had been such a happy day, the day he proposed. It seemed like decades ago, in another life. A healthy life.

She took a careful breath, as deep as she could. "I want it to just be you and me at the very end. Not my mom, not Jen, not anyone but us."

He nodded and swallowed, his perfect throat working. His grip on her hands tightened.

"I'd like to say goodbye to everyone, if that's possible. You know . . . if I can tell I'm winding down but can . . . but can still talk and stuff."

He nodded, then bent so his head rested on their joined hands. He was crying. Of course he was. It was impossible not to, and she was, too.

"I don't want heroic measures," she whispered. "If it's the end, it . . . we have to let it be. I don't want to be a body kept alive by machines just for another day or two. When I go, I want to be . . . me. I know there'll be drugs and stuff, but I want to be able to look at you."

Her hands were wet from his tears. He nodded, unable to speak.

Given the choice, she'd pick his life over hers. Any day, every day. If one of them had to die, it *should* be her, because he was such a gift to the entire world. He was. He was everything.

She bent over so her head rested on his, the two of them folded together like origami. She pulled one hand free and stroked his black hair. Oh, she loved him so much. So much.

"Are you done?" he asked, his voice thick.

"Well, a couple more things." She straightened up. "I don't want to die at home."

He looked up at her. "You don't?"

"No. I don't want you to remember me dead in our bed, or on the kitchen floor, or . . . I don't know. On the toilet."

He half laughed, half sobbed. "Okay. No toilet death. If you do die there, I'll move you so you look dignified, and lie to everyone."

"That's what I'm talking about." She smiled, but her mouth was wobbling. "I want a big-ass funeral, too, where everyone is sobbing, but laughing, too. And really good food and music. None of that church stuff. I want Beyoncé and Bruno. In person, if possible."

He laughed, and his laugh was a sign of his

love, because he knew she couldn't take it if he broke. "Anything else?"

"Yes. Eulogy by Jen, toasts at the after-party from anyone who wants. And then I want to be cremated and mixed in with soil and have a tree grow out of me. They have these urns for that."

He kissed her hands, then looked at her, eyes wet, trying to smile. "What if the tree dies? How shitty will I feel then?"

"Water me twice a week and stick me in the sun. It's not hard, Joshua. Don't be a loser."

"Did you know you can make your loved one's ashes into jewelry?"

"Okay, *that's* morbid. And who would wear that? I want to be a tree. Just don't let Pebbles pee on me."

He pulled her into his arms and held her tight. She adjusted the cannula and then squeezed him back, holding him with all her strength. "I love you," he whispered. "I'm the luckiest man in the world because I married you."

And the thing was, she knew he meant it.

"Tell me you'll be okay without me."

"I won't be."

She said nothing, and Josh was quiet a long moment, the only sound the rhythm of the ocean waves against the shore. "I will be," he said, his voice rough. "I'll be grateful for every day that I got to be your husband."

She turned and wrapped herself around him,

133

and though they tried so hard so many times not to cry, sometimes you just had to. Even when it felt like your heart was being pulled out of your chest, still beating. Even when you had to cough and gasp and would need to up the airflow on your oxygen. Their tears soaked into each other's hair, skin, clothes. But it was okay. Everyone died. Her death was just a little less theoretical than most.

Besides, she had a new project now, unrelated to public space design, and one of which she thought her father heartily approved.

A person had to plan for the future, after all. Even if she wouldn't be there for it.

10

Joshua

Still month two
April, 12:51 a.m.

Why hadn't he gotten a fifth opinion? They'd gone to Dr. Bennett at Rhode Island Hospital, then to Mass General and Brigham and Women's in Boston and, later, to the Mayo Clinic. Every pulmonologist agreed that the treatment plan Dr. Bennett had laid out was the same one they would've followed.

And everyone could see how well that turned out.

Josh should've taken her to Yale New Haven. *And* New York-Presbyterian. And National Jewish Health in Denver. UCSF. Cleveland Clinic. Shit, there had to be places that did better.

Earlier in the day—technically yesterday, he noted—he'd tried to work, but got derailed when a notification from Pulmonary Fibrosis News popped up. A new trial was coming, and the lead researcher was from Yale.

They *should've* gone to Yale. He should've kept looking. If he had, Lauren could well be here with him now, quite possibly even better. He could move closer to her, put his arm around her, kiss her shoulder. She would turn toward him, sleepy but smiling, and they'd kiss, and he'd slide his hand under her shirt and feel the warm curve of her breast.

He jammed his fingers in his hair and clenched his head. He wasn't going to make it through this night. He'd call Jen, but—shit, no, it was way too late. That grief forum he'd found for young widowers and widows? The subreddit group?

No. No. He didn't want to be around more pain.

Time to call AppleCare.

It was that, or he'd start howling or run into the streets or go into the first-floor gym to hit the punching bag, but the last time he did that, Creepy Charlotte had come in (at three a.m.) to do yoga in very little clothing.

Apple it would be. He had an extended warranty, and it was time for that investment to pay off.

He called 1-800-MY-APPLE, so easy to remember from that time when his laptop froze during a system upgrade. It had taken forever, but the person had been wicked nice.

He punched the appropriate buttons and said the appropriate words—*computer. MacBook Air. Software not updating.* Then, finally, he heard a human voice.

"Hi, this is Rory, who am I speaking to?"

"Joshua."

"Can I have your phone number in case we get disconnected?"

Josh gave it, then explained his nonexistent problem.

"No worries," said Rory, his voice chipper. "We can do a safe reboot and see what happens."

"Great," said Josh. Rory gave him the instructions, and Josh pretended to do the things.

"This might take a little while," Rory said.

"Not a problem." Was Rory going to hang up? "Uh, if you could stay on the line till it's up and running . . ."

"Yeah, absolutely."

They sat in amiable silence for a minute or two.

"How's the weather where you are?" asked Rory.

"It's beautiful," Josh said, having no idea what the weather was like at the moment.

"Where do you live?"

"Hawaii. Kauai," Josh lied.

"Oh, man, you're lucky! What's it like there?"

It would be seven o'clock there. The sun would be starting to set, and he'd be sitting on the deck of their house, and Lauren would bring him a glass of ice water with a sprig of mint in it. She'd have a glass of rosé, and she'd curl up next to him.

"It's beautiful. It's Hawaii, right? Um . . . our house is up on a cliff. It rained a little while ago, but it's gorgeous now. Sunset will be soon."

Those sunsets had been incredible, better than any movie.

"Must be amazing."

"Oh, yeah. A real nice place to live."

"Kauai, that's the little island, right?" Rory asked.

"One of them. It's called the Garden Island, because it rains so much. Really lush. They filmed part of *Jurassic Park* here."

"Oh, cool. Were you born there?"

"Yes." Like every person who visited Hawaii, he and Lauren had talked about living there someday. She wanted to raise their kids close to their families, so living in Hawaii would be down the road a bit, once the kids were in college, but when he and Lauren were still young enough to snorkel and surf and hike.

Yep.

The images were so clear, he could smell the plumeria. He'd wear a Hawaiian shirt every day, and their kids would learn the language and be good stewards of the land. Lauren would manage to get a little tan. She'd work on developing parks and help preserve Hawaiian cultural spots and—

"So if I was gonna go to Hawaii, which islands should I see?" Rory asked.

"Well, definitely Kauai," Josh said. "Natural beauty, the prettiest beach in the world at Hanalei Bay. My wife loves to bodysurf, and she says that place is the best." Which was true. She had.

"Maui is fantastic, too. Great hotels and restaurants, plus Haleakalā National Park. You have to see the sunset from there, man. Bring a coat, though. It gets cold. For volcanoes, go to the Big Island."

If the medical engineering didn't work out, he could become a tour guide, maybe. This other version of himself was quite talkative. Full of information.

On the phone with Rory, he didn't have to be Josh in gray Rhode Island. He could be Josh who lived in Hawaii and went fishing and knew a sushi chef who'd make you a roll before the catch was even an hour old. He was outgoing, rather than socially awkward, this Josh who sat in the dark and lied. He sure as hell wasn't Josh Whose Wife Died.

"Where do you live, Rory?" he asked.

"I live in Montana. Also really beautiful, but totally different, I'm sure."

"Are you near the mountains?"

"Sure am."

"Do you get to Yellowstone at all?"

"Oh, yeah, I love Yellowstone. Hayden Valley is my favorite part."

Josh and Lauren had planned on going there. My God. They never would. They *never* would.

"My wife and I hope to get there," he said around the tightness in his throat. "Maybe this summer."

"Wait for September if you can. Fewer tourists."

"Cool," Josh said. "There are bison, right?"

"Absolutely. Big as a truck." Josh could imagine it. Lauren would shriek if they came too close. Nah. She'd be brave. He wondered if they could see a wolf. She loved wolves.

The companionable silence stretched on.

"How are we doing with the download? Almost there?" Rory asked.

"Um . . . yes! Seems like everything's back to normal." Shit. Guess he'd have to hang up now, since he'd been on the phone for an hour and thirteen minutes. "Thanks so much, Rory."

"You bet. You'll get an email survey about how we did, and if you have any other issues . . ."

"No. I'm fine. Uh . . . thank you."

Thank you for being a voice in the middle of the night. Thanks for letting me be someone else for a little while. Thanks for working the night shift. Thanks for never knowing how much I lost.

The survey came. He gave Rory top marks for everything.

11

Joshua

Month three
May 1

The whole world stops when a young person
dies. At least, the world *you* live in.

At first, everyone you know rallies around
you, stunned and grieving, milling around. The
solidarity of loss binds people together. No one
can imagine moving forward. No one wants to.
Stop all the clocks, as the poem instructs.

And time does seem to stop. No one in your
world can ever see being happy again. It's an
impossibility. Nothing will be the same. Nothing
ever *should* be the same. The world is ruined by
her death.

There are the tasks immediately following.
The phone calls. The arrangements. The assignments—you'll go to the funeral home while her
sister goes to the church, and this other one will
order the flowers. There is so much to do, thank
God, because your brain cannot accept what's
happened, and if you stood still for a second,
you might spontaneously explode, like a wineglass shatters with a high note. Your feet are still

moving and someone is pushing food and water on you, and another person is coming in now, and your phone is buzzing with texts and calls, and there's another knock on the door.

You put together the photo collages, the PowerPoint that will show during the wake and reception. You'll make the playlist she requested, pick out readings, order food. For a week or two, the world is filled with the details of death. Family huddles close. Her friends are devastated. Her coworkers can barely function. Her doctor calls to check on you. Her nurses come to the funeral.

For a short time, her death makes you the center of so many lives.

And then . . . it trickles off. There are children to be cared for, homes to be cleaned, food to be prepared. The coworkers still have jobs to do. The friends start getting on with their lives.

The stopped clocks start ticking once more.

Two months and one week after Lauren died, that first day came for Josh. The day when no one called, texted, emailed, dropped by. Not Jen, not Ben, not Donna, not Sarah, not his mother, not Darius, not Bruce the Mighty and Beneficent, not a random former classmate who'd just heard the news.

The first day of his life when his widowed state went unheralded by anyone.

It was *obscene.* Message received, loud and

clear. The world was adjusting to Lauren's absence. Oh, he knew Donna and Jen would never get over her, would think of her every day. But Jen had a husband and two kids. Donna had a living daughter and two grandchildren. They both worked. They had places to go. His own mother ran an entire hospital lab, viewed Sumi and Ben as her siblings, belonged to four book clubs and volunteered through her church. But you think she might have called her only child just to check in. *A fucking text, maybe, Mom?*

No. Nothing.

Josh waited all day in a state of furious, silent martyrdom, hating himself, hating everyone else. Took the dog for a run. Spoke to no one. Checked his phone every ten minutes, then every five, then restarted it in case it had a glitch.

Still nothing.

He could, of course, reach out to someone. Ben would go for a walk with him; all he had to do was ask, and they'd be at the Botanical Center or driving to Boston. It would be better than this ridiculous, pointless anger. But this was a test. A test of *them,* a test of him.

Everyone failed.

By 8:37 p.m., he hated them all.

Fury was creeping into his head like a disease. A red-out was coming.

The first time it happened, he was six, and the school bully—Sam, who was bigger and stronger than any kid in class—had thrown Caitlin's eye-glasses across the cafeteria. Caitlin was a special needs girl and Josh's friend. Joshua didn't remember anything about what happened until he was in the principal's office with his mother, being told that he'd tackled Sam. Josh asked why there was blood on his shirt and why his eye was hurting; it was because Sam had punched him in the face. Josh had hit back, splitting Sam's lip. Both boys had been suspended for a week, but Stephanie took him out for ice cream that afternoon, and when he came back to school, Caitlin handed him a card with her painstaking printing: *Thanks for sticking up for me.*

Another time, when he was ten, his mother had a violently bad reaction to a pepper and had to be rushed away in the ambulance with anaphylaxis. The Kims had come over, but Josh had been like a feral animal, they told him later. It had taken Ben and another neighbor to carry him in the house and hold him down until he came back into himself.

A few days later, after talking to his pediatrician, Josh's mother told him these incidents weren't uncommon for people with Asperger's, as they called it then. The trick was handling it. Distracting himself. She'd given him a sentence to chant when he was little—*The quick brown fox jumps over the lazy dog.* "It has every letter in the alphabet," she said. "Think about it, Josh. Count the letters." It had become a mantra when the red started to flare. *The quick brown fox jumps over the lazy dog. The quick brown fox jumps over the lazy dog.*

At the same time, Ben had taught him to box, or at least, the different types of punches used in boxing. Josh never hit any human, but hitting the bag was . . . cathartic.

Now, at 8:42 p.m., he could see the red rising. Still time to head it off at the pass.

He went to the always empty gym on the first floor of their building and beat the shit out of a punching bag.

Barefisted. The smack of his fists against the hard leather, the exhale with the effort, the sting of the punch, the ache radiating up his arm weren't enough. Harder. Harder. The hiss as he punched the bag turned into exhalations of *ha! ha!* Sweat poured off his body. The exhalations turned into words—*No. No. No. No.* Then, into curse words so foul and filthy he should've been ashamed. But he wasn't. He was furious.

She shouldn't have died. She should not have died, goddamnit, and the motherfucking idiotic way-behind-the-times motherfucking healthcare system fucked her over and left her for goddamn dead and had motherfucking nothing, nothing, nothing to offer her, the stupid sonofabitch ass-hole fucking shit, shit shit *fuck.*

His fury bounced off the walls, echoing, and

his knuckles were bleeding now, his fists sliding as they landed on his own blood, and good, good, the pain felt better than the helpless oppressive nothingness.

Finally, staggering from exhaustion, sweat running down his bare torso, his hands looking like they'd been through a meat grinder, he staggered to grab a towel and mop himself up.

Creepy Charlotte, with her pale blue eyes that were too far apart, smiled at him from the doorway. "Want to grab a drink, Josh?"

"Jesus Christ, no," he said. He got the disinfectant wipes and scoured the punching bag, distantly noting the burn on his knuckles.

"Another time, then."

"No. Never."

"See you soon."

And people thought *he* was bad at reading signals.

The punching bag had done the trick. He was so tired, he had to take the elevator up the two floors to his apartment. He showered, the hot water stinging his hands. When he was done, he went into their room, closing the door so Pebbles wouldn't come in and mess up the bed.

Last week, he'd awakened already knowing she was gone. He didn't reach out for her. That in itself ripped his heart apart all over again. Two months and one week was all it took for his muscles and instinct to adjust. Reaching for her had been his habit in marriage; now, marriage was over, and his stupid body recognized that.

He had stopped checking her side of the bed in the middle of the night. Stopped wondering if she was already up. He didn't call her name. He didn't check his watch, wondering if it was time for her meds or a walk or some breathing exercises. He didn't accidentally reach for two plates at dinnertime, whenever that was, and when he realized he didn't, he deliberately set out two plates, because the acceptance of her absence was worse than the forgetting of her death.

She was dead. It was a fact now, and that was more awful than walking into a room and wondering where she was. He *shouldn't* get used to this. It was grotesque to even consider.

And now, today. May first, the day he had proposed to her four years ago. He'd gotten down on one knee as the crab apple blossoms rained down gently all around them, and asked Lauren Rose Carlisle to be his wife.

He went to her bureau and opened her jewelry box, where he'd put her engagement and wedding rings at some point. He didn't have a clear memory of that, but here they were. He'd give them to Octavia someday, he supposed. Or to Sebastian, for his future wife. Or he could throw them in the fucking ocean, at the beach on Cape Cod, where they'd had so many beautiful days and nights. Maybe he'd just walk into the ocean himself with the rings in one hand, his pockets loaded with rocks to weigh him down. Maybe a passing great white shark would eat him, and he could be dead, then, too.

Two ghosts drifted around their apartment—Lauren, and the Josh who had been her husband, so much more than this empty bag of bones.

For the first time since the night she'd gone into the hospital with the pneumonia that killed her, Josh lay on their bed. Not in it . . . just on top of the covers, staring at the ceiling. He'd had to wash the comforter after Pebbles and her Korean chicken adventure, but Lauren's pillow had been untouched by the sticky sauce. He leaned over and inhaled, smelling her, and the invisible fist of grief slammed him in the heart.

He lay on his back, cradling the pillow, worried that it would lose its Lauren smell. *Don't move,* he told himself, so tired that the thought made sense. *Don't move, and it won't find you.* If he could stay empty, he wouldn't wind up on the floor, howling. He prayed for sleep, for a dream about his wife, but his eyes stayed open.

12:14 a.m.

1:21.

2:07.

3:38.

4:15.

5:03.

5:49.

Light filtered into the room. He could get up now. He made coffee. Opened the fridge. Closed the fridge. Took Pebbles out to pee. Came back up to drink the coffee.

He went onto the online forum for young widowers and widows and asked how people survived this. *Drink lots of water,* people reminded him, his fellow amputees, fellow husks. *Congratulate yourself on getting out of bed or eating something. Get some exercise. Be kind to yourself. Process the trauma,* the forum people said, whatever that meant.

He tried to remember if he'd taken the dog for a run yesterday. Maybe? He could go for a run now. It was drizzly and gray outside. He might have to give Pebbles a bath afterward. That would kill some time. So he pulled on his running shoes and out they went.

People were on their way to work. Lots of raincoats, lots of umbrellas, lots of fast walkers going into buildings. Josh kept running, turning at the river, running at the base of College Hill. His earbuds were in, though he had forgotten his phone, or left it behind subconsciously. Still, the earbuds would protect him. Providence was a small city, and he'd grown up here, gone to two colleges here. He didn't want to see anyone, talk to anyone. They'd blown their chance yesterday.

It was a shock, this continuing world. So many people were *happy.* Didn't they know what was in store for them? *Look at me and despair,* he wanted to tell them, like Jacob Marley's ghost. *I was once you.* He wanted to grab one of those happy assholes and shake them.

He stopped at a red light, then ran when it changed, stepping into an ankle-deep puddle of tepid water. Pebbles's belly was wet and dingy.

God, he *missed* being married. Coming home to someone. Someone to ask where his other sock was. Someone to tease. Someone to touch. He was alone in a sea of people, all of them connected, it seemed. He had his mom. The Kims. Somewhere out there, the biological father who had deserted him before he was born, so what good was he? He had Lauren's small family.

That was it.

What a *shit* idea it had been to work for himself, by himself. Well, it had been incredibly lucky when Lauren was alive and fighting, but it was shit now. He could get a job somewhere, but the thought of leaving the house every day, coming home to it . . . no. Not yet. The literature said not to make big decisions the first year of widowhood.

He eventually found himself running on his own street, having circled back, unsure of how long he'd been gone. Pebbles was panting and filthy. He took the stairs to their apartment, opened the door and looked at the kitchen clock.

11:09.

Jesus. It was, impossibly, still morning.

Wash the dog. Towel her dry. Take a shower. Get dressed. Clean the bathroom of wet dog fur. Eat. Drink.

12:13.

He sighed and closed his burning eyes. Lay down on the couch, but was tormented by visions of Lauren's last hours. He sighed again, got up and headed for his computer.

Pebbles came trotting over, but she was wobbly, favoring her left back leg. "What's the matter, pooch?" he asked, the sound of his voice too loud for his own ears. "You okay?" He ran his hand down her leg, and she whimpered.

"Great, Josh," he said out loud. "Now you've ruined the dog." Pebbles turned to lick his face. "I'm sorry, honey. I'll take you to the vet, okay?"

Yes. Even if she was just a little sore from too much exercise, it would give him something to do. If there was one thing he was good at, it was doctor's appointments.

He called the vet's office and gave his name.

"Pebbles? An Australian shepherd mix?" the receptionist asked.

"That's right."

There was a pause. "I was sorry to read about your wife's death in the paper. She was lovely."

Lauren's obituary had been in the *Providence Journal*, since she'd been a damn impressive woman and had grown up here. "Thank you," he said after a pause, remembering to speak.

"Come in at two," she said. "We had a cancellation."

"Thank you," he repeated, and hung up.

By the time they got there, Pebbles wasn't limping anymore. Still. They were here. It could fill the day.

In person, the receptionist was all-business, which Josh appreciated. He checked in, sat down and waited. Looked at *Cat Fancy* magazine, which was a real thing. Checked his phone. A text from Jen asking him over for dinner this weekend. He answered yes immediately. Thank God. He'd see the kids. It would be noisy. Darius would slap him on the shoulder. He'd be back in the land of the living, in other words. He asked what he could bring. She told him to bring some beer. He would do that.

There was another text from his dentist, reminding him he had an appointment, press *Y* to confirm, *C* to cancel. *C* it was. Wasn't he suffering enough?

The thought made him smile a little. Lauren would've liked that joke.

He glanced at the other clients in the waiting room. An older woman was talking in a baby voice to an enormous cat, who stared with murderous eyes at the Great Dane across the room. The Great Dane sat motionless—perhaps scared of the cat—while his owner read something on his phone.

A youngish woman—thirty, maybe?—sat with a very ugly, patchy dull white dog of indeterminate parentage, and wiped away tears. The dog (he was 93 percent certain it was a dog) looked really old; its bottom teeth—the ones that remained—jutted out, its eyes goopy. Probably here for euthanasia, Josh guessed.

Its owner noticed him looking and wiped her eyes again. "What's wrong with your dog?" she asked.

"Oh. Um . . . she was limping before."

"How old is she?"

"Two and change."

"She's pretty. What's her name?"

"Pebbles." *Interact, Josh,* he heard Lauren say. "Yours?"

"Duffy."

Josh didn't ask what was wrong with Duffy. He didn't want to know, frankly, because he suspected he'd respond with, "Big deal. My wife just died."

The cat growled. The Great Dane whimpered, then tried to climb on his owner's lap.

"My dog's really old," Duffy's owner said.

No shit, Sherlock. "Really?" Josh said. "He looks great." White lies were good for the soul, Lauren used to say.

"He's sixteen."

"That's . . . great." Josh wasn't aware that dogs lived that long.

"I know he's old, but . . . I'm hoping for a couple more years." Her face scrunched as she tried not to cry.

I was hoping for a couple more years, too, lady. "Good luck."

"Thanks."

"Duffy?" one of the techs called, and the woman stood up, old Duffy in her arms, his head on her shoulder like a baby.

"Thanks for talking to me," she said, looking back at Josh.

It was an oddly sweet thing to say. "You're welcome." He should say more. "Feel better, Duffy."

"Good luck with your dog." She waved with her bottom hand, and Josh nodded, forcing a smile. If that dog lasted another month, someone should call CNN.

He looked down at Pebbles, who seemed to agree.

Shit. Someday Pebbles would die, too, and that would be it, his last tie to Lauren, the only pet they'd ever owned together. Their fur baby . . . no, scratch that, he wasn't going there.

But Lauren's dog, still. "I'm sorry, Pebs," he said in a whisper. "Sorry we lost her."

As he suspected, Pebbles was perfectly healthy. "No more than five miles on a run, okay?"

the vet said cheerfully, giving him some anti-inflammatory. "It's great for her, because she's a working dog and used to a lot of exercise, but she's bred for it in spurts, not a marathon. Give her a week off, then ease back into it." He scratched Pebbles's ears, getting a cow-like moo of appreciation.

"Thanks," Josh said.

"We were all really sorry to hear about your wife," the vet added, not looking at him.

"Thank you." He was grateful for the lack of eye contact.

When he got home, he gave Pebbles her pill and a snack, then went to bed and fell into a black, dreamless sleep.

He was awakened by a pounding at the door, an irritable voice calling his name. Sarah. He stumbled to the door.

"What's wrong?" he said, opening it.

"I texted you three times and called twice," she said.

"I was asleep."

"When did you go to bed?" she asked, her voice bossy.

He glanced at the clock. Hours ago. "Um . . . I don't know."

"I thought so. Josh. You have to establish a schedule, buddy. Sleeping for God knows how many hours isn't going to help you move through this."

He bit down on a sharp answer. "What can I do for you?" he asked.

"It's letter day." She pulled an envelope from her bag. "There are two this time, so I just brought them both. I was supposed to bring this one the other day, but I got slammed at work with an emergency placement." Which meant some kid had been removed from his or her home, brought to a stranger's house with a plastic bag of clothes and maybe a toothbrush. She'd told enough stories that he knew. Lauren used to say that Sarah had always been tough, but she had a "heart like a feather pillow."

"That must've been hard," he said, remembering to be human.

"It was pretty horrible, yes."

"Why two letters?"

"She dated this one. I don't know why. Also, I don't know what's in those letters. She didn't tell me, and obviously, I wouldn't look."

She handed him two envelopes this time. One said *Josh, May 1,* the other *Josh #3.* Her handwriting was so round and sweet.

Lauren had had something to say yesterday. Yesterday, when he felt so alone and forgotten. His heart started thumping harder.

Sarah tilted her head. "You okay, pal?"

"What? Yeah, I'm fine."

"We should get together. You know." She shrugged. "Dinner? A movie? An outing somewhere? Let's hang out. It'll be good for both of us."

Her words were a blur. "Okay. Sure. Thank you, Sarah."

"I have to run. I'm going to Long Island for a conference. I'm presenting a workshop on kinship care. So maybe when I get back."

He had to drag his eyes off the envelopes. "Um, that's great. Good for you, Sarah. About the workshop."

She smiled. "Thanks. See you next week, okay?"

"Okay," he said. "Thank you for doing this, by the way. Bringing these to me."

A wave of grief rippled across her face. "Anything for her," she said, her voice growing husky.

He hadn't been much of a friend to Sarah since Lauren died. But she'd been there for him a hundred percent, and for Lauren, too. If he did see her next week, he'd try to remember to ask about the conference, her presentation. He'd try to be a better friend.

He leaned in for an awkward hug, bumping his chin against her cheek. She smelled nice. Clean and . . . outdoorsy. Not like Lauren, but still nice. He didn't like a lot of perfumes or scented soaps, aside from his wife's. But Sarah smelled . . . pretty. "Take care. Have a good trip."

"Thanks," she said, patting him on the shoulder. Then she turned and went down the stairs.

She was good-looking. He'd never really recognized that before, but she was, and it was . . . it was oddly nice to notice. Blond and tall where Lauren had been a redhead and smaller. Attractive, when Lauren had been stunning. To him, anyway. The most beautiful woman in any room, anywhere, anytime.

Time to read what she had to say.

The past two months had taught him to savor this, because as many times as he might reread the letter, the first time was always the best. He would do it right this time.

First, he took Pebbles out for an easy walk. He came back inside, fed the dog her supper and got himself a glass of water.

Then, because the drizzle had cleared and it had become one of those perfect May evenings, he took the letter up to the rooftop garden, avoiding the edge. A seagull was perched on the post, staring into the distance. The spatters of white on the deck said it was a favorite hangout. "Get out of here," Josh said. "Shoo."

The bird didn't even glance at him.

"Seagull. Beat it." Pebbles cocked her head, amused. "Do something, Pebs," he said. She wagged her tail and seemed to smile at the bird.

Fine. Josh wasn't about to go to the edge, and the bird seemed to know it.

He sat on a chaise longue solidly in the middle

of the roof. Pebbles leaped up neatly next to him and curled into a ball.

Josh sipped his water, took a few deep breaths. He could smell something floral—the lilacs that grew down in the courtyard, maybe—and it reminded him of Lauren's soap. "I miss you," he said out loud. Pebbles wagged her tail. The bird glanced back at them, then turned away again.

Okay. Another sip of water. Then, unable to draw out the moment any longer, he opened the envelope.

Hello, Josh, my darling love.

Today is the anniversary of one of the happiest days of my life—the day you proposed. The way the sun lit up those gorgeous trees, you so handsome in your suit, the beautiful, beautiful ring. I felt like the world stopped for a moment. There was that lady in the pink sweats who got all teary eyed and took our picture, remember? And the little boy who wanted to see the ring and asked why you gave it to me.

He had forgotten that. A cute little kid with curly dark hair and long eyelashes, maybe five years old, asking why Josh gave her a present. Then, upon their explanation, he announced that he was going to ask his friend Hayley to marry him on the school bus the next day.

We went out to dinner at Cafe Nuovo, and our family was there, you sly devil, you. Champagne. Imagine if I'd said no! But of course, I never would have, and clearly, you were feeling pretty dang confident. As you should have been. I don't remember what we ate, because I was just floating on happiness, but I'm sure it was delicious.

I hope you remember that today, honey. I hope it won't be all sad for you. Please remember how happy you made me, how perfect that night was, how much I loved the ring you picked out. Maybe you can give it to Sebastian someday, when he's met a woman he wants to marry. Tell him how happy that ring made me. Don't let it be unlucky. Let it be a reminder of that day, and all the happiness that followed.

I love you so much, honey. So, so much. Don't be sad. Okay? That's a stupid thing to ask. Oh, Josh, I can't bear thinking of you unhappy. Put yourself back into that day and remember. It was like a dream, the happiest, sunshiniest, most romantic dream in the world. Please don't be sad.

Lauren

He could almost hear her crying. She had tried so hard not to mourn in front of him. Did he fail her in that regard? Was she able to share that sadness, or did she hide it more often than not? Of course, they'd cried together.

But mostly, they hadn't. They'd made the most of her time. They really had. Their marriage had been so short, but so happy. Yawning terror combined with utter bliss. Their beautiful catastrophe.

He sat there in the sun and did as his wife asked him. He remembered the ring; he and Ben had gone shopping for it together. "This ring is a sign of what's yet to come," Ben said. "Pick out a winner, son." And as soon as he had seen that stunning, simple ring, he knew.

He'd told his mother he was going to propose, and she gave him the biggest hug, then cried, then hugged him some more.

Then he'd gone to the cemetery where Lauren's dad was buried. "Mr. Carlisle," he said, feeling awkward and self-conscious. "I'd like to marry Lauren. I'll take good care of her, and I'll always put her happiness before mine." He paused, then knelt next to the headstone. "She's the most precious thing in the world to me. I bet you know how I feel." And then he didn't feel awkward anymore.

He asked Donna, who pointed out that they'd been dating only a few months (true, but Josh already knew Lauren was the one). Then she caved, and said he was a fine young man and it didn't hurt that he had a lot of money, because people who said money didn't matter were silly, because of course it did.

And then he'd asked Jen. Because Jen was Lauren's hero, and she said, "I'd almost marry you myself, Joshua Park," and hugged him and kissed him on the cheek, a big smacking kiss, and hugged him again.

He bought the suit just for that night, because he didn't have one, and Mrs. Kim said it would be lucky to wear a new suit for the start of a new life. He called Lauren's family and made the restaurant reservation for all of them, the two families, including Ben and Sumi of course, then met Lauren at her job so they could walk down to the park together.

He'd never been so sure of anything in his life. Lauren Rose Carlisle was meant to be his wife. He would've walked a mile barefoot on broken glass just to get her a napkin.

God, the happiness. The smugness that they'd have a long life together. Kids. Vacations, a house with a front porch and a swing in the yard.

Being widowed at thirty had never crossed his mind.

But his wife was right. The sadness shouldn't cancel out what had been so bright and full and beautiful. Just because the cherry blossoms would fall didn't mean you should mourn them on the tree.

"That sounds very profound, doesn't it?" he asked Pebbles. The dog agreed, licking his face. "We should write that down."

Instead, he stayed put, letting the sun warm his face, his arm around the dog, the seagull chilling on the post. He could open the other letter tomorrow or the day after that. Today, he would remember how happy they had been.

12

Joshua

Month three, letter number three
May

Hey there, hottie.

I want you to know that I'm fine. I'm fine as I write this letter—it's been a good string of days, and we're here on the Cape. What a gift this house has been, Josh! Waking up to the sound of the ocean, falling asleep under the Milky Way, being able to have all our friends and family come visit . . . Thank you for being so thoughtful and generous and wonderful.

Your mom is here right now, making us stuffed cabbage with pork, and even though I'm sitting outside, I'm practically drooling. I love your mom. She's so practical and . . . cool. She's a badass, really. Please make sure you visit her a lot after I die. She'll need to take care of you, and you'll need her. She always said getting knocked up was the best thing that ever happened to her.

Sometimes, I dream about my dad,

as you know. But last night, I dreamed that he and I were about to have lunch with . . . guess who? Your father. He wanted to meet you, and Dad and I were going to screen him first. If he was a jerk, we were making plans to beat him up, and laughing so much. Then the dream changed, and my dad and I were in our old backyard, throwing the softball back and forth, like we did when I played in sixth grade. It was nice to see him.

I think these dreams are reassurances that my dad will be with me when I die. So I'm not alone, okay, honey? And you know I'll be watching over you. I'm safe and sound, just like when I wrote this. It's just next-level stuff here in the Great Beyond.

So this is the third month without me, and I'm guessing that you could use some new clothes. I know . . . this is not that big a deal in the scheme of mourning, but since you have no fashion sense and I'm not there to tell you to get rid of those cargo pants and you have an ass that can only be described as Justin Trudeau Level of Perfection—

Josh laughed out loud. She'd always had a thing for the Canadian prime minister.

—I want you to go shopping. At the mall.

Oh, stop panicking! You can do it! Go by yourself, honey. No leaning on Jen or Sarah for help. You're a wildly successful, gorgeous entrepreneur. Stop dressing like Mark Zuckerberg and/or the Unabomber.

You know how I loved clothes. Something new always made me feel fresh and excited to get dressed. It's a little thing, but it works.

Good luck, honey! I love you so much.

Lauren

PS, Give your mom a big hug and tell her how much I loved her. Even though she already knows.

Stephanie did know. Lauren had left her a letter, too. Apparently, everyone got one—his mother, her mother, Darius, Jen, Sarah, even Sebastian and Octavia, which they were supposed to open on their sixteenth birthdays. Mara from RISD, Asmaa from the Hope Center, Bruce the Mighty and Beneficent, Louise and Santino, her coworkers. (Bruce had emailed him a couple of weeks ago to say that he'd fired that nasty Lori Cantore. Personality conflict, Bruce had said.)

So. Lauren had obviously sensed death was coming, but she never said a word. Lauren lived in the moment more perfectly than anyone he'd ever known, and she still managed to write to everyone she loved for when she was gone. Only she could've been that generous, that thoughtful, spending her time on earth so the people left behind would have something from her.

He would never find anyone like her again. He would never try. Once you'd had a love like that, it would be futile to try to replicate it. Everything else would be a hollow imitation.

Was this acceptance? One of the five famous stages of grief, along with anger, denial, bargaining and depression. Someone on the forum had said they didn't follow any particular order—any one of them could punch you in the face at any time. Sure seemed to be that way, Josh thought. His knuckles still stung as a reminder of the anger phase. Sometimes he wasn't sure he was doing this whole grieving thing the right way, thought his particular spot on the autism spectrum mixed things up.

All the more reason to follow Lauren's instructions.

Josh looked at his watch. Six o'clock on a Friday night. Normal people would have plans. He'd had dinner with his mother a few days ago, had gone to Jen's last night and got to read Sebastian a bedtime story. Octavia was talking a little bit—mama, dada, cup—and Jen had tried to get her to say Josh, but she just tucked her head against Jen's neck and smiled sweetly. Both kids had pictures in their rooms of Lauren holding them. Josh couldn't look at those for more than a glancing second, though (the denial bit, probably).

He read her letter again, almost able to smell the salty Cape air, see the achingly blue sky. Maybe he should go there; he had rented the house again for this summer back in January, thinking they'd have longer. Wanting Lauren to have another spring and summer by the sea. If he rented it again, she'd have to live longer, too, right?

Hello, bargaining.

He should let someone else use that house. It was a shame to have it empty. Immediately, he felt guilty that this hadn't occurred to him yet. He texted Asmaa and offered it to her and her fiancé, and asked her to find some Hope Center families who'd like to use it.

The memory of that deck, the sound of the ocean, the seagulls, his wife's laughter . . . Longing, strong enough to make him shudder, hit him like a wave.

Pebbles put her head on his knee. "I have to go to the mall," he said. It felt like he'd be journeying to hell.

An hour later, he was proven right. The mall *was* hell. Teenagers, families, people rushing . . . the place was mobbed. He was jostled, carried along by throngs of consumers, jammed by the great unwashed.

Didn't children have bedtimes anymore? Didn't people want to be outside on this beautiful May night?

"Would you like to try this amazing anti-aging cream?" asked a man, leaping out from a kiosk with a sample in his hand.

"I'm thirty years old," Josh said.

"Never too soon to start! Maybe bring some home to your wife?"

Josh jolted to a stop. "My wife?"

The man pointed at his left hand. "Or husband. Sorry."

Ah. Yes, he still wore his wedding ring. He kept going without answering the man, got stuck behind a cluster of girls all talking loudly in clichéd phrases.

"OMG, I stan him!"

"Yeah, no thanks!"

"She's the GOAT!"

They jolted to a halt outside a cheap-looking clothing store, and he almost ran into them. "Excuse me," he hissed, walking around them, inexplicably furious.

"Super sorry, mister!" one of them yelled, and they all cackled.

"What his problem?"

"Okay, boomer!"

Jesus Christ. He was *not* a boomer. He pictured

tossing them to the side like the Incredible Hulk, flinging them out of his way. Then, because Lauren wouldn't have approved—in fact, Lauren had probably been like these girls, hair-stroking and in love with herself—he pictured them simply in jail instead. Still too mean. Fine. In a room without internet, makeup or hair products.

Speaking of hair, up ahead was a place called Tanglzz. Such a Rhode Island name. His mother had told him he needed a haircut and had offered to do it—he hadn't had one since Lauren died, and it *was* shaggy—but given the bowl haircuts he'd sported as a child, he passed.

"Do you take walk-ins?" he asked the woman behind the counter.

"Sure do!" said the receptionist, and a minute later, Josh was sitting in a chair, a woman with pink highlights washing his hair. "Where are you from?" she asked.

"Providence."

"Awesome!" she crowed, as if staying in his home city were award-worthy. "I'm Britney, by the way," she said, squirting something new onto his head. Yes. Her nametag told him that. "My parents named me after Britney Spears, right?"

Thus cursing her. "That's nice."

"What's your name, hon?"

"James." He'd pay in cash. Telling her his name felt too personal.

"Oh, my God! I got a cousin named James.

Jimmy, we call him. He's in jail right now? But he's not so bad." She scrubbed his scalp with her fingertips.

Aside from sympathy hugs, Britney was the first woman to touch him since Lauren died. He felt nothing. Ostensibly, the warm water and brisk shampoo should've been pleasant. Instead, it was just something to be endured.

"Have you ever been to California?" Britney asked for no apparent reason.

"Yes."

"That's *wicked* awesome. California's the best." She didn't ask which parts of California he'd been to, but apparently anywhere in California was good enough. "Me, I've never traveled much. I went to see my aunt in Pennsylvania once? It was wicked boring. Like, kind of a city? But not really? All these cornfields and antique stores. My aunt? She's only eight years older than I am? So I'm like, 'Girl, where do you pahty?' "

Her voice chattered on, requiring nothing from Josh. She asked what kind of haircut he wanted, and he said "short" so he wouldn't have to do this again soon, and after fifteen or twenty or a thousand minutes, she was done, brushing off the back of his neck.

"There! You're wicked gorgeous now, James." She smiled and squeezed his arm, and he felt bad for disliking her. Left her a twenty for a tip, even though the haircut only cost twelve dollars.

He was weary, but he wanted to do what his wife had told him to do. Still wanting to make her happy.

It had been his life's work, after all.

He walked aimlessly through the mall, past chain jewelry stores and women's lingerie shops and kiosks selling hair extensions and sparkly jewelry, past the crappy food places that sold hot pretzels and ice cream, until he came to a store with men's clothing in the window. More teenage girls, maybe the coven he'd passed earlier, cruised around him. Two of them walked with their arms linked.

Lauren and Sarah had done that sometimes. Maybe they'd been to this very same mall as teenagers, and been much the same as these girls, chattering, self-involved, too confident in their beauty. After all, that's how he'd viewed Lauren the first time he met her. A shallow twit.

Imagine that. The love of his life, the woman he'd married, and he'd given up, what . . . six years with her? No. Almost seven. The thought nearly felled him. If he hadn't been a condescending prick at that party, they might have had *seven* more years.

His heart was racing. He could've had *almost a decade more* with her.

"Hello and welcome," came a voice. "Are you looking for anything in particular tonight?"

Oh. He'd gone in, apparently. "I need some clothes," he said, and his voice sounded strange.

"Great!" the man said. He was young and well dressed, his hair in a perfect swoop off his forehead. "My name's Radley. And you are?"

"Joshua."

"What are you looking for, Joshua?"

He had no idea how to answer the question. "Just . . . everything, I guess."

The answer caused Radley to brighten. "No problem! What size do you usually take? Do you have colors that you like? This is quite . . . cheerful." He gestured at Josh's shirt, which was, he just realized, a shirt Mrs. Kim had bought him in Korea the last time she went—garish red-and-yellow swirls. Cargo pants. Birkenstock sandals with socks.

He probably should've looked in the mirror before leaving the house.

Somewhere, Lauren was laughing. It almost made him smile.

"Whatever you think," Josh said. "I don't have the best taste in clothes."

"Thank God you said that so I didn't have to pretend." Radley grinned. "Okay, let's get started." He began plucking things off the racks, a few shirts here, pants there, jeans, a sweater, more pants, another shirt. Josh trailed behind him, agreeing with everything, seeing nothing.

Seven extra years. He could've been with

173

Lauren for seven extra years, but he'd been a complete and utter asshole.

"These pants are really on trend," the guy was saying. "You can cuff them to be extra hipster, if you must. See the pretty print underneath? Or just leave as is for a more conservative look. I'd French-tuck this shirt, maybe add a vest or a grandpa sweater. This hat would make it super-cute for date night. Here, why don't you start trying things on, and I'll grab whatever else I think you might like." He hung up a dozen articles of clothing in a dressing room, looking pleased, then went back to the racks for more.

Josh closed the dressing room door behind him and looked at the mirror. Lauren had coached him in dressing once they'd been dating a little while, but he'd reverted to his old clothes since her death. They predated her, and somehow it was easier to wear things that weren't attached to her memory.

He really did look like a dork.

He pulled on a pair of cotton pants in a shade of orange—coral, Lauren would've said—a blue T-shirt, a blue-and-yellow-printed button-down.

"I grabbed you a pair of shoes just in case you want to see yourself without those, uh . . . atrocities." Radley slid some brown loafers under the closed door.

Josh put the shoes on. Looked in the mirror.

With his haircut, and the undeniably modern

outfit, he looked different. He didn't look like the hermit genius workaholic with no life, as he used to be, or the stunned-stupid mouth-breathing widower he'd become.

He looked . . . he looked like the guy who'd married Lauren Carlisle. He looked like her husband again.

The pain hit him in the stomach, and he bent over. A keening sound came out of his mouth, and he tried to cover it. Tears rained out of his eyes without warning, and his chest was crushed by the grief.

He could've had *years* more with her.

"Joshua? Joshua? Are you okay?" came the salesperson's voice. The door handle jiggled.

The mirror showed his face, wet from tears, creased in agony, scared, hopeless. How was he supposed to live without her for the rest of his life? His knees gave out, and he sank to the floor, clamping his arms over his head.

The door opened, and Radley stood there, a key in his hand. "Oh, God, you are so *not* okay. What can I do? Should I call 911?"

"My . . . my . . ." He could barely choke the words out. "My wife . . . died."

"Holy Mary. Oh, man, that sucks." Radley sat on the little bench and put his hand on Josh's shoulder. "How horrible."

It was so embarrassing, crying here, almost funny if it weren't so utterly, wretchedly awful.

He was full-on sobbing now, his arm across his face, tears soaking into the unpurchased shirt. He didn't *want* to look like Lauren's husband. He wasn't anymore. He had no right to look like Lauren's husband. He didn't deserve to, not when he'd failed her. Not when he'd given up seven years with her.

Don't be a loser.

Her voice was so clear his head jerked up to see if she was there.

Of course she wasn't. He choked on another sob, then another, this weird, hiccuping thing that he was powerless to stop. He *was* a loser. That was the problem.

"Can I try this on?" asked a guy with an impressive beard, holding up a shirt.

"Can't you see he's having a crisis?" the salesperson snapped. "Jesus! Some compassion, please? Come back tomorrow, and I'll give you forty percent off."

"I'm sorry," Josh managed.

"Don't apologize. Here." Radley—Ripley?— got up and left the dressing room and returned a second later. He held a bandanna in one hand, a bottle of water in the other. "Wipe your face, you poor thing. I'll lock up."

Josh felt a hundred years old. He hauled himself onto the bench and sighed. The hiccuping had stopped.

Not cool, breaking down like this. Not cool at

all. His hands were still shaking. His ribs hurt from crying. He wiped his eyes, blew his nose, drank some water, and when Radley came back, he was under control again, though his eyes were leaking still.

"I'm so sorry," he said. "I didn't see that coming."

"It's totally fine," Radley said. "How long has it been?"

"Three months."

Radley nodded. "Listen. Do you want to get a drink or something? The mall closes in ten minutes."

"That's . . . that's really nice of you, but you don't have to. You've been great."

"I know." He smiled. "And I'm sure you have tons of friends to lean on, but sometimes a stranger is easier."

"Your hair is really cool," Josh said. Why? Why say that? (But it was.)

"It takes forever, but it's worth it, right?" Radley said, waving his hand over his head. "Come on. Let's go get a mangotini or a scotch or something. Really."

It beat going home to a lifeless apartment and grieving dog.

"Okay," Josh said. "I'll take everything, by the way."

Radley's eyes widened. "That's, like . . . a ton of money. Don't feel like you have to. I mean, you have to buy the bandanna, and that shirt, since you slimed all over it, but . . ."

"No. I do need the clothes. Thank you." He started to unbutton the printed shirt.

"No! Stop. Wear those out of the store. Please. For everyone's sake." He glanced at the clothes still hanging in the dressing room. "Are you sure you want everything? Your wallet may scream."

"I can afford it. And it's all nice stuff."

"How would you know?" Radley said, raising an eyebrow and grinning like a stylish elf. He pointed to Josh's red-and-yellow polyester shirt. "I can burn that shirt for you in case you're ever tempted to wear it again."

Josh almost smiled. "My friend got it for me in Korea."

"Does she hate you?" He smiled. "Did she also force you to wear those cargo shorts and those . . ." He paused to shudder. "Birkenstocks?"

"No." Lauren hated them, too. The smile was small, but it was real.

"So maybe you should come here more often. Would you like to take out a Banana Republic card? You'll get a discount." He lowered his voice. "And I'll get bonus points from my boss."

"Sure."

A few minutes later, they left the store and walked out toward the exit to the parking garages, past the mall-based restaurants, all of which had tables set up in the vast food court.

"I can ride with you," Radley said. "I'm car-free at the moment, and I promise I'm not a serial killer. I know a place where no one will bother us and the drinks are cheap. These places?" He gestured to a franchise Josh recognized from their late-night ads for two-pound burgers and bottomless barrels of fries. "I wouldn't eat in one of these mall restaurants. First, I *know* we'd find a hair in our food. Second, it's so noisy! How do people have conversations here?"

As if on cue, there was a crash, and they both looked over. A female server had just dropped a full tray—plates and glasses, liquid and food were everywhere. A giant burger sat right on a man's groin, with french fries littering his pants.

"For fuck's sake!" bellowed the male customer, who wore a T-shirt proclaiming his love of guns. He jolted out of his seat, towering over the waitress. The people around them fell silent.

The waitress put her hands over her face, and for a second, Josh thought the angry man might hit her.

"Hey!" Josh yelled. Redness flared at the edges of his vision. Never a good sign.

"Are you that stupid that you can't even carry a tray?" the gun lover yelled at her.

"I'm so sorry," she said. Somehow, she looked familiar.

"Does that help me? No, you stupid—"

The red flared. "Leave her alone. It was

an accident," Josh called. At least ten people whipped out their phones, sensing trouble. The gun lover turned toward him, his face florid now that he couldn't eat his heart-attack-on-a-plate.

"Food service and retail," Radley murmured. "People treat us like we're scum."

"Is this your problem?" the irate customer asked, coming toward them.

Good. The red flared again. *Bring it on, asshole.* Josh hopped over the little fence that separated the food court tables from the rest of the mall. "I think it is," he said.

"And here comes the mall's violent crime of the day," Radley said. Josh barely heard him.

"You mind your own business!" the asshole said. "You got something to say?"

Contradictory statements, Josh thought. "It was an accident. Cut her some slack." His voice was guttural. Another sign of a red-out. Good.

"Why should I? She dumped food on me, the stupid slut."

Josh's fists tightened.

"You kiss your mother with that mouth?" Radley said.

The man leaned in toward Radley, who didn't flinch. "Watch your back, faggot. You see this shirt? You never know what I might be packing."

Then the man reached behind his back (to grab a gun?) and the red tar surged in Josh's vision. Then his fist *hurt,* and his arm was extended, and

180

the bully staggered back, crashing into a table and then landing on the floor in the puddle of drinks the waitress had spilled.

The crowd started clapping. The man tried to get up, then slipped and fell back down. "My back!" he howled.

Regrettable. Josh had been hoping for a fight. *The quick brown fox jumps over the lazy dog. The quick brown fox. That lazy-ass dog.*

The redness faded. Someone was talking to him. "Josh? Joshua? Are you okay?" It was his new friend. Radley.

"I'm fine."

"You punched that guy."

"Yeah." He definitely had. He looked at his recently abused knuckles, which were a fresh shade of red.

A man came running out of the restaurant with a mall security guard. "Fred!" Radley said. "It's about time! That man was harassing his waitress. Then he threatened to shoot me."

"Do you want to file a report?" the guard asked. "I can call the real police."

"I don't even have a gun!" the bully wailed from the floor.

"We can still press charges for harassment," the guard said.

"Hm," said Radley. "Well, seeing him lying in a dirty puddle of Pepsi is reward enough for me." He turned to Josh. "Joshua? What do you think?"

181

"I'm the one who's going to file a report!" the man barked. "He hit me! That queer hit me!"

Radley tsked. "Hate speech, terrible gaydar *and* a gun lover. Color me shocked."

Josh glanced at him, a little surprised that Radley wasn't more upset. Radley correctly interpreted his glance and shrugged. "This happens more than you want to know."

The crowd was taking pictures of the anus lying on the floor. "Hashtag gun-threatening-homophobe, hashtag Providence-mall," one person said. "What's your name, homophobe? I definitely want to tag you. I filmed the whole thing. Bet CNN will love this."

"His name is Donnie Plum," someone offered. "My cousin used to work with him. He's an asshole."

The security guard asked if Josh wanted to call the police. Josh wasn't sure why he was the one being asked. He *had* done the hitting, after all. "What do you think?" he asked Radley.

"How about you ban him for life from this mall, Fred?" Radley suggested to the security guard. "I'll file a report tomorrow if you want."

"Okay," said the guard amicably.

"Lifetime mall ban," Radley called, and the crowd cheered.

"I already have a hundred and six retweets and a thousand likes!" said the hashtagging person.

"Donnie, you're going viral. Bet you lose your job tomorrow."

Josh and Radley were told they could go.

"Thanks for standing up for me. And the waitress," Radley said as they walked to the car. "You're a total badass. Seriously. That stuff is scary no matter how many times you hear it."

Josh nodded.

As they got in the car, he remembered where he'd seen the waitress. At the vet. She'd had the really old dog. Rhode Island and its two degrees of separation.

Fifteen minutes later, they were in the Falconry, a gay bar over by Providence College. The place was bathed in red light, and the bass of club music pulsed through it. It wasn't horribly loud, or that crowded, though Radley said by midnight, the place would be packed.

They took a seat in a booth, which was spacious and comfortable. The waiter came over. "Drinks, gentlemen?"

"I'll have the watermelon mojito," Radley said. "Joshua? What would you like? Drinks on me, since you protected my honor. Dinner, too, if you're hungry."

He started to say he didn't drink, then changed his mind. "Same," he said.

"Are you hungry?"

"No, I'm fine."

"Nachos, then," Radley told the server. "They're

fantastic here," he said to Josh. "You won't regret it."

It was so strange, being out with someone he didn't know. In a gay bar, no less. After a fight. He couldn't wait to tell—

Nope. He didn't get to tell Lauren these things anymore.

Too bad. She would've loved this story.

Radley settled back and looked at Josh. His blue eyes were very kind. "So. Tell me about your wife."

An unexpectedly direct order. Josh took a breath and let it out slowly. "Um . . . her name was Lauren. She had . . ." How much did Radley want to know? He wasn't good at reading people. "She was diagnosed with a terminal illness about a year after we got married."

"I'm so sorry. She was the love of your life?"

"Yes." It felt oddly good to acknowledge that.

"I bet you two were the cutest couple ever."

Josh pulled out his phone and brought up a picture of them on their wedding day and showed it to Radley.

"Oh, my God, she's a Disney princess." He stared at the phone. "You look super happy."

"We were."

The drinks came, and Josh took his first ever sip of alcohol. The drink was minty and sweet and went down easily. There was a slight, not-unpleasant burn in his throat, which must have been whatever alcohol was in a mojito.

"So, uh . . ." Josh said. Lauren was always the one who initiated conversation. What would she say? "Tell me about yourself, Radley. Is that your first name?"

"Yes. Radley Beauchamp. And my parents were shocked that I was gay. I told them if they'd named me Joe, I'd be an ironworker with a wife and four kids by now." He laughed, and Josh smiled obligingly. "Not much to tell, really. I work at Banana Republic, I have two sisters, I grew up in rural Maine and I'm going to school part-time to become a licensed therapist."

"No wonder you were so good in the store. Thank you for that." To hide his embarrassment, he took a long sip of his drink. Really tasty.

"Thank you," Radley said. "I appreciate it. My parents hated me being gay, because they're the type of Mainers who love camping, Jesus, and squirrel for Sunday dinner. So what's a gay kid to do except leave home and become a shrink?"

"It's a great profession." He assumed so, anyway. He'd never been to one.

"What do you do, Joshua?"

"I'm a medical device engineer."

"That makes you sound very smart."

He shrugged. When the waiter asked if they wanted another round, he said yes.

They talked about life in Providence, drank, and ate nachos. There was definitely some comfort in talking to someone who didn't share his loss, didn't have memories of Lauren, didn't miss her.

"So . . . my wife wrote these letters for me," he told Radley. "That's why I was shopping tonight. She told me to get new clothes."

"Wise woman," Radley murmured.

Josh smiled. "She was."

"Maybe there's more to getting new clothes than new clothes."

"You definitely sound like a therapist now."

Radley smiled. "Sometimes a cigar is just a cigar. And sometimes it isn't."

A man came up to their table and slid in next to Radley. "Hey, Radley. Who's your friend?"

"Joshua . . . whoops, I don't know your last name."

"Park."

"I'm Todd, Joshua, and I think you're super attractive."

"Nope," said Radley. "He's straight and his wife just died, okay? Some space, if it's not too much?"

"Oh, shit, I'm so, so sorry," the man said, backing away. "So sorry. My condolences."

Then Josh was laughing, all of a sudden. Maybe it was the alcohol, because he did feel sort of spinny and light, or maybe it was the other end of his sob-fest in the dressing room, but he laughed and laughed, and Radley sat back and watched him. "His name is Todd," Josh explained. Why that was funny, he didn't know. But it was.

Radley shook his head and smiled. "I'll drive your car back to your place," he said, like a wise old uncle. "I can Uber from there."

"I'll pay for it," Josh said. "These nachos are really, really good."

An hour or so later, Josh was in bed. Radley had typed his name and number into Josh's phone, took a selfie of the two of them for the contact picture and got into the Lyft Josh had summoned for him.

Josh was dizzy and floating and not sad. Well, not *just* sad. He was a little bit happy.

He'd had— Was it true? He'd almost had fun tonight. He'd punched someone. He had clothes that Lauren hadn't bought and had never seen, and for some reason, that made him feel better.

And most of all, he was fairly sure he had a new friend.

"Pretty sneaky, hon," he said, and then he was asleep.

13

Lauren

Sixteen months left
October 10

Dear Dad,
I was going to make a bucket list but decided that was super cliché. There are, however, things I want to do, and I'm aware that I might not have all the time in the world. I want a doggy. I want to eat dessert as often as possible, which I already do, honestly. Um . . . other stuff? The truth is, my life is so happy, it feels wrong to wish for more experiences or possessions or pies (well . . . maybe the pies are okay).

But life is normal now. IPF is a part of my life. I'm not smiting myself with ashes.

You know how so many women say the best day of their life was their wedding day? Not me. The best days (note the plural) are the regular days, Daddy. The days where it's sunny and dry and you can smell the donuts from Knead. When

Sebastian FaceTimes me without Jen knowing and we have our private chats, or he puts the phone down and I just listen to him playing. When Bruce compliments me on something at work, not because he feels sorry for me, because he's not like that, but because I did good work. Sitting up in the garden, spying on the people across the way and making up stories about them.

I'm happy, Dad. I'm really okay, and I'm so happy. Don't worry about me, okay? I love you.

Lauren

Pebbles, their newly acquired Australian shepherd mutt, could dance, walk herself by holding the end of the leash in her mouth, sing along to the radio, sneeze on command and catch a Frisbee in midair.

She also ate toilet paper, was terrified of pigeons, consistently shat underneath Josh's desk and spontaneously peed when she heard the word *ride.*

Cleaning up her sixth pile of poop of the weekend, Josh said, "Don't tell my mother she crapped inside. Our whole house will be bleached." Stephanie *was* on the obsessive side of clean, one of her many attributes. Who else had a mother-in-law who'd clean your kitchen for fun?

Poop aside, life was good. The foliage had been especially bright this year, and they'd spent the day at the Waterman Street dog park, throwing balls and sticks for half a dozen canines as Pebbles tried in vain to herd them. Now, Lauren was on the couch, using her oxygen because it had been a vigorous day. Pebbles was equally tired, curled up at Lauren's side, head on her lap. The silkiest ears in the universe. Sure, Pebbles had chewed up the clicker last night, and she was a bed hog, but these *ears*.

"You doing okay?" Josh asked once the trash was emptied and he'd scoured his hands.

"Yep. A little tired."

He looked at her, squinting as if he didn't believe her.

"A lot tired." She didn't want to tell him too many details every time something came up, husband or not. Her bones felt sore, and her muscles ached and her eyes felt dry and sticky. But *tired* would cover it.

"How about a foot rub?" he asked.

"Is there a woman on earth who'd turn down that offer? Sold, handsome."

He sat down and pulled one of her feet from under the blanket, his hands warm against her cool skin. " 'Did you ever think that you're a hero?' " he began to sing, grinning at her. His voice was adorably off pitch, and she smiled. Goofing around was a conscious effort for Josh, so it made her all the more thrilled.

"Not that song," she said. "Anything but that one."

He raised an eyebrow and kept singing. " 'You're everything I thought I should be.' "

"Wrong words. Please stop or I'll stab you."

" 'I can fly higher than a seagull . . .' "

"Eagle. Keep singing and you won't get laid tonight."

" 'Cuz you are the'— Whoops, song's over." He kept rubbing her feet, smiling at her.

"That was the song Jen picked for the father-daughter dance at her wedding," she said, the memory making tears prick at her eyes.

"Oh. I'm sorry, honey."

"No, no. It was sweet. And it was the perfect song for them." She swallowed.

"What would your song have been?" he asked.

" 'Everything I Am' by Celine Dion," she answered instantly. "I picked it the first time I heard it. I was probably ten." He looked blank. "It's basically the best father-daughter song in the world. I'll play it for you sometime."

"Sounds good."

"Do you ever think about your father?" she asked gracelessly.

His hands paused rubbing her feet, then resumed. "Not really. I never had a father. Ben was a great stand-in, as you know. Taught me to ride a bike and throw a football, which was

191

funny, because he couldn't throw to save his life. We made paper airplanes a lot. Really good ones." He looked at his hands on her feet.

"Ben is the best." She hesitated, then went on. "But just out of curiosity, you never checked Facebook or Ancestry or anything?"

"Why would I? Whoever he was, he left before I was born."

"I don't know. Hovering at the edge of death as I am, these things occur to me." She bit her tongue . . . he didn't like when she made jokes about her health, but he let it go this time and even rolled his eyes.

"Well, don't think about it. And drop the melodrama." He switched feet, his hands strong. The man had skills.

"Do you hate him, honey?"

He didn't answer right away. "I wouldn't go that far. I'm disinterested. He was a deadbeat jerk who abandoned my mother. Why would I want to meet him?"

"Maybe just to see what your ethnic background is? Find out where that black hair came from?" His mother was white blond, and Lauren wondered if maybe his father was Latino or Native American or Italian. "But it's your call, of course."

"Don't . . . don't do anything, Lauren. Don't reach out to him or anything like that. This is not that sappy television show."

"I won't, honey. I was just curious." She paused. "Also, I love that show."

He looked at her sternly. "He's a nonentity. The end."

"Got it." She tickled his ribs with her free foot. "If you promise to bake me a pie with those apples your mom brought over yesterday, I'll have sex with you right here and now. Couch sex, and you know how hot that is, big guy."

"Pie, huh?"

"Those apples aren't gonna eat themselves." She reached for his hand and tugged him closer. Pebbles groaned and rolled over on her back. "The dog read my mind," Lauren whispered.

Josh smiled, and even though she was bone-weary, she knew she wouldn't regret the next half hour. "Move the dog," she whispered. "She's a perv, and I don't want her watching this time."

They made love, laughing here and there, humor interspersed with reverence and lust and a little pride that they could make each other feel so good. After a cuddle, Josh got to work on the pie. Lauren took a shower and had a nap, then answered emails and did some tweaking on the new project Bruce had given her—a courtyard for a new condo complex. Fun.

The pie smelled like heaven, and Josh had cleaned the kitchen till it gleamed. Stephanie keenly believed cleanliness was next to godli-ness, and though Josh had been a slob when

Lauren first met him, his mom's genes were finally clicking into place. That and his fear that a random germ would make her sick.

"Dinner is served," he said. "And please note there's no sugar in here, because the apples were sweet enough, and the pie crust is made with whole wheat—"

"Don't ruin it, babe. Grab a fork and join me."

"It's all for you."

"I'm feeling kindly and big-hearted," she said. "Come on! Share." The truth was, eating too much made breathing more difficult.

Josh took a fork and started eating. No plates necessary.

A knock came on the door. "It's Sarah!"

"Come in!" Lauren called, then coughed. Josh gave her a close look, assessing, always assessing. She wondered how much research he'd done on IPF while she was napping.

"I brought you a pie—oh, my God, it already smells like pie in here!" Sarah laughed. "Great minds think alike. Well, maybe you can freeze this sucker."

"Sarah! You're my best, best friend!"

Josh stood up. "Let me take that from you. Thank you. It's very kind." Lauren almost rolled her eyes. Josh had never really warmed up to Sarah, and he tended to get too formal around her.

Someday, though, they'd be friends. She knew it in her bones. Sarah was such a good person, smart and funny, and she loved dogs, as she was demonstrating by letting Pebbles lick her face.

"Hello, Pebbles, my baby! Hello! Hello! Yes, I love you best, doggy. These two don't even come close." She came over and sat on the leather chair. "How are you guys? What's new and exciting?"

Josh and Lauren glanced at each other. "Um . . . nothing. Nice quiet day."

"So you just fooled around. I get it. Damn you smug marrieds. Josh, please find me a husband."

He looked at Lauren, and she made an encouraging face, letting him know it was a joke. "Yes, of course. It's my top priority." Good lad.

Sarah glanced at the oxygen at the base of the couch. "Rough day?"

"A great day. I'm just a little tired now." Talking about her health was boring. "Hey, did you get the invitation to Mean Debi's birthday party?"

"Yes! When did she deign to like me?"

"I have no idea." Debi was a girl from their old neighborhood who'd been (and still was) a right bitch. "I'm not going. I'm only on the list so she can feel saintly."

"I'm not going, either. I hated her then, I hate her now, I will always hate her. Remember when she told everyone my father was in jail?"

Lauren sure did. Poor Sarah had cried on the

195

school bus, and Lauren had shielded her, pre-tending they were looking at a magazine while she handed Sarah tissues. "Let's have a girls' night that day and do something way better and post pictures everywhere."

"Oh, yes. That's genius. She'll hate that so much." They laughed, instantly reverting to sixth graders, which was the beauty of childhood friends. "She commented on the video you posted of Josh snoring, did you see that?"

"Thanks for that, by the way," Josh said.

"You're welcome. Cinematic genius, if I do say so." Lauren pulled up her Instagram on her phone. The other day, she'd come home from work to find Josh asleep on the couch, a rhythmic snore-puff with each exhale. She'd very gently taped a Kleenex to his nose, careful not to wake him, and filmed him while Pebbles looked on, head tilted with curiosity, startling slightly as the tissue fluttered.

She still thought it was hilarious (and it had thousands of likes, so she wasn't wrong). "Ah, here's what Mean Debi has to say. 'You're amazing to still be having fun, despite everything. Hashtag Praying-For-Lauren.' Oh, my God!"

They laughed more, though Lauren had to pull hard to get enough air. "I hope her birthday cake turns rancid."

"Want some pie, Sarah?" Josh asked, getting up and heading for the kitchen.

"Sure! Let me try yours and see if you're a better baker than I am, in which case I must kill you."

"Understood."

Sarah trailed after him, chatting amiably, and a thought came to Lauren.

Sarah could be Josh's second wife.

Since Lauren's diagnosis, she'd seen a . . . maturing in her friend. Maybe that was something that happened to everyone who had to face terminal illness, their own or someone else's. But while Sarah had always, always been her friend, Lauren knew she was competitive, always wanting to be the prettiest girl in the room, the smartest, the best dancer, whatever. The two of them had always planned to go to school on the Hill . . . Lauren had gotten into RISD via early decision and a rather smashing portfolio, but Sarah wasn't accepted at Brown, despite her straight As. Instead, she'd taken the scholarship offered by the University of Rhode Island. Every time she visited Lauren and they walked around College Hill, Sarah was edgy and a little bitter.

When they graduated, Lauren got her dream job in interior and public space design. Pearl Churchwell Harris, Architects, was located in a beautiful old building on Benefit Street. Sarah got her master's in social work and took a job with the Department of Children, Youth and Families, which was noble and draining and rewarding and depressing. The Lord's work, Lauren said, but it took its toll. And, of course, Sarah wasn't paid nearly enough, whereas Lauren earned enough to be able to find her own place almost immediately. Sarah had lived with her mom until last year.

Lauren wasn't the comparison type; she was Jen's little sister, so she'd learned humility early on. She happily accepted her position as second-best daughter (she was the founder of Jen's fan club, after all). But she could tell that Sarah resented a lot of the surface things. If Lauren wore a new pair of shoes, Sarah's hawkish eyes would spy them. If she bought anything new for her apartment, Sarah would immediately notice it, but not comment. Then there were the not-so-surface things—Sarah's dad was a deadbeat idiot; Lauren had had the world's best father. Sarah had a handful of half siblings she barely knew, courtesy of her father; Lauren had the greatest sister in human history.

So there was jealousy there, and since she had no idea how to combat it, Lauren never addressed it. But it got worse when Lauren started dating Josh. And hey. Josh was perfect and beautiful and everything a person could ever want in a partner. Lauren understood. She believed every woman and gay man on earth would want Josh as a husband. Sarah had a tendency to fall in love fast and hard, and then be dropped. Lauren had asked her to be her bridesmaid, the only one other than Jen. And Sarah had smiled grimly through all wedding stuff, but Lauren knew she was envious.

But whatever competitiveness Sarah had felt melted at Lauren's diagnosis, and truly, she couldn't have been a better friend. She came over at least twice a week, and they went out if Lauren felt up to it. Most importantly, Sarah treated Lauren like a normal person. Unlike, say, Mean Debi, who seemed to think that having a sick friend gave her some sort of special status on social media, because she posted about Lauren constantly. *Thoughts and prayers to one of my dearest friends, who is bravely battling IFP.* Not that Mean Debi ever did anything helpful or kind, mind you. She couldn't even get the initials of Lauren's disease right.

Whatever. Sarah had really come through, and she was fun and pretty and hardworking. It would be nice, she thought, to look down from heaven and see the person she loved best in the world married to her oldest friend. It would be great. It would be lovely.

Pebbles whined, cocking her head to look up at her mistress. "Nothing to see here," she whispered. The dog jumped up on her lap and licked away her tears.

14

Joshua

Month four
June

Dear Joshua,
Hello, my wonderful husband! As I write this, you're sleeping. Naked, I might add. Your shoulders are so ridiculously gorgeous. I am deeply grateful.

It's been strange, trying to imagine you alive while I'm not, trying to think about where you are and how you're doing, what issues might be coming up. I've read some books on grief to try to help you get through this. I know there's not an easy way, and everyone's path is different (I hate that line, don't you? Obviously, everyone's path is different, genius! Duh!)

But everyone's path *is* different.

It occurred to me that aside from all the things we do together, and aside from you running, you don't really have a hobby. (I view the punching bag as more of a coping mechanism than something you actually enjoy doing.) Fly-fishing is a real hobby, for example. Or learning how to sail, since we live in the Ocean State. I bet there's a baseball league for grown-ups in town, and maybe you'd like that.

I think a hobby would be a way for you to do something we never did together. Maybe it will relax you, or tire you out in a good way, or be something that you do at home, like paint. Pottery. (Actually, not pottery. You'd have to give pinch pots and lopsided vases to our friends and family, and they'd have to pretend to like them because you're a widower.)

Would you get a hobby for me, Joshua? It makes me happy to think of you trying something new, something that would interest you. I want you to have free time. I don't want you to be working or grieving every minute of every day. I want you to make new friends. Maybe this can help.

I'll be watching, cheering you on in whatever it is, honey. I love you.

Lauren

He reread it four times, memorizing it, then sniffed the paper, hoping to catch a trace of her smell. Nothing. Just paper.

She was right. He didn't have many hobbies. He designed medical stuff, and he took care of his wife. He liked to travel, but not without her.

He liked to cook, but not for one. The days were too long, and the nights were worse.

A hobby it would be.

Now. What did he like to do?

His mind went blank.

Once or twice a month, he and Ben Kim went for a long walk through the city so Ben could get his cigar fix without Mrs. Kim harping on him. That didn't exactly constitute a hobby, though.

He ran because he knew he had to do something in order not to be a blob of a human, and to exercise Pebbles. He wasn't interested in an art class. His work *was* art, in a way. When he was a kid, his mom had put him in gymnastics to burn off some of his toddler energy, and he kept at it for a few years. But that wasn't something an adult could take up (the idea of him doing handsprings in the park . . . no). He'd played Little League baseball until about seventh grade, when he quit for the robotics team (dork). He hadn't played sports in high school, but had done Model UN (super dork).

To Google he went. *Hobbies for men.* Leather working, out. Microbrewing, out. Guns, no thanks. Too loud, plus he didn't see himself ever shooting anything. Archery maybe? That could be cool. Woodworking . . . nah. Furniture making? In college, he had been sought out as one of the few who could assemble IKEA furniture without direction. Might he have a talent for woodworking? The smell of wood, the satisfaction of a table made by his own hands?

But where would he do that? Would he have to buy a bunch of saws and power tools? Too much trouble.

He called Sarah. "Hey," he said, belatedly realizing she was at work. "You busy?"

"No, no. What's up?" Of course she was busy; she was a social worker for the state.

"Um, well, this is out of the blue, but . . . I've been thinking of taking up a hobby."

"That's good."

"I just don't know what to do."

There was a silence. "Do you want me to suggest something?"

"Yes?" Why had he called her? He should've called Jen, who knew him better.

"Okay. Well, I take karate classes." That's right, she did. She used to come over before class sometimes, because Lauren had gotten a real kick out of it (pun intended), seeing her in her karate getup. "Why don't you come to a class and see if you like it?"

"That would be great. Thank you."

"Okay, I'll text you my schedule and talk to my sensei."

Couldn't she just say *teacher?* Why did she always annoy him? "Thanks, Sarah," he said, aware that she was doing him a favor.

"You're welcome. Gotta go."

• • •

Green Dragon School of Kenpo Karate was in a strip mall over in Federal Hill. Sarah met him there, already dressed in her black uniform, which was cinched at the waist with a black belt.

"Wow," Josh said. "You're a black belt?"

"No, Josh, I'm just wearing this because I like the color." She rolled her eyes, then kissed him on the cheek. "Come on in. Sensei's expecting us."

"Does Sensei have a name?"

"She does. Jane." Josh immediately pictured a tall, strong white woman in her forties, chiseled and hard and militant—a shredded Tilda Swinton. They went into the waiting room, which sported worn blue carpeting, a counter and a line of chairs. Windows showed the larger room with a padded floor, where classes were obviously taught. Freestanding punching bags, kicking shields and myriad other supplies stood neatly on the far side.

"Hello!" cried a woman. She was so tiny he hadn't seen her behind the desk, and he jumped. She was white-haired—sixties? Seventies?—and wore a black uniform with a black belt around her plump waist. Japanese, with a slight accent. "You must be Joshua Park. Welcome! And hello, dear Sarah!" She stood up, not quite five feet tall, he guessed. Four foot ten and a half. Being an engineer made him good at estimating these things.

"Sensei, this is my friend, Josh. Josh, this is Sensei Jane Tanaka."

"Nice to meet you," he said, towering over her. Her hands were gnarled with arthritis, poor thing.

"Have you ever done martial arts before, Josh?"

"No, ma'am. I have a punching bag at home, but . . . no."

"That's okay! We are all beginners at some point. So! We'll do a little karate together, and you can decide if you want to become a martial artist."

It did sound cool. Joshua Park, martial artist.

"Sign this waiver, please. It says you won't sue me if you get injured."

Josh obeyed.

"Now. Come into the dojo. Take off your shoes, then bow to the flag"—a large American flag was tacked to one wall—"and bow to me, your sensei."

He obeyed. The padded floor felt comfortable under his feet, and the room smelled not unpleasantly of sweat and bleach.

"What do you know about karate, Josh?"

"Very little," he said. "It's a Japanese martial art, thousands of years old."

"That's right. Great for exercise, self-defense, discipline. Now, stand here, left foot forward, hip distance apart, weight evenly balanced. Fists up, like so. This is fighting stance."

He imitated her, already feeling like a badass. This was the same as boxing, which Ben had taught him so long ago.

"Wonderful," she said, smiling. She looked like the epitome of a sweet grandmother. "Let's do a little demonstration, okay?"

"Sure," Josh said, smiling a little. It would be cute to watch her do some moves. He hoped she wouldn't strain anything, or hurt her hands by breaking a board or whatever it was you did in karate class.

"Okay, Josh. Try to punch me in the face."

Josh flinched. "Excuse me?"

"Punch me in the face."

"No, thank you," Josh said, glancing at Sarah, who had her phone out, filming.

"Joshua. I'm your sensei. I gave you an order."

"I was not brought up to hit my elders."

"And you shouldn't, unless they tell you to. Come on. Try to hit me."

Ben, even when he was teaching Josh to box, had never told Josh to punch him in the face.

"It's okay, Josh," Sarah said. "She does this to every new student."

"I'm not going to *punch* her," Josh said. "Sorry, Mrs. Tanaka."

"Sensei. Okay, try to choke me, then," she said.

"I really—"

"In this room, I am your sensei!" she barked. "You obey without question! Do it!"

Jesus. Josh frowned, then put out his hands to the air around her soft neck, not actually touching her.

"Is that the best you can do, pussy?" she asked.

"Wow. Yes. I'm not going to choke you, Mrs.—uh, Sensei."

"Okay. Sorry, Joshua. I warned you."

"Actually, you didn't—"

And then he was lying on the floor, facedown, one arm twisted behind his back, smelling the mat, the sound of his body smacking the mat still ringing in the air.

What just happened?

Sensei Jane clapped her hands. "Get up! Now that you see I'm not a helpless little old lady, let's try again. Punch me in the face."

Josh got back up, assumed fighting stance again and hesitated.

"Do it," she said.

"This is not what I had in—"

She kicked his leg out from under him, and he was sprawled on his back, Sensei standing over him, fist drawn. "Kee-ai!" she yelled, and punched. Josh flinched, but her little knobby fist stopped so close to his Adam's apple that he could feel the heat of her hand. "A punch to the throat immobilizes the enemy and can even kill. Up you go, sweetheart. Ready to punch me in the face?"

He climbed to his feet. "I was hoping this would be more—"

She spun, one leg flying up, her foot hitting him squarely in the chest. He landed on his ass. Looked at her. Narrowed his eyes. "I'm ready to punch you now," he said.

"Great! Give it your best shot!"

Josh stood up again and put his fists up.

"Hit me as hard as you can," Jane said. "Right in the face. Aim for my nose."

"Are you going to hurt me?" he asked. "More than you have already, that is?"

She laughed merrily. "Only a little."

Okay, then. He pulled his fist back and let it fly, fully expecting her to dodge or block or something, but her eyes darted to the left, and at the last second, and in slow motion, and also at the speed of light, his fist hit her squarely in the face. He felt a hideous crunch, and Sensei Jane's head jerked back.

"Josh! Jesus! What did you do?" Sarah yelled, and suddenly, there were all these little kids dressed in white, and they were swarming him, and kicking him, and there was a lot of yelling of "Ha! Ha!" and their little fists were sharp, even if they couldn't reach past his waist.

"You hit our sensei! We hate you! We hate you! Kee-ai!"

"Stop it," he said, but the tiny warrior beasts

had grabbed onto his belt and pulled him down to his knees and were now kicking the shit out of him with their tiny bare feet.

"Sarah!" he said, covering his face.

"Attention!" yelled Jane, and suddenly, the kids formed two rows and stood there like little soldiers. Her face was bloody, and Josh stood up, feeling like the world's worst human.

"Children," Jane said, not bothering to wipe her face. "This is what happens when you lose focus. Mr. Park is our new student, and the first one who has ever been able to hit me. Bow to him and show your respect."

"No, please, I'm very sorry," Josh said, but all the little kids turned and bowed to him.

"Now, Joshua, please step outside. Class, one hundred jumping jacks. Violet, count them off while I clean my face."

"One! Two! Three!" a tiny blond girl began shouting.

Josh slunk out of the room, where a dozen parents stared at him.

Sarah came behind him, wheezing with laughter. "You punched an old woman," she whispered, tears streaming down her face.

"I heard that, Sarah," Jane said, holding a towel to her face. "Old? Please. I am seventy years old. My mother is one hundred and four. Joshua, it was my own fault. I glanced away. So! You want to be my student?"

"Um . . . yes. Yes, I do." How could he say no? He'd broken her nose.

"Great! I think you'll do well." She went behind a counter, glanced at him and pulled out a white uniform wrapped in plastic. "Go get changed and join our class."

"Um . . . is there a beginner's class for adults?" he asked, glancing at the assembled parents, who were making no effort to pretend they weren't staring.

"Not at the moment," she said. "There may be one starting in a few months, but for now, you'll take this one. It's one hundred and nine dollars a month, plus forty dollars for the gi. That's your uniform. Go on! Get changed and come back in." Jane went into her office. "Holy shit," she said, poking her head out. "I'm going to have quite a pair of shiners!" She beamed at him, gruesome through the blood, and closed the door.

Josh looked at Sarah, who was pretending to study something very important on her phone. "Thanks," he said. "This is exactly what I had in mind."

"It'll be good for you," she said, struggling to keep a straight face.

"First I hit an old woman, now I get to beat up children," he said.

"See? A hobby. Now listen to Sensei and go get changed." She smiled. "I'll buy you dinner after."

He did as instructed.

The kids glared at him. "Why are you so old?" one little girl asked after she'd been assigned as his partner.

"I'm like a dragon," he said. "Old and wise."

"I can beat you up," she said.

"I believe it."

She punched him in the thigh to prove it.

"Ouch," he said.

"Lyric, no hitting your partner! Give me twenty push-ups," Sensei Jane said from the front of the room. Her voice sounded stuffy from the swelling. The little girl gave Josh a look that said, *Watch your back,* and started doing Marine-perfect push-ups. She couldn't have been more than five.

They kicked the air and hit a punching bag. The kids were damn cute, Josh had to admit. And he liked kids. Even Lyric. He admired the way they didn't trust him or didn't think he was anything special just because he was an adult. The way they'd rushed to defend their teacher.

When class was over, and Josh had been introduced to the parents, one of whom was a former classmate from RISD and two who had known Lauren, Sarah took him to the sushi place next door.

"Did you know I'd be in a class with kindergarteners?" he asked.

"Honestly, no. That was just a gift. I knew Jane would throw you around a little. She does that to

211

all the new students. Well, not the little kids. But the ones who think a four-foot-ten senior citizen can't defend herself."

"I punched her. In the face. Not great advertising," he said.

"Oh, one of the kids distracted her. You'll never win another fight with her again. Enjoy the moment."

He took a piece of spicy tuna with eel and chewed.

Lauren would've loved this night, Josh thought as they ate their sushi rolls and seaweed salad. She would've been rolling on the floor with laughter at the sight of him towering over the little kids. She would've approved a hundred percent.

15

Joshua

On Lauren's birthday, he went into her closet, sat with the last pair of pajamas she'd ever worn and held them against his face, breathing in her smell.

She would've been twenty-nine years old today.

For their third anniversary, the gift was supposed to be leather. He'd gone to the same jewelry store where he'd bought her engagement ring, and picked out a watch with a green leather band. While in the store, he'd also bought her a pair of dangling gold earrings with pearls on the end. They would look so pretty swaying against her hair, he'd thought. Pearls were her birthstone. His plan had been to save them for June, unaware that she'd die within days of his purchase.

It seemed so long ago, that dark February day, the salesperson complimenting him on his taste and saying his wife was a lucky woman.

Today's weather was insultingly beautiful, the air dry and clear, sun shining, midsixties, flowers bursting out of window boxes everywhere. Even the ferns and hostas Lauren had planted on the rooftop garden had come back this spring, despite Josh's neglect of them. (And the seagull, who shat on them. Maybe it was fertilizer.)

Life was everywhere except where he most wanted it to be.

The dogwood tree idea felt stupid today. He wished there were a grave where he could lay a bouquet of flowers. He should've thought about that, should've recognized that Jen and Donna would want somewhere to go.

Someday, he'd plant the tree. Where, he didn't know.

He texted Donna and asked if he could come over. She said yes, and half an hour later, he was in her kitchen, holding her as she sobbed. "I didn't know it would be this hard," she said, her voice muffled against his shirt. "I don't know if I can stand it. My little girl, my baby."

No, he thought. It was unbearable.

"I have a present for you," he said, handing his mother-in-law the box, and when she saw the earrings, she stroked them gently, as if they were alive.

"Her birthstone," she whispered.

"Yes."

She put them on, then looked in the small mirror by the door. "Thank you, sweetheart," she said.

Then she poured Josh a cup of coffee, and they

sat on the porch, Donna's hand on his arm.

"I heard from Jen you're seeing someone," he said after a time.

"Yes. Bill. He . . . he lost his son. Car accident. It's a comfort, having someone who understands. Do you have anyone to talk to, Josh? Another . . . person?"

"I do. Online, but yes." He thought of what Lauren might say. "I'm glad you're seeing someone. I think Lauren would like that."

Donna tightened her grip on his arm. "Thank you," she whispered, then wiped her eyes again.

This day would end. They would both wake up again tomorrow, and the first birthday without her would be over and done with. For now, he'd stay here, with his wife's mother, and let her mourn her daughter.

16

Lauren

Eighteen months left
August 4

Dear Dad,
There are days when I'm still surprised you're gone, when I have this nanoflash of a thought: *Why haven't I seen Dad in so long? It's kind of shitty that he hasn't been over.* Then I remember.

That's kind of how IPF is. I leave the house and take the stairs and think, *Wow, I need to get in shape,* and then remember that, no, it's not that; it's that I have a lung disease. Or I hear a pretty girl's name and think, *That would be a great name for a daughter,* and then remember that motherhood is not in my future. Dr. Bennett told me she didn't recommend it. That I'd be at high risk for miscarriage, premature delivery, pulmonary hypertension, stroke.

I couldn't bear to lose a baby. I can't ask Josh to risk my life for a baby that might not happen.

But never being a mom . . . that was quite a blow, Dad. That took a lot out of me. I can't really talk about that anymore, because some things are just too sad. I think you understand.

On the happy side of things, Josh and I spent a long weekend in San Diego. He had a meeting with someone about something—he was very private about what—so I suspect it was about IPF and how to cure it. We rented a little house up the coast in La Jolla. Everyone is happy in La Jolla, and why wouldn't they be? For one, it's paradise. For two, Dr. Seuss used to live there, and I think his karma still hangs over the town.

Our house had a lemon tree in the backyard with actual ripe lemons on it, and we used them in cooking, because the landlord told us he couldn't keep up with them. Avocados, too, so we ate a ton of guacamole. We went swimming, and snorkeling, and I even tried surfing, and for a few seconds, I stood up and it was AMAZING, Dad! I was so proud that my tragic stuffy lungs could do everything, even though I conked out at three p.m. that day and slept for six hours.

And then . . . we went hang gliding. Well, I went, because Josh is afraid of heights, but he bravely stood on the ground and filmed me. Oh, Dad, it was the best. The place was on a cliff over the ocean, and no one was going up because it was a little too windy. So we sat and waited, then went down to the street to have lunch, and then came back, and it was still too windy. I finally walked over to the guy and said, "Look. I'm dying. We're leaving Tuesday morning. My husband will sign anything you want, but you need to get me up there."

He asked what was making me die, and I told him it was IPF. "Well, shit," he said. "My mom died of the same thing. Get suited up."

Half an hour later, I was ready. Gabe, my handsome and lovely instructor, was strapped to me so I wouldn't crash. He told me to walk/trot to the edge of the cliff, but I RAN, Daddy, practically dragging Gabe behind. I wasn't even a little afraid. Josh yelled, "Go get 'em, babe!" and then the wind caught under the wings, and we swooped up, and I was laughing and laughing with glee. The ocean was so beautiful and the sky . . . oh, it was so clear and blue. I could see the cove where all the sea lions hang out, and the buildings in the distance, but I just wanted to look out at the ocean and sky, and even with the wind roaring in my ears, and being strapped to Gabe, I felt so . . . calm. So happy to live in this beautiful world, Dad. So glad to be me.

Even with everything.

Being in La Jolla was like a vacation from real life, which I suppose is true of every vacation. But my IPF behaved while I was there, and I didn't cough too much, though I needed a nap every day. Not that there's anything wrong with that. Josh said if I wanted to move here, it was a done deal. But I want to be near Jen and Sebastian and Baby X, Darius and Mom, Sarah, Asmaa and Bruce and all the little kids at the Hope Center, even if they're disgusting germ sponges. The trip was wonderful. It was perfect. The two of us are perfect.

Love you, Daddy!

Lauren

Lauren considered divorcing Josh the next week.

The fight came out of the clear blue sky. They'd gotten home from La Jolla, started back in their regular routine. Mara, Lauren's best friend from RISD, called to say that her boyfriend's mutt had had puppies, and would they like one?

219

They sure as hell would.

Pebbles was wriggly, an Australian shepherd–Lab–dachshund–something else mutt, a girl who excelled at licking faces and chewing up shoes. Lauren was in love. That face! Those eyes! The silky ears! The warm little weight against her on the couch!

That very first day of pet ownership, when they were sitting in the living room talking in new, goofy voices, professing their love for Pebbles, Lauren spoke without thinking.

"I'm so glad we got her, Josh! That way when I die, you won't be alone."

The air changed. The puppy, who was gnawing on Lauren's fingers, stopped and looked at Josh, head tilted.

Oh, shit.

His face was stone. Jaw clenched, cheekbones looking ready to cut through his skin, and then a redness seemed to pulse out of him toward her. "This fucking *dog* is not going to outlive you, Lauren!"

She jumped, because she had never heard him yell before, and for a second, she thought it was someone else. But nope, it was her husband.

"Jesus Christ! Don't you *ever* say something so stupid again! What the fuck is wrong with you? How can you say that?"

"I—I—uh . . ."

"How do you not see it?" he yelled, and his

voice was scary. "Don't you ever, ever say something like that again!" He stood up, went to the door and punched the wall next to it, so hard his fist went right through the Sheetrock, and he did it again, and again.

"Honey! Stop! Stop!" Lauren said, running over to him. When she touched his back, he jerked open the door and flew down the stairs. She ran to the window and saw him disappear around the corner.

The puppy was whining. She gathered the little dog against her chest and took a few shaking breaths, heart roiling and churning in a sick, panicked way. There were bloody streaks on the wall. From his hand. From his fist.

She had never seen him like this before.

She closed the door to the hallway and locked it, then slid down to sit on the floor. Tears were streaming out of her eyes.

What should she do? He was almost pathologically even tempered. She didn't even know he could *get* angry, let alone at her. In their entire marriage, they'd had one fight, when he didn't want to go to her office Christmas party because it was too loud and crowded. She said they could leave early, or that he could just come in with her and stay for ten minutes and leave her and she'd get a ride home with someone else, but he wouldn't budge. She'd gone herself, and sulked for the next day, punishing him. This man gave workshops to hundreds of people, after all. He had gone to three colleges where there were many people and noises.

He brought her flowers the next day and apologized. Came to Mara's holiday party a few days later.

But nothing, nothing like this. She had never been scared of him, or his anger, ever. She didn't really know he'd been capable of it.

She sniffed, wiped her eyes on her sleeve and kissed Pebbles's little head. The puppy answered with a snore.

Lauren debated calling Steph to ask if this had ever happened, but didn't want to put his mother in the middle. Instead, she went to Google and typed in a few words: *Asperger's, autism, anger, loss of control.*

And then, after she'd read a few articles that seemed to describe what had just happened to a T, she looked up "anger when your spouse is terminally ill."

Then she called her sister and told her everything.

"Oh, honey," Jen said when she was done. "Can you blame him?"

"It was scary," Lauren said, wiping her eyes.

"Were you afraid he'd hurt you?"

"No! No, of course not. It was just so shocking. Like he went Incredible Hulk on me."

"He's probably repressed a lot of shit. Do you

guys talk about . . . oh, fuck, now I'm crying, too. Do you talk about everything, Lauren?"

"Sort of? We have. I just didn't expect . . . this."

"You struck a nerve." She swallowed loudly. "And if the statistics are right, you were saying the truth." Jen drew in a shuddering breath. "That fucking dog may well outlive you. I think I want to punch a wall now, too."

"What do I do about Josh? I don't even know where he went. I hope he's talking to Ben. I hope Ben kicks his ass, quite frankly."

"I think you should probably just . . . cut him some slack, Lauren. He loves you so much. You're his whole world."

She knew that.

She hung up with her sister, feeling slightly less alone. For the first time, she wondered about her and Josh. Was it selfish of her, being in a relationship that was doomed? Should she . . . divorce him? It had been really easy to picture him as her rock, her hero, but maybe this was too much for any human heart to endure.

Maybe, she thought, tears dripping onto Pebbles's head, maybe it would be better if she cut him loose sooner than later. Because she *would* be leaving him. They both knew that. Divorce might be easier for him to handle. She knew he loved her; that was almost the problem.

Lauren cleaned up the Sheetrock, though obviously she couldn't patch the hole in the wall without the proper supplies. She took the puppy for a walk. She texted Josh, then called him. He didn't respond. She had the immature idea to pretend she felt horrible to guilt him into coming back, but she immediately dismissed it as a teenage move (though tempting, sure).

She texted again, saying that she loved him and wanted to talk. He didn't respond. She called him. It went to voice mail.

She pictured herself going through IPF alone. Well, she wouldn't be alone. She had Jen and Darius, Sarah, her friends, her mother, her coworkers. There would be plenty of people, and maybe a shared burden would be best (because let's face it, she'd be a burden).

He came home around ten that night.

"Hi," he said.

"Hi."

He looked at the wall and didn't say anything else.

"You scared Pebbles," she said. "And me."

"Sorry."

She rolled her eyes. "Shitty apology, Josh."

He stood there with his arms at his sides, looking as if it were the first time he was in his own body—stiff, agitated, foreign. "You can't make jokes about your life, Lauren. Not to me."

"It wasn't a joke, honey. The odds are—"

"No! Stop."

"Joshua," she said, going to him and taking his hands. They felt like dead things, like pieces of wood. "I have a terminal disease. You know this. I know this. The odds *are* this dog will outlive me. Plus, she's prettier than I am."

"Every time you say something that's supposed to be a joke, it's . . . it's like a knife in my chest," he said.

She pressed her lips together. "I'm sorry. I don't . . . I just don't want to be like my mother. I have to be able to make a joke."

"No, Lauren!" He jerked his hands away. "Not about your life! Stop trying to be Princess Butterflies and Rainbows all the time!"

She threw up her hands. "You're the one who just punched a hole in our wall and didn't return my calls for seven hours. Should you be lecturing me about how I should handle my own diagnosis? Just because you're a super-genius doesn't mean you know how to do this. No one does."

The conversation was going off course, and Lauren's throat locked down. Being Princess Butterflies and Rainbows (a new name, and one she kind of liked) . . . that was her thing. She clung to that. It was her defense mechanism.

"Josh, I think we should talk about it if you can . . . if we should . . ." The words were a lot harder to say out loud. "Sit down, honey. Come on. It's me. Let's talk."

They sat. The puppy put her paws on Josh's knee, and he scooped her up, not smiling.

"Honey," she said, "if you can't handle what's coming, then maybe we should . . ."

He looked at her, alarm in his eyes. "What?"

"Maybe we should separate. If this is going to be too hard for you. I would understand that, because I know how much you love me. And if seeing me die—"

"Don't *say* that!" he yelled, and Pebbles jumped off the couch with a reproachful look.

Then Josh clamped his arms over his head and sank onto the couch and just . . . fell apart. Big gulping sobs racked his body. In that moment, Lauren's heart broke all over again. She pulled his hands away from his face and wrapped herself around him. After a second, he hugged her back so hard she could hardly get a breath in.

"Don't leave me," he said against her neck. "Don't leave me. Don't die, Lauren. Don't leave me."

He just kept saying that over and over.

"Oh, honey," she whispered. "I'm so sorry."

Being Princess Butterflies and Rainbows did put up a shield—but she was noticing that the shield was from everything. Maybe the terror was kept at bay, but nothing else was let in, either.

For months, she'd been worrying about Josh after her death. She hadn't worried about him in the here and now, when she could actually do something about it. "I'm sorry, honey," she said again. "I'll do better. I won't make jokes anymore."

He pulled up, his hair crazy, eyes wet. "No. I . . . I know you need to. And I do, too. Just not all the time. Sometimes I need . . ." His voice broke.

"Sometimes you need to punch a wall."

He nodded. "Sorry about that."

"We can get a punching bag for the gym downstairs."

He looked at the floor. "Lauren, I . . . I don't usually . . . I call it a red-out. When I lose my shit like that. I'm sorry I scared you."

"I understand, honey. We're going through a lot."

He nodded and swallowed.

This would be a process, she realized. There'd be curves and veers and long straight stretches, and that was normal. They got to be scared and furious and happy and grateful, and sometimes they could be all those things at the same time.

She climbed off his lap and handed him a tissue, then blew her own nose. They looked at each other, raw and exhausted. "Is there a way to head that off at the pass?" she asked. "You know. To save our walls?"

He nodded. "Yeah. I have techniques. Visualizations, distractions. Creative destruction."

"Oh, I like that term. Like you go out and chop down a tree?"

"Yeah. Or hitting a punching bag. Ben had one in his basement for me."

"Guess what you're getting for a birthday present?"

"Is it a punching bag?" He smiled, looking older than his years, and her broken heart broke a little more.

"It is! How did you know?" She stood up, pulled him to his feet and hugged him. "I'm starving. I'm going to make us both omelets."

He looked at her a long minute. "Are we okay? Do you forgive me?"

"Oh, Josh. Yes, honey."

"Don't ever mention us separating again. Okay?"

"Okay." Then Pebbles pushed between them, and they smiled, and Josh picked her up and kissed her head.

The changes crept in. The diagnosis had been surreal and amorphic at first. But reality was making itself at home, and Josh's red-out . . . it drove everything home.

There had to be time for grief and anger laced together with all that they did have, and that panoply of emotion made Lauren feel more real. She didn't always have to be Princess Butterflies and Rainbows, and she didn't have to be sobbing on the floor. Just because she was terminal didn't take away from the fact that she was also a regular person.

There were the new realities of IPF. She learned to plan her day carefully, so as not to expend too much energy and have a setback. She and Josh bought a lovely teak bench for the shower, and a grab bar, in case she got dizzy or weak. Josh got her a beautiful leather bag to hold her portable oxygen, which she didn't need every day . . . but it was nice that she had a bag that didn't yell *medical device* even if she often had a plastic cannula in her nose.

College Hill was too steep for her to walk to work now. But she did walk around the Brown campus at lunch, because staying fit was important. Louise or Santino usually went with her; Louise was sharp and funny, but Santino was hilarious. He had the best stories about the women he dated—like the one he'd met for the first time, went back to her apartment and found pictures of himself taped to the fridge. Or the one who asked if he'd like to wax her lady bits as foreplay. Like most people who saw her frequently, her condition became normal to them (though Lori Cantore treated her like she was giving away gift-wrapped leprosy).

Bruce the Mighty and Beneficent had brought a twin bed into the staff lounge and made a sign that read *Lauren's sleeping, so fuck off* in case she needed a nap. Lori filed a complaint (sigh), and Bruce called Lauren into his office and made her and Lori Cantore watch as he fed the complaint into the shredder. Dear, dear Bruce.

She, Sarah and Asmaa took a gentle yoga class a few times a week, which was great for keeping her muscles strong, which in turn helped her oxygenation. She went out a couple of times a month with her friends or sister, saw her mom and Stephanie at least once a week. She was planning these days, unsure of how much longer life would be normal, or if a bad flu season would force her to stay in the house for months.

Jen brought Sebastian over every Thursday night so they could babysit while Jen and Darius went out. Lauren loved those nights, Sebastian's funny little questions about how the water got into the tub, or if elephants sleep in nests, or if he could stay with them for nine or seventeen days in a row. He'd fall asleep in their bed, and she and Josh would lie on either side of him, pretending to watch a movie but staring at his perfect skin and long lashes, curly hair and sweet little hands. Their sadness at not being able to have kids went unspoken, but when a few tears slipped down her cheeks, Josh would reach over and wipe them away and tell her he loved her.

Her medical stuff became routine—respiratory therapy, which involved huffing, pursed lips, diaphragmatic breathing, and her favorite, mucus expulsion, which was *just* as sexy as it sounded. She had pulmonary function tests, blood work and checkups.

The goal was to keep things steady. What lung space she had lost to the fibrosis and scarring was gone forever. Every time she got pneumonia, the therapist warned, she'd lose a little more.

Meanwhile, Josh was . . . amazing. Calm, caring, funny and, yes, sometimes sad. The punching bag was used three or four nights a week as a proactive measure, and when he came up, sweaty, his hands wrapped, his mood light, she was proud of them both. He got better at talking about those pesky feelings—she did wonder if she was the first person who'd helped him with that, since she suspected Steph had simply told him yes, life could be unfair, next question please? The wall-punching incident had loosened something in him.

"I was thinking about the Great Beyond," she said one night over a vegetarian dinner so loaded with garlic it had cleared out her sinuses. She tried to keep her voice light, but his head snapped up.

"Are you feeling okay these days?"

"Yes! I feel great today." She cleared her throat. "When my dad died, I thought about it a lot, that's all. And . . . I've been thinking about it again."

"I *don't* want you to think about it."

231

She gave him a look.

"Right. Okay. Tell me more."

She loved him *so* much. "Well, I think it must be this amalgamation of everything you've ever loved and wanted to do. Like . . . you get to be an eagle. Or a baby giraffe."

"Or a shark."

"No one wants to be a shark, Josh."

"Why? No fear, do whatever you want, eat whatever you want . . ." He attempted a smile.

"Kill seals and unsuspecting swimmers? No. There are no sharks in the Great Beyond, Joshua." She pretended to scowl.

"Okay. Well, what else is there?"

"You get to see all the people you love who've died. Obviously. I've got my dad, my grandparents, my great-aunt Mimi. A boy in fourth grade who had leukemia. Peter. We sat on the bus together." She hadn't thought of him in years. Poor little Peter. They'd held hands once. Her eyes stung.

"What else is in the Great Beyond?" Josh asked. "Food, I imagine."

"A make-your-own-sundae bar for sure."

"How about that sushi place we went to in Hawaii? That's worthy of the GB."

She smiled, feeling her shoulders drop a little. Her ending was part of their life now. And she *was* scared . . . not so much of dying herself, but of making everyone she loved so sad. And yes, of course of dying. Dying badly, that was. Would she go out gasping with air hunger, that wretched term? Clawing at the sheets? Or intubated and drugged so she couldn't say some profoundly moving last words?

"I really believe my dad will be there at the end," she said, and then she did cry.

Josh came over and picked her up and held her on his lap. He kissed her cheek and smoothed her hair and said, "Don't be such a loser, babe," and she sputtered in surprise, then laughed.

Thank God for him. Thank God.

Being married to a sick person got Josh a lot of attention from idiot acquaintances and, alas, her mother. "You're a saint, Josh. I don't know how you do it," her mom said one day when she insisted on coming to a doctor's appointment. Lauren was having her blood drawn to check her arterial gases.

"I'm actually sleeping with Tyler here," Josh said, nodding solemnly at the phlebotomist. "Best sex of my life."

Her mom gasped, and then, realizing it was a joke as Lauren laughed (and coughed), glared at Josh.

"I don't like to brag," said Tyler, "but I *do* have a reputation."

"I feel neglected," Lauren said. "*I've* never slept with you, Tyler."

"Text me," he said with a wink. "Hold the

gauze, you know the drill, and voilà! Get out. Go. Leave me."

"Maybe he can be your next true love," Lauren said to Josh.

"I could do a lot worse."

"It's not funny," her mom said. "First, my husband drops dead, and now my daughter is dying."

"Thanks for the reminder," Lauren said. "Can we get Thai food? You want to come, Mom?" Because even if her mother was a little black rain cloud, she was still her mother. "Let's call Steph and see if she can come." Her mom was better behaved when there was a more functional peer around.

Lauren also found that she'd become inspiration porn . . . that too many people bent over backward to praise her for simply being alive. Her social media accounts were suddenly burgeoning with compliments about her boring photos of food and trees. Mean Debi was the worst. *You're amazing! You can do anything! Keep up the good work! #prayers #LaurenStrong.* (Not that she came by or made a casserole or anything.)

Only Jen, Sarah and Asmaa stayed sane . . . Sarah even going so far as to post *yawn* when Lauren posted yet another picture of the sky at sunset. Lauren appreciated that.

She didn't want to be known as Dying Lauren or Terribly Sick Lauren. She didn't want to start a YouTube channel or a foundation (though huge props to those who did, because Lauren would occasionally watch those videos for a lift). She didn't want to document her illness . . . she wanted to think about *living*. Yes, IPF was a big part of it now, but there was no way she was going to post pictures of herself on oxygen to "inspire" anyone. To quote the great philosopher, ain't no one got time for that.

She *did* start a Twitter account under @NotDeadYet0612 with an avatar of a skeleton smoking a cigarette. The purpose was to document stupid things people said, because if you couldn't laugh at them, you might become homicidal. She became quite popular, reporting from the trenches.

> Stranger at my doctor's office asked what I have. Her reaction: "Oh, my God, my cousin's other grandfather? He had the same thing. It was awful. He wasted down to nothing. He didn't even look human in the end. He reeked of death."
> Me: "That's so reassuring. Thank you."
> Some dude on a conference call, asking about my cannula: "Well, we're all dying, really. I could get hit by a bus crossing the street!" How many people actually die this way? Are bus drivers filled with road rage? Why not say "car" or "dump truck"? Poor bus drivers get a bad rap.

Lady in post office when I am innocently mailing a package: "I see that you're on oxygen. Are you sick?"
Me: "No, I just like the buzz."
Her: "Can I hug you?"
Me: "No."
Her: "Let me hug you."
Me: "You touch me, and I'll punch you."

She and Sarah laughed till they cried over that one, and it became their catchphrase . . . *let me hug you.* Never failed to make them giggle. Asmaa, who was sweeter than both of them put together, never got the joke and hugged Lauren every time she heard the line, which just made it funnier.

So she had a terminal condition. Didn't everyone? Everyone *would* die, after all. Lauren's death was just a little more real than getting hit by a bus.

She could live with that. She was living with that. She didn't have much choice.

17

Joshua

Month five
July

He'd started working again, almost every day. Better to do something that might help someone somewhere than watch television. It wasn't easy to concentrate, and his brain would play small, cruel tricks on him. If he finished this phase of the design or read an article about that subject, Lauren would come back. If he could work for an hour, Lauren would come back. If he was just good enough, time would flow backward, and Lauren would be back. Sometimes he thought he heard her at the door or in the kitchen, and he spooled out the notion. Yes, she was back. No, it wasn't the AC clicking on. It was his wife. The past four and a half months had been a bad, excruciatingly detailed dream.

One night, he'd set out her favorite mug next to his. Just to see them together again. Just to pretend for a few seconds that she'd be in this kitchen once more. Even if it was her ghost—and he didn't believe in ghosts. Anything. Anything from her.

There was nothing.

He answered texts and emails and sometimes even the phone. He took Pebbles for a run in the morning, a walk at lunchtime, and, most nights, a romp in the dog park. If a person asked what her name and breed was, he'd answer. Every Tuesday and Thursday afternoon, he went to karate, which was actually pretty fun. Being around five-year-olds with badass attitudes let him escape a little bit. He and Ben resumed their long, rambling walks. Ben had a soft spot for Pebbles and loved throwing her the Frisbee, which Pebbles could catch in midair.

"How are you doing, son?" Ben asked.

"Doing okay." Somehow, those brief talks helped. He guessed it was just knowing Ben was with him that did the trick. They had never needed a lot of words, after all.

The anger would come in red flashes. He lost his car keys one day and tossed the apartment like a DEA agent looking for meth, knowing as he flipped the couch cushions and slammed drawers and barked out curse words that he was overreacting (and would be the one to clean the mess up later). His car didn't start one day, and he kicked it so hard it dented. When his shirt got caught against a chain-link fence during a run, he tugged it, tore it, and then ripped the whole shirt off and split it in half, then tossed it in the trash.

It wasn't the shirt, or the car battery, or the

keys. It was *one more thing,* no matter how small, that he had to deal with. The rage was sickening and satisfying—he'd never kicked a car before, for God's sake, and what good did it do? That thought hadn't stopped him from kicking it over and over. The punching bag in the first-floor gym was earning its keep. If his little karate compadres could see him then, they'd be terrified.

Anger was one of the stages of grief, he knew. It made him feel huge and sick and even a little scared of himself, and when it passed, he was ashamed. "It'll get better," his mother said, staring at his now-calloused, reddened knuckles. "I know it doesn't seem like it, but it'll get easier, honey."

He didn't see how that was possible. Lauren had been the center of everything, it seemed, and now instead of her, there was a black hole with ragged, sharp teeth, gnawing at everyone who loved her, eating them like a snake eats a hapless field mouse, in gulps and fits.

Radley, his first post-Lauren friend, was a relief by comparison. He was often free, leading Josh to believe that either Radley didn't have many friends either, or he was using Josh as a guinea pig for therapist training. Either way, he was grateful, because there were days when it felt like he didn't really exist. That, were it not for a text from Jen here and an invitation from Radley there, Josh felt like he might not be . . . real, somehow. He talked out loud from time to time just to make sure he still had a voice. Pebbles would lift her head and wag, or come over and sit close to him, pressing herself against his legs.

He was so glad he had a dog.

The forum said everything was normal. Others understood and commiserated. It didn't make the problems go away.

One day, Josh was contacted by Chiron Medical Enterprises, a company based in Singapore who'd bought one of his designs. They wanted a device that would help spinal surgeons detect different tissue types in the back to alleviate human error when inserting hardware, limiting damage to soft tissues and especially the spinal cord. It was a good project, complicated but with far-reaching benefits, right up his alley.

The more he sat at the computer, the easier it became to think about the job. His tunnel vision returned, the thought process that had allowed him to succeed so early in life.

He and Lauren had once watched a movie or TV show that depicted some young genius—Sherlock Holmes, maybe, or Alan Turing. The character saw various elements floating in patterns and connections that lit up, invisible to everyone else. Lauren had paused the movie and asked, "Is that what it's like for you?"

"No," he'd said slowly. "It's the opposite. It's

literally tunnel vision. I see the problem, and the next sixteen steps, with the complications sitting on the road ahead, like hurdles I have to jump to keep going. Everything else is blocked out—what time of day it is, if I'm hungry, if it's night or day or raining or sunny. There's just the path to the solution. I think . . . well, I think I'm different because I can shut everything else out and see to the end of the tunnel."

She'd looked at him a long time. "You're remarkable, you know," she said, running her fingertips up his cheek, touching his earlobe. "Utterly remarkable."

He'd been unable to invent anything to help her, though.

Move along, loser, he could hear her say.

Finally, the morning came when Sarah dropped off the fifth letter. It had seemed like an eternity since the last one.

"Want some coffee?" he asked. It was a test for himself to see if he could wait, and also to try to be a good friend to Sarah, who missed Lauren, too, of course.

"That'd be nice. Thanks, Josh."

Shit. He made the coffee, asked her a few questions about her life, tried to pay attention to her answers, rather than the envelope, which seemed to pulse as if it had a heartbeat.

"You must want to read that. I'll get going," Sarah said.

"Oh. Yeah. Okay. Um . . ." He never really knew what to say around her. "Thanks, Sarah."

"You're welcome. See you soon."

He went to his office, leaving the letter there on the counter, and forced himself to concentrate on microscopic fibers and electrical impulses. He set the timer so he'd work until five p.m. Only then would he reward himself with the letter. With Lauren's voice, her words, her presence.

When the timer went off, he leaped out of his chair. Tidied up the apartment, walked Pebbles, got himself a glass of wine—pinot grigio, and yes, it was sweet and girly, but he was a novice drinker still.

Then he went into his study, got the box that contained the other letters, and read them in order—the first one telling him her plan and sending him to the grocery store; the second one instructing him to have people over; the anniversary note; the third letter, which led him to Radley and a better wardrobe; and the fourth, which had him attending beginner karate classes.

And finally, his glass of wine half-gone, he rewarded himself with the latest missive.

A minute later, he put it down, oddly . . . irked.

It wasn't as long as the others. It wasn't as sentimental or funny or personal. It was . . . bossy. Brisk, as if she had better things to do.

Hi, hon! Listen. It's time to get rid of the couch and our bed. In other words, places we had sex. ☺ You can't have memorial sex spots forever. "This is where I shagged my dead wife." No, Josh. Besides, every time you look at those, I bet you picture me, sucking on oxygen and being sick. So give the couch to the community center (don't tell them about the sexy times) and donate the bed frame to the Habitat for Humanity store. You may as well donate my clothes while you're at it. Don't be that creepy loser who keeps all his dead wife's stuff, okay?

I have to go for now, but another letter will be coming, I hope.

I love you, Joshua Park.

Lauren

He'd waited a month for this? This was more like a list of chores than a love letter from his dead wife. She may have been sick when she wrote it, of course. Maybe she'd been tired, or even in the hospital. Maybe he was being a petty asshole.

But still. He needed those letters.

He looked at the couch where Pebbles was lying on her back, legs in the air. Got up and went into the unused master bedroom. He had made the bed the way Lauren had liked it, the pillows plumped, two rows of decorative pillows perfectly in place.

If he got rid of the bed, he could sleep in here again, next to her tree. Maybe. He sat down and picked up her pillow, hugged it to his chest and inhaled.

For a second, he couldn't smell her, and panic flashed through his joints. No! He couldn't lose that! He buried his face in deeper, and there it was, her shampoo and moisturizer, the faintest smell of Vicks and perfume. His heart rate slowed, and tears pricked his eyes.

Her smell would fade away. He knew that. And even though he could sniff her soap and shampoo and perfume and Vicks VapoRub, he'd never be able to smell *her* again.

Death was such a selfish bastard.

The dogwood tree was doing well, fertilized by her ashes. Creepy? Today, absolutely. He almost hated the tree right now; the last bits of Lauren, giving life to something other than her.

"You need to get out more," he said to himself.

Pulling his phone out of his pocket, he texted Jen, Sarah, Asmaa and Donna.

I'm cleaning out Lauren's closet this weekend. Whatever you don't want, I'll donate. It's what she asked me to do.

They were all free Saturday afternoon. It would really happen, then.

He opened her closet door and ran his hand over her dresses and sweaters, blouses and skirts. He picked up the sleeve of a sweater she'd particularly liked and sniffed the collar, then the armhole. There it was—the faint smell of her sweat. Of her.

He'd keep something. A pair of her pajamas.

Someday, he imagined, he might remarry and even become a father. What would he say about that rogue woman's garment he had tucked away? *These are the pj's my first wife wore. Sometimes I smell them to try to remember her. I loved her more than I ever loved anyone, including you, punkin. Sorry!*

Maybe these letters were bad for him. Maybe Lauren had been right, that it was maudlin and keeping him stuck.

But being stuck here, in his grief, his solitude . . . this was his world now.

On Saturday, Jen, Sarah and Donna were all in his bedroom, pawing through Lauren's things while Joshua held Octavia. Asmaa had to cancel; her mother needed her for something, but she asked for a blue scarf of Lauren's to remember her by. The previously pristine room now looked garish and crowded. It was *violated*. Every drawer was open, her closet doors splayed, shoes littering the floor as the women did what women do—talked about clothes.

"This dress is so pretty!" Jen said. "Too bad it won't fit me. Sarah, you take it."

Sarah held it up, a gauzy, breezy outfit with flowers embroidered on the hem. "I'd look like a fairy in it."

"Perfect. You could wear it to a wedding or, I don't know, high tea." They giggled. "Oh, this dress! She wore it all the time on the Cape." It was a long, light pink dress, and Jen was right— Lauren had loved its comfort and color. It had tiny roses stitched along the neckline.

"I'd like to keep that," he said, swallowing.

"Of course, hon." Jen looked at him, her mouth wobbling.

"How's your boyfriend?" he asked Donna, desperate to change the subject.

"He's lovely, Josh. You'll have to meet him. Oh, I remember this shirt! I bought this for her when she was interviewing! She looked so grown up!" Donna smiled despite the tears in her eyes. Josh smiled back, or tried to.

"Oh, my God, she kept this! Jen, do you remember?" Sarah exclaimed, holding up a long black lace dress Josh had never seen his wife wear. "Halloween, when you had that party and she fell into the copper tub?"

"Yes! It was hilarious! Mom, we were bobbing for apples, and she was trying to impress that cute guy Darius knew? She just dove in and pinned an apple against the bottom. With her *teeth!*

She came up with it in her mouth, and drenched all the way to her waist, and her makeup was streaming, and her hair was sopping wet, and she looked absolutely terrifying, like some kind of evil Eve. Oh, my God, we laughed so hard!"

Josh didn't want to hear stories of her trying to impress some other guy. Having a good time without him. Interested in a man who wasn't him. He didn't want to remember that had he not been a stuck-up asshole, he might have been at that party, too.

Their memories of her made her feel too . . . alive. He could just about hear her laugh. The familiar pain stabbed his heart, the blade ragged and sharp. "I'm gonna put Octavia down for a nap," he said as the tot conveniently yawned. "I might doze off with her, if that's okay."

"Sure thing," Jen said. "We'll quiet down." She kissed the baby on her head and said, "Uncle Josh will put you down for a nap, baby girl."

"Nigh-night," she said. She was an early talker, though she showed no interest in walking yet. Josh didn't mind. He got to carry her more that way.

Donna kissed the baby, too, then Sarah did the same, and finally Josh was free.

He took the baby into the guest room. "Time for us to sleep, little one," he said, laying her down.

"No seep," she said, rubbing her eyes.

"Uncle Josh will sleep with you."

"Okay." She was such an agreeable baby.

He lay on the bed and tucked her against him. She put her thumb in her mouth and stared up at him, brown eyes solemn, lashes so long and silky.

"Your aunt loved you," he said, tapping her nose with his forefinger.

"Hi," Octavia answered around her thumb. She snuggled against him, and he put his arm around her. She was the first person to be this close to him since the day Lauren died, and she smelled so good—peanut butter and baby shampoo and sweet breath.

"Nigh-night," she said.

"Night-night," he answered.

"Yuvoo."

"Excuse me?" he asked.

"Yuvoo."

"Oh." He swallowed. "I love you, too, Octavia."

Then she closed her eyes, and sucked harder at her thumb, and within seconds, she was asleep. Josh could hear the women in his bedroom, sorting through his wife's things, and he was so relieved not to have done this horrible task alone, so angry that they were laughing, so lonely after that short note from Lauren, so fed up with himself for being a goddamn moody bastard.

But mostly so glad for the warmth of the baby

next to him. A little genetic piece of Lauren lived inside her.

Maybe Jen would give him Octavia. It seemed only fair.

Two hours later, Donna and Jen had left, taking the baby, alas. They'd also taken the majority of Lauren's clothes, scarves, shoes, purses. Some would be donated, some they were keeping.

Sarah was still here. She, too, had a bag and was scrolling through her phone, at home on the couch with Pebbles at her side.

Would she wear those things? Would he have to see her one day in Lauren's sweater, or wearing Lauren's earrings? The very idea made him feel both gutted and a little vicious. She wouldn't look nearly as good. She'd look like the runner-up she was.

Jesus, he was turning mean. Lauren would hate him these days. Good. He hated her for dying.

"How you doing, Josh?" Sarah asked, pushing a strand of long blond hair behind her ear.

"Fine."

"This can't have been easy."

No shit, Sherlock. "It's fine. It's what Lauren wanted."

She kept toying with her hair. "Is that what's in the letter? A list of . . . tasks?"

"I'd rather not talk about it."

"Sorry. Not my business." She forced a smile.

"So. You mentioned you're going furniture shopping?"

"Yeah. Radley should be here in a few minutes. He lives near Jen, and he's picking up their truck."

"Great." She did her signature move of scooping her long hair to one side of her neck.

"Sarah, we get it. You have long blond hair."

"What?"

"You. You're always drawing attention to your hair in case someone missed that it's long and blond. It's annoying."

Her mouth dropped open. "Wow. So sorry to offend you."

"It's just . . . adolescent, okay? You should be more aware."

She gave him a pointed look. "I'm gonna give you a pass because I think you're really sad today, but in my heart, I'm saying fuck off. I miss her, too, you know."

"I know. Best friends from third grade." Sarah had used that as an introduction every goddamn time she'd come to an appointment with them. Her way of saying, *Hi! I'm important!*

"Second grade, actually."

"If you were best friends, why were you always so . . . pissy with her?" he asked. "You think no one noticed? Even at our wedding, you looked like you bit a lemon."

"Josh! I did not! I was happy for her."

"Yeah. And jealous."

"Yes! And jealous! They can exist at the same time, you know."

"It was more than jealousy. You resented her. Long before we got married. You always felt like you came in second, and you blamed her for it. She felt it, you know. You only became a great friend when she was sick. When it was easy because you finally had something on her. Health."

She burst into tears. "Jesus, Josh! That's so unfair."

It was. But he didn't say anything else. Just shrugged, like an asshole.

"How dare you!" she shouted, jumping to her feet. "How fucking dare you, Joshua? I loved her like a sister. I hate to break it to you, but you're not the only one who lost someone. You're not the first, you're not the last, and you're not unique. This poor-widower-who-can-barely-feed-himself act is getting a little tired, don't you think?"

"I think you should leave," he said, looking at the wall over her head.

"Oh, believe me, I'm already leaving. You're welcome for the help, by the way. Asshole."

She breezed past him and Pebbles, who was wagging her tail, hoping for a pet. A second later, the door slammed.

"Good," he said.

But it wasn't. He'd been a dick, and he felt himself flush with guilt and shame.

"Hello, Joshua! Can I come in?" Radley.

Josh went into the living room. "Hey. Yeah, of course."

"Hey, I passed a woman on the stairs. She was angry and crying?"

Shame heated his face. "Yeah. Lauren's friend."

"Uh-oh. Want to talk about it?"

"No. Let's get this couch downstairs, and then the bed, okay?"

"You're the boss."

Josh and Radley removed the cushions and throw pillows from the couch. Lauren had bought them from her beloved Target, and when, god-damnit, when would he stop thinking of her every second of the day?

"Heave ho," Radley said as Pebbles sniffed and wagged and licked Radley's jeans. They wrestled the couch out the door and onto the elevator, came back for the cushions and pillows, went down and loaded everything into the truck, then repeated the process with the bed.

That one was harder, emotionally speaking.

The bed where he'd first made love to Lauren. The bed where they'd spent their first night as husband and wife. The bed where they'd held each other so close the day of her diagnosis. The last place she'd been in this apartment, that night when she woke up, gasping for air.

"You okay?" Radley asked.

"Yes."

The new mattress would be delivered later today, and the movers would take the old one with them.

They drove to ReStore and dropped off the bed, which was made out of burled maple and snatched up immediately by a young couple.

"Should I tell them it's cursed?" Josh asked.

"Probably not," Radley said. "This place is great. I should totally shop here."

"What's your place like?" Josh asked. It occurred to him that he should have asked by now.

"Unremarkable. I share an apartment in a two-family house," he said. "Nice street. Want to come over some night for dinner?"

No. I never want to go anywhere. "Sure," he said.

"Okay, pal, let's go see what you like at West Elm, shall we?"

It didn't take long. He didn't really care what his couch or bed looked like. He looked for all of three minutes, chose a couch, a floor model that they could take. Then he picked out a bed that, for a chunky fee, would be delivered today. He agreed.

"How about some throw pillows? These ones that look like llama fur?" He looked at the tag. "Oh, my God, I'm half-right. They're Mongolian lamb's wool!"

"Sure," Josh said. "Uh . . . you pick out the colors."

"I think it's important that you pick out the colors, Josh. This is a big step."

He sighed. "Yellow?"

"Yellow is good." Radley smiled. "How about a few other things, too? Something cheery, maybe? These vases are very cute. Oh! And these lacquer trays will make it so you look classy when you eat in front of the TV."

Suddenly, Josh *did* want all new things. He wanted his place to look less like the place Lauren didn't live anymore. "Yeah. Sure. The vases and trays. And . . . uh, how about these book-ends?"

"No need to ask me. I'm just here to nod wisely at the right intervals. As one does when one is a therapist."

Josh picked up a small lamp. A few shelves that seemed ugly but might be cool. A small sculpture that looked like a strand of DNA. A cluster of mirrors. As he staggered to the checkout, grabbing a basket (Lauren had loved baskets), it dawned on him that Radley might need something, too.

"Can I buy you something?" he asked, clutching an armful of boxes and items. "You've been great."

"Oh, no, that's nice of you, but unnecessary."

"Please? As thanks?"

"Uh, sure. Here. This candle." Radley grabbed a candle and sniffed it. "Lemon. Nice."

"How about a chair? You've . . . you've helped me a lot and I feel guilty."

"You do have resting guilt face." He fondled a dark blue chair. "Is this *velvet?*"

"Take it."

"We'll have to ship it to you," the clerk said.

"That'd be great," Josh told her.

"Well, thank you, Joshua!" Radley said. "You're so generous."

Josh looked at his watch, as the day had been endless. Almost six. "I can buy you dinner, too."

When they got home, the furniture guys were already there with the bed, and the mattress was waiting in the lobby. They carried up the boxes and mattress, then helped Radley and Josh with the couch. He tipped each guy a twenty, turning down their offer to assemble the bed. If there was one thing Josh was good at, it was putting pieces together, being an engineer and all. The mattress slid on top, a mattress Lauren had never slept on.

Josh opened the packet of new sheets he'd bought and remade the bed, not caring if he should wash them first. They were blue. His and Lauren's sheets had been white. He opted not to replace the bed's throw pillows. What was the point of useless pillows you just put on the bed, then took off the bed? It looked more . . .

masculine this way. And since he had no woman in his life, masculine it was.

"Sorry," he said to the dogwood tree/Lauren's ashes. "This is what you get for dying."

Radley was doing something he called *zhoozhing* in the living room. Josh wandered in, and the room looked different. Pebbles had already made herself at home on the couch, which was the color of sand, not red, like their old one. He felt a momentary stab of panic. What had he done? Lauren had loved that couch! He hated change! Then Pebbles wagged, her head resting on a fuzzy throw pillow, which would absorb her drool nicely. Radley had moved a chair, repositioned the coffee table and added the little touches. The new floor lamp looked cool. The ugly-ish shelf had gone up with the DNA thingy on it.

"Are you going to cry?" Radley asked.

"I don't think so," he said. He wasn't sure.

"Let's watch something violent and uplifting," Radley said. "*Mad Max: Fury Road*? What food goes with that?"

"Everything," Josh said. "Should I get some beer?"

"That sounds great."

"I appreciate you being nice to me."

Radley tilted his head. "Josh, you're easy to like. We're friends, buddy."

"Good. Good. I thought I was sort of like a test client for you."

"There is that. But no! I mean, I *like* you. You're decent. You have no agenda. You seem to like me."

"I do. And that's . . . that's enough? To be friends?"

"It is for me." He raised his eyebrows.

"Okay. It is for me, too. I just don't want you to be here because you . . . pity me."

Radley rolled his eyes. "Kid, we all have shit that rains down on us at different times. Your time is now. My time was getting beaten up in high school and having my parents tell me I was going to hell. Should we get Chinese? Korean? Thai? Italian?"

They ordered Thai food. Josh walked the two blocks to the nearest packie to pick up beer while Radley sat in a lounge chair in the rooftop garden and pretended to be Leonardo DiCaprio (in his own words).

When he came back, it was a little bit of a shock, seeing the not-Lauren things in the living room. His heart hurt.

But she would like Radley. Would have liked. She'd be glad he had a friend. That he was (oh, detested phrase) moving on.

Tomorrow, he would apologize to Sarah. For now, he tucked the six-pack under his arm and went up on the roof to join his buddy. Like a normal person, no matter how empty his soul felt.

18

Lauren

Twenty-one months left
May 19

Dear Dad,
I think this diagnosis is kind of wrong. I mean, I believe the doctors, but I doubt very much I'm like the other patients. I'm not even thirty, for God's sake. I'm about to turn twenty-seven. They keep saying they don't know how this will play out.

It's really not that bad, to be honest. I'm fine. I'm really fine.

Just wanted you to know.

Love,
Lauren

She *was* fine. Until she wasn't.

In June, six months after the diagnosis, she was doing great. IPF and its grim facts lurked in her closet like a childhood monster, amorphous and dark, waiting. But that monster had never eaten her, had it? So then. Everything made sense.

Because it didn't seem *possible* that she had

something incurable. She'd never even heard of idiopathic pulmonary fibrosis. Some days, she felt perfectly normal. Better than normal, even. So how could her lungs be changing, huh? Hm? Hadn't she given Sebastian a piggyback ride? Hadn't she and Josh had marathon sex the other day?

She was slaying at work, proving herself again and again. How could she be *dying* if she was the company's best exterior space designer? Bruce had just assigned her to a big job for a new T stop in Boston, and she'd spent the day in Beantown, all alone, watching people come and go, reading the pedestrian traffic flow report and staring at the ugly entrance. She was fine. Fine, damn it.

There had to be a mistake. She was just waiting for Dr. Bennett to figure it out.

Of course, there were days when she had to drink two cappuccinos to make it through the workday (but everyone had those days). Days when the thought of taking two flights of stairs to their apartment felt Sisyphean, and her legs felt like lead, and she felt dizzy and weak. But, hello! Hadn't she also made it through a power yoga class? So what if she was short of breath sometimes? She could deal with it. She *was* dealing with it. She was on medication and had an inhaler. Not a big deal. So many people were in the same shoes.

No matter what she Googled, she could not find

a case of IPF where the person had been cured. Not one.

That was *fine*. She would adapt to having a low blood oxygen level. No one could tell her she wasn't going to live a long life. No one. She was freakishly young to have this disease . . . not the only one, but one of the very few. She joined an online forum and talked with other young people with IPF. They agreed; no one was planning any funerals, no sir.

Except all of them used oxygen. All of them had been hospitalized and intubated multiple times.

See? She must not have IPF. She'd never been intubated. Never spent a single night in the hospital.

Until she did.

Lauren had been having a completely normal day at work when she felt something . . . shift in her chest. Something weird, something she'd never felt before. A heaviness. A difference.

She pulled in a breath, but it was off. It was . . . wrong. Her chest jerked, and then fire flashed through it. Suddenly her back twisted in agony—was it a heart attack, did someone just wallop her with a two-by-four?

She sucked in air, but it wasn't enough. Panic slapped her hard, and she tried again, but no, nothing. Was this a nightmare? *Wake up! Wake up!* Her chest was working, up and down, up and down, almost like she was choking on something, but deeper down. Oh, God, she was going to die.

She pushed back her chair and said, "Call . . . 911 . . ." and slid to the floor, buzzing with adrenaline, but utterly weak. Her hands flailed near her throat, pulling at her collar, and God, the pain! Her chest hurt like nothing she'd ever felt before, like someone had rammed an arrow clear through her. Her back was spasming in torment, and she couldn't breathe, couldn't *breathe.*

She fought. She fought like a wild animal in a trap, gasping in horrible wrenching sounds, her legs flailing, foot connecting with Santino as he tried to help her sit up. Her coworkers gathered round, saying things, putting their hands on her, but she couldn't hear them, she was heaving and the sounds that were coming out of her—animal sounds, desperate and feral—drowned out everything.

Louise was on the phone, yelling. "My coworker can't breathe! She has a lung problem and she can't breathe! She's *dying!* Hurry up, hurry up!"

"Somebody do something!" Bruce yelled. "Where the fuck is the ambulance? Somebody, help her! Jesus Christ!"

Josh. She was going to die without Josh. She fought harder, kicking, gasping.

Then Sarah was there; yes, yes, they were going to meet for lunch, but there was not enough air, damn it, she didn't want to die. Sarah knelt beside her and held her hands, which were clawing at her throat. Bruce was sobbing and Louise was chanting, "Fuck fuck fuck fuck," and all that seemed to be far away, because she was losing consciousness, oh, God. If she did that, would she die?

"Slow and easy, slow and easy," Sarah said, her voice stern and calm. "Help is on the way. You're going to be okay. Slow down, try to relax. Got an inhaler handy? Someone get her purse."

Lauren locked eyes with Sarah, gasping like a fish out of water. Sarah was here. Sarah of the great sleepovers, Sarah who could do such good French braids, Sarah who cried so hard when Lauren's dad died. She wanted to thank her, but all that came out was a high-pitched squeak.

"Back off," Sarah snarled at the coworkers. Then the inhaler was in her hand, and she gave Lauren a hit, but it was hard to get the medicine into her lungs. Sarah repeated the action, then again. A little better breathing, but the chest pain . . .

"Josh," she croaked.

Sarah pulled out her phone. "I've got this. You just breathe, easy and slow, easy and slow." Her voice was calm and firm, and Lauren forced her brain to repeat *easy and slow, easy and slow.* "Josh, it's Sarah. Meet us at the hospital. Lauren's having trouble breathing. The ambulance is already here."

Then the paramedics were in her view, and someone put a mask over her face, and there was medical talk, but everything was going gray. Sarah gripped her hand. "I'm right here. You're gonna be fine. Stay awake, okay?"

Lauren fought against unconsciousness. It felt like a truck was parked on her chest. The mask was helping and smelled funny, but her chest, her chest. *Your lung collapsed,* said a part of her brain, but all she could think about was *breathe, breathe, get the air in there, breathe, breathe, breathe.* Then she was in the back of the ambulance, and they were moving. The paramedic talked to her, but she couldn't hear, or wasn't listening.

She forced her eyes as wide as possible, then felt the slip of her eyeballs as unconsciousness gained a step. *No. Bite me.* This was no gentle faint, no coughing fit, this was a battle, and she would fight it viciously, fight the suffocation, fight the grayness. *No. No. I am* not *dying.*

At the ER, doctors and nurses swarmed her. *Patient collapsed at work, given three hits of albuterol, friend says a history of IPF, limited breath sounds both sides. Pneumothorax. Intubate.* Then Lauren was floating, and a doctor was hunched over her face, opening her mouth.

Unconsciousness won, but it was okay, she was being helped, and then she was just . . . blank.

There were dreams, strange dreams and sounds

of hissing and squeaking. She dreamed she could fly. She dreamed that she was lost and couldn't find Sarah's house, so she took an elevator down to a train but remembered that she was married and had to go home to Josh. She thought she was in Hawaii in their beautiful sunset house, but Hawaii smelled like flowers, and it smelled sharp and bitter here. She dreamed that she was in a tree house, but everyone had forgotten about her, and the ladder was gone, so she would have to live there, and there was no bathroom.

She dreamed her father was here, and she wanted to get on a train with him to go to New York City, but he said no.

She woke up, throat aching. She gagged. Josh and Jen were there, telling her it was okay, she was safe, she was getting better. Lauren tried to smile, but fell back asleep.

The next time she woke up, Josh was there, and her mother, looking like hell.

"Hi, honey," Josh said, leaning forward. "You're intubated, so don't try to talk. You have pneumonia, and your lungs collapsed. But you're better now. Just take it easy."

"You almost died," her mother wept. "Oh, honey, you almost died. I couldn't *live* if you died! Don't you know I already lost your father? Please don't die!"

Josh didn't take his eyes off her, but his perfect lips twitched, and she knew what he was thinking . . . *Shut up, Donna.* Or maybe he did actually say it.

She squeezed his hand. "It's been four days," he said, and oh, she loved his voice. "They kept you sedated so you could breathe better. But you're okay." He kissed her hand. "I love you."

She fell back asleep.

They extubated that day or the next . . . time was slippery in the hospital. She was exhausted in a way she'd never felt before. Even moving her eyes or smiling took effort.

She had almost died. There was no avoiding that fact. It slept with her there in the hospital, amorphous no longer, but a sharp steel blade. It was real now. She woke up thinking about it, and she took it with her to sleep, and it was there in the foggy places in between.

Josh was always by her side. Always. Jen and Sarah were there often, and her mom, who cried a lot. When she was a little more alert, Darius brought Sebastian in, who was fascinated that her bed could go up and down with the push of a button.

Her voice was raspy, and she was given milkshakes that tasted grainy, nothing nearly as good as an Awful Awful from Newport Creamery, she said, so Josh went out and got her one. She'd lost weight, apparently. She'd always been curvy with a little tummy Josh said was the sexiest thing on earth . . . that tummy was flat now. Weird.

She'd had pneumonia, the resident told her. Nonobstructive atelectasis, bilateral . . . in other words, two collapsed lungs thanks to pneumonia combined with IPF. Her O2 sat was so low they intubated her and fought the pneumonia with IV antibiotics.

Dr. Bennett came. She'd been in daily, apparently, but Lauren didn't remember. Her presence was reassuring; she projected an air of calm, like . . . like Florence Nightingale, or a homesteading wife from long ago who'd put a poultice on Lauren's chest and a cool cloth on her head.

"I'm so glad you're better, Lauren," she said, pulling up a chair next to Josh. He needed a haircut and a shave, but damn, he was so handsome. Lauren smiled at him, reassured when he smiled back. "We almost lost you," Dr. Bennett said.

"Yeah," said Lauren, her smile dropping. "It felt that way."

Josh gave her a sharp look.

"This kind of episode is going to happen from time to time," the doctor continued. "The absolute best thing to do is get in to see me the second you feel *any* additional difficulty breathing. Even if you're imagining it, or it's caused by a weather change, I want to see you. No toughing it out, because every time you get sick, you lose a little lung capacity, and it's gone forever."

"Gotcha," Lauren said.

"And, Josh, you have a background in medicine to some degree, right?"

"Sort of." His voice was flat.

"I'd like to teach you to listen for changes in her breath sounds with a stethoscope."

"Yep. Fine."

"We can play doctor," Lauren said to him.

He didn't smile back. Not even a flicker.

"I'll be in tomorrow," Dr. Bennett said. "Keep up the good work, and I'll see if I can discharge you."

"Thank you," Lauren said. Then she fell asleep.

She sent Josh home later that evening so he could shower, take a walk with Ben Kim (Yoda to his Luke Skywalker, Lauren always said), see his mom and bring Lauren the dinner Mrs. Kim had made for them.

She also needed some time alone. Once the sweet nurse left after taking her vitals, Lauren closed the door, got back in bed, and took a few slow breaths.

She didn't have asthma. She wasn't someone who coughed a little more than usual. Her lungs were not going to get better. She would die from this disease. She didn't know when, but she did know how.

She was terminal. It wasn't *if* . . . it was *when*. It was coming. A decade, or a half, or a year or a month, but last week, she and Death had wrestled, and this time—*this* time—Lauren had won.

Barely.

Her lips trembled. She swallowed and considered the facts.

Her life would be short.

For a few minutes, that was all there was. She would die young. She would not grow old. This kind of feral fighting to breathe, these hospitalizations would happen again and again until she lost. Until she died.

Her eyes filled with tears.

At the sound of footsteps in the hallway, she looked up, expecting Josh.

It wasn't Josh. It was a father, carrying a small, heartbreakingly thin child with no hair, no eyebrows and a cannula in her nose. Lauren knew it was a girl because she had on a flowery hairband. The little girl didn't lift her head from her father's shoulder, but she saw Lauren and smiled. Instinctively, Lauren waved.

Then they were past her doorway.

As quickly as she could, Lauren got up and went to the door, dragging her IV pole with her. She looked down the hall, but the little girl and her father were gone.

"You okay, Mrs. Park?" the nurse asked.

"Um . . . a little girl and her dad just went past?"

The nurse nodded. Her eyes filled with tears.

"She didn't look so good," Lauren said, her own tears falling.

"I can't discuss another patient," the nurse said, but her mouth wobbled, and Lauren knew.

The little girl was terminal, too.

Lauren stood there, leaning against the door-frame on her weak and shaking legs, for as long as she could.

When Josh came back, shaved, adorable, smelling delicious and holding food, they ate, him sitting on the foot of her bed. Sumi had made that fabulous sticky chicken with sesame seeds, and Steph had contributed grilled brussels sprouts and mashed potatoes with sour cream to put some meat on her bones, Josh reported.

When they were done and Josh had cleared the plates, Lauren patted the bed again. Josh sat down, kissed her hand and then looked at her. His expression grew somber.

"So, honey," she began, holding his hand tight in hers. "I think we need to talk."

"Okay," he said.

"I'm going to die from this," she said, her voice shaking. "Not today. But I . . . yeah." It was the first time she'd said it aloud. "I'll die from this."

"No. No, you're not. We have to stay positive."

"Well, I've been—"

In a rare move, he interrupted her. "I've already talked to someone at Johns Hopkins. They have something really promising in development. You're on the list when human trials—"

"Josh, please. We have to be realistic."

"—start, and so far, the results are fantastic."

"In mice," she said. He wasn't the only one researching IPF.

"Yes. In mice." His jaw tightened.

"I need to talk about the future."

"And you will be fine in the future," he said.

"Joshua!" she said, then coughed. "Please listen."

"No!" he barked, then lowered his voice. "No, Lauren. You're not going to die. I won't let you."

"Okay, God." She forced a smile. "Good to be married to the Almighty. If you were a mere mortal, this might be a disaster, but lucky for me, you won't let me die."

"Don't," he bit off, staring at the wall. "The cure is right on the horizon."

"For *mice*." Most of these promising mouse cures didn't make it to human trials. And even if they did, most of the patients with IPF wouldn't be alive when that day came.

"There's a trial coming in about a year that has—"

"Are you going to sit there and ignore what I have to say, or are you going to be my husband?"

His face cracked a little. "The trial . . . it looks good," he said, but a few tears slid out of his eyes.

"I'm glad," she whispered. "I hope it works."

They sat in silence for a few minutes, the shadows lengthening as night crept toward them.

"I saw a little kid today," she said, looking at the doorway. "Maybe five years old. She's not gonna make it. She was so thin, and her skin was yellow. But she *smiled* at me."

He bowed his head.

So he knew, too. That her life would be short.

"Honey," she whispered, "aside from a miracle cure, I'm going to die from this. And I need to wrap my head around the idea, because I've been pretending it's not true." She paused, took a slow, careful breath. "It is true. It's something we need to accept."

"I will *never* accept this." His voice was low and fierce.

Her eyes filled. "I need you to. So we can have more in our lives than me being sick."

"No. I won't accept it." But he bent over so his head was resting on her lap, and she felt his shoulders jerk. She stroked his shiny, shiny black hair, smoothing in her teardrops as they fell.

"Josh," she said as gently as she could, "if you're sad for the rest of my however-long life, I won't be able to stand it. I'll die of a broken heart before I die from this stupid lung thing. I need you to be with me, not trying to cure me." She started crying in earnest now and had to cough. "I'm scared, and I don't want to be, and I can't be brave without you. I want to be like that little girl. I want to smile on my last days. I want to love the rest of my life, and I can't, Josh, I can't if you're not right here with me."

"Oh, honey, I am. I'm here." He got into bed with her and held her tight, her tears soaking into his shirt as she cried.

She didn't want him desperate and working to find a cure, the days sliding past as he Googled and researched and called people at Stanford and tried to invent something that would Roto-Rooter her lungs. Because in the end, she would still die. She knew that now. And if she only had a little while left, be it months or years or even a miraculous decade, she needed him to be here. Present. Happy to be married to her.

"I understand," he said, his voice rough. "I'll do whatever you want. Be however you want."

"I only want you."

He raised his head, and his eyes were so sad. "I only want you, too," he whispered.

"I know," she whispered. "I know, honey." The sadness, the grief, the fear were suddenly crushing. He gathered her in his arms and held her so close.

That little girl would never have this.

Lauren was the lucky one.

"Think of what a hot widower you'll make," she whispered.

And, because he was the best husband ever,

because he could read her so completely, he said, "I think I might have a chance at Beyoncé."

The hospitalization changed her. Being able to admit that her life could end at any minute, having been that close to death, and having Josh understand where she was—it triggered something unexpectedly joyful. She beamed at her mother when Donna came to visit, let her nephew push the buttons to raise and lower her bed, looked at Sarah's matches on OkCupid and offered advice, sent Darius to get her and Jen a double order of cheeseburger sliders from Harry's. "I'm also eating for two, in solidarity," Lauren told him. And later, when Josh was lying next to her in her hospital bed, she let her hands wander.

Life was good. Life was here, and she was in it. She was with the living, and she was damn lucky.

She didn't see the little girl again. Didn't know her name to ask after her.

When she was finally discharged, two days after Dr. Bennett promised, the ride home seemed so full of color and beauty, she felt new, her nose practically pressed against the window. It was summer! It was so green! The sky was unbelievably blue, and it seemed like every business and residence was in a competition for most beautiful window box. You could almost forget what season it was when you were hospitalized.

Sarah had been at the apartment, Josh told her, and when they went in, Lauren practically cried at the welcome sight of the place. It felt like she'd been gone for years, not ten days. Someone—Steph, no doubt—had baked a coffee cake, which was still warm and made the whole apartment smell like cinnamon. On the kitchen table, there was a vase full of yellow roses and a note that read, *Welcome home, you two!* in her mother-in-law's blocky printing.

"Wow," Lauren said. "I'm so happy."

"Are you crying?" Josh asked. "Such a sap."

"I am. And I'm stanky. Those CNAs did their best, but I do *not* smell good. See you soon, pretty boy."

Oh, the shower, that beautiful shower. Lauren spent forty-five minutes shampooing, shaving her ridiculously furry legs and scrubbing her skin with the almond-lemony shower gel she loved. When she was finished, she was a little tired, but it was worth it. Thunder rumbled in the distance, and Lauren looked out the window, the view so familiar and beloved. The formerly clear skies were clouding over, since New England could never make up her mind about weather.

Home. She'd never take it for granted again.

"Hello, big boy," she said, walking into the kitchen in her silky pink robe, naked underneath. She wrapped her arms around Josh's waist and pressed her face against his shoulder.

"Nope. First I feed you, then I shag you."

"I accept." She sat down to grilled salmon over an arugula salad, vegetable fried rice. It smelled like heaven—ginger and garlic—and suddenly she was ravenous.

"Who brought this?"

"I made it, thank you very much. I'm upping my cooking game."

"Huh. Being hospitalized has its upsides."

"Glad you think so." He smiled. They were both so giddy that she was home that even a mention of her illness couldn't put a damper on their moods. They ate—and ate—then had fat slices of coffee cake.

God, it was good. Josh cleared the dishes, then led her to the couch and pulled her back against his chest, his arms around her.

"Don't I smell nice?" she asked. "Better than the hospital?"

"You do. Fish and flowers. My favorite combination."

For a while, they just sat and looked out the big windows at the lights of the city, smeared by a thunderstorm. The distant rumble and pattering rain sounded so pretty and gentle.

"Listen," Lauren said eventually. "That whole lung collapse and intubation . . . I'm sorry you had to go through that. It must have been terrifying."

"Yes, it *was* all about me, now that you mention it."

She laughed and snuggled closer. "I know IPF is part of my life, but I still want to love it. My life, that is. Every day. Every hour. I want to have fun and do things and go places and be irresponsible and eat bad food—just once in a while, don't panic—and . . . and all that stuff. I don't want to be constantly checking myself to see if I'm okay."

" 'Get busy living, or get busy dying,' " Josh intoned in his best impression of Morgan Freeman.

"Don't you Shawshank me. But yes."

He turned her to face him, and his eyes were shiny. "You're the best thing that ever happened to me, Lauren. That hasn't changed. That will never change." His voice grew hoarse. "And, yes, I'm terrified of losing you."

"I'm so sorry, honey." Hot tears slipped out of her eyes. "I don't want to die. I don't want to be sick. I don't want to leave you, but I'm here now, and that . . . that has to be enough."

He looked at her for the longest time. A tear escaped, and she wiped it away. His eyes were so kind and gentle. That flame was still there, lighting up her heart. "Okay," he finally whispered. "It will be enough. I'm still gonna keep trying to find a cure, though. Obviously."

"Just not twenty hours a day, because I need you. Right here. With me, not attached to the computer."

"I get it. Yes, ma'am."

She kissed him, his lips so soft and wonderful. "I love you with all my heart."

"I love you with all my liver." He grinned, and she was abruptly laughing and crying. He knew. He understood. He always did.

"Okay." She wiped her eyes. "So am I gonna get laid, or what?"

The answer was yes. He was gentle and slow and maybe a little too careful, but they were together, where they belonged.

And it was more than enough.

19

Joshua

Month six
August

Josh had intended to make things right with Sarah, but she'd taken a vacation just after his outburst. If she got his text, then email, she hadn't answered.

He was tired of himself as he was. He hated the word *widower,* hated the oppressing sense of fatigue that started every day. The other day, his friend Keung in London had emailed him. Said he was thinking of Josh because—wait for it—his grandmother had died, and he was really grieving, man, it was so hard, such an empty space in his life, he wanted to reach out to Josh, who'd understand.

Josh looked up her obituary. Old Gran-Gran had been ninety-seven. No. He did not understand. He wrote a furious response, sent it and then blocked Keung's number and email address. It wasn't like they'd been close anyway. Who needed a friend like that?

He unblocked Keung the next day and apologized for being an asshole (even if Keung should've been a teeny bit more sensitive).

Josh wanted to make his wife proud. He wanted her approval. After the unpleasantness with Sarah, and the resentment when she, Donna and Jen had gone through her things, the angry email to Keung, he needed to do something to show he wasn't that guy . . . to her, and to himself.

He wanted to do something good. Something Lauren-ish. Something that required him not to simply throw money at a cause—last month, he'd donated a chunk of money to the Hope Center's latest project, which was turning a parking lot for a former podiatry office into a children-run community garden. Asmaa had gotten a grant to buy it, but she asked him if he'd like to donate to get the tarmac ripped up, buy supplies and plants, etc. "We'll call it the Lauren Carlisle Park Children's Community Garden," she said. "Even if you don't donate a dime, we're naming it after her."

"I'll donate more than a dime," he said. "But let's just call it Lauren's Garden." He told Jen and Darius about it, too, and Donna, and his own mom, and they all donated, too, as he knew they'd want to.

But he wanted to do more than just write a check, so he met Asmaa at the garden site. They were struggling to design an irrigation system, he offered a solution, and just like that, he became a volunteer. A couple of times a week, he showed up to shovel dirt, help the younger kids make trellises for peas and beans for next spring. He helped them figure out where to put the paths and where to put the beds. His mom, who was quite the gardener, brought in plants that would grow again next year, and showed the kids how to deadhead the flowers.

It was exactly what Lauren would have done. The Hope Center was where they remet that perfect night when he saw her and *knew,* without a shadow of a doubt, that he had been really, *really* wrong about Lauren Rose Carlisle.

He was functioning. He'd started cooking and eating better. He took better care of Pebbles because the dog deserved it, and looking into her eyes gave him some sense of connection. She had lost Lauren, too, so he tried. Brushed her and threw the Frisbee to her in the dog park, rubbed her belly and told her she was a pretty girl. He was tidying up the apartment more regularly. He let his mom cook him dinner a couple of times, understanding she needed to be needed, and that, like him, she was better with actions than words. He texted or called Donna every third day. He started babysitting for Jen and Darius, the way he and Lauren had.

But God, he still felt so empty. He wasn't in constant agony anymore—it had been almost six months—but he wasn't better, either. He went to karate and managed to smile and even laugh there; hard not to with all those little warriors. Same at the Hope Center, and when he got to see Sebastian and Octavia. He and Radley did something once in a while, too—drinks or food or a movie at Josh's.

But those were a few hours. Three or five hours in a week that lasted one hundred and sixty-eight.

He adjusted the calendar on his computer so it only showed two days at a time, because looking at the days and weeks and months and years ahead of him . . . it was just too hard. All that time would come and go, and still Lauren would not be back. Ever.

Darius called him one muggy Saturday morning. "Dude, there's a marathon today. It raises money for rare disease treatment and research. Jen and I are running with the kids. Sarah, too. You want in? It's a 5K. You can handle it, right? Sorry I just told you about it. Jen is giving me a dirty look right now, because I was supposed to call you last week."

Josh wasn't used to this kind of rushed decision, to spontaneity. It made him nervous. "You want me to sponsor you?"

"No, brother. Just run with us."

"Oh." He winced, then silently chastised himself. "Yeah, okay." Why not? He liked running, more or less, and had nothing else going on this weekend. Radley was in Chicago, doing the residency part of his low-residency program.

Besides, Radley had gone above and beyond already, and Josh didn't want to give him friend fatigue (another term he'd learned on the forum). "Sure. I'm in."

"Excellent! Meet us in an hour. Texting you the info now. See you there, buddy."

The race started at Providence College, the beautiful Catholic school on the other side of the city from Brown and RISD. Josh brought Pebbles; Sebastian and Octavia loved the dog. He paid the entry fee, filled out a form holding the organizers free from liability should he drop dead at some point—it *was* pretty hot—and got a chip for his shoelace.

"Are you running in honor of someone?" the lady at the table asked.

"Um . . . yes. My wife."

"What's her disease?"

Such a weird question. "Idiopathic pulmonary fibrosis."

The woman knew enough to flinch. "I'm so sorry. If you want to write her name on your number, go right ahead."

"No, thank you." The last thing he wanted was for people to know he was a widower, which would compel him to talk about his beautiful wife with strangers who would say stupid things like *she's at peace now* and *heaven has another angel.*

He found Lauren's family at their meeting spot and exchanged the usual awkward, sad hugs. He gave Jen a kiss on the forehead, and managed not to pull away from Donna. Sebastian declined to hug him; he hadn't been the same around Josh since Lauren died. Poor little guy was only four.

"High five?" Josh suggested. Sebastian shook his head, and Josh wanted to cry. Once, the kid had run into his arms. Now, he knew Josh was broken somehow. Luckily, Pebbles came to the rescue and began licking Sebastian's face, getting the kid to giggle and wriggle. That dog was worth her weight in gold.

"Unca Josh!" Octavia announced.

"Hi, peanut," he said, his voice husky.

He remembered to ask Darius about work and ask Donna about Bill. People kept coming by to say hello, which Josh hated. Too reminiscent of Lauren's funeral.

And there was Sarah. She looked at him, then looked away, her face tight. Super. He needed to apologize, but he sensed she wouldn't make it easy.

"Hey. Got a second?" he asked.

"Sure!" she said, fake smiling.

They walked a few yards away from everyone else, to the shade of a tree. It was a brutally hot day, already ninety, and muggy. The shade felt nominally better. Sarah's smile dropped.

She looked tanned; he forgot where she'd gone,

but it didn't matter. Her blond hair was lighter than normal, pulled back in those complicated braids. She wore blue running shorts and a matching tank top. She was very fit, he noticed. Athletic, even. Was that new, or had she always been?

"What's up?" she asked.

"How was your vacation?"

"Great." She raised an eyebrow.

"Where did you go?"

"The Outer Banks." She stared, waiting. Expectant and righteous. Which, he supposed, she'd earned. He should do something with his hands, which seemed to hang awkwardly, so he tried to put them in his pockets before remembering that he had no pockets. He put his hands on his hips, then let them fall again.

Peopling was hard.

"Well?" Sarah asked.

"Right. Listen . . . I said some stupid things. Unkind things. About you."

"Yes. You did."

"Yeah." His shoulders relaxed a fraction. "So we're good, then?"

She twitched. "Excuse me?"

"Um . . . are we okay?"

"No, Joshua. You haven't apologized."

He blinked. "I just did."

"No, you just acknowledged your assholery. You haven't apologized at all."

"Oh." He wished he had Pebbles, but she was

with Darius and Sebastian. "Well, I'm sorry."

"Shitty job, Josh. Try again." Her face was hard, mouth tight. She looked like she might spit acid at him in another minute.

He blew out a breath, trying to give her what she wanted. "I'm *very* sorry?" She shook her head. "Sarah, I'm sorry for what I said." He paused. "You were a good friend to Lauren. She appreciated you."

Sarah had her hands on her hips. "Still not feeling it."

"I'm *deeply* sorry."

"Do you even have normal human emotions, Josh? Because what you said cut me to my heart, okay? There was *nothing* you could've said that would've hurt more. So a few crappy sentences aren't going to cut it."

"No," he said.

"What?"

"No, I'm not sure I have normal human emotions. I did with Lauren. But . . . not so much anymore."

Sarah's face softened, becoming quite pretty and not like she was going to spit acid anymore. She opened her arms, so he had to hug her, which he did, but not too hard and not too long.

"I'm forgiving you for her sake. Let's have dinner sometime, though, and really talk."

More talking? Shit. "That'd be great. Thank you."

"The race is starting. Let's go."

Thank God. He joined Lauren's family. Sebastian and Octavia were gleeful at being pushed in running strollers decorated with blue and green streamers. Darius, the former football player, was in admirable shape, and Jen was, too—they both did that kind of exercise where they threw truck tires and did one-handed push-ups till they vomited. Sarah had run cross-country in college, if he remembered correctly. And he ran, too, so it wasn't like he was a slacker.

Except, apparently, he was. Within a quarter of a mile, he was working hard to keep up. Sarah's legs were inches longer than his, and Darius and Jen had a game going on where each kid got to be in the lead for a few strides before the other overtook them. Josh, on the other hand, was hurting. Leg cramps. Side pain.

At the one-mile marker, his face felt tight and fiery. Why was this so hard? He should be able to do three miles in his sleep. He ran five almost every day.

Ah. He hadn't eaten today. Or last night, now that he thought of it. Had he had anything to drink other than coffee this morning?

No. "You guys go ahead," he called. "I'll catch up."

Sarah didn't pause, her braids swinging as she continued.

"You okay?" Jen asked over her shoulder.

"I didn't drink enough this morning. See you at the finish line."

"I'll slow down for you, Josh," Darius said.

"No, Daddy! Run faster!" Sebastian demanded.

"It's okay," Josh said. "You go ahead. Pebbles needs a drink, too." Yes. Blame the dog.

He swerved to a water station, accepted a water bottle and drank it, watching them get farther and farther ahead. That was fine. He'd never mastered talking and running at the same time anyway.

He gave Pebbles the rest of the water, then continued running. The heat, the thickness of the air . . . ugh. He hadn't thought to put on sunscreen, either. No baseball cap to cut the ruthless glare of the sun.

A woman was running at about the same pace. She was pushing a tiny stroller that could only fit a newborn. Should she be out so soon after giving birth? Josh wondered. Scientific curiosity got the best of him, and he angled over to look at her child, peered in, then flinched.

Not a baby. A very ugly dog with a bald, fat stomach and scraggly, grayish-white fur.

"Hi!" said the owner.

"I thought your dog was a baby."

"Oh, he is. My fur baby! Hey! I know you! Don't I? Have we met?"

It was the woman from the vet's. Rather a shock that her dog was still alive.

"We both use Dr. Kumar."

"Right!"

Also, he'd seen her spill a tray of drinks on someone. The night he'd met Radley, and punched the rude man.

"So this is . . . ?"

"Duffy, remember? Duffy, say hi!" Duffy didn't move, lying on his side, his tongue hanging out. Josh was tempted to ask if he might have died, but then again, the poor woman would find out soon enough. "What's your dog's name again?" she asked.

"Pebbles."

"Oh, right. Like Pebbles and Bamm-Bamm?"

Josh had no idea. "Yeah."

"This is a great cause, isn't it?"

"Sure." Again, the running-and-talking thing . . . difficult.

"My brother has Ehlers-Danlos syndrome. You know . . . the one where your joints are loose and they dislocate all the time?"

"Uh-huh." The rhythm of his feet on the pavement was hypnotic, echoing a little, almost soothing.

"So he's doing okay, but there's no cure. Yet. He needs pain relief, mostly. He doesn't seem to have the vascular part. Thank God."

"That's good." Was it because Josh was running that he couldn't quite see the people lining the streets? Or was he—

"He's only twenty-two, poor kid. And you

288

know what? People think he's an addict, because he's really thin. The pharmacists won't fill his pain meds because they think he's a junkie, and even though his doctor called—" She glanced at him. "Are you okay?"

Nope. No, he wasn't. "I . . . uh . . . I think I need a breather."

And then his knees buckled, and the pavement was gritty against his cheek. Pebbles licked his ear with great vigor.

The woman's face appeared suddenly, her dark ponytail touching the ground. "Yikes," she said. "Should I call 911?"

"I think . . . I fainted."

A medic on a bicycle was there almost instantly. "Stay where you are, sir," he ordered, kneeling next to him and taking his pulse. "Another one down," he said into the radio on his collar. "Told you we'd have at least a dozen." He looked down at Josh. "Sir? What day is it?"

"Saturday. I didn't eat this morning," Josh said. "I'm fine. I'm dehydrated." He tried to get up.

The guy pushed him back down. "Stay here. I need to assess you. You people make my job hard. A 5K in this weather isn't for everyone."

Faint-shaming. Not cool. "Sorry." Then again, Josh and his ilk also kept the guy employed, so maybe the EMT should be a little more gracious.

"Do you know where you are, sir?" People ran past, gawking, telling him to hang in there.

"Yes. I'm in Providence, Rhode Island, home of the fourth-largest self-supporting marble dome in the world, doing a run to raise awareness for rare diseases. Can I at least sit on the sidewalk?"

The medic and Duffy's owner helped him to his feet, and one of the spectators quickly offered him a chair. He sat, and the medic took his blood pressure. "Ninety over fifty, sir. You are definitely dehydrated. And running on an empty stomach? That's just dumb."

"Thanks. I know. Sorry." It was embarrassing to be the subject of so much attention. He petted Pebbles's head, and she licked him some more.

"Do you want me to wait with you?" Duffy's owner asked.

"No." God no. "You keep at it. Thank you."

"No worries! Sorry to leave you. It's just that my brother's waiting for me at the finish line."

"Have fun," he said, and she was gone. Good stride, nice muscles in her legs. People were pretty decent, if you gave them a chance. He needed to remember that more.

Josh was given an electrolyte drink, made to sit with an ice pack on his head, then released with a warning from the surly medic. Josh thanked the person who'd loaned him the chair (another nice, decent person), then cut across a block to get to the finish line back on PC's campus.

"There you are!" Jen exclaimed. "Everything okay? We heard someone fainted!"

"I'm fine," he said. "Just took it slow. The heat, you know?"

Sarah raised an eyebrow. It seemed to be a thing of hers.

His mom, Ben, Sumi and Donna appeared; Donna had called his mother, they said, and the Kims tagged along, too. The Kims were lugging coolers and two picnic baskets, never ones to skimp on food. They found a spot under a tree and ate, and Josh felt significantly better. Octavia, who finally had learned to walk, toddled around, anointing everyone with drooly kisses and buttercups. In the distance, the white-robed priests strolled the campus, and Pebbles ran off to intercept a Frisbee.

"You doing all right, son?" Ben asked, sitting next to him.

"Yeah."

"Missing your wife, of course."

Josh nodded. Ben put his arm around his shoulders.

"She was a flower," the older man said.

"She was a whole field of flowers," he said, and Ben nodded.

Neither said anything else, and Josh was grateful for the silence and the company. Ben was the only one who could pull that off. Silence was good. Silence let him imagine his wife here, playing with the kids, chasing them around, giving piggyback rides. Well, of course she'd been too weak for that. But in his mind, she was healthy, and the kids begged for more, and she'd chase them and roar and swoop them up in her arms until she flopped down on the grass next to him. She'd put her head in his lap, maybe, and he would feel real again. Not this fake version of himself, the ghost of Lauren's husband.

But once, he *had* been Lauren's husband. He was proud of that. The two feelings would have to make peace.

"I should get going," he said. He stood up, helped Ben to his feet and gave him a brief hug.

He was the first to leave, but the urge to get home was strong. He stood up, fist-bumped Sebastian and then Octavia and steeled himself for the goodbye rounds.

"I left something under your door," Sarah said. "I would've brought it if I'd known you were coming." The eyebrow lifted again.

A *letter.* A Lauren letter. God, he needed that today. So much.

"Thanks," he said. "I'll text you about getting together."

He said his goodbyes and headed out. As he walked away, he felt his shoulders drop and the tension leave his legs.

Peopling was hard. It was worth it about half the time, but it took a lot out of him. Pebbles seemed to agree, because she curled up in a ball in the back seat of the car on the way home.

The letter was waiting when he got there.
Josh, #5
This time, he didn't wait. He tore it open right there in the foyer, despite that fact that his shirt was salty with dried sweat. He was desperate to hear her words.

Dear Joshua Park,
I love you. I love you! I love you so much. I love that you're half-Swedish. I love that you look nothing like a Swede, not because I have anything against blond hair and blue eyes, but because it's just cool that you're a black-haired boy. I love your arms. I love your talented hands. I love that Mrs. Kim taught you to cook. I love how smart you are, even when you tune me out because you're in your mind palace. I love that you never know what day it is. I love you. You are the best husband in the entire world. No. The entire planetary system, and hell yes, I'm including Pluto on that list.

How are you, honey? Are you doing okay? Settling into a routine yet? I would say that I miss you, but I imagine that I'm haunting you in the really sweet, reassuring way, and NOT in the creepy-little-girl-from-that-terrifying-movie way. WHY did we watch that? Why?

At any rate, sweetest heart, I'm hoping that this month, you might start reaching out a little bit. I know you're a loner, and yes, it was totally hot when I met you. But I don't want you to fall back into that because of . . . well . . . loneliness. I don't want you to be stuck because I died.

So I was thinking maybe you could do some volunteering. Asmaa can put you in touch with a project you'd like. Maybe you can do something with the home-less veterans, you know? Or be one of those folks who picks up trash on Sunday mornings? Maybe you can be a Big Brother or something.

You're too good to waste, Josh. I want the world to get to share you, my truest love, my heart, my honeybun. You have so many gifts. The world is lucky to have you, and I was the luckiest of all.

I love you, honey. Forever.

Lauren

He had tears in his eyes when he finished reading.

Sometimes, when they were married, they'd have the same idea at the same time. He'd call her from the market and say, "I was thinking of making chicken Parmesan for dinner," and she'd squeal and say, "I was literally texting you this very minute, asking if you'd make chicken Parm!" Or sometimes he'd say, "Turn on the subtitles, okay?" at the very second she was reaching for the remote to do just that.

"Soon," she once said, before her diagnosis, "we won't even need words to communicate." He liked that idea.

It was the same today. "Great minds think alike, honey," he said aloud, his voice husky.

No one would ever know him the way she had.

But they could know him a little. After all, he was the man who had won Lauren Carlisle's heart. The luckiest guy in the world.

20

Joshua

Month seven
September

*T*hey were in Hawaii, but it was the Providence apartment, or maybe it was the Cape
house they'd rented. At any rate, they were by
the ocean, and it was sunny and beautiful, and
he could hear the gentle roar of the ocean. The
breeze skimmed their skin, blowing Lauren's
hair against his neck. She was laughing, leading
him into the bedroom, wearing a filmy white
nightgown, barefoot, no makeup, that cute little
tummy, sexy as hell.

He was kissing her again, actually kissing her.
She was real, she was back, she was his again. "I
can't believe you're here," he said.

"Of course I'm here, silly," she said, and her
voice . . . he'd forgotten how much he loved the
sound of her voice, huskier than when they first
met, but so beautiful.

"You came back."

"I'll always come back, honey." Then she
pulled him closer and slid his shirt off his
shoulders, unbuckled his belt and pulled him
onto her, falling back on the bed.

"I missed you so much," he said.

"I know, Josh. You've been amazing. So brave and good."

"You can be dead if you come back like this, okay? I don't mind, as long as I can see you."

She laughed, kissing his cheek, mouth, neck, sliding her hands down his back, to his hips, tugging him closer, opening her legs, and she—

He jolted awake with a raging hard-on and only the sleeping dog next to him.

"No!" he yelled, punching the mattress. "Goddamnit!" Pebbles leaped off the bed and ran into another room, but for the love of God, Josh did not want to wake up. It was like losing her all over again.

If he was going to have a sex dream about his wife, couldn't he at least finish it? He flopped back on the bed and closed his eyes, but he knew it was no use. He wasn't going to fall back asleep. His erection tented the sheet. God, it was embarrassing. Ridiculous. He had a boner for his dead wife and nothing to do for it, aside from the obvious. But he didn't want to jerk off. He'd probably cry, and the combination was too pathetic, even for him.

He closed his eyes and tried to recapture the dream, but already, it was breaking apart, like fog. The hard-on stayed.

Ridiculous.

It had seemed so real. *She* had seemed so real. Missing her was a gaping maw, an ache in his whole body.

The clock read 3:06 a.m. The loneliest hour in the world.

Jen said dreams were visits from the dead, but to him, it felt like torture, to have been in that dreamworld and to have to come back to find Lauren dead.

Growing up Lutheran, he'd gone to services regularly with his mom—St. Paul's, a beautiful old church in Providence with lots of stained glass windows and hard wooden pews. It was a nice community—his mom loved the outreach and community service they did. It was good enough in that respect, but the idea of God reaching down to help here and there, of an afterlife . . . harder to swallow. Maybe it was the science geek in him. Maybe his birth father was an atheist, and it was genetic. The idea that God was waiting in the sky somewhere, deciding whether or not to answer your prayers . . . it didn't make a lot of sense.

He remembered when he was about eight years old, and a tornado had flattened an entire Kansas town. He and his mom were watching the news report, which showed only one house standing in the entire neighborhood amid acres and acres of rubble. "It's a miracle," said the weeping owner about his own survival. "My wife, she was sayin', 'Spare us, Lord, spare us,' and the good Lord held us in the palm of His hand and saved us."

In the house next door, the entire family had been killed, including a six-week-old baby.

"Why didn't God save the neighbors?" Josh asked his mother. "Didn't they pray?" Even then, he was cynical. "I bet the baby's parents were praying."

"God listens," his mother said. "But He's not a grocer, okay? Just because you pray for something you want doesn't mean you're going to get it."

"So why pray?" asked Josh.

"Why *not* pray?" she answered. "Eat your broccoli." She paused. "It's nice to think that someone else is out there, someone who loves and understands you. And God helps us all. Just maybe not in the way you think, or the way we want Him to."

Not exactly a passionate argument for the power of prayer. Josh was twelve when he dropped the belief of God completely. Oh, church was fine— he liked the sameness of the service, the music at Christmas and Easter. He liked that his mother was so well regarded by the other parishioners. No one ever made a fuss over her lack of a spouse, and they always told him what a good kid he was.

But for him, the experience was more about the smells of candles and lemon wax, the handshake from the pastor, who had a certain celebrity about him in his robes. Josh had taken Lauren a few times when they were engaged, and a few times afterward, before she was diagnosed. He liked the cooing of the church ladies as Stephanie introduced Lauren, and he loved seeing Lauren charm everyone.

So Josh had nothing against church. He just didn't believe in God. Or the Great Beyond.

Until Lauren had gotten sick, that was, and then he understood. There might not be any atheists in foxholes, and there were *definitely* no atheists in the ICU. You can't be an atheist when your twenty-seven-year-old spouse is fighting to breathe, her eyes wide, clawing at her throat. You can't be an atheist when you see her intubated and still. Or when they tell you there's no cure for what she has.

He'd prayed. He asked God to forgive his earlier lack of faith. He accepted the prayers of his mother's church friends, the prayer chain they set up for him, the rosaries Sumi Kim (a Catholic) fervently offered, the quieter, more poetic prayers of Ben (a Buddhist). Josh *begged*. There was nothing pretty or ceremonial about his praying, no sir. He asked God for time, for a trial drug to work, for a miracle reversal. Of course he did.

And then, after God failed to save her, when God said no to the prayers and left Josh alone in the world, lost and stunned and bereft, he became an atheist again.

It just made more sense. If anyone deserved to live, it had been Lauren.

He looked at the clock again: 3:22. With a sigh, he got up to work and give Pebbles a snack to apologize for scaring her.

A few days after the marathon where he so distinguished himself, he asked Sarah out for dinner. A nice restaurant, one he hadn't ever been to before, to avoid memories of Lauren. They ordered a bottle of wine, and Josh had half a glass. He'd written up a few index cards to remind him of things to ask her, because he tended to go blank when interacting with people he wasn't a hundred percent comfortable with.

1. *How is your mother's knee replacement working out?*
2. *How is your grandfather?*
3. *How was your vacation? Did you eat any good food? What was your favorite thing to do out there?*
4. *How is work going? It must be hard to deal with some situations. What do you do to relax?*

And the last . . .

5. *How are you doing without Lauren?*

Chances were low that he'd manage to ask that one. But he referred to the first index card, asked, and Sarah started talking in a friendly-enough way.

Lauren was the one who'd been good at this. With her, Josh picked up on cues, listened to her talk to people, watched her face as she smiled or frowned or nodded. He always felt more present, more at ease with himself and other people when he'd been with his wife. She was the key to his being fully engaged. He remembered to nod as Sarah paused, asked a follow-up question and tried to smile at the right places. He referred to card number two, then three when her answer was brief.

They ordered their dinners; fish for him, steak for her. Card number four.

He hated that everyone looking at them would assume they were on a date. He wished he could somehow communicate that he still loved his wife, that this was her friend, that he was absolutely not interested in her *that way.*

The food came. He took a bite of trout. It was pretty good. "How's your steak?" he asked Sarah.

"Good. How's your fish?"

"Good."

The conversation was not exactly rapier sharp. How long had they been here? Two hours? Three? He sneaked a look at his watch. Thirty-nine minutes.

Aha! He thought of something to say. "I bought a vase the other day. From Hawaii."

"Cool. What does it look like?"

"You know. It's . . . blue. And it has white on it. Like a cresting wave."

"Sounds pretty." She cut another piece of meat.

"Yes." It was gorgeous, in fact. One of a kind, handmade on Kauai, at the same shop where he and Lauren bought a sculpture on their honeymoon.

"You guys brought me a beautiful paperweight from Hawaii."

"Did we?" Lauren had bought dozens of gifts, it seemed.

"Yes." Sarah poured herself a second glass of wine. "So about all the shitty things you said to me, Josh."

"Yes. Still sorry."

"You know what? Everything was true. About how I was pissy and jealous." She shook her head, her eyes getting shiny. "Lauren was . . . sparkly. You know? She sparkled."

"Yes," Josh said. It was the perfect word for her.

"And . . . well, it wasn't always easy to be known as 'Lauren's friend.' All through elementary school, and then even more in middle school and high school, I was sort of like this . . . appendage." She pulled a face, then did her hair swoop, and Josh felt an unexpected little sunburst of affection for her. That hair swoop gesture . . . she did that when she was nervous. Now that he had that information, it wasn't so annoying.

"You know, it's depressing when you're everyone's second choice," Sarah continued. "I only had her. Everyone else in our circle was Lauren's friend. I was there, and I'd known her the longest, but I wasn't in the inner circle. Never slept over at their houses, or invited them to mine. Lauren was my best friend, and I didn't really need anyone else, you know?"

He leaned forward, setting down his fork. "I do. I understand completely." How shocking, that he had this in common with Sarah. He'd never wondered about Sarah's other friends. He'd had no reason to.

She smiled sadly. "Of course you get it. So anyway, Lauren was too loyal to cut me off, but I wasn't . . ." She shook her head, started to do another hair swoop, then stopped herself with a half smile at Josh, silently acknowledging her habit. "Whatever. Everything came easily to Lauren. Friends, guys, grades. She was so pretty and fun. Everyone wanted to be around her."

Josh nodded. "I felt the same way. She could've had . . . I don't know." Who was that character Lauren had so crushed on? "She could've had Jon Snow. But she picked me, and I'm still not sure why."

Sarah smiled. "Ah, she adored you, Josh. Right from the start."

"And she always thought of you as her best friend. When we first started dating, she never said your name without the title. 'My best friend, Sarah. Sarah, my best friend.' "

Sarah wiped her eyes. "That's nice to hear." She swirled the remaining wine in her glass, studying the deep golden color. "When she got sick," she said quietly, "I thought it had to be a joke. Like, if anyone should be the dying friend, it should be me. Like she was too golden to have anything but perfection."

Josh stifled the urge to wish it *had* been Sarah. He'd already thought it a number of times, anyway. He felt ashamed of that, of thinking Sarah's life was worth less. She was someone's daughter, too. Someday, someone would love her the way he loved Lauren. She'd probably become a mom, and she'd be a really good one. He shouldn't judge.

"I was going to dump her as a friend," Sarah said quietly. "In college. She got into RISD . . . I didn't get into Brown. She lived in the coolest student housing ever; I was at URI in a triple with the girl in the top bunk drunk-puking on me four nights a week. Lauren was here on the Hill, so happy and confident that the world was hers, and I felt completely unremarkable by comparison. It bugged me so much I was thinking about transferring somewhere."

"Why didn't you?" he asked.

Sarah shrugged. "I had a good scholarship at URI. In my mind, I was brave enough to go out west, to California or Seattle, but in reality, I was in Kingston, thirty minutes from home. Every time I saw Lauren, she was telling me how fabulous and interesting school was, how cool her professors were . . . she was majoring in clothing design originally. I don't know if you knew that."

"I did."

"Yeah. So she was taking classes like History of the Little Black Dress or whatever, making her own beautiful clothes, while I was slogging through statistics taught by these sleepy adjuncts who never bothered to know my name. I didn't even know what I wanted to major in."

"That's not uncommon," Josh said. *Good job,* he could just about hear Lauren say. *Good sympathetic listening.*

"So. I was sick of her sparkliness. Her perfect life. Her happiness, honestly. I was tired of comparing myself to her and coming up short. Everything about her was cool. Her married sister, her hot brother-in-law, her field of study." She poured the remaining wine into her glass. Her eyes filled again with tears. "I wanted something crappy to happen to her, because it seemed like nothing ever did. So you were right. I was bitter and petty."

"Why didn't you, um, dump her?" he asked, a little fascinated.

"Her father died. And she was completely heartbroken." Sarah wiped her eyes carefully, so as not to smudge her mascara. "The first bad thing that ever happened to her. Mr. Carlisle . . . he was the best. I still remember her voice when she called me. I knew right then and there something horrible had happened."

And so Josh learned that Sarah's own father had left when she was eight, popped out a few new children with his next two wives and had to be ordered into paying child support by the court. Sarah was her mother's only child, alone to bear the contentiousness of the divorce and the neglect from her father. When Sarah did visit her father in Arizona, she was forced to babysit her younger half brothers and a stepsister, courtesy of her father's second wife. Sarah had adored that little girl, but once her father divorced Wife Number Two, she never saw her again.

"So her family life . . . that was just one more thing she had that I didn't. Did you know the Carlisles ate together every night? Every night! My mom worked nights, so I always made my own dinner. Frozen pizza and shit like that."

Josh made a noncommittal noise. He and his mom had eaten together every night, too, and at least once a week with the Kims. Once in a while, his mom would go out with her friends or attend a lecture, in which case the Kims had him sleep over and treated him like their own son. From the age of eight until fourteen, he'd spent every afternoon at their house, fixing things in the basement with Ben, cooking with and being spoiled by Sumi.

The image of Sarah opening a cardboard box and eating pizza alone was awfully sad.

They ordered dessert, and the evening, which had been dragging earlier, was now quite . . . pleasant. Interesting. There was something to be said for this after all, this . . . interaction. Mining of information.

"Something happened to Lauren after her dad died," Sarah said. "She grew up, I think."

Josh nodded. "I thought so, too." He hesitated, feeling slightly guilty. "The first time I met her, I thought she was a twit."

"Are you serious?" Sarah exclaimed. "I thought it was love at first sight!"

"Second sight," he admitted. "And I think you're right. She had an easy life, and she was missing a little . . ." He paused to find the right word.

"Gravitas?"

"Yes. Exactly." Was he *gossiping* about his wife? He pushed his fork into the unnecessary whipped cream that accompanied his cheesecake, making a pattern and then smoothing it out and repeating the motion carefully, finding peace in the repetition. "But the next time we met, she was different. There was more . . . there was more to her. And she was only eighteen that first time. She had the right to be . . . young. Carefree. Goofy."

Sarah nodded and wiped her eyes, managing a smile. "She was awesome when she was goofy."

That was the truth. Lauren could make everyone laugh, herself most of all. How many nights had she fallen asleep giggling at her own joke, or starting a tickle war with him? She'd laughed in her dreams, even. "What were some of the goofy things you guys did together?" he asked.

"Oh, God. We used to write romance stories in school about our teachers and pass them back and forth. We'd torture Jen if I was sleeping over, spying on her, hiding in her closet to scare her later. Lauren loved talking in an accent with strangers. Russian was her best, I think."

He hadn't known that. The little tidbits were better than the dessert. Things he could take home later and play over and over. He felt unexpectedly grateful to Sarah, sharing all these prized memories.

The server came over, asked if they'd like more coffee. "Just the check, thanks," Sarah said, so that was the end of the evening, he guessed. It was strangely disappointing. He'd never enjoyed Sarah so much, this different, more honest side of her (and yes, hearing stories about Lauren).

"How are you doing with the letters?" Sarah asked when the server left.

He was silent a minute, considering his answer. "They're . . . they're good. They help."

She waited for more, but he didn't offer anything else. "Asmaa told me about the children's garden, and how you're volunteering there. Lauren would really like that."

His throat tightened at her words. "Thanks," he said, his voice almost a whisper.

"You made her so happy, Josh."

He looked at the crisscrosses in the whipped cream, then smoothed them out and remade them, more carefully this time.

It's okay to show how you feel, Lauren had told him on more than one occasion, especially after her diagnosis. *You'll be surprised at how kind most people are.*

Easier said than done. But he forced himself to look at Sarah and gave a nod, abruptly glad that their dinner was over.

21

Joshua

*Still damn month seven
because time seemed frozen,
letter number seven
September*

It was only a few sentences, but those sentences made his joints zing with adrenaline and a little horror.

My sweet darling Josh, hello!
I have a wicked fun thing for you this month. You ready?
See a medium.
Oh, come on! Why not? It'll be fun. You know you want to see if there's a GB, my darling atheist. Give it a shot! You never know. Maybe I'll appear and we can sneak off for a paranormal shag. Or maybe I'll be busy doing angelic, miraculous things and you won't hear from me. If that's the case, know that I'm doing THE LORD'S WORK saving children from being hit by buses, rescuing kittens, etc.

But I know what I believe: I believe in you and me. Forever.

I love you.

Lauren

She had to be kidding.

She wasn't kidding.

This . . . okay, he would need help for this one. His mother was out; being Lutheran, her religious focus had been on ideas such as Jesus died horribly for you, you wretch, and therefore you should make casseroles for potluck suppers. Mrs. Kim, though, was a hard-core Catholic and had saints for every occasion.

He picked up his phone and called their land-line, since they were of the demographic who only turned their cell phones on if they wanted to make a call. "Ben? Hi, it's Joshua."

"Hello, son. What's new?"

"Um . . . do you know any . . . uh . . . any mediums?"

There was a long pause. "I think you better talk to Sumi," he said. "She loves that crazy woman on TV. The one with the hair?"

"Yeah. Lauren did, too." Which is probably why she gave him this ridiculous task.

"Hang on, Josh." He passed the phone to his wife, saying, "Josh wants to see a medium."

Sumi squealed with joy. "Oh, my darling, this is wonderful! Wonderful! I'm sure Lauren will come through for you, sweetheart, she loved you so! *Loves* you. You won't regret this, these people, they've been blessed with a gift, it's amazing, do you watch *Long Island Medium*? Or *Mama Medium*? They're so gifted! I've been to a few of these, so I'll send you a list, okay? Oh, this makes me so happy! So happy, Joshie. It will comfort you. You should take your mother! Wouldn't that be fun?"

"Oh . . . yeah, no, she's not . . ."

"She's not *yet!*" Sumi cried. "She will be!"

"Maybe we don't mention this to her," Josh said. He could already picture her eye roll. He already felt dirty himself.

"I'll email you the list, okay? Or do you want me to come over?"

"Email is fine."

"Okay, darling! Bye!"

Two hours later, there was a knock at the door. Josh got up from his computer and opened it to see the Kims and his mother.

"I couldn't stop her," Ben murmured as Josh was enveloped in Sumi's hug. "Sorry."

His mom came down the hall. "There you are," she said. "I hear you're going to try to make contact with the dead." She raised her eyebrow.

"Mm," he said. So much for Sumi keeping this a secret.

"You're too skinny, so we thought we'd cook," his mom said. "Do you want a glass of water?"

313

"I'll take a beer."

"Oh, you drink now? My only child doesn't tell me that he's lifted his self-imposed lifetime ban on alcohol." She sighed dramatically, opening the fridge, then gave him a smile. Their own language . . . *You could call a little more. I care about everything you do. I'm still here for you.* He gave a nod. Message received.

Ben sat down next to him, holding his own beer. "Sorry about this," he said. "I tried to hold them off."

"No, it's . . . it's nice," Josh said. He could almost hear Lauren's laughter now. She loved how Steph and the Kims were almost a single unit and descended upon them at will.

He missed that laugh. God, he missed it.

His mother and Mrs. Kim fussed and sautéed, simmered and chatted, slipping Pebbles a treat here and there. No wonder the dog stole food.

But it was comforting, his two moms laughing and talking, Ben asking a few questions about Josh's latest project, taking a look at the plans. Ben had been an engineer himself before he retired, though his work had focused on city water systems. There was life back in the apartment. Fresh air and . . . well, a little happiness.

They ate, and then Sumi took out a piece of paper with at least twelve names on it, complete with phone numbers and websites.

"I can't believe you managed to wait till after dinner," he said.

"I know!" she said. "I've been dying to show this to you, but your mother said we should feed you first. So." She pointed to the first name on the list. "This one I like because her tarot readings are good. Not phony. Hi, Pebbles, yes, baby." She handed the dog a piece of pork, then pointed at the paper again. "This one, nice, but not always on, you know? When she is, she's super. Angela? She's amazing, but you can never get an appointment, she's *that* good. If you're lucky, a person cancels and you can get in. This guy here, I like him a lot, but sometimes I think he's making things up. Every time I go, he tells me I'm about to meet my soul mate. Which, come on. I have a wedding ring on, mister! I already did that!"

Ben smiled. "True. She did."

Josh cleared his throat. "How many of these have you been to, Sumi?"

She leaned back in her chair. "All of them. I've been doing it since my mother died in 1992."

"Wow." That was a lot of money down the toilet.

Ben glanced at him with a little shrug and a smile. "Whatever makes her happy."

"Even I went once," Mom said.

"What?" Josh almost choked with surprise.

She shrugged. "Why not? It was fun. He said

there was travel in my future, and there *was* travel in my future."

He rolled his eyes. "There's travel in everyone's future, a person could say."

She laughed. "It was an experience, Joshua. Be open to new things."

"I'm trying. I just can't believe you didn't tell me."

"Why not?" she asked, sipping her tea.

"Because you tell me everything."

"Clearly not."

"Is there anything else you're hiding? Do you have any more children? Did you secretly marry my birth father?"

"Joshua." She gave him her best *calm yourself* look. "I have no idea where your father is or even if he's alive."

"Your psychic didn't tell you?"

"I never asked." She ate a piece of broccoli. "But in case you were wondering, your grandmother watches over you and loves you." She winked at him.

Josh sighed. "I think this will probably be a waste of time." He glanced at Ben. "Will you come with me?"

"Oh, I wouldn't miss it," Ben replied.

He chose the medium named Gertie because it felt like an honest name. There was one named Moonflower, another named Ariella Borealis,

316

which Josh did *not* think was her given name and which therefore presented credibility issues.

Gertie Berkowitz, however . . . that was a name you could trust.

On the appointed day, he and Ben drove to Tiverton, a wealthy little town on Narragansett Bay notable for its meandering stone walls, water views and gracious homes.

Ben was the perfect person for this day, with his implacable sense of calm. Josh could've invited Radley, who'd come over the other night to watch a movie, but he had the feeling Radley would be too chatty. He could've asked Sarah or Jen, but . . . no. It might've been too emotional for them.

Josh had been careful when he booked the appointment, which he did simply by calling her 401 area code number (another good sign . . . it wasn't an 877 or a 900 number). He blocked his own number before dialing so she couldn't look him up that way. He gave his name as Joshua—no last name, in case she was the Googling type, picked a time, and that was it.

Being a man of science, he read up on mediums. Most would speak in generalities and watch you for clues. At best, Josh thought, they were simply very empathetic and good at reading people, hoping to give comfort. At worst, they preyed on the grieving by asking leading questions, then parroting back the information. "Was water significant to your mother? She's showing me water." Honestly. Who didn't have some connection with water? People were 72 percent water on average. Everyone had some beach, river, pond, creek, salt marsh they loved. And then the bereft person would say, "Yes! We went to the beach when I was little!" and the psychic would say, "Yes, that's exactly what she's showing me."

Not exactly proof of the afterlife.

He was only doing this for Lauren. She'd thought it would be fun. He wasn't convinced.

It was a beautiful, sunny day, and the drive twisted through farmland laced with rock walls. He and Ben didn't say much for most of the drive, which was their way . . . only speaking to observe something especially interesting. The five turkey vultures eating a dead raccoon, for example.

"Poor vultures," Ben said. "They do us a service by eating carrion but get no credit."

"True," said Josh. There was a metaphor in there somewhere, but his brain was buzzing too much to find it.

He glanced at the clock. "We're gonna be way too early," he said.

"Should we stop at Dunkin'?"

"Okay. Yeah." Being in Rhode Island, where there were more Dunkins per person than anywhere in the world, it wasn't hard to find one.

Josh pulled into the parking lot. "What would you like?"

"An iced coffee. Thanks, son."

Josh went into the familiar, thick smell of the store. Since they were both Rhodies from birth, Josh and Lauren had never gone on a road trip of more than fifteen minutes without stopping for Dunkin'. Every time they went to the Cape, or Mass General, the airport, to Jamestown or Westerly, they'd hit Dunks and get their fix.

When was the final time they'd been? What was the last time he'd bought a coffee for his wife, such a small thing, but so precious? It would never happen again. He wished someone had told him. "Hey, pal, your wife will die soon, so this is the last time you're gonna buy her a coffee. Savor the moment, okay?" He wished he'd been able to know *all* the last times so he could have enjoyed them, taken in every detail, every molecule of each moment. The last time they made love. The last time she laughed. The last time they held hands while walking.

"Hi," the teenager behind the counter grunted. "What can I get you?"

"One hot coffee, black, and one medium iced latte with whipped cream," he said.

He ordered, waited obediently, then took their drinks to the car. It was only then he realized he'd gotten Ben the drink Lauren always ordered.

"I . . . I got you the wrong thing," he said.

319

"It's okay. This looks great." Josh got in the car and wiped his hands on his jeans. "You okay?" Ben asked.

"Yep." After a second, he remembered Lauren telling him to share feelings with people who loved him. "I'm a little nervous," he said. "Do you believe in this stuff, Ben?"

"Well . . . I believe we have a soul, and it moves on." He took a pull of his drink. "In Korea, we have all sorts of traditions honoring the dead to let them know we miss them. Then I married a Catholic, and some of that has seeped in. So the short answer is . . . sort of, but nothing specific."

"I think it's complete bullshit," Josh said. "Lauren wanted me to do this, though."

"Well, then, it can't be too bad an idea. But it also could be complete bullshit, as you say." His face crinkled like crepe paper as he smiled.

Josh started the car. If he did somehow get duped into thinking Lauren was "there" or "here," whatever that meant, how would he feel? Would he spend the rest of his life at Gertie's, chatting with his dead wife? You know what? He'd take it. But what if Gertie said, "Sorry, kid. I got nothing"? Would he be furious? Crushed? A dolt for hoping for any crumb whatsoever?

Gertie had said on the phone that he could pay her at his discretion. She had a thick Rhode Island accent, leaving off the last consonant of words and adding an *R* after a vowel, per state law. "Pay me whatevah y' think the readin's wehth, Jawshuer deah."

"You have arrived," announced his iPhone. Josh pulled into the driveway of a modest, well-kept gray-shingled Cape, the yard graced by what had to be a three-hundred-year-old tree, based on its circumference. It was a good sign, that tree. He didn't know why, but it reassured him.

"Don't give her anything to go on, okay?" Josh asked Ben as they got out of the car. "Try not to nod or say, 'Yeah, his wife died from a lung disease.' Just let her talk."

"You've told me that three times, Josh. I think I've got it." Ben clapped him on the shoulder. "I'll sit silent and stone-faced, okay?"

"Sorry. And yes. Thank you."

Before they even knocked, the door opened, making Josh jump. "Hello!" said a small, white-haired woman. Her face was extremely wrinkled, her eyes hooded like a turtle's. "I'm Gertie, your psychic medium. Come in, come in, sweetheart." Her accent was thick and comforting. "You're Josh—can I call you that?" He nodded, and she turned to Ben. "And you are . . ."

"Ben. Nice to meet you."

They followed Gertie into her little house, which was full of photos of family members. Cardinals were her favorite bird, apparently, because images of the red bird were every-where—on the curtains, throw pillows, framed photos and cross-stitched samplers. It looked like a classic old lady's house—too much furniture, outdated carpeting and the comforting smell of lemon Pledge.

In one corner, there was a round table, covered with an orange vinyl tablecloth. They all sat. Josh had already begun to sweat. His neck muscles locked, and his fingers felt tight with anxiety.

"So here's how it works," Gertie said. "We sit here, and I light this candle and say a prayer, and we ask your loved one to come forth. They show me signs, and I tell you what they are. Sometimes, I'm not one hundred percent sure what it means, so you'll have to help me."

Ah, yes. The leading questions. They'd say, "I'm seeing the number four. Is that meaningful? No? Think about it. They're telling me four means something. Birthday? Death? Anniversary? Fourth floor of the hospital? Number of kids? Did you have four cats throughout your life? Four tires on your car?" And you were supposed to think your dead loved one was floating around you.

Why was he here? It wasn't as if Lauren would know if he blew off her suggestions. Great. Now he felt guilty on top of sweaty and anxious. Ben was studying his hands, stone-faced and silent, as promised.

Gertie patted his hand. "Josh, there's nothin' to be worried about. I'm a nice Christian lady, I go to Mass every week, so there's no demonic spirits or the like, no sir."

"Got it," Josh said.

"The messages come fast, and I might miss something, see? But mostly, those who've passed on just want to reassure the livin' that they're right as rain, and you'll be together again. This life here? This is just a tiny piece of our true lives."

Okay, boomer. Straight from *Mediumship for Dummies.* Josh's hopes were not high.

Gertie lit the candle, said the Our Father. The kitchen clock ticked loudly. A car drove past. Gertie had a little whistle coming from her nose every time she inhaled, and Josh suddenly wanted to laugh (or bolt). Ben caught his eye and squashed a smile.

Then Gertie tilted her head, seeming to look at the floor. "Oh," she said, "you lost your wife."

The urge to laugh vanished.

"Is that right?" Gertie asked. "Just say yes or no."

"Yes."

"I'm so sorry, dear." She closed her eyes again. The breath whistled in her nostrils, and Josh's heart was pounding, and didn't she hear that? Could he offer her a tissue? How had she known about his wife? Was it because he still wore his wedding ring? Had she Googled him after all? How many widowers did Rhode—

"Her name started with an 'L.' Laurie? Not quite. Lara? Laura?"

How the *fuck* . . . He cleared his throat. Ben's eyes were slightly wider than usual. "Lauren," Josh said, his voice strange.

"Right. Good. She's showing me . . . a bed. Hospital bed. She was . . . she was real sick, aw, jeez. She was at the hospital a lot."

Josh said nothing, but his heart was like a wild horse in his chest, kicking against his ribs. The clock ticked. Ben remained granite-still. Gertie's nose squeaked.

Okay, he shouldn't give her that much credit just yet. Josh was young. How many thirty-year-old men came to a psychic to speak to their dead grandfathers? *Wife* was a good guess, and saying she was very sick was a fifty-fifty bet.

But the name thing . . .

"You were with her at the end. You got in bed with her. She's showing me the two of you snugglin' there. Is that right, hon?"

He tried to control his breathing. "Yes." Again, what self-respecting husband whose wife was breathing her last *wouldn't* get into bed with her? The stallion in his chest kicked just the same. He did not want to remember that moment. At all. Ever.

Gertie smiled, but was still staring at the floor. A nose-squeaking breath. Another. "She's showing me children. Did you have kids?"

324

Ah. Okay. She was just good at guessing, then. "No. We did not."

"Did she have any before you?"

"No."

"Well, she's showing me two kids. The girl is a little bit of a thing. A toddler. The boy's older. They're . . . they . . . are they biracial? One of their parents is Black?"

Sebastian and Octavia. Holy shit. Josh managed to nod.

"My God," Ben breathed.

"She's showing me her name and pointin' to the girl. Is the girl named after her? Not the first name, but the second? A middle name?"

The horse in his chest kicked again. "Yes."

"The boy's name is . . . starts with a T. Tyrone. Is that right?"

"That's his middle name," Josh whispered.

"She's showing me the number four." Four was not . . . it didn't . . . His mind was turning to tar.

"Is that meaningful to you? Birthday? The month of April? Did she die on the fourth of the month?" No. No. Nothing.

It was Ben who answered. "The little boy is four years old."

Well, holy shit. That was true.

"The little boy sees her, too, sometimes. He talks to her. Kids' defenses are lower, so they can do that." Gertie blew her nose, and when she inhaled again, the squeak was gone, thank God, and shouldn't he be concentrating? Gertie tilted her head and looked at the floor once more.

"Lauren wants you to tell their mother she watches over them. Is she their big sister? No. Aunt. She's the aunt of those kids, and their mother is her sister. Oh, they were close. How she loved her sister."

"Yes." How the *fuck* did she know this?

"Now she's showing me flowers. Lots of flowers. She wants you to see the flowers."

"Okay."

"No, nope, she's stuck on the flowers. Is there something special about the flowers?"

"I . . . I sent her flowers a lot," he whispered.

"No, not that. She's bein' specific with the roses. Somethin' special there. Are roses special in any way? Do you know someone named Rose?"

"Rose was her middle name."

Jesus God in heaven. And then, Valentine's Day. Their anniversary, the rose petals on their bed.

How could Gertie know that? She handed him a tissue, and he realized tears were streaming down his face. It wasn't a good feeling, this, this . . . uncertainty, this longing, the roar of grief that his Lauren was really gone, truly dead, on the other side.

"And what's with the tree? She's showing me a special tree. In a pot near the window."

Her dogwood tree. Ben's eyes were comically wide now, though his face was the same.

"She says that tree is linked to her somehow, and she—"

"Stop! Stop. I—I—I . . . Please stop," Josh said.

Gertie looked at him, her turtle eyes kind. "I'm sorry, darlin'. Am I going too fast for you?"

"I don't . . . I never . . . really believed in this," he said. "It's . . . a lot." Ben reached across the table and squeezed his hand.

"Aw, of course it is, hon," Gertie said. "It can be very overwhelming, especially if you don't believe."

The horse in his chest was bucking and rearing. Josh mopped his face and wadded up the tissue.

Gertie's head tilted again. "She has more to say. Her presence is very strong. Do you want to hear it?"

Of *course* he wanted to hear it. How could he not? "Yes."

Gertie tilted her head to the side. "She's showing me that you work with . . . little things. Little things you build. You . . ." She tapped her fingertips together. "You make them? You . . . you make things on a computer, but she's showing me a hospital, too."

"He's a medical device engineer," Ben blurted. Josh didn't even care that he told. Gertie was close enough.

327

"That's it! That's her way of making sure you know she's really here. She's proud of you, Josh. Very proud. You two were wicked happy."

"Yes. Yes," he said, his breath coming hard. "Look. I know she loved me and her sister and the kids, and I know what I do for a living. But . . ." His voice broke. "Does she have anything to say to me?" He rubbed his forehead hard and tried not to look at Ben, for fear he'd start sobbing. "Something for now?"

Gertie stared at the floor again. "She wants you to know she's not alone. Her grandfather? No, her father? Did her father pass? Yeah? They're together. She's a beautiful soul, your wife. She laughs a lot. She's happy."

Good. Good. He only ever wanted her to be happy.

His heart cracked just the same.

"Okay . . . yep. Yep. She says you'll get married again. She's pointing to her ring fingah, then showing me the number two. Your second wife. You already know her, but you don't . . . you're not aware that she's gonna be important in your life." Gertie laughed. "She's showing me a penny and droppin' it. Like, the coin hasn't dropped for you yet regardin' this woman."

"Sarah, maybe?" Ben murmured. Josh heard the words, but they didn't register.

Gertie tilted her head again. "You blame your-self, she says. But you were wonderful! She's showing me over and over again how good you were, how you took care of her. She wants you to stop feeling guilty. You couldn't have done any more. She's tellin' me you were perfect. Drop the guilt."

That was a message mediums often gave their clients, Josh had read. It also happened to be completely appropriate to his case.

He took a tissue and wiped his eyes. Gertie smiled at the floor. "So much love between you two," she said.

The pain in his chest was crushing. *Please come back,* he couldn't help thinking. *Please come back.*

"She gives you signs, Josh. You aren't seeing them. She wants you to see the signs."

He nodded.

Then Gertie turned to Ben. "You're not his father, but she says you're like one, and she thanks you for bein' there for Josh."

Ben's stoicism crumpled, and he put his hand over his eyes. Gertie patted his arm. "She's showing me a paper airplane? You're throwing it? Did you make paper airplanes together, you and Josh?"

Ben nodded, his shoulders shaking.

"And there's another woman she's showing me. Like a sister, but not. Purple sparkly dresses . . . did they take dance class together? Something with dancing. She wants you to tell her she's with her. She's strugglin', too, the not-sister. Best friend, that's it. Her best friend."

Sarah. He'd have to call Sarah. This would mean the world to her.

Gertie nodded. "Okay, she's stepping back. She wants you to be at ease, to be happy, to know you'll be together again in the next life." She was quiet for a minute, then blew out the candle and looked at the two men. "Hoo! That was a good one, I think! Don't you?"

Josh wrote her a check for $500. She hugged him hard, and then hugged Ben, and they left, not speaking. He drove to the end of the road to turn around; it was a dead end, facing the water. But he just sat there a minute, his hands shaking.

"You okay, son?" Ben asked.

He looked out at the bay, the water sparkling in slices of blue and silver under a sky heavy with creamy cumulus clouds.

"It was shocking," he said.

"Yeah. Very specific."

His hands were choking the steering wheel. "The thing is," he continued, "does it make any difference? She's still gone. What good does this do? Does it change anything? Do I go back every week?"

"I think . . . I think it's just nice to believe she's not a hundred percent gone."

"She's gone enough. I don't want signs. I want her." His throat was killing him, and he dashed his hand across his eyes. "Sumi said you have a church thing tonight. I'll get you back."

"Josh, if you want to talk more, son . . ."

"No. I'm fine."

They drove back to Providence in silence. A thunderstorm rolled in, and when they pulled up onto his old street, Ben asked if he wanted to come in. Josh refused, thanked Ben, gave him a quick hug and then called Sarah. "Can I come over?" he asked, even though he was already headed her way.

She said yes.

She opened the door a few minutes later, wearing a David Bowie T-shirt and running shorts. Her apartment was somewhat untidy and unremarkable—piles of papers on her desk, a few coffee cups scattered about, mail on the counter.

"Hey, Josh," she said. "To what do I owe the honor?"

"I saw a psychic today," he said without preamble. "She said Lauren showed her a person who wasn't a sister but like a sister. Purple sparkly dresses at a dance recital or something."

The color drained from Sarah's face. "Jesus, Josh. A little warning next time?" Then she turned away. When she spoke next, it was a whisper. "It was the eighth-grade talent show. We wore purple sparkly dresses and danced to Soulja Boy. 'Crank That.' We were awesome." She took a shaky breath. "The psychic knew that?"

"Apparently. She said to tell you Lauren is still . . . with you."

Sarah put both hands over her face and started to sob.

Hug her.

He did. She hugged him back. He felt something loosen inside him and, after a few seconds, became aware of the fact that he was crying, too.

It wasn't horrible.

In fact, it felt kind of great, just to cry with someone who had loved Lauren, too, and not worry, just for a second, if he should be doing something different. No. Hugging was . . . it was okay.

"Oh, Josh," she whispered. "I'm so sorry for the two of us."

The thunderclap took them by surprise, and they jumped apart. Josh straightened, wiped his eyes on his sleeve. Sarah got a tissue and blew her nose.

"You want to see a movie?" she suggested, and for some reason, that sounded perfect to him.

"Something violent," he said.

"A war movie."

"Horror," he countered.

"Whatever you want, pal. You just talked with your dead wife. You get popcorn *and* soda." She smiled at him, and he felt himself smiling back.

"Thanks, Sarah," he said. "You're a good friend."

Almost to his surprise, he realized it was true.

The psychic had mentioned a woman in his life who would be his second wife. Someone he already knew.

He wasn't ready to think about that, though. Not today. Maybe not for a long, long time.

But it was there just the same.

22

Lauren

Twenty-five months left
January

Dear Daddy,
Help me. Oh, Daddy, please help me.
Please don't let this be true. I'm so scared.
Please help me, Dad. Please let this be
wrong.

Lauren had had three appointments with Dr.
Bennett, the pulmonologist. Three appointments in three months, with a few reschedulings
because of snow and the holidays and the thrill
of making new traditions. They had had the
Kims and Stephanie over for Pepero Day, a
sweet Korean holiday that seemed to exist
solely to celebrate friendship. Then there was
Thanksgiving—the big meal at Jen's, including
Stephanie, then dessert at the Kims', because all
four of their kids had been home and had wanted
to see Josh and meet her. They had a brunch
that weekend with all their local friends, and
Lauren had felt so happy and grown up, cooking
and cleaning for her former classmates and

colleagues, showing them their beautiful home.

Then it was Christmastime, and they had their first major fight over Josh not going to her office party. They made up, of course, went on the holiday stroll and celebrated Jen's birthday. On New Year's Eve, they hosted a party—Sarah and her date (who passed out on the couch before nine p.m.), Louise, Santino, Bruce and Tom, Mara, Asmaa and her honey, Jen and Darius. Even with the drunk guy, it had been a blast, and they'd gone up to the rooftop to watch the fireworks. The Kims had had them over for lunar New Year, another big celebration, and had invited Lauren's mom, too, which was awfully nice.

In other words, it had been easy to forget that she was a little out of breath for no apparent reason.

But now the holidays were over, and Lauren had no more excuses. She kept telling herself not to be nervous. They'd already said it wasn't cancer. No sign of a tumor on her chest X-ray, thank God. But they wanted an MRI now, too.

She was *fine,* she reminded herself. Young. Healthy. Blissfully happy. Sex at least three times a week, usually more. Yoga classes and the gym on the first floor. Did she get out of breath? Of course! That was the point.

She was just . . . tired. She had asthma, and maybe chronic bronchitis. If she felt weary and heavy sometimes, wasn't that just *because* she worked out? It was a *good* sign, damn it.

It was that intern in the ER who'd first given her that tremor of fear. That *pause.* No one wants a doctor to pause before reassuring you.

But she'd been tested for a lung infection. A virus, though she tested negative for everything they could test for. Low-grade pneumonia on top of asthma? Chronic sinus infection with post-nasal drip and acid reflux?

They couldn't quite pin it down.

"Just a few more tests," Dr. Bennett said, and Lauren felt a flare of fear and anger. *Diagnose me or tell me I'm healthy, for God's sake,* she thought, her face reddening. "This is a tricky case," the doctor continued. "I want to be sure we get it right."

Not super reassuring. "I'm really fine," Lauren replied. *I could like you. Give me a clean bill of health, and we'll be great friends, I promise.*

"Outpatient Testing will call to schedule you in the next day or so," Dr. Bennett said. "If you feel worse, call me right away."

"I'm fine. I feel great."

"We'll talk soon."

Shit. No martinis with Dr. B., then.

And then there was Josh, hovering, glancing at her when she coughed. "Honey, I'm *fine,*" she snapped one night. "Can you please not bury me yet?" He didn't answer. She huffed and went to bed, and he came in a half hour later and took her in his arms and said he loved her. It was impossible to stay mad.

Two more X-rays, two CAT scans, one high-resolution CAT scan, a pulmonary function test, a second pulmonary function test, one bronchoscopy (even with sedation, that was nasty). The questions were endless and irritatingly repetitive: Was she a smoker? History of asthma? Pneumonia? *Tell us again how your father died. When did you go to Hawaii? Where did you stay? Swim? Eat? Were you exposed to asbestos, silicone dust, heavy metals, contaminated air-conditioning systems, moldy foliage, pigeon droppings?*

"Of course I've been exposed to pigeon poop!" Lauren yelled the umpteenth time she was asked. "*And* moldy leaves! Hasn't everyone? Just give me some damn cough medicine that actually works!"

So when Dr. Bennett called her and asked her to come in "with your husband," Lauren was almost relieved. Finally, they'd figured it out. Some weird pneumonia she'd caught on the plane to Hawaii, probably.

"Have a seat," Dr. Bennett said when they arrived at her office. "And please, call me Kwana."

A good sign or a bad sign, to be on a first-name basis with your doctor? Lauren felt cold, suddenly.

"Hi, Kwana!" she said, as if being cheery would make everything okay. "I love your hair." Over the holidays, Dr. Bennett had gone from shiny, straight hair to multiple braids twisted into a bun. And hey. If she wanted to be called Kwana, that was *fine*. They'd get out of this appointment, Kwana would apologize for being so aggressive, when gosh, it was just this one thing, here was the cure, and absolutely, she'd love to come out for drinks one night!

Except Lauren's heart was beating too hard. She took a slow, deliberate breath. All good. No cough, not right now, see?

"Does it take forever, those braids?" she asked. Talking about hair was much, much better than anything Lauren could think of at this moment.

"It takes a while, yes." Kwana seemed to be very still. Josh took Lauren's hand. His was sweaty.

"Okay," said Kwana. "We've done every test we can, and we did a couple twice. It looks like idiopathic pulmonary fibrosis." Lots of syllables in that one. "We had a tough time diagnosing it because we wanted to be sure. It's not a common disease in someone so young."

"Okay," Lauren said. So they had a name for it, and she'd take medicine and it would clear up.

She looked at Josh. His face was gray. *Nope. Gonna ignore your face, babe.* "What's the plan, then?"

There was a pause. Another fucking *pause,* and suddenly, Lauren was shaking. She couldn't look at Josh, because . . . because . . .

"Now, don't panic," Dr. Bennett said. "What happens with this disease"—*disease?* That sounded horrible!—"is that your lungs create a fibrous tissue. Scarring. We don't know why. Some people who work with asbestos or fine particulates get it. Yours is called idiopathic, because we don't know why you have it." She paused, looking at both of them in turn to make sure they were following. *My husband is a genius, lady,* Lauren wanted to say. *You don't need to slow down for him.*

On the other hand, Lauren was having some trouble hearing. There was a persistent, high-pitched buzz in her ears. Defense mechanism, probably, to block out—

"The problem is, the scarring takes up room in your lungs. That's why you've had problems breathing."

"I really haven't! I mean, just a little. Once in a while."

Kwana nodded. "Right. And it's great that we caught it early. There are some very good medications that can slow this thing down."

"Great!"

"And oxygen to help you when you're short of breath."

"Wait. What? I don't need to be on *oxygen?* I

mean, I fainted one time! Twice! But one time after a long hike and not enough hydration, and the other time, because . . . because . . ." Her voice had the hint of hysteria in it, and she let it trail off.

"Well," Kwana said gently, "there will probably be times down the road when you will need it, and it'll make you feel significantly better. A lot less tired."

"But I'm fine. I mean, I really feel quite . . . quite good." She looked at Josh. He didn't look at her. He wasn't blinking. Just staring at Dr. Bennett.

Oh . . . shit. He shut down like this when big things happened. He just got really, really quiet. Like when his favorite professor had died a few months before they got married. He didn't talk, he didn't cry, he just went into this . . . nothingness. When she'd called his mom to ask if he was okay, she said he'd done the same thing when her father had died when Josh was twenty.

But they had *died*. She wasn't about to do that. Whatever was wrong with her, she'd handle. Joshua Park would not have a sick wife. She wouldn't put him in that position.

"Okay," she said, sounding more like herself. Good. Good. "So the meds, maybe oxygen in the future . . . anything else?"

There was another *pause*. "We'll get into respiratory therapy to maximize your lung function."

"Got it. Sure. And how long does this last?" No answer. "I mean, when will I be back to my old self?"

Kwana—Dr. Bennett—didn't answer for a second.

"What is the cure, *Kwana?*" Lauren asked loudly.

Josh turned to look at her, finally. Finally. "There is no cure," he said quietly.

The words took a few seconds to land.

"What?" Lauren shouted. Then, freakishly, she laughed. "Well, *that's* not helpful." She looked at both her doctor and her husband, then swallowed. "Seriously?"

"There's no cure at the moment, no," Dr. Bennett said. Lauren didn't want to call her Kwana anymore. Nope! They weren't going to be friends.

So if there was no cure, then that meant . . . well, it meant she'd have to deal with this the rest of her life.

Huh.

"I don't want you to panic," Dr. Bennett said. "This is a serious illness, but you're only twenty-six, Lauren. We honestly have no prediction for how well you'll do. Okay? You're very healthy otherwise. Let's not envision the worst just yet. I'm starting you on a medication called Ofev, which is very effective in slowing the fibers and scar tissue. A lot of patients swear by a combination of Chinese herbs, so I want you to try that as well. I've got all the information here."

"Okay," Lauren said, slightly reassured. "Great. Um . . . what's my long-term prognosis?"

"I don't want to jump the gun here."

"Tell me anyway," she said.

Kwana looked at Josh, who gave a small nod. "Well, our last line of defense is a lung transplant."

"Would I be okay then?"

"We'll cross that bridge if we have to, okay?"

Lauren looked at Josh.

Skin still gray. Jaw locked. Infrequent blinking. *Oh, no. No, no. No thank you.*

Josh knew a lot about medicine. A lot.

"Am I . . . am I going to get better?" she whispered.

Dr. Bennett leaned forward, folding her hands together. "Lauren, I'm very sorry, but as your husband said, there is no cure for this. There are some promising treatments on the horizon, but right now, I have to be honest with you. With IPF, the fibers keep growing until breathing becomes impossible. A lung transplant would be the final step. Otherwise, it's a terminal disease."

The world stopped. No sound, no smells, nothing. Just complete stillness.

Terminal. Final.

Terminal?

Lauren swallowed. Her eyes felt huge and cold. "So . . . I'm going to die?"

"We're not sure what your trajectory is going to be. There are only a handful of known cases in people so young."

"Can you answer the question? Am I going to die from this?" That loud voice, so rude.

Kwana didn't take offense. "We can't make any predictions. *Especially* in your case, since you're not even thirty."

"No predictions except that I'll die?" she squeaked.

"She will *not* die from this," Josh said, his voice hoarse and fierce, and for a second, hope leaped in Lauren's heart. She was married to a certified *genius* who just happened to make medical devices. He would figure this out in a matter of weeks, *Kwana.*

"This is a lot to process," Dr. Bennett said. "I recommend that you stay off Google and just read the literature in this packet."

"Why?" Lauren's voice was hard and loud.

"Because you should get your information from experts in the field," she said, handing over a folder. "Trust me."

She didn't remember leaving the building or getting into the car, but she must have, because Josh was driving, and they were gripping each other's hands, hard. Lauren stared out the window, vaguely registering the familiar sites—

the Big Blue Bug, Rhode Island's most famous resident. The capitol dome, the Superman building—so called because in the old television show, Superman had jumped over it, making Providence famous. There was Kennedy Plaza, the old Brown and Sharpe building. They pulled onto their street, into the parking lot, got out and walked into the building in silence, still clutching hands. She started toward the stairs, then walked through the lobby instead and pushed the button for the elevator.

The stairs would leave her breathless.

Tears gathered in her throat, and she swallowed hard.

The second they walked into the apartment, they both went to the couch and opened their laptops, almost exactly in sync, the only sounds their fingers on the keyboard.

Yeah, so Googling *wasn't* a great idea. She had to give Dr. Bennett credit for that.

The prognosis for a person with idiopathic pulmonary fibrosis was three to five years. Life post–lung transplant, so long as there were no complications, could last as long as five years. But lung transplants were tricky.

So, best-case scenario, Lauren *might* live to see forty.

But probably not.

She felt dizzy. Was this a dream? Was this whole life a dream, with her wonderful husband

and all their happiness, their beautiful apartment, the honeymoon, the trip to Paris? Would she wake up in her childhood bed, groggy and confused, Dad still alive?

She squeezed her hands together, because pinching herself felt too cliché. If she was thinking about things like clichés, then it couldn't really be happening, right? Also, the pillow on the chair across from her needed plumping. And she was hungry. Grilled cheese, maybe? So she probably wasn't stuck with a fatal disease. She probably wasn't dying.

Words from the computer floated in her brain. *Final treatment. Terminal. No cure. Breathing becomes impossible. Three to five years. Quality of life.*

Three to five years.

Last week, they'd gone sledding with Sebastian. Jen told her they were trying for another baby, and they got so silly, talking about celebrity baby names. And sure, Lauren had gotten out of breath laughing. But so had . . . yeah, no. She was the only one.

For a second, that moment came back to her, the warmth of her sister's house, the cocoa, the laughter . . . the way she couldn't seem to fill up her lungs with enough air.

Because her lungs were filling with fibers.

Oh, Jesus. Oh, God.

"Let's go to bed," Joshua said, and she jumped

at the sound of his voice. It was two o'clock in the afternoon, but he was right. Bed was the only option. They stripped down to their underwear and got in under the puffy duvet, then wrapped their arms around each other so tight it hurt.

They were both shaking.

No words. Not then. Neither one of them was crying. Not then. Not yet.

The truth sat in the room with them, dark and heavy, waiting to be let into their lives, their bed.

She would die young. Josh would be widowed.

She was not going to get better.

She had a terminal disease.

She had really wanted a baby instead.

23

Joshua

Month eight, letter number eight
October

Dear Josh,
I hope you're doing well, sweetheart. Eight months is a long time. I hope you're feeling happier and more energized these days.

So this month's task is pretty straightforward. Do something for your professional career, and try something you've been scared of doing.

You've got this. I believe in you.

Love,
Lauren

Well. That was a pretty crappy letter, if he was being honest. He'd gotten changed and poured a half glass of wine for this? He stalked around, his bare feet silent. Pebbles lay asleep on the couch, oblivious to his mood.

"A shitty letter, Lauren," he said out loud. "Sorry, was I taking too much of your time?" Was she too busy to write more than a few sentences?

Was he getting to be too much of a responsibility, and she only had a few Chicken Soup for the Soul platitudes to toss his way?

Rage swept through him, red and tarry, blotting out everything else, and before he could switch gears, before he could call his mom or Ben, before he could get to the gym and hit the heavy bag, before the quick brown fox could jump over anything, the red tar was everywhere and he was drowning in it. A far-off, still-calm part of his brain guided him to the cabinets. He heard a smashing noise and more yelling, and there was pain in his foot, a distant pain, and then he slipped and his head thunked against the floor and he was out.

He woke up to Pebbles licking his face. Her breath was awful. "Hi, puppy," he said, and his throat was sore and scratchy. Also, something was sticking into his back.

He was lying on the kitchen floor.

He sat up, wincing, and felt the back of his head. A good-sized lump was there. And there were shards of porcelain everywhere.

Polka-dotted porcelain.

He picked up a piece and looked at it. Lauren's coffee cup. She'd used it every morning. Actually, she'd bought four of them, because, she'd said, they'd be everyone's favorite. And they had been. Even his mother had liked them, and she wasn't a person who cared a whole lot about mugs. He remembered a weekend morning when Lauren had had her "three moms" over for coffee cake, and they'd all drunk from these mugs.

From the look of the mess on the floor, he'd broken each one. Yep. Four little handles scattered amid the ironically cheerful destruction.

There was a knock on his door. He went to it, limping slightly, and opened it. Creepy Charlotte.

"Hey, I heard some noise. You okay?" She looked him up and down. "You're bleeding, you know."

"Stop stalking me, Charlotte."

For a second, he wondered if Gertie the Medium had meant Charlotte, but if so, he would take that $500 back, thank you very much. He closed the door in her face, went back to the kitchen and surveyed the mess.

Nice job, asshole.

If Pebbles stepped on the broken mugs, she might cut her paw. He put her in the guest room to keep her safe, though she gave him a disappointed look. "Sorry, honey. I'll be back in a few minutes."

The cut on the bottom of his foot was fairly deep. He cleaned it out with hydrogen peroxide, welcoming the burn as punishment, and wrapped it in gauze. Then he cleaned up the kitchen and bloody footprints.

No more of Lauren's mugs to taunt him from

the cupboard each day, and a new scratch in the floor from his rage.

He'd had more red-outs in the past few years than he had in the rest of his life combined. Now that the rage had passed, he felt ashamed. Lauren had been busy just staying alive, and so what if her note was short? He was a shitty and ungrateful husband—widower—for not being more appreciative of these letters, even if this one wasn't his favorite. She'd been busy trying to live.

Josh sighed, got Pebbles and went up to the garden, careful to avoid looking over. Instead, he looked up at the sky. Almost sunset now. October's days were notably shorter, and Josh was relieved. August had been wretchedly hot, the weather and humidity seeming to suck the color and life from everything and replace it with sepia-toned pollution or bland, not-quite-real air from the AC.

After seeing Gertie, he'd fallen into a funk. He wanted to feel completely different after the visit—*my wife is in heaven and she sees me!*—but it didn't bring Lauren back. Was there a heaven? Maybe? He hoped so, for her sake.

But his problem wasn't the afterlife. It was the here and now. He skipped karate classes, not wanting to bring his gloom to the little kids, and emailed Asmaa, saying he had a big project to finish, so he couldn't help out at the center as much this month. She wrote back kindly, saying to take his time, and they'd be happy to see him whenever he could make it in.

It seemed so long ago that he'd been a married man. That his wife and he had sat in the rooftop garden, or at the Cape house, or downstairs, the two of them made safe by love.

Do something for his professional life, and try something he was afraid of.

He sighed. Pebbles jumped up next to him and put her head on his leg, and he petted her silky head, grateful for the perfect forgiveness of a dog.

Each year, Johnson & Johnson sponsored a giant medical device conference, and he'd gone every year since he was twenty, except for last year, when he was afraid to leave his wife. He could go again; he'd been thinking of it himself, more for a change of scenery than anything else. It was next week, so that would take care of Lauren's request for this month. But it didn't have the kismet feeling the volunteering letter had . . . the feeling that they were still in sync somehow, that she'd been able to read his mind.

As far as the "do something you're scared of doing," he wasn't sure what that meant. He'd presented at this conference before, and while he didn't love crowds, he wasn't phobic or anything. He just left when it got too overwhelming or loud.

What had Lauren had in mind?

He would never know.

A few days later, he flew out to San Francisco for the conference. He let the now-familiar refrain of the grieving run through his head. *The last time I was on a plane, Lauren was* . . . He'd posted on the forum about this, and it was a common experience; every experience clashing with a recollection of loss. For five hours, he stared out the window, watching America drift past below.

When they landed, he took a car to the hotel where the conference was held, signed in, got his badge and went up to his hotel room, which was very clean and generic, and on the second floor, per his request. He unpacked, ironed his shirt and looked at the conference program, marking which presentations and speakers he wanted to see. He knew some of them. Plenty of people likewise knew his name, because for a thirty-year-old, he was kind of a big deal. When he couldn't stall any longer, he brushed his teeth and went downstairs to the conference rooms and displays.

Shockingly, it was a relief. All these people who didn't know, all these people who just wanted to talk to him about work, new products on the market, trends in design, new technology.

For two days, he was immersed in the field he loved, the only one he'd ever considered working in. He went to the keynote lunch, given by a billionaire inventor who believed in global healthcare and pandemic preparedness. In workshops, he was greeted with respect and recognition. Twice, he saw his design for the neonatal monitoring bed in presentations, which gave him a quiet flare of pride.

Chiron Medical Enterprises, the company in Singapore who'd hired him to design a smart scalpel for spinal surgeries, was a sponsor of the conference. He'd sent them the final design and specs just last month. Alex Lang, the CEO, and Naomi Finn, the COO, found him and asked him to dinner. He accepted.

They met in the lobby and took a town car to an impressive restaurant at the base of the Bay Bridge, that other unsung wonder of San Francisco. Alex and Naomi flattered him, talked shop, told him funny stories and generally schmoozed him.

Sure enough, by the end of the second bottle of wine, the pitch came. "Josh, we'd love to have you work with us exclusively," Alex said. "You could live in Singapore, or you could stay in Rhode Island. And let's be honest, you can name your salary and benefits package. We want you to head up the design team, and we're willing to do what it takes to make it happen."

"That's very flattering," he said.

"Have you been to Singapore?" Naomi asked. "It's amazing. Seriously. I've lived in seven major cities, including Sydney and Paris, and Singapore is the most beautiful of them all."

He nodded, remembered to smile, and for a few minutes, he let himself picture being the type of guy who could live on the other side of the planet, who could walk cheerfully into a glass office and have two administrative assistants and a gaggle of engineers to do the mundane parts of his job.

"Fly out, on us," Alex said. "Have a look around. Bring your—hell, I don't know if you're even married."

The question was like a baseball bat to the head.

Answer, he told himself.

The pause was going on too long.

"I'm not," he said.

Naomi said, "That wedding ring is just to scare off any interested parties, then?"

They didn't know. They didn't *know.* If he told them now, he'd see their expressions change from interest to pity, or shock or compassion. "It's a cultural thing," he lied.

"Another one of the great things about Singapore is how multicultural it is," Alex said, and Joshua was off the hook as the pair extolled the benefits of the city-state.

When the conference ended the next afternoon, Josh was exhausted from all that time with other people. But he didn't want to go home just yet. The idea of going back now, in late October when the leaves had fallen in a heavy rain and windstorm and the city would be gray and dark . . . He decided to be spontaneous and stay.

Cookie Goldberg, his virtual assistant, switched his flight and booked him for another two days at the hotel. Then Josh texted Jen, Donna and his mom. Jen responded by saying that they might have to keep Pebbles forever, because Sebastian was so in love with her. She texted a picture of the boy, sound asleep, Pebbles sleeping next to him, her head on his pillow. Sweet.

Aside from a similar conference a few years ago, during which he'd never left the hotel, he hadn't been to San Francisco, not properly. A little sightseeing would kill some time. Had Lauren ever been here? He didn't think so.

So no memories, then. For now, he could be a guy who wasn't married, wasn't widowed. He could just be a normal person.

San Francisco was balmy, beautiful and overly gentrified. So many homeless people, so many new glossy, sleek apartment buildings to house the wealthy. He considered designing a pop-up shelter that could be folded and moved, but ten seconds on Google showed him it had already been done by a plethora of architects. He went to Japantown and Haight-Ashbury. Bought some gifts for the family. In Lower Pacific Heights, he stared for half an hour into a window of an aquarium store that had mystically beautiful tanks, filled with living plants and exotic fish, then ordered one to be shipped to Sebastian for a Christmas gift.

When his stomach growled, he ate lunch at the bar of a small Italian restaurant and watched the Red Sox lose to the Yankees. He imagined living in a number of Victorians, so different from their—his—loft. Were the people inside these homes happy, living in such a beautiful place? Was anyone widowed, wailing on their floor the way he'd wailed?

He walked and walked, soaking up the sunshine, admiring gardens and dogs—seemed like everyone had a dog in San Francisco. Pebbles and her friendly ways would fit right in. He found himself looking at the Ghirardelli sign, and stood in line to get an ice cream cone. It was worth the wait.

"Excuse me," said a young woman, maybe twenty, twenty-five. "Do you know how to get to the Golden Gate Bridge?" She wore a backpack and had pretty red hair. Almost the same color as Lauren's. Her eyes were green, though, not like Lauren's whiskey-brown. Give her a pair of contacts and a different haircut, though, and they could've passed for sisters.

"Sorry, I don't," he said after too long a pause.

"No worries! Have a nice day!" Off she went,

looking at her phone, probably texting her friend that she'd just met a creepy guy.

After a minute, he followed her. He had no destination in mind, and seeing the sunlight bring out the colors in her hair, so very, very close to Lauren's . . . it seemed like a beacon. Where was she going again? Ah, yes. The Golden Gate Bridge.

He'd never seen the Golden Gate Bridge up close. He was afraid of—

Do something you're afraid of. He was afraid of heights.

Thoughts of the girl forgotten, Josh summoned a Lyft to the bridge, suddenly on fire to be there as soon as possible.

It was more beautiful and graceful in real life than any photo. The sun was shining, and against the violently blue sky, the bridge did seem to glow. It stretched impossibly far across the water to Marin County. Sailboats and shipping vessels dotted the water, and birds flew above the bridge, below it, between its cables.

The bridge was ridiculously high. Really. It was *unnecessarily* high. Surely he could skip this and have a drink at the Top of the Mark and be done with it, right? Wouldn't that be easier? He could just . . . just . . . yeah, nope, he was already here.

Already, his heart was pounding at the thought of walking across it. Was he dizzy? He felt a little dizzy. A lot of people fell off this bridge, didn't they? No. No one fell. They . . . they jumped.

Shit.

Sweating, he started walking. Fast. He was wearing his hiking boots—the last time he'd worn them was with Lauren when they drove up to Acadia National Park last fall, but he couldn't think about that right now. He had panicking to do.

Just keep going, he told himself. *Haul ass. Get across and take a Lyft back to the hotel.*

He walked as fast as he could, staring straight in front of him, concentrating on the people. Cars shouldn't be allowed up here. That was a *horrible* idea. Cars were so heavy! Had this bridge ever snapped, or was that just in disaster movies? Shit. What about earthquakes?

Oh, God. He glanced to his left to see if the city was crumbling, and saw the water below him. Far, far below him. That was a mistake, looking down. His knees buckled, and suddenly he was on all fours, heaving for breath.

"You okay, mister?" someone asked.

"Yep," he said, his voice sounding overly loud.

"Are you having a heart attack?"

Probably. "Afraid of heights."

Could he get up? He didn't think so. His heart was shuddering in his chest, and his shirt was damp with sweat, despite the cool temperature and breeze.

He felt the tremor coming, felt the earth begin

to shudder . . . no, nope, that was just a pickup truck. But what about the wind? Was the bridge swaying? Was it about to break, and all these people would fall to their deaths, screaming, clawing, all the cars and trucks pouring into the bay, the noise thunderous and—

"One step at a time," came the voice. "You got this, bud. You can do it." A white hipster dude with a red beard reached out a hand and pulled him to his feet. "Deep breaths, yeah?"

"Yes," Josh said. He knew all about deep breaths, after all. All that respiratory therapy he'd done with Lauren.

It worked. His fear dropped from a ten to about an eight and a half. The hipster dude beamed at him. "So awesome that you're doing this. Good for you. He's afraid of heights," he added to the few onlookers. Most people ignored him, cruising past, looking at their phones or taking pictures. He appreciated their lack of interest.

"Need an escort?" Hipster Guy asked. "I'm walking to meet up with some friends over on the other side."

"Um . . ." He didn't have much choice, did he? He was on the damn bridge. He was stuck. He would take this up with Lauren later. In his imagination, anyway. Maybe it would be good to fight with her.

"I'm David," said the hipster. "From Arkansas originally, but you know, the culture out here is so intense, and I came out to see a friend a few months ago? And I was like, dude, I'm staying. Seriously. Arkansas can*not* compete with this place. Also, weed is legal, right? Just another perk."

Walking *was* slightly easier with David, because David did not stop talking to draw a breath. He was overcoming some issues of his own, right, doing great, eating clean, and he was so psyched to see other people, you know, confronting their fears and the past and future, and wasn't it, like, crazy that the world was so beautiful even with all the shit going on?

Josh tried not to look at anything other than the pavement in front of him, though his peripheral vision showed the cables that made the bridge stand. Would one snap? Would it hit him in the head and send him tumbling over the side, or would it hit him in the throat so he'd bleed out, clutching at the geyser of blood? Would this cause a chain reaction that would then send cars careening into pillars and the bridge crashing into the water, the people screaming—

"We're halfway across, dude," David said. "Let's take a minute so you can look around."

Josh stopped. He was shaking violently, but his knees hadn't buckled again. He kept his gaze fixed on the ground. If he didn't look up, did it count? It would. It did.

But Lauren would want him to see the view.

She loved new experiences. She loved heights, the ridiculous woman. She'd never backed down from anything, at least not that he knew of. That time in La Jolla, when she went hang gliding, and she was so happy, so *alive.*

He raised his eyes slowly, slowly, got his gaze about a foot off the ground, saw the glittering water, then looked back at the beloved pavement. If he ran, how long would it take him to get back on solid ground? Bicyclists whizzed past on the walkway, and hey, wasn't it a *walk*way, did they have to be so fast, and what if a car jumped the lane and killed him, and all these people, really, did they all have a death wish?

Don't be a loser.

Lauren's voice was so clear . . . the fond way she had said that line, the challenge he'd always accepted. He gripped the railing and forced his head up and kept his eyes open. For a second, the scene swam in front of him, and he thought he might vomit, or faint, or fall, but then the view came into focus.

San Francisco's buildings, white and sharp against the sky. Alcatraz. Marin. Boats and birds. He turned around and saw the Pacific spreading out, so blue and vast.

It was . . . stunning.

I hope you can see this, honey.

A deep breath that didn't quite work. Another one. Another, slower one. *Relax and breathe,* he used to say to his wife. *Relax and breathe, nice and slow.* If she could do it, so could he. After all, she'd been facing death. He was just being a wuss.

The blue was so intense against the sunlit bridge that the air seemed to shimmer. "It's beautiful," he said, though his knees were still shaking.

"Right?" David asked.

"Right."

"Check it out, dude. Fog's coming in." David pointed behind them, to the San Francisco skyline, and there was the legendary cloud bank, tumbling over itself. In seconds, it had erased the view and swallowed the bridge. Josh couldn't see the water, or the city, or the sky.

"I should get going, man. You headed to Marin? We can walk together if you want."

"No, no. I'll go back to the city. Thank you."

"You cool?"

"So cool." Josh stuck out his hand. "Thank you, David. This meant a lot to me."

"A pleasure . . . uh, what's your name?"

"Joshua."

"A pleasure, Joshua! Take care, dude!"

Some people were simply, undeniably decent. Radley. Jen. Darius. This guy.

The walk back was easier. Piece of cake, really, since he couldn't see how high up he was. He wove through the other pedestrians, dodged those taking photos. Dang. He should have taken a picture for Laur—

Nope. He couldn't take pictures for her anymore.

That thought would've dropped him a few months ago. This time, it only stopped him for a few seconds.

Then, he pulled his phone out of his pocket and took a shot of the bridge, the upper reaches fading into the now-gray sky. He texted it to his mom, Jen, Radley and Ben. Then, after a second's pause, added Sarah to the chat. What would Lauren say?

Walked over the Golden Gate Bridge like a boss. See you later, acrophobia.

He hadn't been a loser. He'd done something he was afraid of.

His wife would've been so proud.

24

Joshua

Month nine
November

On a cold, dark evening in November, Sarah came by with a letter.

"I have a date, or I'd be more sociable," she called as Pebbles whined and barked and wagged. "Bye!"

"Have fun," he said, picking up the envelope.

A date, huh? She did look really pretty, her hair shiny, red lipstick on. He knew she dated—well, Lauren used to tell him about her misadventures, and there was the pyramid scheme guy who'd come to his first, disastrous dinner party. But he'd never met her *boyfriend* per se. He'd just seen her a few days ago when Radley and she had come over to watch a movie, and she hadn't mentioned anyone, so maybe this was just another bad first date in the making.

Well. He had a letter from his wife to read.

He went through his pre-letter tradition— shower, clean clothes, a half glass of wine. Then he picked up the letter, holding it carefully, studying her handwriting, the fat swirl of the *J*, the long tail of the *a*.

Joshua, #9

Counting this letter, there were only a few more waiting for him. After that, she'd really be gone.

Nine *months* since she died. How could he have lived this long without her? It seemed like nine years, nine decades. Every memory was so precious, and yet . . . his throat tightened to think about it . . . every memory also receded further into the distance. Sometimes, he felt like he was remembering the memory, not the actual moments—remembering the times he remembered their wedding, going over every minute they'd spent together . . . well, except her last day. That one could stay suppressed for eternity as far as he was concerned.

He wanted to think of *her*, in real life. He wanted to hear her voice, smell her scent, not just describe it to himself. He'd watched the movies they'd taken of each other. Every one. He watched their wedding video at least a hundred times. He scrolled through thousands of their pictures on his computer.

He looked like a different person in those photos. He looked so . . . young. Even in the pictures where she had a cannula, or she was in the hospital, he looked happy, assured and in love. Dazzlingly in love, confident that he was loved back just as much.

At least he had given her that. All his love, his whole heart. He'd known such happiness, such love every damn day. And these letters reminded him of that.

With a deep breath, he opened this one reverently, slowly.

Hello, honey!

How are you? I wish I knew what time of year it was so I could give you better things to do . . . you know, like if I knew it was winter, I could say, "Make a snowman with some random children!" (Except you might get arrested on suspicion of being a pedophile, so maybe not that.) Or if I knew this month was May, I could say, "Plant a garden!" (Better! Make sure you do that in May!)

Last month's "task" was lame, and I'm sorry for that. I was trying to be well-rounded and wanted you to do something related to your career. It sounded like the advice you'd get in a fortune cookie. "Do something you're scared of." Lame, Lauren! (But if you did, I'm SO PROUD OF YOU!)

So this month's is better. But also worse. But better. You ready? You are? Good.

Kiss a woman. Not a peck on the cheek

to Jen or my mom . . . kiss a woman not related to you by blood or marriage.

Josh felt abruptly ill.

You can do this. You never have to see her again, but I'm guessing it's time. It's been nine months. Time for me *not* to be the last woman you kissed. Moss will grow on your lips if you don't use them. Everyone knows that. It will get too weird if you wait much longer (assuming you haven't already slept with half of the East Coast). And once you pass a year, it might take on too much significance. Do you know what I mean?

He didn't. He had not once considered kissing anyone since her death. He *absolutely* wanted her to be the last woman he kissed. Ever. In his entire life.

I know what you're thinking . . . that you'd be disloyal to me if you kissed someone. But it won't be, because if you did what I asked, I'm a tree now, and you need to start thinking about your future, which, aside from my tree-ness, I'm not in. Them's the hard facts, honey.

I'm so sorry. It's not what I would've

chosen, but then again, Josh, we were so happy. If my IPF helped bring us what we had . . . that beautiful, intense love . . . then maybe I *would* have chosen it.

But that's a letter for another time. As I'm writing this one, I want you to know I'm happy. We're sitting in your mom's living room on a Sunday morning, and she's making cinnamon rolls and it smells like heaven.

I love our life. I think I love it even more because of IPF, because yes, every day is a gift (sorry to sound so sappy). Would I be this appreciative of everything, from the smell of cinnamon to the sight of you in the shower? I don't know. I'd like to think I would, but I don't know. I DO know I love you more than I ever thought possible. You just brought me a glass of peppermint tea and smooched me, which brings me back to kissing . . .

Remember that song (you probably don't), but there's a song that says, "A kiss is just a kiss." This kiss you're about to have doesn't have to be a great kiss, or a meaningful kiss. Just do it, as they say. You might even like it, and that would be wonderful as far as I'm concerned. You're a great kisser, and that talent shouldn't die with me. Okay? Okay.

But, honey, our life together ended. I want you to have a new life. I hope with all my heart that these letters are helping you. Who knows? Your second wife could be burning them in the sink. But I think not.

I love you, honey. I want you to be as happy as you made me.

Lauren

He drained his wine and poured some more. Drank that down fast, too. Looked at Pebbles. "She wants me to kiss someone. A woman. You don't count, sorry." He raked his hands through his hair, tugging.

He knew how her mind worked, and in Lauren's head, it all made perfect sense. A nice kiss, just to get it over with. Enough of a kiss to—maybe—stir some feelings, even if they were simple lust.

He did miss kissing. God, he missed it. He missed sex and hugging and touching, and laughing and her hair, and her softness, and her breasts and her legs and her feet and her neck. He missed kissing every part of her. "There is nothing hornier than a marathon makeout session," she used to say, her voice breathless, face and throat flushed, rosy with love.

He called Radley. "Got time for a drink?" he asked.

"I do! Where?"

An hour later, he and Radley sat at the Eddy, the type of bar that had drinks containing egg whites and burnt rosemary and eucalyptus-infused ice cubes, which Josh knew because he was sipping one right now. Liquid courage and all that. He could see why Lauren and her friends had loved "drinkies," as they called it.

Radley, who had chosen a much more manly drink—Coopers' Craft bourbon, straight up—was delighted at the letter's task. "God! I wish I'd met her! She sounds like an angel with a dirty sense of humor."

"That's a perfect description."

"So how do you feel about this?"

Josh cut him a look. "Please, no therapy tonight."

Radley laughed. "Okay. Why am I here, other than the fact that I make you look cooler?"

"Do you know anyone who would kiss me?"

"I would kiss you. Right here, right now."

Josh laughed. "That's very kind."

"A woman, huh?" He tapped his black metal ring against his glass. "Do you like this ring, by the way? I'm thinking it's a little much."

"I like it."

"Okay, good. You look nice, by the way, but untuck your shirt a little, like this, so you don't look like my grandfather." He reached over and tugged Josh's shirt on the left side so it hung free, then took a sip of his bourbon. "Five more months at Banana Republic, and then I'll be a licensed therapist. I cannot wait. I'll have an advanced degree and can fix people for a living." He smiled, and Josh smiled back.

"That's great, Radley." *I'm proud of you,* he wanted to say, but who was he to be proud? He'd had nothing to do with it. "Um, it's really impressive. Working and going to school full-time . . . it's a lot." He paused. "And also, you're a good friend."

"True, true," Radley murmured. "Throw me a party in your fab apartment when I graduate?"

"Of course. I'll even cook."

Radley smiled. "Thank you! Okay, back to the kiss. I know someone. Yes. She's wicked nice, a little Worcester, you know? A girl-gangster vibe, a little roller derby . . . tats, piercings, leather, the usual. But super pretty. Wicked, *wicked* pretty. And she's a very nice person. Really fun."

"What's her name?"

"Cammie. Should I text her right now?"

Josh felt sweat break out on his forehead. "No, no. Uh . . . no. I'd like to think about it."

"Let's do it. No time like the present." Josh winced, but said nothing as Radley's thumbs began flying over his phone. Radley narrated as he typed. "Hi, Cams, I have a friend who would love to meet you for a date, okay? He's a doll, but he'll be nervous. Been off the market for a while. Love you!" He looked up at Josh. "There."

"I feel a little sick."

"That's a good sign!"

Seconds later, Radley's phone chirped. His face lit up. "She says she's in, text me his info." Radley looked at him. A few more taps, and Josh's info was delivered. "Let's order some food, okay? I'm starving."

Cammie was indeed wicked, wicked pretty. In fact, Josh's mouth dried up when she walked into the same bar four days later. Holy crap. She wore a formfitting white dress with a deep V in the front, high-heeled red shoes and a red leather jacket, and everyone in the bar turned to look at her. Dark tumbling hair, very long but natural-looking eyelashes, red lipstick. She had a tattoo of black barbed wire around her wrist, and somehow, it all worked.

She was *incredibly* hot. You know. If he was being objective.

"Josh, right? How you doin'?"

He closed his mouth and stood up. "Hi, Cammie. Uh . . ." His brain wasn't working. "Nice . . . nice to meet you. Um . . . is Cammie short for anything?" Was he making sense? It didn't seem like it.

"Short for Cameron," she said. "My mom was hooked on those shows where girls had boy names. *90210*, *Gilmore Girls*, you know." He didn't, but nodded anyway. "Is Josh short for anything?"

He hesitated. "Joshua."

"Oh, right." She extended her hand for him to . . . kiss, it seemed. He took it and shook it awkwardly, as if it were Pebbles's paw. "Very nice to meet you, Joshua," she said. "I was totally psyched when Radley texted the other night." She sat down, and Josh did the same. "What a doll that guy is, right?"

"Absolutely." He swallowed.

"How did you meet him?"

"He . . . he helped me in Banana Republic and we . . . well, we became friends." He opted not to tell her about the sobbing.

The server came over, his eyes glued on Cammie's breasts, which, to be fair, everyone could see a lot of. It *did* seem a shame to hide them. "Welcome to the Eddy. What can I get you?"

"Grey Goose straight up with a twist of lemon, stirred," she said.

"A woman who knows what she wants," the server murmured to her cleavage. It took him another minute to force his eyes to Josh. "Sir?"

"Oh, I'll have, um . . ." Josh fumbled with the menu. "The Apple Double Dutch?"

The server couldn't keep from a slight eye roll. It *was* one of the more precious drinks on the menu. "Any food for you two?"

"We'll have a charcuterie board, hon. Some meat, some cheese, you choose for us," Cammie said, and Josh liked that she was bossy and friendly at the same time. The waiter drifted away, leaving them alone.

She smiled. Wow. Could he be attracted to her? She was certainly beautiful. Tall, curvy, great legs, confident. She also seemed nice. There was nothing not to like so far.

"So Josh, tell me about yourself, honey. Radley says you're a good guy."

"I'm a medical engineer." *Boring, hon,* he could almost hear Lauren say.

"What does that mean?"

"I design medical devices." *Still boring.*

"Like what? Like . . . I don't know. Stethoscopes?"

"Well, those have already been designed, but yes." He ran through some of his easier-to-describe devices—the needle that sensed blood flow, the chair for people with mobility issues.

"Oh, pissah!" she said, clapping her hands together. "I mean, that's awesome, Josh. You must be wicked smart. My uncle Lou? He could use one of your chairs. My God, that man does not take care of himself. Diabetes, but does that stop him from drinking regular Coke all day and eating shit? No. It does not."

Their drinks and food came, and the waiter smiled again at Cammie's breasts. Josh took a swallow of his cocktail, which was really quite delicious.

Cammie took a delicate bite of cheese. "So tell me, Josh, how is a good-looking guy like you in need of a . . . whatchamacallit. A matchmaker."

Here it came. It was still so hard to say. "My wife . . . died last winter."

"Oh, *fuck* me. Hon, I'm so sorry."

"Yeah. Thank you." He took a big swallow of his drink, appreciating the warmth and floatiness that wafted through him. Girly drink or not, it was doing the trick.

Stay in the game, Josh. Don't be a loser.

Cammie leaned forward and covered his hand with her own. Her eyes were impossibly blue. Blazingly blue. Did people still wear tinted contact lenses, or was she just blessed with actual turquoise eyes? "So you're lonely," she said.

Such a simple sentence. He felt himself getting choked up. *Do not cry now, loser.* Another swallow of the appley drink. He nodded, then shrugged, trying for a smile.

"Aw, honey, you poor baby. Of course you need a little guidance, then. Ease back into the dating scene. Radley was a hundred percent right in texting me."

His drink was gone, and so was hers. His head felt a little detached from his body, but when she gestured to the waiter for a second round, he didn't contradict her. "Where are you from?" he asked.

"Worcester." She pronounced it "Wistah,"

instead of "Wooster" like everyone else in New England, marking her as someone who'd grown up there. The waiter brought their second round and food. Josh's drink tasted even better now.

"So what do you do, Cammie?" he asked.

"A little of everything, frankly," she said. "I'm a hairstylist part-time."

"Your hair *is* very pretty," he said. "So shiny." Was that a dumb thing to say? Probably.

She beamed. "Thanks!" Maybe not, then. She picked up another piece of cheese and nibbled on it with her perfect teeth. Her lipstick somehow did not smear on the cheese, or her martini glass, for that matter. Women and their magic. Their good smells and lotions and makeup and hair stuff.

He liked women.

Josh realized he was a little drunk. Not necessarily a bad thing in his case, socializing-wise, and he'd walked here, so driving would not be an issue. "What's your dream job?" he asked, surprising himself. *Thanks, alcohol!*

"Oh, my God, I can't believe you asked that. What a great question! Most men are just interested in . . . well. You know." She straightened up. "I would *love* to have my own business. A salon, but also a cocktail bar, right? Get this, though. It's just for women."

Josh sat back, the better to listen (and not wobble).

"So you come in, see, and you get your nails done or hair cut"—Cammie gestured extravagantly—"and there'd be this makeup bar, like at Sephora? Except not grubby. Super clean. And so you could beautify right there for a small fee after your mani or haircut, with a consultant or not. Your choice. And then—this is the genius part if I do say so myself—you go to the back room, or maybe the front room, and there's cocktails and a cute bartender!"

"Amazing!" Josh said.

"Right? So you could talk with your friends, make some new acquaintances, maybe, and hang out." She sat back, pleased by her pitch. "I'm gonna call it Shine, because, like, your nails, your hair *and* your personality can all shine."

"What a great idea," he said sincerely. "I would go there. I mean, if I were a woman."

"I know! Tell me the truth. Your wife would've loved a place like that, wouldn't she?"

"She definitely would have. And all her friends would've, too."

"See! I just gotta save some more money, and then it'll happen. Dream big, my ma always says. So in the meantime, I do a little of this and a little of that. I'm saving up." A big smile.

He did like her. Very much.

They smiled and sipped and chatted, and while there was a pleasant rolling feel to the floor, Josh was actually having a good time.

"Tell me more about your wife," she said, and he did. He told her about how happy they were, how many fun things they did, the places they'd gone, how even when she was at her sickest, Lauren never stopped being positive and kind and perfect.

Cammie had tears in her eyes. "I hope I meet someone like you someday, Josh," she said, which was odd, because that day was today, wasn't it?

"She wrote these letters for me to read every month after she died," he said, again surprising himself. "She said she wanted to walk me through this first year without her."

"Oh, my God." Cammie's mouth wobbled, and she took a cocktail napkin and carefully wiped under her lashes. "That's beautiful."

"I thought so, too."

"Your guardian angel."

He hated that term, but . . . "Exactly. And every month in the letter, she gives me something to do, so I'm not just sitting around our apartment, lost."

"Seriously? What does she tell you to do?"

"Well, the first thing was just go to the grocery store. Then, you know, have people over for dinner. Get a new couch. See a, um . . . a medium."

"Oh, my God! How was that? Was it amazing? I'm a total believer."

"It was pretty incredible," he admitted.

"My cousin? She has flashes like that? Totally random, but it knocks your socks off. Like once? She said my grandmother had made my dress for my first Communion? She's like, 'Grandma is showing me the dress she made for your first Communion,' and I'm like, 'Oh, my God, I loved that dress.'" She smiled fondly at the memory. "It had pockets. Then my mother said that my cousin *would* know that because Gran made all the first Communion dresses for her granddaughters, but still. She knew about the pockets, right?"

"Yes," Josh said, though he wasn't sure if that was an appropriate response. "This lady was very . . . accurate."

"Such a gift. God bless her." She made the sign of the cross, and Josh's eyes followed her hand up to her shiny hair, then down to her lovely cleavage, then left, then right, and whoo! His eyes were getting a little rebellious, weren't they? A little maverick, those eyes.

Their second round of drinks was gone, the room was spinning slightly, and Josh decided, what the hell, he'd tell her. "So for this month, my wife wanted me to kiss someone. A woman."

He probably hadn't needed to add that last part.

"Seriously? That was her thing for you?"

"Yes."

Cammie's brilliant eyes welled again. "I think that's so . . . kind. So fucking romantic."

"Me, too," Josh said, though again, he wasn't quite sure his answer was appropriate, since he couldn't exactly remember the last sentence out of Cammie's mouth. No more drinks for him.

"I don't usually kiss my clients, but I'm gonna make an exception for you."

"Thank you." He smiled. A second later, a distant bell chimed. "Wait. What . . . what did you just say?"

"I'll make an exception for you, sweetie. Abso-fuckin'-lutely."

"You called me . . ." What was the word she used? "A client?"

"Sure." She shrugged. "But I could see us becoming friends, too."

So nice! "Me, too." What were they talking about again? "Um . . . the client part."

She tipped her head, her shiny hair falling to one side. "What about it, hon?"

"Why am I your . . . client?"

She frowned. "Oh. Radley didn't tell you?"

"Tell me what?" Josh asked.

She rolled her eyes, then smiled. "Okay." She lowered her voice. "I'm a working girl."

"Sure. You cut hair."

"And I'm *also* a working girl." She laughed a little, a nice sound.

But Josh's foggy brain couldn't quite make the . . .

"I'm a member of the oldest profession," Cammie said, clearly amused.

The riddles weren't helping. He didn't quite get it and sensed he didn't want to.

She leaned forward. "I'm a consensual sex worker," she whispered.

"Oh," Josh said. A second later, he remembered to close his mouth. "Radley . . . Radley knows this?"

"Of course! That's why he called me, Josh."

"Oh." He rubbed his hand across his face. "I thought we were on a . . . date."

"We are, hon. You just pay me afterwards."

"Oh." He was saying that a lot.

"I'm my own boss, and I make quite a good living," she said. "Another year, I'll have about a hundred grand for Shine."

"Wow. That's . . . wow."

"I like the work," she said and she gave him a wink. "Do you have a problem with a woman who does this for a living?"

"Is it legal? Like, are you breaking the law right now?"

"Not a hundred percent legal. But I pay taxes. I tell the IRS I'm a consultant. Which, you know, I like to think I am."

"I see." Was *he* breaking the law right now?

"Check, please," Cammie called, and the waiter

came over. Josh felt like he was blinking a lot. He took out his wallet and left a big tip.

"Should we go to your place?" Cammie said.

"Here's the thing," Josh said.

"Let's talk outside," she whispered. "In case there's any undercover po-po around here."

He followed, because he wasn't sure what else to do. Undercover po-po? That would suck! Was he about to be arrested? Oh, God, what would his *mother* think? She'd kill him. Jen would never let him see the kids again, and—

It was a cool night, and the air helped the brain fog lift. They walked down the alley, like any good prostitute and her john. About halfway down, Josh stopped.

"Cammie, I don't know how this works, but—" he said.

"That's fine, sweetie. We can do whatever you want. You just have to Venmo me three grand."

Jesus. That was a lot. Not that he'd ever paid for sex before, but that was a very high hourly rate. *Focus, idiot,* he told himself. "What I mean is, I don't know how it works, but I don't need to know because . . . I don't want to sleep with you." He felt himself flush, afraid he might hurt her feelings. "Also, I feel like I might be breaking the law," he said. "Which I generally don't do."

"Oh. A good Catholic boy?"

"Lutheran."

"Most of my clients are Catholic. I mean, this *is* Rhode Island."

"Right."

Cammie thought a minute. "Okay. Here's the deal. You're sweet. You're lonely. I love your story, and you're cute. I'll kiss you for free. Anything else, you pay."

"I didn't *want* anything else. Not because you're not beautiful or . . . you know. You're very sweet and likable. And beautiful. I'm just . . ." He swallowed. "I'm still in love with my wife."

The words sounded huge in the alley.

"Aw, sweetie. I get that. I do." She leaned against the brick building. "I would kill to have someone be that in love with me."

"I'm sure there are *many* people in love with you," he said honestly.

She shrugged, smiling. "True. I just haven't found the one, as they say. Well." She tilted her head. "You ready to be kissed?"

"Oh. Um. Sure." His face felt hot, and his hands were clammy.

"You want tongue?"

"No, thank you."

"God. The manners on you." She smiled, then leaned in and kissed him, their lips interlocking. His hands went to her waist. Her lips were very smooth and firm, and it was . . . nice. Quite nice. Lovely, in fact. He didn't hate it. It just felt . . . new.

Then he pulled back. "Thank you."

"You're welcome. Thank you, too, hon." She wiped a little lipstick from the corner of his mouth. "We could be friends, you know."

"I'd like that."

She ruffled his hair. "Okay. Well, I got another date at ten, so if you don't need me anymore . . . ?"

"I'm good. Thanks."

"Okay. Can I call you an Uber? I'm getting one for myself."

"I'll walk. Take care, Cammie."

"You too, hon. See you around."

He started walking toward the river, then turned around. "Hey, Cammie."

"Yeah?"

"If you want an investor for Shine, let me know."

She folded her arms and gave him a fond smile. "You. You're the sweetest thing ever. I just might take you up on that."

He lifted his hand and turned around. The walk should clear his head. Two cocktails were one and a half too many, he thought. He pulled out his phone and tapped Radley's name.

"Hello, hello!" Radley said.

"Cammie's a working girl," he said.

"I know. So how was it?"

"You set me up with a prostitute."

"I thought I made that clear."

"You did not."

"Whoops. Um . . . are you super angry?"

"No," he said. "She's great. Very genuine."

"Did you . . ."

"Kiss her? Yes. And that was it."

"Got it. Let's try to be more clear with each other moving forward, okay?" Radley said.

"I'm not the one who—"

"I have a date. Gotta run. Bye!"

Everyone had a date tonight, it seemed. Jen had asked him if he would babysit so she and Darius could go out (his mother had leaped at the chance when he said he was busy). Sarah had mentioned she was going on a rare second date. Radley now. Cammie, even if hers was a business transaction.

Well, he'd had a date, too. Sort of.

Cammie wasn't his type, of course. His type was Lauren. He'd only ever been in love once. He might not ever be again.

But he'd kissed a woman tonight, and it had felt nice. He hadn't crumpled in grief, he hadn't yearned for more. More than anything, he was glad it was over.

Lauren had been right. Get it out of the way, keep moving forward. "Did *you* know she was a consensual sex worker?" he asked her out loud.

He'd bet she was laughing somewhere in the Great Beyond.

He hoped so. She'd had the best laugh in the world.

25

Lauren

Thirty-five months left
March

Daddy,

I am a smug married. I love being married. Marriage is the best thing ever, and I can't believe how happy we are. We've been married for five weeks, and every day is like a dream come true.

Our wedding—shoot, Dad, would you like to hear about our wedding? You would! Great! I know you were there in spirit, but this is my official update to you, assuming you can read in the Great Beyond.

All signs were pointing to doom. First, I caught a cough from one of the little germ sponges at the Hope Center, because I've been volunteering, reading and doing art projects. Anyway, I had this cough for a month. Then I apparently lost six pounds (coughing burns a lot of calories) and had to have my dress tightened. Then there was a huge storm two days before the wedding, and it was expected to park over Rhode Island for the whole weekend and either snow or rain or both. The downside of choosing Valentine's Day for your wedding.

The storm blew out to sea. Thanks for that, Dad! And my cough seemed to disappear. You are one good guardian angel.

So . . . I got to the church early for the rehearsal the night before. It was chilly, but it had that good church smell, you know? Candles and incense, furniture polish and good intentions.

I stood there for a few minutes and thought of you, Daddy. You've been gone for six years now, and I can't believe so much has happened to me without you. This especially. You would love Josh. You would've pretended not to like him at first, but you would love him like a son. He would've asked for your blessing before he proposed, and you would've lectured him on how special I am, then hugged him and tried not to cry.

And at the wedding, you would've walked me down the aisle. You would've tried to smile and you would've patted my hand, happy tears in your eyes. You would've called me your little girl and told me how beautiful I looked. You would've shaken Josh's hand and told him he'd better take care of me.

So, standing there in the church, all by myself. I pretended you were there, and I pretended to link my arm through yours, and I walked down like you were next to me, and I cried my damn head off.

How could I be getting married without you? Why couldn't you have lived, Dad?

You were the best father, Dad. The best.

For a second, I thought I would be a wreck for the wedding, mopey and weepy, like Mom. But I guess I got it out of my system, and when Josh came in, he could tell I'd been crying, and he said how proud you'd be of me. He told me how he went to the cemetery and promised you that he'd take good care of me and never let me feel unloved.

You see, Daddy? I picked a winner. I know you love him, Dad. I know you approve.

Okay, back to the happy stuff. The day of, I was SO happy. I was just floating, Dad! I also looked gorgeous, if I do say so. Darius walked me down the aisle. (Mom passed when I asked her. Sigh.) But hey! Darius is the world's best brother-in-law, and Jen is damn lucky, too. Sebastian was our ring bearer and the CUTENESS!

My dress was so pretty . . . I tried to pick out something my daughter will want to wear someday, and not something that would make her scream with laughter. (We hope to have at least two daughters, like you and Mom did, Dad, because where would I be without Jen?) So it was Audrey Hepburn fabulous, as you no doubt saw. Josh wore a suit—I thought he was handsome in cargo pants, but MY GOD. I saw his face and thought, *I am so lucky. He loves me. He loves me!*

His mom was happy-crying through the whole thing. It was so sweet. I didn't peg her as a crier, and there she was. She blew me a kiss as I walked up the aisle.

Daddy . . . when we said our vows, Josh's voice was so gentle and . . . perfect. Neither of us cried. It was almost too important for tears. I looked into his eyes, and I never meant anything more in my life when I said I would love, honor and cherish him all the days of my life.

The reception was so much fun. Even Mom had fun. There were toasts, and Jen bawled and was also hilarious, and we all danced till we dropped. Seriously, I thought I was going to faint at one point, the downside of wearing a wedding gown. But at one point, when we were slow-dancing, Josh whispered, "You know what I want?" and I said, "What's that, honey?" and he said, "I want to take my wife home."

And Daddy, that was everything. Wife. Husband. Home. Us.

Yes, he carried me over the threshold.

It was perfect. I'm so happy, Dad. Know that. Feel that. Your little girl is so happy.

In retrospect, the incident during their honeymoon was the first big warning.

Their rented house sat on a huge cliff overlooking the ocean and was impossibly pretty. The flowers, the wild roosters crowing at all hours, the abrupt and glorious drenching rains followed inevitably by a rainbow, and the clear, warm water . . . it truly was paradise. How did people visit Hawaii and leave? Lauren didn't know.

Plus the great married sex. There was a safety now, a comfort and security that gave her the ability to let go of any inhibitions, knowing that if it was awkward or silly or just didn't work out (for example, her pathetic attempt to talk dirty), they'd laugh and move on and learn together. Long hours in bed, walking naked around the house, eating pineapples and mangoes, feeling like a goddess in this tropical utopia with her man . . . the happiness brought her to tears sometimes.

Forever. All the days of my life. Forsaking

all others. The beautiful words of the wedding ceremony kept echoing in her head, so full of promise and meaning, enacted every time they made love, every time they talked. They had deep conversations about their childhoods, and she learned things she'd never known about him, and told him things she'd never told anyone, and their love deepened and grew even more.

At night, if he fell asleep first, she'd stare at his beautiful face, her heart thrumming with love. She would take such good care of him. Make him so happy. He deserved everything, her hardworking, earnest, brilliant, quiet, kind and sometimes awkward husband, and she would give it to him.

They ate sushi and poké and tried to pronounce long Hawaiian words properly. The beach was an easy walk downhill from their cliff house, and the walk back was good cardio, enough to make her winded and sweaty. Every day, they swam and played in the waves, lay on the sand and laughed when it rained on them and just waited till the sun came back out a few minutes later. They tried surfing . . . Josh was physically perfect but adorably clumsy, but Lauren caught a few waves, and the feeling of being propelled by the force of the ocean made her giddy.

One day, they drove to the western side of the island to see the Nāpali state park and maybe Hanakapi'ai Falls. It was a rugged trail, but they both loved hiking. They packed food and lots of water, and got lost in paradise. Holding hands when they could, walking through the thick forest, swatting mosquitoes. The birdsong was almost deafening.

At the base, they stood in awe at the four-hundred-foot falls, the mist shimmering, the walls of the hills bursting with moss and ferns that grew right out of the shale. They swam in the frigid water, laughing and wrapping their arms around each other. Ate the picnic lunch they'd packed, then sat in a silence that wrapped them in honey-golden contentment and wonder.

But the ascent was harder; a brief rain shower had turned the trail to slick mud. They stopped to rest a few times, and Lauren felt so tired she wondered aloud if she could just lie down and grab a nap. Her limbs felt heavy and achy, but what choice did she have? When they finally made it to the car, both damp with sweat, she was breathing fast and hard. Josh, damn him, caught his breath almost immediately. She shouldn't be this winded, she thought. She was in great shape, she'd drunk plenty of water, had two granola bars, a sandwich and mango slices, she . . . whoops . . . things were graying out, and she seemed to be flowing down toward the earth, just like the waterfall.

The next thing she knew, she was lying on the ground, staring at a flower, because there were flowers everywhere on this island. So pretty. They should move here. Also, it was hard to breathe. Her damn asthma. It felt like there was a leather belt cinched around her chest, getting tighter with every second.

"Honey! Lauren! Honey!" Josh was there, and she tried to smile, but her chest hurt, and her breath squeaked.

"Inhaler," she whispered. He was already fumbling in the backpack and quickly pulled it out and handed it to her. She took a hit, then another, and her breathing eased a bit.

"Your lips are blue," he said, and his voice was shaking.

A small crowd had gathered. "Want me to call 911?" someone asked.

"No," she said at the same time Josh said yes. He scooped her up and carried her to the side of the road to wait.

"Thank God you . . . work out, babe," she said, still puffing. "It'd be so embarrassing . . . if you had to drag me." Big breath. "For you, that is. Not me." He smiled, but it didn't quite fool her. He was worried.

Blue lips. That was a first. Residual cold from the swim? The elevation? Some weird allergic reaction to the fruit?

The EMTs gave her oxygen and said fainting wasn't that uncommon after this hike, especially if a person wasn't in great shape.

Rude. She *was* in great shape. She just had asthma. "Ride in ambulance, check!" she said as they unloaded her at the hospital. "This was thrilling. Thanks, guys! Mahalo!" They did that cool thumb-pinkie wave and wished her well.

Josh's face was somber, but she reassured him. The ER doctor wasn't worried. He gave her a five-day course of prednisone, listened to her lungs and said she sounded like someone with asthma. "It's probably the exertion coupled with the difference in humidity, but everything else looks good," he said. "Make sure you drink lots of water and have a good dinner tonight. Your oxygen saturation is ninety-five, which is on the low side of normal. You might be a little anemic, given that you're a woman who gets her period, which can also cause a drop in O2 sats. You said you're on your honeymoon, so if you've been hitting the mai tais, back off on that, because alcohol can make you dehydrated, which doesn't help anything."

"Killjoy," Lauren said. Mai tais were the new love of her life. Ah, well. There was always tomorrow.

It took Josh a full day to stop checking to see if she'd faint again. She had to admit, she kind of loved being treated like a delicate orchid. The honeymoon progressed with no further incidents . . . just love. And fun. Joshua got a tan. Lauren's nose sunburned a little. They took an inner tube ride down an old plantation canal through the rainforest. Snorkeled with turtles and brilliant-colored fish. They went jet-skiing, and saw a pod of spinner dolphins who played with them for a few minutes before darting off into the cerulean ocean. One night, they ate at a little shack-like restaurant and heard a Hawaiian singer, and the music was so lovely and happy. Lauren sat with her back against Josh, and the singer dedicated a song to "the young lovers at table four." So, so romantic.

Best of all was going back to their pretty little rented house each night, giving their food leftovers to the stray cat who had marked them as softies, and watching the sunset, holding hands.

It was hard to leave.

"We'll come back," Josh promised. "Every few years, how's that? This house, every time. Maybe we can even buy it if it ever goes on the market."

Sometimes she forgot he was wealthy. Well. *They* were wealthy now. Josh wouldn't sign a prenup, even when she had said she wouldn't mind. "That would indicate a lack of faith in our future," he'd said in his serious way. "And my faith in our future is absolute." Lauren asked Stephanie what she thought, and Steph smiled and said, "Josh has never once made me question his judgment. I'm not going to start now."

So yes, a house in Hawaii wasn't out of the question. And hey, she made a decent living, too.

It wasn't like she brought nothing to the table.

Back home, her dry cough returned. After a couple of weeks, she went to the doctor, who drew blood and tested her for the usual viruses, and everything was negative or normal.

So she didn't worry.

Just before the wedding, they'd moved into a bigger apartment in the same mill building where Lauren had lived. It had more character than Josh's building, so he sold his place and they bought a three-bedroom with access to the rooftop garden.

Oh, the joy in making it lovely and warm—her specialty, after all. She turned one bedroom into his study and got lounge chairs and a table for the garden up top. He had to sit in the middle of the roof, given his fear of heights, which she thought was cute. The second bedroom could be for guests, though they agreed they'd eventually want a house. For now, the apartment was absolutely perfect. They had friends over, like real grown-ups. One Sunday, they made dinner for their mothers, Jen, Darius and Sebastian, who now called Joshua "Unca Josh." Seeing him play with her nephew was a preview of coming attractions. Oh, he'd be such a good father! Maybe even as good as her own.

Though Josh was a workaholic, Lauren made him limit his computer time on weekends so they could cook together, take walks, go to the farmers' market and buy beautiful mushrooms and tomatoes. Work was going great—Bruce the Mighty and Beneficent loved her and gave her some plum assignments. They had him and his husband, Tom, over for dinner, and moved from boss-employee to friends.

At her annual review, she got a nice raise and an office of her own, which made Lori Cantore hiss with jealousy. Lauren didn't care; Lori was just that type, and she had Louise and Santino as work friends. The first thing she put on her desk was a picture of her and Josh, taken in the lush yard of their house on Kauai, the glorious sunset in the background.

Every Thursday night, she volunteered at the Hope Center, and helped with the open house on the first Sunday of each month. Josh donated a 3-D printer and hit up RISD for a grant. (They had ignored Lauren when she asked, but for their golden boy, anything. It was for a good cause, so who cared how it got done?) She saw her sister for lunch at least once a week, and she and Josh babysat so Darius and Jen could go out.

Twice a month, she made sure to go out with her girlfriends—Sarah, Mara, sometimes Asmaa and Louise, too. She didn't want to be that woman who disappeared after marriage, and while being with Josh was her absolute favorite thing, she wanted to remind both of them that she had other people she loved.

Every morning, Josh made her breakfast. He cooked her dinner once a week; she loved cooking, and he didn't, but it was the thought that counted. He set up a weekly flower delivery for her office, so every Monday as she shook off the faint melancholy that the weekend had ended, there was a fresh bouquet of flowers in her office, never with lilies, because they gave her a headache. The fact that he remembered that about her was as romantic as the flowers themselves.

He still worked a lot, often leaving bed while she slept. On the nights when she did something without him, he worked, and if she fell asleep watching a movie on a Sunday afternoon, she'd wake up to see him with his laptop, working on a design that would save humanity from whatever problem he had in his sights.

One night after they'd made love and lay tangled in the bed, heart rates returning to normal, she said, "Do you remember the first time we met? You told me I was too pretty and shallow. You could barely deign to look at me."

He looked at her with a half smile. "I do remember."

"Was I so bad?"

He shrugged. "You were so . . . different from me. So confident and popular and . . . socially graceful. But I think even then, I knew."

"Knew what?"

"Knew you'd be trouble." His hand grazed her ribs, tickling her.

Oh, God, she loved him. She loved *them*. His hermit days were over, thanks to her, and he learned to live more like a human and less like a feral raccoon. He emptied the trash before it was overflowing and tried (though failed) to wipe down the counters so they were spotless. He said he loved her daily, and he still blushed over the words sometimes. He made small talk with her mother and hugged Jen awkwardly when she came over. And when he looked at her with those dark-flame eyes, she felt him in every cell in her body.

Life, as they say, was perfect. Every day was so full, so peaceful, so bright with joy and warm with contentment. When she thought of the future, Lauren felt a palpable thrill zing through her blood. Babies. (They would be *so* cute! Maybe Josh would do that DNA test so they'd know his ethnic background on his paternal side a little more, since Steph claimed not to know.) They'd take vacations. Buy a house. Raise a family and grow old together.

More than anything, she loved thinking about that . . . the endless unfolding of days.

There were little irritants, of course. When Josh was immersed in a project, he'd apparently lose his sense of hearing and she'd have to wave her hand in front of his face to get him to say hello to his mom. He relied on her to do everything social in their lives, whether it was going to a movie on a Friday night or deciding how to spend Christmas. He didn't have friends of his own—not really, not like she did, and sometimes she wished he had a monthly poker game so she could have a night alone in the apartment.

But those things were so small.

She still missed her dad, still wanted to show him everything, every project she worked on, whether it was a new bus stop or a tiny park along the river. She missed him on her birthday, shocked that she was turning twenty-six without her dear old dad.

Most of all, she ached with the loss of a grandfather for Sebastian . . . and her own future children. Darius's father was still alive, but Josh had never met his. There'd be no grandpa for their kids, except for sweet Ben Kim, who had already offered to stand in when the time came. There were moments when, walking home from work, she'd look at the sky and think, *Can you see me, Daddy? Are you still here?* Writing those letters to him . . . they helped her feel like he was still there.

When she started feeling seriously tired, she thought she might be pregnant, birth control or not. She practically skipped to the drugstore to buy a test. She didn't tell Josh—she'd show him the stick if it was positive—and peed on it at work.

Negative.

Drat. Not yet. Well, that was okay. They were young, they still wanted to take a few big trips before kids. But the tired feeling didn't lift.

She started eating better—spinach a few times a week, more protein—and it helped a little. But when the fatigue hit, it wasn't like being sleepy . . . it was like her whole body was leaden. Her cough was still there, though sporadic, and she noticed she needed to clear her throat more often. Her GP told her she had bronchitis and acid reflux, chronic allergies. She took Claritin and Pepcid, and occasionally steroids if her asthma flared. She tried a new type of inhaler. It sort of helped. She started doing weight training in addition to yoga and power walks. Running tended to exacerbate her asthma.

When they had been married for seven months and autumn was bursting into color all around them, Lauren fainted again, this time at a work site, banging her head on a concrete post. Bruce the Mighty and Beneficent freaked out at all the blood, and he fainted, too— not exactly Pearl Churchwell Harris's finest moment as a company. They were both taken to the hospital and put in side-by-side stalls in the ER.

"You always say to make an impression," Lauren offered, holding a wad of gauze to her head.

"I was picturing something slightly less gory," he said.

"How bad is my cut?" she asked, taking the gauze off. Eesh. Lots of blood.

"Don't show me! Jesus! Do you want me to fire you?"

"You're such a wuss," she said. Josh was already on his way. She texted Jen, filling her in on the melodrama. Heads bleed a LOT, she typed.

"If we lose this account, it's your fault," Bruce said. "Eat breakfast, for the love of God."

"I *do* eat breakfast. I have protein and carbs and fresh fruit every damn day. I just have low blood pressure." She glanced at the monitor over her bed. Her blood pressure *was* low—94/52. O2 sat 93, heart rate 88, all fine. "Be nice to me, or I'm throwing this gauze your way."

"Nurse? Can you sedate her or something?" He covered his eyes with his hand.

The resident came in and drew the curtain between her and Bruce. "Time to staple that closed," she said cheerfully.

"Can we make my boss watch?" Lauren asked.

"Of course," the woman said, smiling.

"Stop it!" Bruce ordered. "I'm very fragile."

The doctor explained what she was about to do—clean the wound, lidocaine and staples—but Lauren was abruptly sleepy. How much blood had she lost? The staples went in without fanfare, tugging at her scalp a little.

Then Josh burst in. "Honey! Oh, my God, sweetheart, what happened?"

She opened her eyes and smiled. "Hi, babe. Sorry to worry you."

"Your wife bleeds like a Romanov," Bruce called.

"Hi, Bruce," Josh said. "Lauren, what happened?"

"I fainted and hit my head on a pole."

He sat on the edge of her bed and kissed her hand. "Poor thing." It was so good to see his face, warm with concern and love. Maybe he could lie down next to her for a cuddle and a nap.

"What about me?" Bruce asked. "I had to watch her blood spurt out of her head like a frickin' faucet."

"You're also a poor thing," Josh said.

"And heroic," Bruce added.

"That too."

"It wasn't *that* bad," Lauren said, lowering her voice to an exaggerated whisper. "Everyone knows Bruce is a baby."

The doctor was done stapling. "I'm gonna check with my supervisor, okay?" she said. "Be right back."

Be right back in emergency room lingo apparently meant *when you've aged a good year,* because it took hours for the senior doctor to come in. By this time, Bruce was gone, having given Lauren the next day off and orders to never bleed in his presence again.

"Is it possible you're . . . you know. Pregnant?" Josh asked, that light in his eyes glowing.

"Anything's possible," she said, squeezing his hand. It had been a couple of months since that other pregnancy test, and she hadn't been that religious with birth control.

"I hope you are." There it was, his unguarded, unfiltered love. Her heart pushed against her ribs so hard she was surprised it didn't fall into his lap.

"Well. I can toss the birth control anytime."

He thought about that a minute, her serious husband. "Actually, I have a Christmas surprise in mind. Not that you being pregnant would cancel it out or anything."

"What is it?"

"It's a surprise. Don't ask. Don't look at me like that. Fine. You broke me. I'm taking you to Paris for Christmas."

Her fatigue evaporated. "Paris! Oh, my God, Josh, really? Really?" He nodded, and she kissed him, threading her fingers through his silky hair, feeling him smile against her mouth.

Paris at Christmas! Oh, how stinking romantic! And classy! She'd bet there were no Frosty the Snowman inflatables in Paris, no sir.

"Excuse me," came a voice. It was the senior

doctor, the resident behind him, smiling. "We just wanted to take a listen to your chest. Your O2 sat is a little low."

"I have asthma," she said. "And bronchitis, on and off."

"Mm," he said, putting his stethoscope in his ears. "Breathe in and hold. Exhale. Breathe in. Again. Again. Now cough, and breathe in again. Really deep this time. Good."

When he was done, he didn't look at her. "I'd like you to see a pulmonologist to be on the safe side," he said. "We can refer you to someone. Dr. Yoshi, get Kwana Bennett's number."

"Her inhalers never work for long," Josh said. "And she has a dry cough. They said allergies first, then mold, on top of her asthma. She gets tired pretty easily."

"Well, aren't we full of complaints?" Lauren muttered.

"Right," said the doctor, who was as warm and inviting as marble in the snow. "Give Dr. Bennett a call. Good to meet you. Take care."

"Such charisma," Lauren murmured as he left, and Dr. Yoshi, who was signing a tablet, snorted. Ah. An ally.

"Is there anything I should know?" Lauren asked the young woman.

"I'm really only treating your scalp wound, and I'm a first-year intern. Come back in ten days, and we'll take those staples out." She didn't look at Lauren or Josh.

"Why did he listen to my lungs? Was there something weird?"

"Your O2 sat is low. It's under ninety-five."

"But ninety-three is good, right? I mean, it's still an A." Lauren smiled.

Dr. Yoshi didn't smile back. "It's a little low. It's a good idea to see a pulmonologist, not just your regular doctor." She paused. "If you're on asthma meds, they should be doing better for you, so you probably just need them adjusted."

There. Nothing to be scared of.

But a cold slither of fear twined around her ankles.

Josh looked uneasy, too. She squeezed his hand, and he squeezed back.

But she felt fine the next day and the day after that, and any fear subsided. She called Dr. Bennett, got an appointment in three months' time.

October was truly gorgeous, the yellow leaves and brilliant blue skies putting on quite a show. Thanksgiving was a loud, happy affair at Jen's.

At Christmas, they did go to Paris, wandering the rainy, ancient streets, marveling at the architecture, the statues, the creperies. They rented bikes and rode in the cold air along the Seine, and looked at Notre-Dame's reconstruction. She bought presents for Sarah, Jen and Asmaa on

Boulevard Saint-Germain and a tie for Darius at Dior. They ate and made love in their lovely hotel room, drank coffee outside under heaters. The only downside was that France was unaware of the miracle invention known as half-and-half.

On their last night, they took a pedicab down through the Christmas village along the Champs-Élysées, delighting in the lights and smells, strategizing where to eat after they went up to the Arc de Triomphe. It was five or six flights of narrow, winding stairs, and Lauren felt a little winded and dizzy at the top. Asthma. Cold air.

But she didn't want to think about that when the Eiffel Tower was glittering with lights, when the Christmas village stretched all the way back to the Tuileries, when they were young and in love and able to take a trip like this.

They stood there, looking out at the City of Light, arms around each other. "We're so lucky," Josh said.

Nearby, a young man dropped to one knee in front of a pretty woman and offered up a ring. She burst into tears and threw her arms around him. "Oui! Oui! Bien sûr!" she laughed.

"I hope they're as happy as we are," Lauren said, then kissed her husband. She had tears in her eyes. Tears of gratitude, that was all. Gratitude and awe at all life had to offer. She was going to ignore that little slither of anxiety. It would be wrong to let it into their golden life.

26

Joshua

Month ten
December

Sarah had dropped the December letter off early, because she was going to Arizona to visit her father and myriad half and stepsiblings for a week.

The task was a shock, and Joshua was not at all sure how to feel about it. For the first time, he questioned Lauren's decision.

For one, it wasn't her business.

For two, it might hurt his mother.

For three, it was a lot harder than any other month.

> Hello, my darling!
> I hope last month's task went well and you are no longer a widower who hasn't kissed anyone since the tragic death of his wife. (I hope it was great, for the record.)
> So this month's is on a very different note, and you might not like it, which is absolutely fine. So let's cut right to it.
> Meet your father.

You told me once that never knowing your father—which was his mistake, don't get me wrong—has always made you feel a little disposable. And I understand that, honey. If I had met your father, the first thing I would've done is kick him in the nuts. Maybe you deserve that chance, to call him out (and kick him). Or just see what he looks like.

I could be wrong about this, Joshua. If you hate this idea, don't do it. I just want you to have some kind of answer. We talked about it on our honeymoon. Do you remember?

Even if this guy is as different from you as he could possibly be, maybe—*maybe*—it would feel like a puzzle piece clicking in. If nothing else, it's a distraction, a project. At best, it would give you some kind of closure.

You know I only want the best life for you, Joshua, my truest love. But this one is up to you.

I love you, sweetheart.

Lauren

He did remember that night, that conversation, and his heart gave a surge at a memory he hadn't accessed yet, the fresh wave of love and longing, so deep he could feel it radiating out from his bone marrow, through muscle and tendon, all the way to his skin.

They had spent the day swimming and paddle-boarding and goofing around at the beach in Hanalei Bay, truly one of the most beautiful places either of them had ever seen. The water was so clear, the waves big enough to be exhilarating. They swam all morning, took a nap on a blanket under the shade of the palm trees, got lunch at a little takeout shack, went back in the water, the epitome of a newly married couple—in love, young, attractive, demonstrative, laughing. Blissfully ignorant of the future.

Afterward, they drove back to their house on the cliff to watch the sunset. There were two rainbows that evening, followed by the pounding rain that was so frequent on the Garden Island. Then they'd gone to bed, like any good honey-mooners, and made love in a long, slow session. He could smell the sunscreen on her skin, and her faint, citrusy perfume, salt and sweat, and lying there afterward, he blurted out the thing he'd thought since about their fourth date.

"I never thought I'd find someone who would really know me, and love me anyway."

The words hung there in the dark, and Lauren was silent.

Then she propped herself up to look at him. "Why, sweetheart?" she asked, and her voice was so gentle.

He shrugged.

"I don't know. I never . . . loved anyone before you. I felt like there was something wrong with me. Something that couldn't . . . connect."

"We all feel that way, I think."

"Did you, though?" he asked. "Or were you just waiting for the right guy?"

She kissed his shoulder, her hair cool against his skin. "I was waiting for you."

He pulled her close, still amazed that this beautiful, smiley woman was his wife. "I guess I always figured I'd be the wrong guy. For any-one."

"You grew up so loved, though," she said, and it was one of her tiny flaws . . . she hated to let people sit with a negative emotion. "Your mom's only begotten son, Ben and Sumi call you their favorite child . . ."

He thought a moment. "That's true. But . . . well, I had two parents. One never stuck around even to meet me. Never wrote, called, visited, asked for a picture." He shrugged. "It made me feel . . . a little . . ." His voice trailed off the way it so often did when he tried to describe feelings. "A little expendable. Unimportant. And growing up without having a dad, not even a shitty dad who only came by once a month . . . it made me different. Plus, Rhode Island isn't exactly the most diverse state. The other kids would always ask what I was, if I was Latino or Asian or

Arabic, and I couldn't even answer. My mom just wouldn't discuss it."

"Those Swedes and their secrets."

He smiled a little. "Yeah."

She kissed his shoulder tenderly, her hair falling across his chest. "Oh, honey. I wish we'd been friends when you were little. I would've punched anyone who made you feel bad."

"It wasn't that, really. It was more . . . a hole in my life where a father should've been. A void."

There was a long silence.

"Did you ever try to find him?" she asked.

"No."

"Would you ever want to?"

He thought on that. "I don't think so," he said. "Not at this point in my life, anyway."

She tucked her head against his shoulder, sliding her cool arm across his stomach. "You have the biggest heart," she said. "You'll be such a good dad. We'll have the most beautiful kids in the world. Smartest, too. And they will adore you."

It was just what he needed to hear, with his secret fear that there was part of him that was locked away, uncaring and dead. She pressed a kiss to his chest, and another to his neck.

"Should we practice making babies?" he asked, feeling a smile start across his face. "So we get it right when the time comes?"

"Yes, please, husband." She laughed, a sound as beautiful to him as the morning birds.

What a perfect day that had been. What a beautiful, perfect day. He would always have that day, proof that he could be utterly, completely happy.

And now, remembering that conversation, pressing the memory into his heart, he could see he had given her some reason to think that he would like to meet his father.

He knew his father's name . . . it was listed on his birth certificate. Christopher M. Zane. But first, he'd have to talk to his mom.

The next day, he sat in his childhood home. His mom had made pot roast for him, Sumi and Ben. Sometimes she insisted on being the one to cook, since Sumi took care of that most of the time.

They ate dutifully, Sumi sneaking some seasoning out of her purse and dashing it onto her plate, then Ben's as Stephanie's back was turned. Josh smiled, and she passed him some. Ah. Bulgogi spice mix, the magic of paprika, garlic, ginger and brown sugar. A pity that thirty years of living next door to the Kims hadn't made his own mother a better cook. She viewed meals as a necessary evil, good Lutheran that she was.

"It's delicious, Mom," he said, winking at Sumi.

"We have happy news," Sumi said. "Hana's

expecting again. Five months along! We thought she was too old, but guess what? She's still got some good eggs."

Ben chuckled. "Their oldest is a senior in high school. So much for retirement, but a baby is always a blessing."

There was a pause.

"How *wonderful!*" said Stephanie, too emphatically. She carefully avoided looking at Josh.

So here it was. The awkward moment as the Kims realized Stephanie wouldn't be a grandmother, or Josh a father, and that Lauren was still dead.

Sumi looked at her hands. Ben cleared his throat.

"Congratulations," Josh said, getting up to kiss Sumi's cheek, clapping Ben on the shoulder the way Darius would have. Like a normal person.

"Thank you, Joshie," Sumi said, though her voice was subdued. "We're thrilled."

"Do you think they're hoping for a boy or a girl, or do they care either way?" he asked, and so it was that he had to make pregnancy small talk with his old friends, feeling the tug of grief like a riptide.

He and Lauren had wanted four. Back when they were unaware of the cruelty of illness and the hubris of that kind of thing . . . as if you could go up to some divine deli counter and just put in your order. *We'll have four kids, please. Two girls, then two boys. All healthy, please. Oh, and could you throw in a Golden retriever?*

"Oh, no, it's six fifty-two!" Sumi exclaimed. "We have to get home for *Jeopardy!*"

"You can watch it here," his mom said.

"And get creamed by you and Josh? No, thanks," Ben said. "A man has to maintain some pride."

Josh smiled. He and his mother *did* tend to get every answer right, except in the pop culture categories. With Lauren, they'd been unbeatable as a team. He'd also told Ben he needed to talk to his mom alone.

"I also ate too much and have to get out of these pants," Sumi added.

"I love you both," Josh said. "See you soon."

"What's on your mind?" his mom asked the second he closed the door. "Was it their new grandchild?"

"No. Did that bother you, though?"

"No," she lied. "It's wonderful. Why would it bother me?"

They stared at each other a minute, the subject of children lurking between them. *You can talk about your feelings, you know,* Lauren would say. Then again, this was his mother. Feelings hadn't been discussed a lot.

What the hell? "Of course, I'm sad Lauren and I didn't have kids," he said.

"Well. That would've been irresponsible,

given her condition." She looked at the floor to avoid his eyes. Logic had always been her go-to response for anything. Josh said nothing.

"Do you want dessert?" she asked. "I made an apple cake. Coffee milk?"

"Sure." She was a better baker than cook.

His mother cut the cake, put a dollop of Cool Whip on the side and cut herself a piece, too, then poured them both coffee milk, Rhode Island's weirdly delicious state drink. She sat down heavily across from him. She was still a striking woman, his mom, with her blond hair and piercing blue eyes. They had the same nose, the same slight cleft in their chins. Otherwise, he must have been his father's boy, so to speak. It wasn't uncommon that, when Josh was a kid, people had assumed Ben was his biological father, given Josh's straight black hair and dark eyes.

"So what's up, Joshua?" She always could read him better than anyone else.

Except Lauren.

"Well, Mom . . . I was hoping you could tell me about my father."

She flinched and took a hostile bite of cake. "When did you start lobbing bombs in conversation?"

All his life, when he'd asked about his father, Stephanie had been like this. Cold enough to let him know his questions weren't welcome. Irritated (or hurt) by his interest. By the age of ten or so, he'd stopped asking. All he knew was that they'd dated briefly, his mother had gotten pregnant, and his biological father left, never to return, call or write.

"I'm sorry, Mom. I know you don't like talking about it, but . . ."

"Well, it came out of nowhere, and I'm not prepared to talk about it."

He nodded. "Is there some way I should've eased into that?" This *was* his mother. She should know he lacked social dexterity.

She shrugged and fluttered her hands. "I can't think of how." She sighed. "Fine. Eat your cake. I need a minute." She took a sip of her coffee milk, glaring at him.

He obeyed. One bite. Two. Some Cool Whip, a staple from his childhood. Three bites.

"So," she finally said. "He was tall, dark, handsome, irresponsible. What else do you want to know?"

"You met in college, right?"

"Yes. He was in graduate school in Boston."

Josh let the silence rest between them. "Anything else, Mom?"

"Do you have a form I can fill out? It would be more pleasant than this."

He almost laughed. "I'd like whatever information you have."

"Are you sick? Do you need a family history?" Her forehead crinkled with worry.

"No. Not at all. Not sick."

She sighed. "He left me when I was four months pregnant, Joshua. He knew what he was doing, too. I told him the minute I found out, and he made the choice to—what do you kids call it?—to ghost me. He is *not* your father. He was an unpaid sperm donor who left us both."

"I know that, Mom." He sighed. "The thing is, I have too much time on my hands. I miss Lauren." His voice broke. "I don't have that many . . . people. Outside of you and Ben and Sumi, I have two relatives that I know of—your cousin, and her daughter. I'd just like to . . . see where I came from, genetically speaking."

"Oh, so you *do* want to meet him! I see!" She tossed down her fork, and it hit the plate with a clatter. "You think after thirty-one years, he's going to take you to a ball game and teach you to catch?"

"No. I would just like to meet him. One time." He hadn't been sure of this until the words left his mouth.

She said nothing, though she may have hissed. Then she anger-ate her dessert, stabbing her fork through the innocent cake like she was murdering it, chewing fiercely. She chugged her coffee milk.

"Mom," he said gently, "you are the person I most admire in the world. You and my wife. That will never change. What you did, having me alone when you were still a college student, graduating, working in a highly competitive field, raising me to be a good person . . . it was remarkable. *You* are remarkable."

Her face softened just a little. "That's true."

"The way you loved and took care of Lauren . . . and me . . . don't think for a second that I will ever, ever forget that."

She looked away, her mouth trembling a little, her equivalent of a sobbing wreck.

"But I'd like to meet my father. It won't change anything. I just want to . . . know."

She wiped her eyes on her napkin. Took another bite of cake, a sip of coffee milk. "You know his name."

"Yes. Christopher Zane."

"He was from Indiana. His parents had a farm. He was getting his degree in . . . gosh, what was it? Environmental engineering. Or agricultural engineering. Something like that. He was at MIT, I was at Harvard. He went to Notre Dame for his bachelor's, and on our first date, he got mad at me because I didn't know who the Fighting Irish were." She rolled her eyes.

Josh's head was buzzing, even as his brain memorized the facts. That was more than his mother had told him about his father in his entire life.

"We dated for six weeks. I was a strict Lutheran, remember, and I thought premarital sex was for slutty girls, got carried away and had unprotected

419

sex. I was stupid, I was in denial, so I told myself I had just skipped a period or two." She sighed. "I knew, though. I kept hoping I wasn't." Her head jerked up. "Don't get me wrong, Joshua. You're the best thing in my life. I don't regret you for one second."

"I know that."

"Good." She patted his hand, then resumed stabbing her cake. "So when I couldn't pretend anymore, I took a test and voilà! Pregnant. I told him. We fought. Abortion wasn't on the table, not for me. We talked for about two seconds about getting married, but it was already clear we weren't going to work. He said he'd 'pay his share.'" She made air quotes around the words. "Then he went off on a project of some kind, some summer program, said he would call me when he got settled, and I never saw him again. I sent him a letter at his MIT address, which was the only one I had. It came back. His email address was defunct. I called him at his last known phone number. It was disconnected. That September, I called MIT, and they said he was no longer enrolled there."

Silence settled over the kitchen. Outside, sleet started pattering against the window.

"And that was it, sweetheart," she said, her voice gentler than when she'd started.

There was an unpleasant pressure in Josh's chest. What kind of person turns his back on his unborn child and just disappears? For decades?

"Is he still alive?" Josh asked.

"I don't know." She sighed. "I put his name on the birth certificate because I wanted evidence, I think."

"Why didn't you try to track him down and ask for child support?"

"I didn't want it. Honestly, I would've lived in a box on the street before doing that." She shrugged. "But my father was still alive back then, so he made sure we didn't have to. I transferred to Brown, and they gave me a stipend, and between that and what Papa gave us, we were fine."

"Did you ever Google him? Just out of curiosity?"

She pulled a face. "Yes. Once, when you were about ten. He was teaching at Northwestern and lived in Chicago. Or he did twenty years ago. So there it is. Everything I know. He completely abandoned us. Never looked back. So there you have it for when you plan your joyful reunion."

"It's just curiosity, Mom. And something to do."

"You could dig ditches. You could clean toilets. Volunteer at a shelter for battered women."

"Okay, okay. I get it. And I do volunteer at the Hope Center. Also, I just got my red belt in karate. Everyone else's mom was there for the belt ceremony. I was sorry you couldn't make it."

There. She smiled. She'd laughed so hard when he told her about his kiddie karate classes.

Her smile faded. "Josh . . . I kept my old post office box in Cambridge for ten years. You know. In case he wanted to contact me and hear about you." Her eyes filled. "He never did."

He inhaled slowly, held it for a second, then exhaled. "He sounds like quite a dick."

"Can't argue that point."

"Do you know anything else, Mom?"

"No." She shook her head and wiped her eyes. "His loss, Joshua. You are the best son in the world."

He got up and hugged her, his fierce Viking mom. "I love you, Mom." She hugged him back hard, then kissed his cheek soundly.

"I love you, too. Do what you have to do."

"Thank you."

"You're welcome. Finish your cake."

Joshua found Christopher M. Zane with four clicks on Google after entering his father's name, educational history and the word *engineer.*

And there he was. A photo and everything.

Christopher M. Zane had graying dark hair, olive skin and brown eyes, a square solid face, aquiline nose and a crooked left incisor that showed clearly when he smiled. Josh's left incisor was also crooked. Identically crooked.

Objectively speaking, Josh could admit his

father was handsome. A bit like George Clooney, but not as pretty, as Lauren would say.

He stared at the picture.

He looked a lot more like his father than his mother. A *lot* more.

Josh was always surprised to be noticed for his looks, given that he spent so much time in his own head. His sloppy, pre-Lauren, pre-Radley attire was chosen for comfort, and when he did put in the effort—like buying the suit he'd worn to propose to Lauren—he was pleased. He cleaned up nice, as Sumi told him.

But now, looking at his future self on the screen there . . . maybe he didn't like the way he looked so much anymore. Not that this man had done anything significant in Joshua's life other than ejaculate. Well, that and walk away.

Christopher M. Zane, now a PhD, taught civil and environmental engineering at the University of Chicago. A graduate from Notre Dame, he had "studied at MIT," got his master's from the University of Chicago, a doctorate from Northwestern, was now tenured at the University of Chicago and a frequent guest lecturer. He'd taken a sabbatical in South Africa three years prior. He was married and had three children.

So Joshua had siblings. Noted.

Josh didn't let emotion get in the way. As when he worked, his tunnel vision served him. He signed up for a record-finding service, and several minutes later, got his father's address, phone number, previous addresses. Christopher M. Zane had gotten a speeding ticket in 2018. He'd been a part owner of a now-closed café in Wicker Park. Here was a picture of him at the opening, his arm around his wife, three kids. "Christopher Zane, his wife, Melissa, and their three children, Sawyer, Ransom and Briar"—apparently, they wanted their kids to join the rodeo—"at the opening of Deep, Dark and Delicious, the latest café to open in Chicago's funkiest neighborhood."

A half brother and two half sisters with cowboy names. He studied their faces. Melissa was blond and blue eyed, and two of the kids were as well, but Ransom looked like her father.

And like Josh.

How strange, to see someone who undeniably looked like him after thirty years of being an only child. Thirty-one, to be precise.

The café had closed two years later. Ah, well.

He Googled his father's address, hit street view and saw that his father lived in a gracious old Victorian in Oak Park. Lovely neighborhood. A real estate search let him see the old listing and all the rooms inside. He saw the windows in the master bedroom, the smaller, cozy bedrooms his half siblings had. The kids had had to share a bathroom, and he could imagine the bickering that took place there. Big kitchen. A sunroom overlooking the backyard.

It was a nice house. Really nice. The kind he and Lauren might have bought.

A few more search terms, and Joshua learned that his paternal grandparents, Mike and Kerry Zane, owned a huge dairy farm in Rolling Prairie, Indiana. Two thousand cows, all the equipment and buildings necessary, everything very shiny and modern. There'd been a beautiful old home on the property as well, with a wraparound porch, four bedrooms and a six-stall barn for horses.

The farm had sold for $12.2 million fourteen years ago.

Funny, to think that his ancestors were wealthy.

Fourteen years ago, Joshua had been choosing colleges based on their financial aid packages and scholarships. Stephanie was frugal and had started saving money for his college before he popped out of her uterus, but her salary had never been anything more than modest until the past couple of years, when she moved into what might be considered comfortable. Before she'd gotten knocked up, Josh's mom had planned to go to medical school. She was getting an online master's degree now, thirty-one years after Josh had been born.

He clicked back on the two photos of his father.

He called Cookie Goldberg. "What do you want?" she said by way of answering.

"I'm going to Chicago tomorrow," he said. "Book me a flight and find a quiet hotel, okay?"

27

Joshua

Month ten
Still December

Seventeen hours after calling Cookie, Joshua sat on a bench outside the building where Christopher M. Zane, PhD, was holding office hours. The sun was mercilessly bright, the sky a cold, brittle blue. The bench itself was iron, but Josh barely noticed the freezing temperature. No. He was watching the doors of the building where his father taught and held office hours.

Thank God Sarah had dropped the letter off early. Otherwise, he might have missed this window, since the semester was ending in a few days.

Right now, he was hoping that his father would use the main entrance when he left. He'd printed out the university's photo and the one of his father's family at the café and kept close watch on the door. Kids came in and out of the building, bundled against the cold. It was cold in a way the Northeast never was—a dry, biting cold that cut through every layer Josh had on. It was fine. He didn't mind.

"Can I help you?" someone asked. She smiled and shifted her backpack.

"I'm waiting for Dr. Zane," he said.

"Oh, he's in office hours. He's my professor."

"Really."

"Yeah. He's great. One of the best in my program."

Josh didn't respond. She tilted her head, and he remembered to speak. "Glad to hear it."

"Well. Happy holidays."

He nodded. "You too."

As she left, he returned his attention to the door, and right then, a man came out, dressed in a heavy winter parka. He held on to the railing, moving a bit stiffly. He was tall and held a briefcase in one hand. His hair was salt-and-pepper gray. He looked like George Clooney.

The man waved to a student, then took a left and started walking west.

Josh got up, grabbed his leather bag and jogged up behind him. "Professor Zane?" he said, his voice calm. He felt calm, too. He felt . . . nothing, really. A distant curiosity.

"Yes?" His father turned. Up close, he looked older than his pictures, shadows under his eyes, the skin on his face starting its downward journey into laxity. Still handsome, though.

"Joshua Park." He didn't put out his hand.

"Do I know you? Are you a student or alumnus?"

"No." He paused. "I'm your son."

That expression . . . *the blood drained out of his face.* Joshua watched as it happened. Christopher M. Zane's face turned utterly gray. His eyes widened, and he bent over, hands on his knees. "Oh, my God. Oh, my God."

Josh didn't offer to help him. He waited, and after a few seconds, his father stood up, breathing heavily. He took a step backward, his breath fogging the air. His eyes were wet, Josh observed, and he was unsteady on his feet.

Which meant nothing, of course.

"Hey, Dr. Zane! You okay?" called a student.

"Yeah. Yep, fine, thanks. Thanks." He shook his head a little, took a few deep breaths, then looked at Josh's face. "My God," he said, and his tears overflowed. "My God."

"Can we go somewhere to talk?" Josh asked. "Or do you need an ambulance?"

"No, I'm fine . . . just . . . my God. I never thought . . . I never expected to . . ."

"Is there a café or a restaurant nearby?" There was. Cookie had researched it and sent him four places. She didn't know the reason for his visit, and she'd kill herself before asking.

"Yes. Um, this way."

They didn't speak, though a few times, someone said, "Hey, Professor," or "Hi, Dr. Zane!" Joshua's father didn't acknowledge their greetings. Maybe he didn't even hear them. The cold air put some color back into his face, and he kept glancing at Josh, who returned his looks calmly. He waited for feelings to come. They didn't. They probably would, he imagined. Just not yet.

On the next block was an Irish pub. Christopher Zane opened the door and held it for Josh. Inside was dark and warm.

"Chris! How you doin'?" called the bartender.

"I'm good, Tim, I'm good." So he was a regular here. No introduction for Josh. "Hey, we're gonna take a booth in the back, okay?" He turned to Josh. "What would you like to drink?"

"Coffee."

"Coffee and club soda, Tim," he told the bartender. "We'll save you the trip and take them with us."

An interminable minute later, and they had their beverages.

It was almost four, and already getting dark. Josh followed his father to the booth farthest in the back. They took off their coats and sat. It was a nice pub. Rather ordinary, but homey.

"So this is . . . quite a surprise," Christopher said, taking a big breath.

"I'm sure it is."

"How old are you, Joshua?"

"Thirty-one as of October fourteenth." The worst birthday of his life, this last one. The first without Lauren. The first as a widower.

"Jesus. God. I . . ." He took a long pull of his club soda. "I guess I should ask what you'd like to . . . do. Or say."

"I wanted to meet you. Ask you a few things."

"Right. Right. Of course." He scrubbed a hand across his face. "Sorry, this is a lot to take in." Another swallow or two of club soda. "Uh . . . how is your . . . your mother?"

"Alive. That's all you get to know."

Christopher flinched. "Fair enough."

"I know you're married and have three children with cowboy names. I know where you grew up, where you went to school, that you have a sister named Eileen. I know your parents sold their farm in Indiana and now live in Arizona. I know you owned a café in Wicker Park."

"Jesus, the internet really does tell all." He blew out a breath. "Do you want money?"

Josh couldn't help a bitter laugh. "It's a little late for child support."

"I mean, I do owe you. And there *is* money. Now. There wasn't always. The farm sold—"

"I know, and I don't care. I want you to tell me how you could leave a pregnant twenty-year-old and your unborn child."

Christopher M. Zane leaned back in his seat and looked at the ceiling for a long minute. When he looked back at Josh, his eyes were full of tears.

"I don't have a good answer for that. There *is*

no answer, other than I was a shitty, stupid kid—"

"You were twenty-five."

"And as immature and stupid as a sixteen-year-old." He drained his club soda. "Let me text my wife and tell her I'll be late. Hang on a sec."

Josh waited.

Christopher texted, then turned off his phone and put it in his coat pocket. Josh appreciated that. The man took another deep breath. "Listen, I can't justify what I did. Walking away, I mean. I didn't plan it. I was taking part in a summer project in Austin that year, and I fully intended to go back to Boston. And then I stopped home in Indiana. I hadn't told my parents about . . . you. Or Stephanie." He looked at his hands. "They . . . my parents, that is . . . they were so happy to see me."

Josh waited. "My father immigrated from Pakistan when he was seventeen." Ah. So that's where Josh got his dark hair and eyes. "He worked ninety hours a week for ten years as a janitor and a farmhand before he could buy his first piece of land. Thirteen acres. He ended up with eight thousand. I was the first person on either side of the family to finish college. My mom didn't even finish high school."

Christopher stopped to let that sink in. Or just to gather his nerves, maybe. Josh had to hand it to him; he wasn't tap-dancing around.

Josh wasn't really here to listen to the story of

432

his invisible grandparents and their American dream, but it was interesting. Pakistan. He was Pakistani. Cool. He'd have to do some reading on the culture and history. After all, it wasn't his ancestors who'd dumped his mom.

"Is your mother also Pakistani?" Josh asked.

"No. She's white. Her parents didn't approve of her dating a . . . well, they had ugly words for my father. So they kicked her out, and they got married when they were really young."

"You think they'd approve of you walking out on your pregnant girlfriend?" Josh asked, his voice almost amiable.

"God, no. I never told them. They . . . were so proud of me. I was supposed to be proof that they'd made all the right choices. I wasn't supposed to be an idiot and get a girl pregnant."

"And yet you did."

"Yes. Joshua, I have no excuses here. I was scared and selfish and entitled and weak. I couldn't go back to MIT, and so I dropped out. I—" His voice broke. "I just stayed. Like a coward. Like a selfish asshole."

He wiped his eyes. Josh was unmoved.

"The longer I stayed, the easier it got. I told myself your mother would go back to Sweden."

"Why would she go to Sweden?" Josh asked. "She grew up in central New York. She spent one semester in Sweden. She's a second-generation American. She knows maybe ten Swedish words."

"Oh. I . . . I thought she was *from* Sweden, for some reason."

"Wrong."

"Well. It doesn't excuse what I did. But that's what I told myself. She was back there, they had . . . uh, better healthcare and, oh, shit, I was so stupid and self-centered and grasping at any straws. Call it magical thinking or wish fulfillment or me just pretending she'd floated off to a better life, becoming a doctor. After a while, I believed it. I pictured her in Sweden, having the baby—you—there, raising you there."

"She moved to Providence. Transferred to Brown, because they gave her more money than Harvard. I was born at Rhode Island Hospital. She didn't go to medical school. She couldn't, not with me." He let the guilt sink in. "She kept her old post office box in case you ever reached out."

There was a long silence.

"I never did," his father acknowledged.

"I'm well aware of that."

Christopher M. Zane had a hard time making eye contact. "I want to tell you that . . . my decision haunted me. Not that I did anything about it other than drink. I *hated* myself. I flunked out of my master's program and had to restart a year later. I knew I was being weak, but . . ." He shook his head. "But the longer it went on, the harder it felt to undo any of the harm

I did. Eventually, I told myself you were both better off without me showing up and begging for forgiveness, because what I did was . . . unforgivable."

"Did you even know that I was a boy? Did you bother to find out?"

His father looked at him, blinking. More tears fell from his eyes, Josh observed impassively. "No," Christopher M. Zane said. "Once a certain amount of time had passed, I told myself it was for the best."

"For you, clearly it was."

"I don't know about that. I think it made me a far worse person. I've lived with that shame for thirty-one years."

"Good. You should be ashamed."

His father nodded.

So there it was. His father had been a shallow, selfish idiot. Josh sipped his coffee, which was tepid now, and thought he should design something for that problem. A heating cube that would warm your coffee or tea without making it taste old and bitter, the way the microwave did. Honestly, if there wasn't something like that already on the market, he'd whip one up and sell it in a heartbeat.

It was comforting to think of himself back home, at his desk, rather than here, with the man who didn't even know Josh had been born.

"If I could do it over, I would have made very

different choices," Christopher M. Zane said quietly. "When my wife and I had our first child, I went into a very . . ." He sighed. "A very bad place. I kept thinking about how much I loved him, and how I'd thrown you away, and I was afraid to love my boy."

Josh felt his first flicker of sympathy. The kid didn't do anything, after all.

"I couldn't tell my wife, and I . . . I started drinking again. She threatened to kick me out, I got sober, got counseling. Then our daughter was born, and then our second girl, and it helped. By then, I felt it was too late to try to find you and Stephanie. Too much time had passed."

"You could've tried."

"Yes. Believe me, I know that. I try to be a good father to them, but I can never stop feeling doomed in some way because of what I did to you. If the universe ever took one of them, I'd probably deserve it." His voice broke.

Drama queen. Still. Either he was a fantastic Method actor, or he was genuinely affected by Joshua's surprise appearance, because the tears continued to rain down.

"I don't think the universe works that way," Josh said.

"I'm so sorry," his father said. "I'm so very, very sorry."

Josh inclined his head a little bit, acknowledging the words.

His father wiped his eyes on the cocktail napkin, blew his nose, then folded his hands on the table, and Josh realized with a start that those were *his* hands, twenty-five years from now. Same shape, same knuckles, same shape to the fingernails.

"Do you love your kids?" Josh asked.

His father's eyes filled again. "I do."

"Good." He figured he should add something. "They have unusual names."

"My wife picked them out. I didn't feel like I—oh, God, I'm making this all about me. But I didn't feel like I deserved to name anyone. If my kids' names sound like something you'd name a dog on a horse ranch, well. They're fine. They're good kids."

Josh almost smiled.

"Can I ask *you* some questions, Joshua?"

"Sure." Why not?

"Was your childhood . . . okay?"

Josh nodded. "It was. It was very happy. I'm sure my mother could've used some help, but she figured it all out."

"She was brilliant."

"She *is* brilliant. No love lost for you, though."

"I don't blame her in the least." He hesitated. "Did she ever marry?"

Josh considered not answering. Then again, why not? "No."

Christopher nodded, looking at the table. "I had

hoped . . . I pictured her marrying. I hoped you might have a nice stepfather."

"Nope." He had Ben, though. The memory of Ben, teaching him to ride a bike, making paper airplanes, made his chest ache. He *had* had a father. A great father. He still did.

"Does she need money? Do you?" Christopher asked.

"We would both burn your money at this point," Josh said.

"If you needed it, that's the least I could—"

A red flame danced in Joshua's left eye. "Dr. Zane. We don't need your money. If we were starving, we wouldn't take it."

His father nodded. "I get it. And I respect that." The red flame died down.

They sat in silence for a few minutes. A few people had come into the pub, but they were at the bar. Snatches of conversation and laughter floated past like smoke.

"Um . . . what do you do for a living, Joshua?"

Google would tell him whatever he wanted to know, so Josh figured he might as well. "I'm a medical device engineer."

"Really! That's terrific! So . . . uh, what do you focus on?"

"Pediatrics, mostly. Some surgical devices. Adaptations for minimal invasiveness and pain."

"That's wonderful. That's great, son." He

438

winced. "I'm sorry. Force of habit. I call a lot of my students that. Midwestern thing."

"It's okay. I am your son, I suppose. Genetically, if nothing else."

"I can see a little bit of my father in you."

"Please don't do that."

"Right. Sorry. It's hard to know the right thing to say."

"I understand. This is an unusual situation."

"Are you always this . . . self-contained?" his father asked with a faint smile.

"Most of the time, yes."

His father's smile grew. "Good for you." Another pause. "Where did you go to school?"

"RISD, Brown, MIT."

"Wow. So you got your mother's brains." Neither of them acknowledged the coincidence of them both going to the same school. Stephanie had never breathed a word when he'd been offered a spot at MIT.

"And where do you live now, Josh?"

"In Providence."

"You and your mother are close?"

"Yes."

"Good. I'm glad to hear that." He hesitated. "Are you married?" he asked, nodding at Josh's left hand.

Josh looked at his wedding ring. "My wife died ten months ago. Idiopathic pulmonary fibrosis."

His father's face fell. "Oh, no. I'm so sorry."

"Yeah. Me too."

What would Lauren do at this moment? What would she have him say? If she were here, how would she make this situation easier? She'd wanted him to have some kind of closure, some kind of peace.

"Listen, Dr. Zane—"

"Oh, God, please. Call me Chris. Or . . . or whatever you want."

"Okay. Chris." The name felt strange in his mouth. He paused, trying to gather his thoughts. "Look. Not having any contact with you . . . it left a mark. I didn't grow up hating you, and my mother never mentioned you in any way, except to tell me you left before I was born. But I always did feel a little . . . thrown away."

His father nodded, his mouth wobbling. "I'm so sorry," he whispered.

"But I've had a really good life. My mother is the best, and I have . . . I have people. And my wife, she was . . ." His eyes stung. "She was incredible, and we were very happy." He cleared his throat. "So you didn't ruin me. I never knew you, so you couldn't. But I always wondered how I could be . . . tossed away like that."

Chris nodded. "It had nothing to do with you," he whispered fiercely. "Nothing. I was selfish. Completely self-absorbed. That's the reason. I took the easiest, most cowardly path possible. I let your mother deal with everything alone, and

I believe I'll have to answer for that someday. I carry that with me. Every day, Joshua." His voice broke.

They sat in silence for a few minutes. Tim the bartender asked if they wanted a refill, and they both said no.

There was a perfectly symmetrical *H* carved into the table, and Josh traced it with his forefinger. A master carver, with the seraph base perfectly even. Well done.

"Why don't you stop?" he asked his father.

"Stop what?"

"Feeling guilty." He dragged his gaze away from the *H* and looked at his father's face. "I don't say this to be unkind, but we were probably better off without you."

Chris gave a pained nod.

"It seems like you're a better man now than you were then."

His father bowed his head. "I appreciate that more than I can say," he whispered.

Josh looked at him. Weird, to think that half of his DNA came from this stranger. Then he stuck out his hand. "I forgive you."

His father's mouth opened slightly. He took Joshua's hand and gripped it tightly. Josh squeezed back, and they stayed that way for a long minute before Josh withdrew.

"Do you . . . do you want to meet my family?" Chris asked. "Your . . . siblings?"

441

"Oh, God, no. I don't see a reason to put this on them."

He couldn't tell if his father was relieved or disappointed. "Okay. Um . . . would you like to see pictures?"

"Uh . . . sure." Huh. They had that in common, that hesitation of speech when they were unsure how to answer.

His father pulled out his phone, turned it back on and tapped the screen, then handed it over. "That's at Christmas last year," he said.

Josh looked at the screen—three kids, the girls in red dresses, the boy, tall and gangly, wearing a blue crewneck sweater. The older girl—Ransom—looked cheeky, and Josh felt a faint smile at the idea. He had a cheeky half sister who looked like him. Last week, he hadn't known that.

"They look happy," he said, handing the phone back.

"Thank you," Chris whispered.

"What kind of things do you do together?" he asked.

"Oh, we, uh . . . well, we all like games and movies, so once a week, we have family night. And we go bowling sometimes. Ransom and Sawyer love baseball, so we go to a Cubs game once a year or so. Um . . . we do yard work together. Sometimes we go to the lake. We, um . . . we have a place up north. In Wisconsin."

"That sounds nice."

More tears fell from his father's eyes. Well, Josh hadn't inherited that trait. He was not a weeper. Sometimes, he wished he were. "You don't have to tell them about me," he said.

"I . . . I might."

"That's up to you. I don't plan on visiting you again, Chris. I don't need a father. I think it's too late for us to be anything to each other."

"I looked for you. On Ancestry.com. I thought maybe you'd . . . put yourself out there to track me down. One day, my kids will probably find out they have a brother."

"Half brother." Josh paused. "That'll be a difficult conversation."

"It will be." His father studied his face. "Are you *sure* there's nothing you want from me? I would do anything to at least try to make it up to you. To start, at any rate. This has been such a shock, but I'm so glad to see you. I truly am."

Josh inhaled slowly. "Thanks. I just wanted to meet you. I wondered what you looked like. I wanted to know what kind of person you are." He paused. "My wife thought I should. She thought it would be good for me. I think she was right."

His father's face spasmed, but he got it under control. "Okay. But if you want, just reach out . . . you know, for anything. Anything at all. If you change your mind, if you're ever in Chicago, we could—"

"Right now, the answer is no. But thanks."

"Can I give you my card just in case?"

"Sure."

Chris pulled out his wallet, withdrew a card and wrote a phone number on the back. As he did, Josh committed his face to memory.

If being fatherless had left a mark on Joshua, abandoning a child had left a scar on Christopher M. Zane. He looked older than his years, careworn.

At least he'd had the grace to admit his wrongdoing without trying to justify it.

They got up from the table, and Josh could see that his father's hands were shaking as he tried to zip up his coat. It was oddly touching.

Chris pulled out his wallet and left a twenty on the bar. "Leaving us so soon?" Tim the bartender said.

"Yeah. Tim, this is Joshua. Joshua Park."

"Nice to meet you," Josh said.

"Tim," Chris blurted. "Would you mind taking our picture? Josh, if that's okay with you."

He hesitated. But his mom would want to see it, he suspected. And if not, well, he would have it, and in some small way, it would be nice to have a picture of him and his father, no matter how unimportant he had been for all these years.

Lauren would have liked that.

His father handed over his phone, and Josh did the same. They stood side by side. "Okay, look

444

at me and smile," Tim said. Josh obeyed, and then he felt his father's arm around his shoulders. "Next phone, one, two, three, done. How do you like them?" He handed back the phones.

"Tim . . . this . . . this is my son," Chris said, and his voice shook.

It was the first time Josh had ever heard a male voice say those words. His chest felt a strange, not-unpleasant ache.

Tim's eyebrows raised. "Wow. Nice to meet you, man."

"You too."

Josh looked at the phone. There they were, father and son, and standing next to each other. That crooked incisor gave it away.

"You have . . ." Chris pointed to his own crooked tooth.

"Yeah." They looked at each other and smiled, and that ache in Josh's chest grew.

It was fully dark now, colder than ever. The streetlights cast puddles of light at regular intervals down the road. "Do you need a ride?" Chris asked.

"No, thank you," Josh said. "I'll walk."

"Okay." His father stood there, an inch or so taller than Josh. "Can I give you a hug?" he asked, and his voice shook.

"I'm not really the hugging type," Josh said.

"Of course. Sorry. I have no right to ask."

Don't be a loser.

"Ah, fuck it. Why not?" he said, and he hugged his father hard, felt the man jerk with a sob. For a second, they just stood there, arms tight around each other.

Then Josh let him go. "Take care, Dad," he said. He smiled, turned and walked down the street, following the path of light.

28

Joshua

Still month ten
Still the unending month of December

Josh was ignoring the holidays this year. They were hard to avoid outside in the real world, so he went out as little as possible, still trying to adjust to the fact that he'd met his father, and trying to ignore Christmas.

Lauren had been a Christmas zealot. It felt grotesque that the holiday was happening without her.

Then Jen asked to come over one Saturday afternoon, and Josh said yes instantly. He'd missed her, he realized. The apartment was a mess, even though he'd hired a cleaning lady, a nice woman Asmaa had referred from the Hope Center, but he'd been working a lot, and takeout containers were scattered around. Pebbles was shedding, which didn't help, so he vacuumed and made the bed. Showered, put on clean clothes, put on coffee and rummaged for cookies or something in his pantry. Ah. Mrs. Kim had brought over those Korean sesame seed cookies, and he seemed to remember that Jen loved them. Yes. He was sure she did.

He hadn't seen Jen without Darius or the kids for a long time. They'd been a team when Lauren was sick, the two people who loved her the most.

He thought for a minute about his half siblings out in Chicago. It was strangely pleasant to know they were there. His mother had looked at the picture, shrugged, and said, "He looks old." The subject was then closed. And Josh had put his father's card in the box with Lauren's letters, a way for him to tell her he'd done it. He didn't think he'd ever want to see Christopher Zane again, but you never knew.

The knock came on the door, and Pebbles went wild. She loved everyone, but she greeted Jen with particular joy. Maybe she knew this was as close to Lauren as she could get. Maybe they smelled similar, the two Carlisle sisters.

"Pebbles! Hello, my baby! Hello! I missed you!"

Josh waited, accustomed to the dog getting love first. Eventually, Jen straightened. "Hey, how are you?" Jen said. She hugged him. "Good to see you. Oh! I like what you did here! Is this coffee table new?"

"No. The couch is. You've been here since I got it. But the rug is new." He'd seen it on an auction site Lauren had registered for, and thought it would look nice against the old floors. "Coffee?

Cookies? We— I have your favorite. Sumi's sesame cookies?"

"Oh, yes! No coffee, please. Got some milk? Soy milk? Almond? I'm easy. Oh, wow, this couch is really comfy. I like it."

It was her way of saying she didn't mind that he'd changed things. He'd moved stuff around, even put some away. The small vase they'd gotten in Hawaii. A bowl of oval, gray stones, all from the beach on the Cape, each one meticulously chosen by Lauren. He couldn't get rid of them, but he didn't have to look at them every day.

Josh plated the cookies, poured himself some coffee and some soy milk for Jen and brought everything to the living room, sitting next to her. "You look good, Jen. How are you doing?"

"Good," she said, though her eyes instantly teared. "Horrible. I miss her constantly. It's like a hole in my chest, and I swear I can feel the wind blowing through it."

He covered her hand with his and said nothing.

"I went to your psychic," Jen said. She took a cookie and ate it whole.

"How was it?"

"It was good. It's shocking. So get this. I walk in, right, and I don't know why I'm there except that I *miss* her . . ." Her voice choked off, and she took a swig of milk. "And immediately, Gertie says, 'Your sister is showing me a newborn baby. Are you pregnant?' " Jen started to cry. "And I am, Josh. Not even a month, but I am. You're the first person I've told, outside of her and Darius."

She turned to him and buried her face against his chest, sobbing, and he put his arms around her. "I'm so happy for you," he whispered as she bawled. "This is great news."

His wife would never know this baby, never hold her, never kiss her, never even have a photo with her. He understood Jen's tears. His own were seeping into her hair.

"I hate that life is going on without her," Jen said wetly. "I hate it."

He wanted to agree, because he knew exactly how she felt. He gripped Jen by her shoulders and made her look at him. "This is wonderful, and no one would be happier than Lauren. Except maybe me." He squinted at her. "You know, I'm thinking Josh is a beautiful name. It's time for me to have a namesake, and I'm totally available as godfather."

It wasn't great patter, no. But he was trying. He could not let Jen feel anything but joy radiating from him. He had to look after her. She was his family.

"What if it's a girl?" she said, taking in that shaking breath that meant she was done crying.

"Josie? Joshilyn? Joss? We can figure something out."

She laughed, and Josh's heart contracted.

Lauren would appreciate that. She'd be grateful that he made her sister smile.

"Jen," he said, "this thing about me being your brother-in-law, you being my sister-in-law . . ."

"Yeah?" she asked, frowning. "Don't tell me you have a crush on me."

"Well, of *course* I do," he said, though he didn't and never had, but this was how people connected, he understood, this light flirting and teasing. "But it gets complicated, explaining how we're linked. Maybe I could . . ." He hesitated. "Maybe I could just call you my sister."

Again her eyes filled with tears. "You're the best, Josh," she said, grabbing another cookie. "You're the best. I always wanted a baby brother. I used to dress Lauren up in boy clothes, did you know that?"

When she left a while later, taking all the cookies at his insistence, he went into his bedroom, looked at the dogwood tree, which was obscenely healthy, and had a good cry.

Thank God for the internet. Josh ordered gifts for the kids, Jen and Darius (a gift certificate to a really nice restaurant with his own babysitting services thrown in), his mom, Donna, Radley and Sarah. He'd had to go out for coffee the other day, and every damn couple seemed pink-cheeked and healthy and in love, every family filled with the holiday spirit, happiness oozing out of them like radioactive sludge.

Not that he was bitter.

God, he was *so* bitter. A year ago, Lauren had needed to measure out her energy carefully, but they'd still done every Christmas tradition, baked dozens of cookies, listened to Christmas music ad nauseam, put out the reindeer throw pillows and Santa mugs. No one had told him it would be their last Christmas. No one told her.

He felt like an aging, brittle piece of paper that would disintegrate if touched. He stayed away from people as much as he could. However, he couldn't avoid Christmas completely.

He and Radley went to the Eddy—sometime in the fall after Josh's date with Cammie, they'd started meeting there every Wednesday night. This Wednesday, however, was a mistake—the place was mobbed with Christmasy people, and music, and decorations, and drinks. Josh told Radley about meeting his father, needing almost to yell over the noise, and God, Josh was going to start screaming and stabbing people with the fancy toothpick that speared the cranberry garnish in his drink.

Focus on someone else, loser, he could imagine Lauren saying. "Do you have plans for the holidays, Rad?" he asked.

"You mean, besides the retail hell I live and

breathe?" He took a sip of his bourbon and waved to someone he knew.

"Yeah, besides that."

"No. I plan to order Chinese food and watch horror movies."

Lucky. Josh took a sip of his smoked grapefruit martini. "Why don't you come to my mom's house? Christmas Eve. She has a big party. The Swedes love Christmas."

"Really?"

"Yeah. She'd love it. She's been dying to meet you." He hesitated. "And I'd be very . . . grateful to have you there."

"I'd *love* to come. Thank you, Joshua." Radley's face was endearingly sincere.

"I got you a present," Josh said. "Can I give it to you now? It'll be crazy at my mom's."

"Of course! I love presents!"

Josh pulled a box out of his messenger bag. "Sorry I didn't wrap it," he said.

"You have the right to hate Christmas this year, Josh." He opened the box to reveal a bracelet made of strands of leather clamped together with three steel rings. Each ring had a word stamped in hangul characters.

"It's Korean," Josh explained. "My friend Ben helped me. This says 'friend,' this one says 'kind person,' and this one says 'brother.'" He waited, hoping it wasn't too much.

Radley stared at him a second, then put his

453

hand over his eyes to hide his tears, and Josh knew he'd done well.

"I love it so much," Radley said, putting it on. "My God, Josh, it's perfect. Are you sure you're not gay? Seriously, thank you." His mouth wobbled. "You know, I try to keep my own family out of my head, but holidays are . . . well. They're hard. And this . . ." He gestured to the bracelet. "This means so much to me. Thank you."

"You're welcome. You've been really kind." He thought back to that night in the Banana Republic dressing room. Radley had been more than kind. He'd been practically a guardian angel. "Besides," he added, "I always wanted a brother."

Radley got up and hugged him, and Josh hugged back, glad for his friend, awkward with the affection. Radley wiped his eyes and sat back down, and Josh was grateful when the conversation turned to Radley's evil Human Behavior professor. That was one of the best things about Radley, Josh thought as he watched his pal talk with great animation. He carried the conversation 90 percent of the time.

As they were leaving, Radley said, "Let me just go say hi to that guy over there." Josh paid the bill, then tried to wind his way through the packed bar to get to the exit. It was deafening in here, and he hated crowds. His anxiety jumped, but he reassured himself that he'd be home soon, on the couch with Pebbles, not a goddamn Christmas ornament in sight.

He waited behind a server, who was squarely blocking his way. Josh went to her left—nope. Right—nope. He tried to make eye contact with the people at her table, but they stared at her like she was the living Buddha as she answered their questions.

It was taking a *long* time. He tried to move past again, but the server apparently had no peripheral vision, because she, too, seemed oblivious to his presence. She was detailing the Eddy's elaborate drinks. "Um, that one has, uh . . . um . . . butter-washed Wild Turkey, maple, Pierre . . . something, and some . . . chocolate shavings? No, bitters! Chocolate bitters. It sounds gross, but, um, I've heard it's really good."

The maître d' glared at her. It wasn't a great sell, to be fair. Josh tried once more to get around, but nope, she was completely blind in her left eye, apparently, and the people at her table still would not make eye contact with him. He sighed and stared at the server's long dark hair, which was pulled into a braid. Cut that off, and he'd have a good strong rope.

"Okay," said the waitress, "so you *do* want the cinnamon in it, but not burnt? Um, I'll ask. Sure! Okay. But Chopin, and not Grey Goose. Got it. And Chopin is gin? No, no, of course. It's vodka.

Got it. And you want lemon in that? Juice or a twist? Got it."

He doubted she did. The patrons were being ridiculously particular, especially given that the restaurant was jammed.

Finally, she turned and almost bumped right into him. "Sorry, was I in your way? Oh, hey! It's you! Hi! How are you?"

It was the woman from the fun run, the one with the ancient dog in a baby stroller, who'd helped him when he passed out. "Hi," he said. "Right. The race."

"Yeah. You fainted! How are you now? I mean, obviously, you lived. But you were okay?"

"Yes. A little dehydrated, that was it."

"Good. I'm glad." She stood there a minute, smiling at him.

"You gonna put that drink order in sometime? Like, ever?" said one of the patrons at the table. Christmas tended to bring out the worst in people, Josh observed.

"Yes! Sorry! I will. Right now." She smiled again at Josh.

"How's Duffy?" he asked, a little shocked that he remembered the dog's name, then internally winced. The dog had to be dead by now.

"He's great! Thank you for asking! The vet gave him these supplements and some steroids. He's like a new dog. Seriously. It's like he's thirteen again."

456

How old *was* that dog? "Good. Oh, and your brother?" He'd had that condition where his joints popped out. Ehlers-Danlos, that was it.

"Oh, my *gosh,* you're so sweet to remember. He's good! Thank you."

"Well. Happy holidays."

"You too! Happy New Year!"

"Were you *talking* to a *woman?*" Radley asked when they were finally out on the sidewalk.

"Yes. We go to the same vet."

"Well, good for you, Joshua," Radley said. "Hey, it's snowing! Beautiful, isn't it?"

"It is."

Lauren had loved the snow. She used to stare out the windows in the darkened apartment and watch, sipping cocoa.

Her memory was everywhere.

"I'll see you on Christmas Eve, okay?" he said. "I'll text you my mom's address."

"Thanks, brother," Radley said. He held up his wrist. "I'm never taking this off."

On Christmas Eve, Radley arrived at Stephanie's promptly at five thirty, wearing an appropriately dapper suit for someone who worked in a men's clothing store. His arms were loaded with packages.

"It's so nice to meet you!" Stephanie cried, taking off her apron. She was wearing her *Free Mom Hugs* T-shirt with a rainbow heart, in case anyone missed the fact that she was very accepting, and hugged Radley tight. "I'm so glad you're here! Thank you for being my son's friend! I know he's a burden." She sent Josh a smug look that clearly said, *I delight in embarrassing you in front of your friends.*

"Wow, Mom," Josh said, but he smiled. It was all so normal.

"I've been dying to meet you, Ms. Park. Josh says you're the world's greatest mom. Is this true?"

"It is! Oh, Josh, thank you, honey. Also, Radley, you have to call me Steph. Or Mom, if you like, honey. Joshua says your family lives far away? So sad at Christmastime."

"Well, unlike yourself, they're homophobic assholes, so not that sad." His eyes met Josh's, and Josh gave him a chin jerk, acknowledging that he understood the white lie. It *was* sad. "But Joshua has officially adopted me as his brother, so I guess you totally *are* my mom."

"How about another hug, then!" Stephanie said, and Radley got a second, longer hug. When they broke apart, Radley had tears in his eyes. Josh gave him a manly lean-in hug and introduced him around to those who had not yet met his buddy.

It was quite a crowd—the Kims, who'd have their own kids over tomorrow; Jen, Darius, Sebastian and Octavia; Donna and her now-steady boyfriend Bill; and Sarah with some guy she'd dug up (he could already tell it wouldn't last); as well as three people from his mother's lab who didn't have family in the area.

Bill, whom Joshua had never met, was holding Octavia, and while he seemed like a perfectly nice guy, it gave Josh a pang. The familiarity, the contagious sadness that it was not Lauren's father who was here, that Donna's boyfriend would never know her daughter.

"The legendary son-in-law," Bill said, shifting the baby so he could shake Josh's hand. "I've heard so many great things about you. Merry Christmas."

"Really nice to meet you," Josh said, faking good cheer. "And, um . . . same! Great things."

It was crowded and noisy; Sebastian was strung out with excitement, making Octavia overly excited, too. The strangers from the lab were all very chatty and conversational, Darius and Radley were apparently in competition to become his mother's favorite son, bending over backward to help and compliment her. Donna and Bill were trying to keep Octavia happy, Jen was busy checking NORAD with Sebastian, the Kims were trying to woo his mother into taking another vacation with them, and now telling Donna she should come, too.

Guess they were all in the acceptance phase.

Suddenly, the red tar rose in his vision. How

dare everyone be happy? This was *Lauren's* holiday. The first Christmas without her, god-damnit. He wanted to bellow out his rage and pain; he wanted to kick Darius, who was telling some story that had half the room howling with laughter; he wished Sebastian would quiet the fuck down; he hated that his mother had done everything she always did on Christmas Eve. Where was the space for Lauren? Where was the acknowledgment? He didn't want to soldier on. He wanted to . . . break something.

He pictured himself standing under cold water, cooling the rage. *The quick brown fox jumps over the lazy dog. The quick brown fox jumps over the lazy dog.* Cold water. Yes. The waterfall in Hawaii they'd hiked to. That cold water, Lauren in a bathing suit, giggling as she wrapped herself around him.

Oh, Lauren.

Ben came over. "Need to step outside, son?" he murmured, a firm hand on his shoulder.

Just like that, the red was gone. Josh was being an ungrateful ass. All these people loved him, and he was about to have a meltdown like an overtired toddler. He glanced at Ben, shook his head. "Sorry. I was just . . . having a moment."

"It's understandable, Josh. We're all thinking of her. All doing our best."

"I know."

"Honey, would you put the gubbröra in the red bowl?" his mother asked him with a perceptive look.

"Sure thing, Mom."

He nodded at Ben and did as he was told.

Over dinner, Jen's pregnancy was announced, and they all drank champagne, with apple juice for the mama-to-be and kids.

Then Jen raised her glass and said, "To my sister," and they drank again, and Jen started crying, which made Donna cry, and Octavia joined in, and soon everyone was crying.

Except Josh (and the lab people). The tears didn't come. He couldn't talk around the lump in his throat or the ache in his chest. He nodded at the table, then picked up Octavia and brought her in to see the Christmas tree.

He was so tired. So tired of Lauren being dead. So tired of grief. Tired of well-wishers and hugs and a family that didn't have Lauren in it anymore.

Sarah came in and put her arms around him and Octavia. Didn't say anything, just leaned her head on his shoulder, and the ache in his chest became a knife, a dull, serrated knife that just about killed him.

Merry fucking Christmas.

"Thank you, Sarah," he murmured. The lights on the tree winked, and Josh felt a hundred years old.

• • •

He'd been smart enough to turn down invitations for Christmas Day, though his mom had hounded him to go to church with her, and Jen had pleaded with him to come watch the kids open their presents (at six a.m.). The forum had told him he could do whatever he wanted this first year of holidays without her, and so without much thought, he found himself heading east on I-195. Pebbles slept in the back seat, occasionally rousing to press her nose against the window.

The sky was gray, and there was no snow on the ground. Once he passed New Bedford, there were hardly any cars. Everyone was already where they were supposed to be. Everyone but him.

The Cape was quiet for the season, and the house they'd rented last summer was unoccupied. The shades were drawn, giving off a melancholy, lonely look. He pulled into the driveway, got out, and the smell of the ocean hit him hard. The thunderous crash of the surf brought him right back to the last time he'd been here. When he was still a husband. When his mission in life was to look after his wife.

Would the code to the door lock still work? Should he peek in the windows? No. It would hurt too much to see this place, empty without her laugh, her smile, her sparkliness.

Pebbles ran delightedly around the outside of the house, peed, then raced down the steep path to the beach. Josh followed. The smell of salt was strong, and the ocean was wild and beautiful, thanks to a full moon tonight and a tropical storm down the coast. Waves broke as far as he could see, a roiling white surf in a pounding, ceaseless roar. Pebbles fruitlessly chased a flying seagull, then found a stick and ran around with it, playing fetch with herself, dashing into the waves, then darting back.

Josh sat on the damp sand and looked at the view.

He could walk into that water and be dead of hypothermia in a relatively short time. Or drown, though he'd prefer hypothermia. The water was probably just above freezing, and he didn't have a lot of body fat. If he swam out far enough, nature would take him. And wouldn't it be appropriate, to die here? Would Lauren come for him the way she had imagined her father would come for her? Would they finally be together again?

What did he really have in this life that was worth keeping?

A lot, he knew, thinking of Octavia's soft warmth in his arms, of Jen's love, his mother's constancy. Ben and Sumi. Radley. Darius. Sarah. All of them. Pebbles, who well might follow him into the ocean and drown herself, and he couldn't let that happen.

But he stared at the crashing waves just the same.

He imagined going back up to the house, and instead of it being empty and cold, everyone was there. Lauren, healthy and pregnant, her whole family, all of his. Instead of last night's exhaustion, it would be so happy. So filled with joy. Because that's what Lauren did. She made the world happy. Everyone who knew her was better because of it. The house would smell so good, and they'd laugh, and he'd hug her and put his hand on her stomach, and after everyone had left, they'd go into their bedroom and make love to the sound of the waves.

He bent his head. *I miss you,* he thought. *I miss you so much. I don't want to live without you anymore, Lauren. I've done a good job, haven't I? Please come back. The letters are running out, and I need you. I can't live without you anymore. It's too hard.*

He got up, walked to the water's edge and stood there. A wave sloshed over his shoe, the bite of the Atlantic at first sharp, then numbing. He took a step in, his ankles and shins instantly frigid. Pebbles barked in delight, leaping next to him. Another step, so that the waves crashed above his knees. The undertow was strong, and when it tugged at him, he backed out.

"Come on, Pebbles," he said, and she obeyed. The wind was fierce, and his ears burned with the cold. He didn't want Pebbles to get too cold. He certainly didn't want her to be sucked out by the ocean.

They walked back up the path to the house. Josh let Pebbles into the car, and she decided then it was time to shake. With his shoes still squishing water, his pants plastered to his legs, he started the car and drove home as the darkness deepened.

29

Lauren

Fifty-one months left
November

Dear Dad,
I hope you've been watching, because you're going to be a father-in-law again pretty soon! Sure, sure, Darius is perfect, but I'm 10,000 percent sure you're going to love Josh just as much.

I'm in love, Daddy! First time ever, not counting Orlando Bloom (who will always have a corner of my heart, of course). But everything I ever hoped for is here with Josh. Everything. He makes me feel safe. Cherished. Beautiful. Like nothing bad could ever happen as long as we're together.

Check us out, Daddy. I know you'll approve.

Love,
Lauren

Fate. Destiny. Guardian angels. Tarot cards. Voodoo.

Whatever the case, Lauren knew that dating Joshua Park was just a formality. As soon as she saw him at the Hope Center, she knew—she just *knew*—he would be hugely important in her life. Their first date had only confirmed that. She had a lot to learn about the details of his life, but he was, as they say, the one.

They were extremely different. He worked alone, staring at his computer screen, headphones on, talking with a slew of subcontractors he rarely saw in person. He had one employee, a virtual assistant named Cookie, whom he'd never met but who handled things like his travel arrangements, meetings, billing and other mysterious assistant things. His business card said only *Joshua Park, Biomedical Engineer.*

In the years since their first and less-than-pleasant meeting, Joshua had gotten a master's of science with a focus on biomedical design from Brown *and* a PhD in mechanical engineering from MIT. You know. As one does. That thing he'd designed when he was eighteen, in his second year at RISD, because of course he started college young . . . that thing was a special chair geared for people who had to sit for long periods of time due to mobility issues. The chair monitored the occupant's heart rate, blood oxygen level and weight; provided moisture detection in case of incontinence, excessive sweating or edema leakage; and had vibration settings to stimulate lower extremity circulation. It could cool or warm the person seated in it, and could also boost them out if they wanted it, and lower them back in. It was also quite comfy and fun, which Lauren knew, because it was one of two chairs in Joshua's apartment.

The design had sold for just under $10 million. Thud.

"What did you do with the money?" Lauren had asked when, a month or two into their courtship, he'd volunteered this information.

"I paid my mom back for college. Set some aside for grad school. Banked it. Started a 401(k). Set up a scholarship. You know."

"No, I don't, since I've never made ten million dollars." She smiled. "Did you do anything fun?"

He thought about that. "I sent my mom on a vacation," he offered.

Turned out, he'd sent his mom and her best friends, Sumi and Ben Kim, on a *monthlong* vacation, first-class airfare and hotels, so they could visit Korea, Thailand and Australia. Private tours in the big cities, a designated credit card so he could pay for all their expenses.

"Did they love it?" Lauren asked, hands clasped in front of her.

"They did." And that was that. But he smiled, and his smiles could say more than ten thousand words.

Joshua Park owned his apartment—a soulless

but expensive two-bedroom in a new building near the river. It was a sharp contrast to her tiny but beautiful loft in a refurbished mill building, complete with original creaky floors and brick walls. While her apartment was cozy and charming, Josh's was bleak, aside from the view of the capitol's beautiful dome. He had a kitchen table but no kitchen chairs, two plates, two forks, two glasses. His living room held the medical chair, a couch, a huge TV, and a giant desk with five different computers. His bedroom contained a bed with one pillow. No art, no rugs, no throw pillows. He didn't have a car but did have a retirement fund.

Aside from food, she couldn't see that he spent money at all, adopting a painfully dull cargo shorts and T-shirt look that made him look seventeen years old.

"So being a spendthrift," she said. "Not a problem, I'm guessing?"

"The money's there if I need it," he said. "But I can't think of anything I need right now."

"Except for the love of a good woman," she said. "Which money can't buy, of course."

"I have that," he said, and her heart thrilled, because they hadn't said those words yet. Then he grinned. "My mom. She's a *very* good woman." And because he was so serious and quiet much of the time, his joke meant all the more.

Oh, she had it bad.

His second patent, which he finished while still at RISD, was a needle that could sense blood flow under the skin of newborns and children, minimizing bad sticks and bruising (and misery). He could've sold that one; instead, he made the design free, as Jonas Salk had done with the polio vaccine. He co-designed a battery-powered tool that replaced the old-fashioned mallet orthopedic surgeons used in joint replacement, then reworked the design for pediatric patients. Now he was working on a warming bed for premature babies that would sense drops in their heart rate and breathing.

He was incredible. Brilliant, philanthropic, hardworking, focused, driven, kind.

He also lost track of time, went days without showering and had terrible eating habits—takeout way too often, or dinner consisting of Flamin' Hot Doritos because quite often, he simply didn't hear the buzzer or see the text from the delivery service. He made several pots of coffee every day but forgot to take more than a sip or two, resulting in numerous mugs lurking on flat surfaces, the bitter smell of old grounds thick in the air.

In essence, he was a hermit. A beautiful hermit with a bad haircut and terrible clothes.

"Why don't you have your own company?" she asked, sitting one night in his sad living quarters. "You know, a giant eco-friendly building with meditation rooms and massage therapists roaming the halls, looking for tight shoulders. On-site daycare, company retreats in the Himalayas . . ."

He smiled. "You could design the space for me."

It *was* her profession, after all. "Done. I'd even give you a discount."

"I'm not really that kind of guy. I like being alone." He blushed a little. "But I also like having you here."

She felt a warm squeeze of pleasure. "And why is that?"

He shrugged, biting down on a smile. "You smell nice."

"Better than stale coffee and old pizza?"

"Let's not get crazy." Then he kissed her, his mouth slow and warm, his hands pretty damn excellent for a guy who didn't get out much, and yes, she was in love.

Since Josh had virtually no social life and communicated with people only via technology and only when absolutely necessary, she tried to open up his life a bit. He wasn't agoraphobic . . . he just worked a ton, and was on the shy side. Socially awkward, rather than socially anxious. He hated loud noises, like fireworks or roaring motorcycles, which made him agitated, saying the sound hurt his brain. In groups, he had a time frame before he would shut down like a phone that abruptly lost its charge—a half hour at first, then an hour as she wooed him out more and more. But he also said he had fun, once he relaxed a little. He told her he was on the spectrum and wasn't great at picking up cues all the time. "So if I'm being a jerk, please tell me," he said one night, in bed, post-nooky.

"Ditto," she said, smoothing back his hair. His earnestness . . . it got her right in the heart. "For the record, you were wonderful this past hour."

She took him hiking, surprised that he could outpace her when, to the best of her knowledge, his only form of exercise was walking from kitchen to desk to bedroom. Then again, her asthma was worse at different times of the year. But if she got out of breath, he'd stop and look at her with those dark, dark eyes lit with that gleam of light, and she'd feel so *seen,* so protected and loved, that maybe it wasn't the asthma. Maybe it was just love stealing her breath.

Love at second sight. Even though he'd insulted her way back when she was a twitty freshman, she had to give him points for being right. She *had* been shallow. She had been measuring her worth in cuteness, good cheer and popularity.

She didn't anymore. Her father's death, her mom's change in personality, the birth of Sebastian, her involvement in things like the community center, her desire to do well at her job . . . she'd grown up.

She wanted to be worthy of a person like Joshua Park.

Three days after they had run into each other at the Hope Center, when she had boldly taken fate by the horns and asked him out, Lauren was in a committed relationship. Just like that. There was no conversation or discussion—they just were. They talked every day. Texted more than that. Saw each other a few times a week, then nearly every day. She woke up smiling because of him, and even though she was generally a happy person, she now understood what had been missing in her life.

Him.

His deep, calm voice caused a physical reaction that made her insides tremble and thrill. When she saw him, she was propelled into his arms by nothing short of pure joy and a truckload of endorphins.

Love wasn't hard. It wasn't complicated. They didn't have to talk about monogamy or commitment. "I want to see you again as soon as possible," he said on their first date, so forthright and unguarded that she felt a rush of protectiveness.

She would take such good care of him. He was so pure, and she would make a beautiful life with him. For him. Because of him.

And he took care of her, too. He admired her work and understood its complexity, unlike most people, who thought she was an interior decorator or landscaper, rather than the designer of how space would be used. He was so focused on her as she talked about it that, at first, she felt shy. This guy saved *lives* with his *brain,* and it was kinda sorta hard to compete with that. But he asked for her perspective on things, readily admitting he didn't know anything about what made a park pretty or what purpose a public square had or what pedestrian flow meant. And he listened to her answers about how public spaces could be the soul of a city or college, how they could transform the bleakest industrial park or poorest neighborhood.

His attention, so focused and singular, made her feel bathed in warm, golden sun. No guy she'd dated had ever been so interested in her. Most had just waited for their turn to talk, or interrupted her or mansplained till she cut them off. Other guys bided their time (generally fifteen minutes) until they could see if she'd put out that night.

Josh *saw* her, heard every word, and made her feel . . . important. The most important person in the world.

Which, to be fair, was not the most common experience for Lauren. Jen was the superior sister, a fact Lauren would not dispute. Growing up, her mom always assumed her second daughter was fine, which Lauren was. Her mom had been a teacher, and her patience for kids dried up before she came home. Jen was fabulous, and Lauren was her biggest fan. Her dad had thought both his girls had hung the moon.

Men Lauren's age . . . most of them were still teenagers, no matter what age their driver's licenses showed.

So to have this beautiful, brilliant man tilting his head when she talked, his brows drawn together, not missing a single word she said . . .

To have this kind, gentle man asking her if he could hold her hand and later, kiss her, and later after that, unbutton her blouse . . .

To have him ask if she'd like to have dinner with his mother, because "she's dying to meet you" . . . it was like the best dream she'd ever had. No hipster pretentiousness, no millennial cynicism, no mansplaining superiority even though he was a bona fide genius who was making the world a better place.

He told her on their fifth date that he had wondered if he'd ever meet someone. That he'd never expected to get married, because his place on the spectrum put a lot of people off. That women didn't have patience for him. That he wasn't tall enough. That he didn't know how to flirt.

Lauren thought he was utterly delightful because of those things, not despite them.

Also, had he just actually said the word

married? She didn't ask him for further explanation, but she sure as hell replayed that sentence ten thousand times.

She didn't wonder if they should take things more slowly. Didn't wonder if anyone else was out there. She deleted her dating apps the night of the Hope Center opening.

He was the one. And so was she.

He was equal parts smooth and dorktastic. He unabashedly loved his mom, who raised him single-handedly after her boyfriend had abandoned her. Josh saw her and the Kims every Wednesday night for dinner. If his mom texted him a cat video, he'd watch it, and *love* it. Yes, he lost track of time and was often late and didn't have a Pavlovian response to texts and needed her to explain things like body language, only watched the same two TV shows (*The Great British Bake Off* and *Star Trek*). Yes, he desperately needed a decent barber. It didn't matter. He videoconferenced with the likes of Bill Gates and Bono—Bono!—and presented workshops on up-and-coming fields of biotech. Several times when they were out walking, deans from RISD and Brown had literally run to catch up to them to say hello to their prodigy.

Joshua also held the door for her and took her to the nicest restaurants as ranked by Providence .com (he was big on research). He was unabashed in telling her she was beautiful, smelled good, had smooth skin. He sent flowers to her home and office, sometimes twice in one day, forgetting that he'd already done it.

His work was so important, and he was so wonderful, but left on his own, he might stay in his apartment for the rest of his life, lost in his mind palace. So she scheduled time off for him, putting it into his phone so he'd get a reminder an hour before that he was due to shower and answer the door when she buzzed. She would text him and tell him to stretch and drink a glass of water and eat a vegetable, and he'd answer with a picture of a carrot and the words *thank you.*

They took walks in the cold winter air, went to student shows at the Providence Art Club and RISD, where Josh was always fawned over (justifiably) and Lauren was not (irritatingly). She cooked for him and introduced him to the wonder of roasted broccoli, which he had never tried before.

There was a *lot* of soulful gazing. It sounded cheesy, but it was . . . it was like coming home. Kissing was the best. Long, hot makeout sessions on various pieces of furniture or on a bench at the Roger Williams botanical gardens.

And sex . . . oh, God, sex was . . . it was fun and amazing and it had moments of utter . . . reverence. Because this was the last man she was ever going to have sex with. This was sex with the man she'd marry. This was the father of her future children, children she loved already.

When he asked her to meet his mother and the Kims, she was as nervous as she'd ever been. After all, Josh only loved a handful of people, and at least half of them would be at this dinner. She wore a modest dress, tried to look effortlessly perfect and natural in the hair and makeup area (which took hours) and called her sister eight times to get pointers on how to impress potential in-laws.

She didn't have to worry. Stephanie, a tall, striking blond woman who looked nothing like Josh, opened the door, took a critical look at Lauren, and then said, "I approve. Come on in."

She did, glancing at Josh with wide eyes. He shrugged.

The Kims, by contrast, fell on her. "At last!" Sumi cried. "Joshie has been telling us great things! Oh, sweetheart, you're lovely! Stephanie, the babies they'll make!"

"Let's not get ahead of ourselves," said Ben with a wink.

"That took . . ." Josh looked at his watch. "Sixteen seconds. Lauren, this is my mom, Stephanie Park, and our best friends, Sumi and Ben."

The photo albums were next. Stephanie, who seemed warmly amused by this whole "meeting my son's girlfriend" experience, brought out the photo albums of baby Josh and told the story of moving into this very house, eight months pregnant, having just transferred from Harvard to Brown. The Kims practically adopted her; Sumi had been Steph's birth coach.

"The cutest baby ever!" she said, clapping her hands. "No offense to our own four."

"They were funny-looking, it's true," said Ben.

Lauren drank in the pictures—the Kims throwing baby Josh a Baek-il, his one-hundred-day birthday. Steph laughing as Josh chewed wrapping paper on Christmas morning. Josh dressed in a little suit for Easter. Josh riding a bike, his face fiercely focused as Ben ran alongside him. At one of the Kim daughters' weddings. His high school graduation. Pictures of him in front of the first-year quad at RISD.

It looked very much like a happy, full life.

Stephanie was the director of the Rhode Island Hospital lab, overseeing a staff of about twenty. Once Josh turned eight, he'd gone to the Kims' house after school, which explained why he spoke Korean. The Parks were always included in holidays.

A small family circle—no mention of the deadbeat dad—but a loving, happy circle just the same.

"Tell us about yourself, Lauren," Stephanie asked at dinner.

"I work as a public space designer, which means I design everything from a bus stop to a park to a doctor's office. I have an older sister,

Jen, and she and her husband have a little boy. My mom still works as a reading consultant for the public schools, and my dad . . ." Her voice choked off unexpectedly. "My dad died when I was twenty."

"So sad," said Sumi, patting her hand. "Do you like Korean food?"

Lauren smiled. "I love it."

"I can teach you to cook, just like I taught Joshua!"

"I will *not* teach you to cook," said Stephanie, smiling. "I'm a fair gardener, though. And a great baker."

"Wait till you see Mom's peonies this spring," Josh said, and it warmed her through and through. Spring was months away, but he was planning on her being there.

Le sigh.

"Josh has never brought a girl home before," Ben murmured, leaning in. "We were a little surprised, to be honest. In the best way, of course." He smiled, and Lauren's toes curled in her shoes. They liked her. Thank God.

After they all cleaned their plates, Lauren practically wrestled Sumi for the honor of clearing the table. She and Josh loaded the dishes and washed the pots and pans together.

"You're doing great," he whispered in a rare moment of picking up on the unspoken.

She let out a breath. "I'm so nervous."

"Mom likes you. And the Kims *love* you."

After tea and coffee, Josh announced it was time to go, his "time spent with loved ones" meter expired. A bit to Lauren's surprise, Stephanie pulled her into a hug.

"We should have lunch," she said. "So we can really get to know each other."

"I would love that," Lauren said.

When they got into her car, Josh turned to her. "You okay?" he asked.

"I'm wonderful. I love them. They're so nice, Josh."

"Yes." He smiled.

"I hear you've never brought a girl home."

"No. Definitely not one I wanted to marry," he said.

There it was. That certainty. He looked at her a long minute, then kissed her on the lips, so gently. Joy filled her with a warm, buoyant, golden light.

"I love you," she said, and they both laughed, then kissed, and kissed some more, and Lauren's eyes were wet with tears of happiness.

He proposed on the first of May, a day when the blossoms on the crab apple trees were so thick they looked like pink whipped cream. He'd picked her up from work, and they walked hand in hand along the Providence River, just past RISD. Josh said he'd had a meeting with a company that day, explaining why he wore a suit she had never seen. The light was soft and golden, the breeze causing pink petals to drift and float, and then he was down on one knee, holding up a small velvet box.

The ring was an emerald-cut diamond set on either side with smaller diamonds, stunning in its simple beauty.

"Will you marry me?" he asked, and she just looked at him, smiling with more love in her heart than she knew it could hold.

"Damn right I will," she said. Of *course* she would. It was just a formality. She was meant to be his wife, and he was destined to be her husband.

As they kissed, she made a vow. She would do everything in her power to make a beautiful, happy, meaningful life. The last thing she would ever do was break this man's heart.

30

Joshua

T he letter had sat there for a few days now, throbbing like a wound in his mind. He dreaded reading it. He was dying to read it. But after this, there would only be one more, and once these stopped, he didn't know how he would face the future. Couldn't she have done this for two years? Five? Ten?

Finally, with a sigh, he sat down, patted the couch so Pebbles would leap up next to him, then opened the letter.

Hello, honey.
If you're still reading these, I guess you still want to hear from me. I'm glad, Josh. I know one thing. Even if I'm dead, I would never really leave you. I don't know what or how that looks right now, but I remember feeling my dad around me. I hope you can feel me there with you sometimes, just enough to reassure you.

So it's been a good long while since I

483

died. I hope your new normal isn't too isolated or sad. I hate the idea that I've made your life sad. We had shitty luck with the IPF, but God, we had the best luck with each other.

I've been thinking a lot here on Cape Cod, listening to the ocean, trying to imagine what your life will be like eleven months after I die. I hope you at least gave some thought to meeting your biological father. If you do decide to meet him, I hope and pray it goes well. I hope whatever you decided, you know that the last thing you could ever be is disposable.

He had to stop for a minute and take a few breaths. She'd been right about that meeting. It had given him something. A face. A story to fill the void. A sense of peace. And it reinforced the knowledge that Ben Kim was the greatest man Josh had ever known. He felt even closer to him after meeting his biological father.

I think about when I first came to your apartment, and it was such a mess. Hopefully, I broke you of that habit and our place is neat and clean.

"It is, honey," he said.

I remember how you went for days without going outside, how you never went to the rooftop unless I ordered you to. I remember how when we were dating, I'd be the only person you saw sometimes for days at a time.

I don't want that to be your life now, Josh. And so . . .

I think you should buy a house. That's my job for you this month, honey. Start looking for houses. One with a yard for Pebbles, grass for you to cut, a garden where you can grow tomatoes, because you love tomatoes fresh from the vine, warm from the sun. I want you to have neighbors to wave to, and I want you to shovel some old lady's walk when it snows. I want little kids to ring your doorbell on Halloween. I want you to walk out to the mailbox and chat with the nice folks across the street. Our apartment was great, but it's pretty isolated, and even I couldn't win over that couple from the second floor. Plus, Creepy Charlotte scares me (if she's your second wife, I'm going to kill you, FYI).

He laughed out loud. Creepy Charlotte had opened her door the other night the second Josh had come home from a run. She was wearing a towel only. "Did you knock?" she'd asked.

"Absolutely not," he said, running up the stairs before the towel could "slip." He'd definitely gotten better at reading people this past year.

> What do you think, babe? You don't need to buy a house right now (but you can afford it, don't forget). Maybe just start looking. Take Sarah. She loves open houses.
>
> It's a way to start thinking about a life separate from where we lived so happily together. Because that life is in the past now. It's time to start making something new.
>
> I love you so, so much, Joshua Park.
>
> Lauren

He thought a minute.

Shopping for houses . . . sure. It was fun. He liked seeing open houses, just like anyone.

But leaving this place? That life wasn't past! She was wrong. His life was right here, in the place where they'd lived. He'd bought the new couch, the new bed, as she'd asked.

But it was *not* time to leave.

He wadded up the letter and threw it across the room, whereupon Pebbles leaped on it. Josh cursed, got up and took it out of her drooly mouth, smoothed it out and looked at it. Some of Lauren's handwriting smeared, which made him feel like utter shit.

He pulled out the ironing board and iron and smoothed the letter out. "I'm sorry," he said. Pebbles wagged her tail and barked.

He knew Lauren wanted the best for him. He also knew that a lot of her suggestions had done some good. Seeing his father had put to rest some of his feelings. Kissing Cammie had been pleasant enough. Buying new clothes had brought Radley into his life.

But leave the apartment where they lived together? Where they'd made love and cooked and watched movies and figured out her care? He couldn't imagine it. He didn't want to feel *more* distant from her.

A new couch and bed was one thing. A new place? Every corner of the apartment was infused with her. It was a shrine in some ways—the photos of her, the paintings she'd chosen, the towels, the napkins. Everything was a reminder of loss as well as of Lauren. Anything new was similarly in her memory—*I bought this when my wife had been dead for six months and four days. I bought this to hang where our wedding photo was.* It hadn't erased her in any way; it had made her absence all the more noticeable.

Time for the punching bag now.

• • •

"I don't want to live somewhere else," he said to Ben a few hours later.

"Yeah, those fists are telling a story," said Ben, smiling kindly. "Try to wrap up next time."

They were sitting in the basement of the Kims' house, Ben's man cave all these years, a place where Josh had spent many hours building things from the bits of metal and wood Ben offered him. The room smelled faintly of spices with a hint of smoke from their fireplace upstairs. It was one of the places Josh felt safest in the world.

But not tonight.

Ben handed him a length of wire, thin enough that Josh could twist it. Yes. It was good to have something to do with his hands. Better than a fidget spinner, anyway. Ben knew him well.

"You'll never be ready, son. But you'll do it anyway. And after some time passes, it won't feel so wrong."

"I don't want time to pass," Josh admitted in a low voice, not looking up. "Every day is a step away from her." His voice broke, just a little. The image of her last day flickered at the edges of his brain, and he shoved it away. Twisted the wire. Bent it. Threaded it through a loop. Lauren on the beach, on the bed, on their wedding day. Anything but that last day.

Ben said nothing, but another moment later Josh felt the older man's hand on his shoulder.

Ben was right. There was nothing to say. Time would pass. Time had already left him behind. He handed the wire, now a small box with a lid, to Ben and stood up. "You're right. Thanks, Dad," he said, and for a second—just a fraction of a second—he could smell his wife's perfume. He headed for the door.

"Hey." Ben's voice stopped him. "You don't get to call me Dad and then leave without a hug."

Josh wasn't a hugger. Well, he didn't used to be. Seemed like he was getting pretty good at it. Ben's eyes were shiny when they pulled apart. He patted Josh on the cheek, and Josh smiled.

Nice to have someone who didn't need a lot of words. Nice to have a father who understood him so well.

Frank the Realtor had just about squealed when he heard Josh's budget, which Josh had given as "probably not more than $2 million."

"I have *plenty* to show you," Frank said breathlessly. "When are you free?"

Josh called Sarah and Radley to see if they wanted to come along. "Oh, my God, absolutely," Radley said. "It'll be the only time I get to see inside some of these beauties."

Sarah, too, was thrilled. "I love seeing other people's houses," she said as they approached stop number one.

"Such a voyeur," Radley said.

"Exactly."

"Hello!" said the Realtor, cantering over to meet them. "Joshua Park? So nice to meet you! I'm Frank!"

"Gay," Radley muttered. "He's eye-fucking me already."

"He's eye-fucking Josh's bank account," Sarah murmured.

Josh ignored the naughty children and got out, shook hands and introduced his friends. "They're—"

"We're getting married, and Josh is buying us a house!" Radley exclaimed, gripping Sarah's arm. "So generous!"

"Really, Josh, you didn't have to. But we're grateful," Sarah added, fixing Radley's hand so they looked more natural.

"Wow, that's super fun!" said Frank, the poor slob, looking slightly confused.

"Let's go in," Josh suggested, then whispered to his friends. "Why are you lying?"

"It's more fun this way," Radley whispered back. They approached the monstrous house, which was one of the great Victorian beauties on College Hill. Josh had always thought it was a museum, truthfully.

"So this is a five-bedroom home with a fully updated kitchen, attic space, separate garage and—"

"We'll just look around and ask questions as

they arise," Radley said. "Come, precious, let's wander." He led Sarah inside, holding her hand if she were the queen and he her devoted foot servant.

The house was beautiful, that was for sure. Huge, too. It had a big entrance foyer with a sweeping staircase, formal dining room on one side, giant paneled living room on the other.

"Look at these stairs!" Radley exclaimed. "I would sweep down in my dressing gown every single morning. These stairs are made for drama."

"You could carry me up to bed every night," Sarah said.

"And *totally* ravish you!" Radley said. He tried to pick Sarah up, but failing (he was a scrawny thing), he and Sarah nonetheless ran upstairs, laughing like hyenas.

Josh and Frank trailed behind. "You'd have fifty-five hundred square feet," Frank said. "Five full bathrooms, two half baths, central air, a really gorgeous master bath—"

He stopped in the doorway of the master bedroom. Radley and Sarah were rolling around on the king-size bed like puppies.

"I *love* me a hard mattress," Radley said with a Southern drawl.

"I *love* me a hard man," she returned, and they dissolved again into laughter.

"Um . . . they're so . . . in love," Josh said.

"Whatever you say," Frank said, doubt heavy in his voice.

The house had a study, a beautifully redone kitchen, a dining room, family room, office, butler's pantry (whatever that was), a formal living room, the aforementioned five bedrooms.

"The yard's a little small," Josh said, looking out the back window. "And I think the house is a little too large."

"Are you two planning on having kids?" Frank asked Radley gamely.

"We are," Sarah said. "God willing, we'll have eight."

"We're waiting till the wedding night to consummate the marriage," Radley said. "Sarah didn't want to, but I insisted. I want to be pure for my bride." They darted out of the room, where they could be heard gasping with laughter, congratulating each other on their funniness.

"Sorry. They're idiots, but they're mine," Josh said. "What else have you got?"

"You want to stay in Providence proper, right?"

"I think so," Josh said. "I honestly haven't thought about it until recently."

The next house was another breathtaking beauty, and about a third smaller than the first house. But again, the backyard was teeny. Pebbles wouldn't be able to run anywhere.

Maybe Lauren was right. Being in a neighborhood would be good for him. The mill building was gorgeous, and while Josh was cordial with his neighbors, he barely knew them (and didn't see any reason to change that now).

But working outside in the yard, or sitting on the porch, saying hello to neighbors as they walked . . . well, it could happen. Especially with his two goofy friends. They'd help break the ice. He pictured Octavia and Sebastian there, Darius grilling up some brats on the grill, Jen holding the new baby. "Maybe something with a little more room outside."

They looked at a third house, but it was down by the capitol, right near the train station, and Josh would be driven crazy by the noise. It was also new construction, and very new money, which Josh supposed he was, but he was not the type who needed to brag about his Venetian glass drawer pulls and Italian marble island. "I'm so over this subway tile, all-white kitchen," Radley said. "But this island, babe. Think of the *filthy* things we could do up here."

"Ooh. Chop those vegetables the way Mommy likes," Sarah said in a breathy voice.

More staggering, more wheezing, more apologies from Josh.

"Are you actually interested in buying a house, or is this just because you're bored?" Frank asked. "It's okay if you are. People do it all the time."

"No, I . . . I just started looking. These two are

just comic relief. My wife died in February, and I . . . I guess I need a change."

"I'm so sorry," Frank said.

"Thanks." Hopefully, his tone shut that conversation down.

"Describe the perfect house for you," Frank suggested, sitting at the island and gesturing for Josh to do the same.

The perfect house would have Lauren in it. Their kids.

Don't be a loser.

Josh took a deep breath and exhaled. "I don't want a mansion. This is too . . . imposing. It's beautiful, but it's too . . . sterile. The other houses were too much like museums." He thought a moment. "I want a house where my family can visit. A big yard for my dog. A decent kitchen. I like to cook." He liked to cook for others. Cooking for himself was boring, and depressing to boot.

"Got it," Frank said. "I have a place in mind, actually. It's not in Providence, but it's just over the line in Cranston. It backs up to Narragansett Bay, and it's a nice old house with great woodwork and some stained glass windows. Big but not grotesque. It needs some work, but the bones are great. Want to see it?"

"Sure." Radley and Sarah would, that was for sure.

Twenty minutes later, they arrived at the house, a fat older house, not quite a Victorian, not quite

Arts and Crafts, not quite Tudor . . . a little odd, really, with its steeply pitched roof and lead-paned windows. Big yard. The back led to a set of stairs down to a dock overlooking Narragansett Bay.

It smelled like the ocean and pine trees.

They went up the deep front porch, which wrapped around one corner. It would be nice and shady in the summer, he imagined. Frank fumbled with his key.

"Sorry we were acting like children," Radley said, smiling. "We're his friends. This guy here is solid gold, but he needs a laugh every now and then."

"Children are much better behaved than the two of you," Frank said, glancing at Radley. Maybe he *was* eye-fucking. Josh didn't know about these things.

Frank found the right key, opened the front door, a solid oak relic flanked by lead-paned windows, and in they went.

"Holy shit," Sarah said. "It's . . . wow."

They wandered around in silence, Frank wisely letting them see for themselves.

Beautiful woodwork, stained glass and beams greeted them in the living room, which clearly had remained untouched since it was built—the craftsmanship and style were from another era. It smelled a bit musty, but not in a bad way . . . just in an old-house way.

Whoever lived here last had been fond of ugly wallpaper and paint colors. The dining room was a violent shade of purple but sported a fireplace; the kitchen was mac 'n' cheese yellow, with the original glass-paned cabinets painted blue. At some point, the owner had updated the counters to yellow Formica, and the floor was chipped vinyl.

The house went on forever . . . a small study with chestnut floor-to-ceiling bookcases against orange-painted walls. There were multiple fireplaces and porches. There was a sunroom, wallpapered with a pattern that resembled splotches of blood, and, continuing the body secretions color palette, bile-green shag carpeting.

Upstairs, it was uglier . . . the previous owners had put in awkward modifications here and there—dividing one bedroom into two with a shaky wall, installing a casket-sized shower in one bathroom and, for some mysterious reason, building a closet around the claw-foot tub. Three bathrooms were carpeted. Every upstairs window would need to be replaced, and some would have to be custom-made. Four bedrooms plus a very cool attic suite on the third floor that had a sitting room with slanted ceilings and funky little windows, a good-sized bedroom and full bathroom. "This used to be the maid's quarters. Perfect for a teenager," Frank said.

Outside, the large, wooded yard led down to the

water. There was a workspace over the garage, its windows looking over the bay, where, come summer, there'd be a plethora of sailboats, no doubt.

"The Edgewood Yacht Club is over there," Frank said, "if you're interested in boating."

He pictured Lauren sitting on the deck of a sailboat in a big floppy hat, smiling at him. "I'm not really a boat person," he murmured.

He could always sell it, probably at a profit once he got rid of that tacky wallpaper, over-hauled the kitchen and updated the bathrooms. He kind of liked the rambling nature of the house, the fact that it wasn't just one thing. It was full of nooks and crannies and secret closets, beautiful banisters and a creepy cellar.

It was, he thought, a little bit like him. Awkward on the outside, yet lovely within, if you could put in the work. The house was to Josh as Josh had been to Lauren—needing an overhaul, but full of potential.

He bet she would've liked that analogy.

He could picture Sebastian and Octavia playing on the porch with their little cars and trucks and animal toys, watching fireworks on the Fourth of July. The yard was plenty big enough for a dog, or even two. Darius and Jen could come and stay; he could almost hear Darius's big laugh as he grilled. Plenty of room for every-one.

And, in the study with the broken fireplace, a little girl could curl up on that window seat and read all day. She could color in the sunroom and make a fairy house under the big maple trees, the way Lauren had told him she had done as a child. Stand at the counter and help Sumi and Ben make kimchi.

This little girl . . . she was not Octavia. She was . . . his.

His future daughter. Shy like him, black hair, pretty eyes. She'd love to read and build things. She could sleep in the front bedroom with the big windows and run down the ornate stairs on Christmas morning. She could sit in the deep claw-foot tub at bathtime, and he would push her hair back from her face as he tucked her in at night, and—

"I'll take it," he said to Frank. "Excuse me a minute."

He bolted outside and stood under the bare trees, looking toward the water. His heart jack-hammered in his chest, and for a few seconds, his vision blurred, but the cold air helped. It wasn't a red-out. It was something like panic. He was breathing too fast. *The quick brown fox jumps over the lazy dog. The quick brown fox jumps over the lazy dog. The quick brown fox.*

"I'm sorry, Lauren," he said out loud. "I'm sorry." He leaned against the pine tree, its bark rough against his back.

That little girl was the first time he'd pictured a future without his wife that wasn't bleak and solitary. The first time he'd imagined the possibility of being happy without Lauren. Of loving someone not linked to her. The first time he'd imagined having a child who wasn't theirs.

He took in a slow breath and let it out, then another. Wiped his eyes.

Don't be a loser, he could almost hear her saying. *This is exactly the point.*

31

Joshua

Month twelve
February

The rush of buying the house carried him along for a few weeks. He'd shown it to Jen and her crew. Sebastian had proclaimed it "the best house in the world for hide-and-seek, Uncle Josh!" and Donna had clucked over how extravagant it was, "but you deserve it, of course." His own mom had simply told him how proud of him she was, and then picked out the room she'd like "when Sumi, Ben and I come here for two weeks every August." Ben proclaimed it perfect for Josh.

After the whirlwind closing, Josh went back to the house with Radley and Sarah. The neighborhood was quiet; Josh assumed some of the houses were second homes that filled up in the summer. The former owners had agreed to sell him some of the furniture, which was great . . . some of the stuff was quite nice, and the house was too big for him to furnish on his own.

He figured his two friends would be good people to give him advice on where to put stuff

. . . and help him feel less lost in this place. He didn't plan to move in for some time, although Frank had told him that the market was hot for loft apartments like his, and he'd be thrilled to list Joshua's.

But the apartment was where he and Lauren had lived. Josh wasn't sure if he was *ever* going to sell it. He didn't have to decide right away, but he did need to get his ass in gear and earn some more money.

Chiron Medical Enterprises, the company in Singapore, had sent him a case of wine and reminded him they'd love to host him, whatever he decided about their job offer, which was still on the table.

Right now, Radley was peppering Sarah with questions about why she went into public service instead of the more lucrative private counseling.

"I wanted to go where the need was greatest. The kids in the system . . . it just sucks so bad for them. Most of the time, they're taken out of their homes at a really awful moment, then plopped into a foster home. No matter how nice the foster family is, it's traumatic. So if I can be their friend, or their rock, during that time . . ."

There was a lot of nobility in that answer.

"Do you think you'll ever burn out?" Radley asked.

"Absolutely. It seems like everyone in the department does. But for now, I'm good." She stood back and surveyed the results of the furniture placement.

"When you go to private practice, we can be partners."

"That would be so fun, Radley." She smiled at their friend, then looked at Josh. "How are we doing, Josh? You like where we put this?"

"Yes," he answered before he looked at it.

"Great! Well, I have to run. I've got a date."

"Not so fast," said Radley. "Spill."

"He's a telemarketer," she said sheepishly. "Timeshares."

"Oh, my God, honey," Radley said, recoiling. "Is the dating scene that bad?"

"Yes."

"Any port in a storm?" Radley asked.

"I just think if I comb through enough manure, I'll find my diamond."

"You deserve someone great, Sarah," Josh said, surprising himself. "You sell yourself short."

She tilted her head to look at him. "Thank you?"

"You do. Don't go out with the telemarketer."

"Hey. He's employed, unlike half of the men I meet."

"Maybe you date crappy men so you'll always have an excuse for why you're single," he said.

"Josh!" Radley said. "You need to work on your filter, honey." He looked at Sarah. "He's right, though."

"Oh, fuck you very much, both of you," she said fondly. "I'll text you later. Miracles happen. He could be a good person. See you guys soon."

She left, and Radley sighed. "If I was straight, I'd marry her."

"Really?"

"Sure. Maybe. Or not. I don't know. The idea of sex with a woman makes my testicles retract. What shall we do next, Joshua?"

"I was thinking," he said. Should he filter this next thing? "Um . . . would you like to live here? Maybe? You could have the third floor. And when you start seeing clients, you could use the space over the garage. But if you don't want to, it's okay."

Radley's eyes were wide. "That's a very big offer. Are you sure?"

"Yeah. It's too big for one person."

Radley sat back. "Well, Joshua, that's incredibly kind of you. But you won't be alone forever. You'll find someone again."

"I'm not . . . it's only been eleven and a half months." He swallowed. "I would love to have you. If not you, I'd probably find someone else. A tenant or something. I . . . I might be traveling more in the future, and it would be good to have someone here when I'm gone. Dog care and . . . that kind of thing." He paused. "Companionship."

Radley sat quietly for a minute. "My lease runs out in March. We'd have to have ground rules about privacy and all that. You might get sick of me."

"True." He felt his lips tug in a smile.

"Maybe we can do a trial run. Six months, and if it's not working or either of us feels uncomfortable, no hard feelings. I mean, I need my own space, too. And I'd insist on paying rent. A token amount, but still."

"Okay."

They looked at each other, then Radley leaped to his feet and hugged him. "Oh, my God, this is so exciting! Can I go see my floor?"

Josh laughed, and Radley ran upstairs. "This house is fucking beautiful!" he yelled behind him.

Good. He wouldn't be alone. Radley never talked about it, but Josh knew money was tight. This would be a win for them both.

As ever, he thought of Lauren. *You would love him,* he thought. *He's my best friend, outside of you.*

In two weeks, it would be their fourth wedding anniversary. And right on the heels of that, the first anniversary of her death.

A year. Would the grief magically lift? Would it get worse? He supposed he was about to find out.

On February 14, Josh started drinking wine at noon. Funny that a year ago, he had been a teetotaler. Well. Widowers deserved to drink, especially on a crap day like today. It was dark and sleeting out, the perfect atmosphere for misery. Nothing like New England's shitty winter weather to underscore the mood. He went into his bedroom and brought the dogwood tree out to the living room and sat it next to the couch.

"Let's watch our wedding video," he practically snarled. Great. So he resented the tree now. And why shouldn't he? It was feeding off his dead wife.

He pulled up the video on the TV. It had been their tradition to watch it on their anniversary. Three whole times. *Thanks for killing her, God. If you exist, you're an asshole. Go ahead, strike me down. I'm ready.*

There was Darius, beaming like a proud papa as he walked Lauren down the aisle. Her mother sobbing, Jen beaming, his own mom teary eyed and smiling. Ben looking so dapper as best man.

And Lauren, so full of life and light that she truly did glow. No tears for her that day—she'd been all smiles. The most beautiful expression on her face, solemn yet joyful, as she looked in his eyes and said the words. "I, Lauren Rose Carlisle, take you, Joshua Stellan Park, to be my husband."

His own voice had been steady and sure that day, and he remembered knowing with every molecule in his body that this was right. They belonged together.

Their first dance hadn't been slow and romantic. It had been "For Once in My Life" by Stevie Wonder. Happy, bouncy, a song that brought a smile to everyone, and their guests had clapped along as Josh and Lauren spun and laughed and goofed around on the dance floor. No practiced routine for them, no sir. Just pure, unadulterated joy.

And now he was alone, day-drinking and crying. He pulled Pebbles onto his lap and let his tears seep into her soft fur while she licked his head. Just last year, Lauren had left a path of lit candles to their bedroom. It turned out to be the last time they'd made love.

A *year*. A fucking year without her. He wasn't proud of himself for surviving it. He would've cheerfully died if it were up to him. He should've been hit by a bus, and the laughs they'd have in the Great Beyond if that happened . . .

He would never love anyone the way he'd loved her.

It took him some time to notice the red envelope that had been slipped under his door.

Lauren's handwriting. *Happy Anniversary.*

A yellow sticky note was attached to the envelope, in different handwriting. *There's one more left after this one. Take care today. —Sarah*

His hands shook as he opened it. It was one of those overly expensive cards made with tiny swirls of paper, practically a sculpture. Two hearts intertwined, all the colors of the rainbow where the hearts intersected.

Inside there was only one line, in her fat, pretty handwriting.

I will love you forever.

"I love you, too," he said, his voice rough with emotion.

He was so, *so* grateful she'd thought ahead, thought of him without her.

But he *missed* her. He missed her so much that his knees gave out, and he slid to the floor and let his head fall back against the door.

Then Pebbles was there, wagging, licking him, whining, nudging him hard with her herder's nose. "Okay, okay," he said, wiping his eyes on his sleeve. "Message received." He was treated to a full face-lick from the dog. "You're a good girl," he said, hugging her. "Such a good puppy."

He went back to the couch, looked at his watch: 1:16 p.m. Just ten hours and forty-four minutes until this endless day was over.

On February 22, Joshua held a jesa ceremony to honor his wife on the anniversary of her death.

He'd been talking more frequently to Ben since he'd met his biological father. This day needed to be marked, and Ben came through, as ever, with the idea for a jesa, a Korean tradition to honor the dead. It was usually reserved for ancestors, Ben had said, but who cared? He had described the ceremony in great detail, and to Josh, it sounded perfect.

He'd gone to the Kims' the day before, and his mom took a rare day off to help cook. There were Korean foods and some of Lauren's non-Korean favorites, all in some kind of order to pay homage to her life.

Now all that food sat in five rows on Josh's coffee table—the dessert row, which contained chestnuts, pears, apples and persimmons, as well as clementines, which had been Lauren's favorite fruit, and yakgwa, the honey cookies she had loved. Donna had brought chocolate chip cookies, Lauren's childhood favorite, and Josh added them as well. The next row held pickled herring (another Lauren favorite), kimchi, shrimp and stuffed clams. Then came the soups—fish, vegetable, chicken noodle. The next row of food contained the sticky chicken she loved, and jeon, the vegetable-imbued pancakes. The final row, farthest from where Josh would sit, contained a bowl mounded with rice and another type of soup—beef turnip, Korea's traditional soup for the dead, and a bowl of sand.

Ben had brought over a small rice-paper screen, which was set up at the other side of the coffee table, the idea being that Lauren's spirit would come and sit on the other side of it. On the table was a picture of her taken on their wedding day, her eyes shining, her skin perfect, her lips curved in a smile full of love. Next to the table was the dogwood tree, a full foot taller than it had been last year.

Josh knew he would do this jesa only this once. That after today, the first year would be over, and all those firsts would be done. But he needed to mark this day somehow, and the whole year that had passed. He'd invited everyone close to her—Jen and her family, Donna and her boyfriend Bill, Sarah, Radley, Asmaa, and Lauren's boss, Bruce. Sumi and his mom, and Ben, of course.

When everyone had arrived and stood in the living room, he opened the living room window to let in her spirit. A few seconds later, he closed it. *Hope you made it inside, babe,* he thought, swallowing the lump in his throat.

Jen's face was already wet with tears, and Sebastian's eyes were round and solemn. Octavia was asleep on Darius's shoulder. Donna and Bill held hands, Donna's eyes red-rimmed. Sarah and Radley stood together. Asmaa stood next to Bruce, her arm through his. Ben had his arm around Sumi. Everyone watched in silence.

Josh knelt in front of the table and lit the incense—ironic, since Lauren hated incense. *Don't let that keep you away,* he thought, almost smiling. Then Jen handed him a cup of rice wine, which he circled over the table. He'd spent all week studying the ceremony notes Ben gave him, but if he got some wrong, he was sure Lauren would forgive him. He poured a little wine into the sand three times, then laid a pair of chopsticks across the rice bowl.

He turned to Donna and bowed to her, the mother, and then repeated the gesture to Jen, honoring her family. Tears were on everyone's cheeks now, and all was quiet except for the sound of sniffling.

Josh stood and faced the photo of his wife, his heart gripped in a vise. "Lauren Rose Carlisle Park," he said, his voice surprisingly steady, "I call your name as the year changes, and the day on which you died has come. I will love you forever and will never forget your love, as big and wide as the heavens. In your honor, I humbly offer you this meal." Then he knelt in front of the table, looking at her picture for a minute, then bowed so his forehead touched the cool floor.

He stayed there a minute, tears flooding his eyes. So much love, so much sorrow. *I miss you,* he thought. *Please be safe. Please be happy.*

When he rose, his mother handed him a tissue and gave him a nod of approval, squeezing his arm.

"Thank you all for coming," he said, his voice breaking, and then Jen was hugging him, and his mother, and Donna and Sarah and Darius, Sebastian wrapping his little arms around Josh's legs, everyone, everyone gathered around him and held him in their love . . . not just for Lauren, but love for him.

"We love you, Josh," Jen said fiercely.

"We do, brother," Darius said.

"I love you, Uncle Josh."

"I love you, son." *I love you. We love you. We love you.*

He started to cry then, and surrendered to it, sobbing in the embrace of their love. They weren't just here for Lauren. They were here for him.

"We do get to eat," he said finally, and everyone laughed.

"Good. I'm starving," Jen said, squeezing him harder before releasing him.

He knew there was a proper way to serve the food and such, but he was done with the formality. This was enough. His guests helped themselves, his mother and Sumi handing out forks and plates and chopsticks. Donna poured wine and Darius opened beers. Josh went to the window and looked out, the cold air feeling good against his skin.

Sarah came and took his hand. "She would be so proud of you," she whispered. "She always was. You did it, Josh. You made it through the first year."

He nodded, and then he hugged her. "Thank you for sticking by me," he said.

She nodded, took a shaky inhale, then let go.

"How was your date?" he asked.

"It was as bad as you guys predicted," she said, wiping her eyes. "One of his icebreaker questions was 'If you were going to kill me, how would you do it?' "

He laughed. "Wow."

"Another one bites the dust," she said. "Hey, would it be okay if I put on some music? Some of Lauren's favorites?"

"That would be great," he said. She went over to the iPad and started clicking away.

Ben appeared next to him. "You did great, son," the older man said. "She was . . . she was a special girl." There were tears in his eyes.

Josh hugged him. "Thank you, Ben. For being my father. For helping me."

"It's an honor."

Josh patted Ben's shoulder. "Go get some food."

"What about you?"

"I'll be there in a minute."

It was good to have a little distance from the throng, but he was so, so glad they were all here. A year ago, and for the two years previous, he had only thought of them as Lauren's.

This past year, they had become his as well, some more than others, but all of them taking him into their hearts.

He was lucky. They had walked with him through this long, lonely year. He was *damn* lucky, not just to have been Lauren's husband, but to have all of these people as well.

Then he saw a movement in the far corner of the living room, and his heart jolted. For just one second, he saw his wife, wearing the long pink dress she'd worn so often that Cape Cod summer. Her hair was loose, and she wasn't wearing her cannula. She was watching Sebastian and Octavia, who were playing on the couch, a faint smile on her lips.

Then she turned to him and smiled in full, that smile that just staggered him. Her brown eyes sparkled with laughter, as they had so often. For that one second, he saw once again all the love she had for him, all the joy.

He didn't look away. He didn't even breathe, hoping the moment would last forever. Then his eyes swam with tears, and when he blinked, she was gone.

32

Joshua

Month thirteen
March

He did not read the letter Sarah left in March.

Instead, he emailed Alex at Chiron Medical Enterprises and asked when would be a good time to visit. Then he called Cookie, who booked him a flight, and he flew to Singapore a week later.

At the Chiron headquarters, he told Alex and Naomi his terms. He'd take the job but would need to be based in Rhode Island, though he'd spend two weeks out of six in Singapore. Way to rack up those frequent-flier miles. They said yes immediately.

He was introduced around, given a first-class tour of the beautiful city, taken out for dinner and to meet the woman who would be his Singapore-based assistant. Over dinner, he told Alex and Naomi he was a widower, and it had been just over a year. They expressed their condolences, and no one said anything more about it.

His salary was less than he'd made some years,

514

but it was steady, had good healthcare benefits, six weeks a year of vacation (because everyone but Americans knew the value of significant time off). He'd also get bonuses based on patent and design implementation. Alex and Naomi suggested he hire two engineers and an assistant to work in Providence.

It was time for a change.

33

Lauren

Fifty-seven months left

Two years and one month after her father died, and the day after she graduated from Rhode Island School of Design, Lauren Rose Carlisle had made a list.

A really important list.

The past twenty-five months had been tumultuous. When her father died the spring of her sophomore year, she was thrown into a tarry pit of chaos and grief. Dad had been the world's best, and his death was so shocking it changed Lauren's world. The rest of her college time was spent in the weird limbo of loss where she went through life, eating and showering, doing projects and papers and hanging with her friends and sister. Sometimes she found herself laughing, and it came almost as a surprise. Sometimes, she'd stop abruptly in the middle of a sidewalk, asking herself, "Am I awake right now? Is this really my life? Are you seriously saying I will *never* see my father again?"

The fabulous Dave Carlisle, beloved by all, hated by none, devoted husband, adoring father, excellent neighbor, dog lover—sweet Dave Carlisle who ran two miles a day and didn't eat dessert, just slumped over at his desk one afternoon, a half-finished container of strawberry yogurt next to him. No profound last words. No family holding his hand, whispering how much they loved him.

Lauren had *worshipped* her dad. No man was perfect, of course . . . except her dad. He was funny, corny, indulgent enough, strict enough, and went through life happily stunned at his great luck in marrying Donna, the love of his life. Daughters? What could be better than two perfect girls? Nothing! Lauren knew it was a rare dad who could make both his girls feel like they were his favorite. When Jen had sweet little Sebastian, just five months before her dad's untimely death, he had cried at the sight of his grandson, and later sent flowers to his wife and *both* his girls, congratulating them on their new status in life—grandmother, mother, aunt.

At the age of twenty, Lauren would've been hard-pressed to find a single time her father had let her down, been irritable with her or shown her anything but love and wonder. Darius, Jen's husband, had been pronounced "almost as wonderful as Daddy" by Jen herself, to which Darius said he'd have to up his game.

"Are you kidding, son? You're fantastic," her

dad had said. "You just take care of my little girl."

Lauren herself had ridiculous standards when it came to dating. She and Sarah would argue cheerfully over this; Sarah thought everyone deserved a chance, and Lauren . . . Lauren didn't want to waste time on anyone who showed the slightest red flag. She had seen how a real man should treat a woman. She didn't want anything less.

Her dad's autopsy showed a massive aneurysm. It wasn't fair. He had deserved better, the kind of guy who'd pull over to change a flat for anyone, who paid off the balance of a family's layaway at Christmas. Dave Carlisle should've died heroically, running into a burning building to save babies and puppies (and he *would* have run in, and Lauren had no doubt he would've saved everyone). He should've died with a smile on his face, surrounded by the three women who loved him, his baby grandson on his chest, full of gratitude for the love he had earned in his life.

But . . . "life sucks and shit happens" and all the other bumper stickers told Lauren that she had to swallow this bitter pill—a baseball-sized pill—and keep living.

Sometimes grief brings a family together; sometimes it pushes each person into a corner. Sometimes it does both. She and Jen had always been good to each other; Jen was five years older, and Lauren adored her appropriately. Jen had set the bar unfairly high with her grades and career in environmental law, her beautiful, kind husband, her perfect baby, and Lauren cheerfully acknowledged this.

But when their dad died, they grew closer, and the age gap mattered less. They called each other a few times a day, whispering their grief and shock, crying with each other. Lauren went to visit all the time, holding Sebastian, laughing at his sweetness, crying because her dad wasn't there to see it. As time passed and the shock of grief lessened, they just got closer.

Lauren's relationship with her mother, on the other hand, shriveled. Donna had always been the competent, brisk, all-knowing, all-powerful parent, but when her husband died, she crumbled. It was completely understandable. A love like Donner-n-Dave's, as Rhode Islanders pronounced it, didn't happen often. They had been the envy of all who knew them. Donna didn't seem to notice that her daughters had also lost someone incredibly important. Her focus was on herself, which wasn't exactly a surprise, as Jen and Lauren discussed. She'd been a good mother, totally solid, but not the kind who paid a lot of attention to her girls. As a teacher, her students ate up a lot of her patience. She wasn't cruel . . . it was just that the girls (especially Lauren) were something of an afterthought. *Husband, job, community, and oh, yeah, two daughters, too!*

Lauren had always felt that if she were, say, kidnapped, it would take her mother a week or so to notice she was gone. "Shoot, where's that Lauren got off to?" she might say, failing to notice the ransom note taped to the door.

But her dad . . . her dad would've charged to her rescue.

When he died, the family seemed diminished by a lot more than one-fourth. It was like 90 percent of them were dead, too.

Grief, you see, is lonely for everyone involved. Mom had lost her life partner. Jen didn't have the luxury of grieving the way Lauren did, not with a baby to care for, and her sorrow had to be dealt with in bits and pieces. And Lauren had to live with the knowledge that Dad wouldn't see all the important milestones of her adult life— graduation from college, job, first apartment, getting married, having kids. He was just . . . gone.

It was thoughts like those that could bring a person to her knees.

But she was her father's child, and with the help of a good therapist, her sister's love, Sarah's rocklike friendship and the new friends she made in college, she kept on moving forward. She was a weeper, thank God, so there were no repressed emotions.

She wanted to live a life her dad would be

proud of. That *she* would be proud of. Parents die. Disney taught that right from the beginning. When the tears came, sometimes predictably, sometimes taking her by surprise, she gave herself five minutes for a full-on sob, then got back to the stuff at hand. She changed majors. Got a good internship that morphed into a job offer.

And then, that day after graduation, she made her list.

Lists had magical powers, Lauren thought. All that crap about writing down your dreams and checking in? It worked. It had gotten her through college, especially after her dad died, keeping her focused and punctual.

This list would be different. It would be a life list.

She went to her laptop—who was she, Jane Austen?—and dared to dream big. No one else would see it, after all, so why not put it all out there?

When she was done, it felt good. It made her feel oddly safe. Over the next few years, she looked at it periodically. She liked checking back in and crossing things off. She'd add things, too. And somewhere along the line, she started writing to her dad about the things on the list, or just life in general. It never failed to make her heart ache in the most painful and wonderful way, this little communication with her dad in the Great Beyond.

She got three promotions in her first two years at Pearl Churchwell Harris, Architects, putting in long hours, hitting it off with her boss, Bruce Churchwell, the Mighty and Beneficent. With her third raise, she left the apartment she shared with two other women and got a tiny one of her own. She made time for her sister, mom and friends. She dated, though very casually. She volunteered at a community center and rode her bike on the weekends.

And then, life changed with the kind of pulse that makes the world stop for a second, that lets you listen to the breath of stars and ocean. The day you recognize your life will never be the same.

That moment came on a Friday in early February, and a snowstorm earlier in the week left Providence looking snug and warm, like a movie set. Walking to the Hope Center, Lauren had delighted in the prettiness of the city; going home, she wasn't sure she saw a thing.

Oh, no. Her mind was too busy for that, even as her breath fogged in the cold air, and cars drove carefully down the snow-narrowed streets.

She needed to document this night, to talk with someone who would understand that this was it, the day she saw her future. Someone who would cherish her news and not say the wrong thing, but would understand the glow, the ember of something beautiful.

Her dad, obviously.

She came home to her little apartment in the old mill building, flicked on the lights, shrugged out of her raincoat and slipped off her painful, beautiful high heels. Usually, she took a moment to appreciate her home—she was a designer, after all—but tonight, she had things to do.

She wanted to do this properly, because it felt so momentous. Almost as if writing to her dad would make it official. So, not wanting to rush it, she went to the kitchen and took out a bottle, trying to make every movement deliberate, special, memorable. She unscrewed the cap and poured the wine into one of the very cool (and cheap) wineglasses she'd bought from IKEA. Held it up to the light to appreciate the lovely golden color.

She took her wine to the velvet couch her mother had told her not to buy. ("Why would you want a red couch? It looks like it's drenched in blood.") Settled herself, took a sip of the wine, set the glass on the coffee table and opened up her laptop with a great sense of anticipation welling in her chest.

Lauren had just come from the opening of the community center where she volunteered. Two years ago, she'd suggested to Asmaa Quayum, the director, that the place needed an overhaul. Four grants later, after countless hours of pro bono design work and sweat equity from dozens of volunteers, the Hope Center had opened its new and beautiful doors to celebrate the transformation.

The event had been packed with donors, community members and the kids who'd helped paint and decorate. All three bosses from Pearl Churchwell Harris were there, smiling approvingly. Jen and Darius had come (her mother had not, but that was probably just as well). The RISD interior design class had come, as well as half a dozen former classmates.

Including one surprise guest.

Lauren took a deep breath, a sip of wine, and opened the list she'd started three years ago now. She'd updated it a dozen or more times, this path for her life, when she had felt a little lost and uncertain, when she wanted to reassure herself, when she felt lonely or unsure . . . or just when she wanted to feel close to her father. Some of the things on the list were to be expected, some were a little silly, and some were completely sincere.

Things to Do in the Next Five Years

1. Get your dream job.
2. Find a great apartment.
3. Make a difference in the community.
4. Have little kids run up to you because they adore you.
5. Do something that would make Jen proud.

6. Buy and wear a really fancy dress to a significant event.
7. Meet the man you'll marry.

She started typing.

February 6

Dear Dad,
Do I have news for you.

Today was a big day. My first solo project opened! The Hope Community Center. This was a big deal, not just for me but for Providence, Dad. We need a place like this, and even though it was there before, it was kind of grim and industrial, not to mention underused.

Not anymore!

There were so many happy families there tonight . . . I admit, I felt a little holy and saintlike. But seriously! Saintlike! Parents now have a cool place to hang out, take classes, meet each other, and it's all free. Kids have all sorts of activities—art, dance, computer classes. There's a teen hangout room. A toddler playscape. And it's so flippin' pretty! Natural light, great flow, cool colors (none of that primary color shock wall look, you know what I'm saying?).

The party was fantastic. A few local restaurants donated the food and drinks—stuffies and hot wieners and a raw bar from the Eddy. We had Del's lemonade for the kids, wine and champagne for us grown-ups.

Oh, Dad. If you had been there, you would've been so proud. I was thinking about you so hard, knowing you wouldn't have missed the opening for the world. For a second, I thought I could feel you there. I swear I caught a whiff of Aqua Velva. Thanks for that, Daddy.

I wore my fancy dress. (Armani!!! Don't worry, I got it online for cheap, and don't forget, I did apparel design for a year and a half.) For the opening tonight, I wanted to look the part, like a successful public space/interior designer who works for a great firm and represents the Providence community. Because, even though it still surprises me, I am that person.

Back before you died, I admit that I was a little unfocused. I mean, winning *Project Runway* was basically the only plan I had for the future. (Thanks for loving me just the same.) I'm so glad I'm not designing clothes and am doing this instead. Seeing those families tonight was incredible, Daddy. Feeling like they have this gorgeous place, partly because I helped . . . I felt really proud. And humbled, and lucky, and just overjoyed. What a great job I have! Next stop, I want to overhaul an ER waiting room, because I was there two weeks ago. (Dad. I have asthma. Who knew?) Anyway, it was so frickin' ugly I almost cried. If you're sick, you should be able to be somewhere that doesn't look like Jean Valjean's prison cell.

But I digress. You know how I wanted little kids to run up to me because I'd done something great? It happened. Asmaa, the director of the Hope Center, gave her speech to welcome everyone. I didn't know she was going to do this, but she said the NICEST things about me. How hard I worked, how I went above and beyond the call, how I made this place a second home for so many. And yes, I've been practically living there the past year, and I do love the kiddies. But she surprised me, and my eyes filled with tears, and Jen put her arm around me, and my bosses were beaming, because they're really nice, but also because of the great PR.

Then . . . much to my complete shock . . . Asmaa called me up to the podium to say a few words, and Jen hugged me and had tears in her eyes, and all the kids who've been helping or hanging out and painting the walls . . . they all ran up to me and hugged me and they were saying, "Go, Lauren! Go, Lauren!" and it was the happiest moment of my life. I have no idea what I said, but it doesn't matter. Jen said it was perfect, bless her.

I wish you could've seen me, Dad. I wish that so much.

Lauren got up, blew her nose, took a hit of her inhaler, since crying made her chest feel tight, and noticed that her mascara was at Terrifying Raccoon level from the bittersweet tears. She washed her face, got into her pj's, put her hair into a ponytail and got back to her laptop. Took another sip of wine, settled into her couch and decided that once she was done with this update, she'd have that Pepperidge Farm coconut cake in the freezer for dinner, because she hadn't eaten much at the opening. And also to celebrate, because . . . well . . . something important was coming to an end. Even more importantly, something else was about to begin.

Before we get on to the last thing on my list, Daddy, I have a little story to tell you.

When I was a freshman, back in the good old days when you were alive, I went to a party. Which, you know, I did probably more than I should, but in hindsight, thank God I had fun then, because your death really took the wind out of my sails, Father. So I'm glad I got some irresponsibility in when I could.

Anyway, I was at a party, and I may have been underage drinking (I was, so go ahead and haunt me). And then this ripple went through the room, this shiver of excitement through the herd . . . because HE was here, the king of RISD, the golden boy, the future bazillionaire. Joshua Park.

Who was this young man, you ask? Let me tell you.

Joshua Park is:

A) extremely, extremely handsome.
B) apparently a certifiable genius who skipped a year in high school.
C) the inventor who designed something when he was 18 YEARS OLD that sold to a huge medical company for a ton of money. And then he kept doing things like that. He donated the design of something that will save premature babies and has been on CNN. Based

on the rumors, he was about to invent time travel.

He was a senior at this particular party, and everyone was looking at him like he was Prince Harry. RISD's pride and joy. Word had it that already, he had endowed the school with a million buckaroos.

Josh is also wicked handsome (I mentioned that, didn't I?), and too cool for normal activities like parties, so he's not just a genius and already killing it professionally . . . he also has this loner hot guy vibe. So there he is, and this swarm of people enveloped him, like bees crawling over the hive. Of course I was watching (we all were, and his name was being murmured through the crowd like a wave, *Joshua Park, Joshua Park*).

And then, the weirdest thing happened. I wanted to . . . I don't know. Rescue him. I wanted to save him. He looked so stone-faced and uncomfortable, blinking a little too much, like he'd been inside for a week and had gotten his first glimpse of the sun, like a sad (extremely handsome) earthworm. My heart just went out to him.

So you know me, Dad. Save him, I would! Give him someone to talk to, someone who could help him relax and not pump him for info on how much he's worth. Who doesn't love your little girl, right? I'm nothing if not adorable, charming and a pretty good flirt (your daughter, after all).

I had no plans to jump him, kidnap him, rob him or trick him into marrying me. I just figured I'd meet the Golden One and befriend him and sure, see if the old Carlisle charm would work.

It didn't.

I twisted and wove my way over, waited the appropriate amount of time as the throng told him how wonderful/amazing/ brilliant he was, and finally, had my chance.

"So you're Joshua Park," I said. "The man, the legend."

He didn't answer. Looked at me and looked away.

"I'm Lauren Carlisle. Freshman, apparel design." I smiled and hair-tossed (my hair was longer then, and, again, I was eighteen).

He looked at me and gave a tiny eye roll.

"What?" I asked.

"I wasn't aware RISD had a clothing design major," he said.

No, of course not. He was too erudite to know that.

"Do you have something against clothes?" I asked, bristling like an adorable hedgehog.

"No."

"Good. I wouldn't think so, since you're wearing clothes. I mean, technically, they are clothes, if also a sin against humanity." I smiled (charmingly, trying to give him a second chance). He was wearing baggy tan cargo shorts and an orange POLYESTER T-shirt, white athletic socks and sneakers.

No smile for my comment. He was clearly looking for someone else to talk to. This only made me try harder.

"How are you liking your semester so far?" asked I, taking a sip of my drink.

He shrugged.

"Not the most talkative guy, are you?"

Then he looked me up and down and said the following, which, yes, I remember word for word. "I imagine that because you're pretty, you think people won't notice that you're also shallow and not that interesting."

My mouth dropped open, Father dear. Also, I was chewing gum, and the gum came tumbling out, but I did catch it. "Wow," I said. "That's incredibly insulting. You don't know me."

"I don't need to know you."

I think my head actually jerked back. I mean, I was just being a normal, happy, friendly college student. We had talked for all of fifteen seconds, and yet he had decided I was shallow and boring? BORING? I was many questionable things, but boring was not one of them!

I squished my gum into my napkin and dropped it in his drink, a move I am proud of to this day. "Has anyone ever told you that you're condescending?" I asked.

"No."

"Then please, let me be the first. You're incredibly condescending. No wonder you don't have any friends."

And then I went over to talk to my friend Mara.

I glimpsed him a couple of times before he graduated that spring, but we never talked again.

Until tonight. Are you sensing the anticipation, Dad?

The open house was in full swing, and suddenly, I felt on the alert. Not in a scared way, but just . . . aware. The way you can tell a thunderstorm is coming before you even hear a thing. It took a few minutes, and then I saw him, and I recognized him immediately. He hadn't changed, even though it's been six or seven years. Still wicked handsome. Still dressed pretty badly (ill-fitting jeans and the ugliest Western shirt I've ever seen).

But this time, he was standing alone.

Looking at me.

He raised his chin in recognition, and when I was done chatting with the city councilman, I went over.

"Hello, Joshua Park," I said.

"Hello, Lauren Carlisle."

"You remember me?"

He almost smiled. "Your picture is in the foyer."

So it was, among many photos hung there to thank the contributors and sponsors of the renovation. "Well, we did meet once," I said. "You insulted me at a party my freshman year."

"Also, I insulted you at a party your freshman year."

Then he smiled, and so did I. "This doesn't look like apparel design to me," he said, looking around. (He *did* remember me!)

"I changed majors my sophomore year."

"And look at you now."

My heart felt suddenly too big and

hot for my chest. It wasn't that he was (extremely) handsome . . . it was the . . . the *recognition*. The way those five words . . . honored me. Almost like he was impressed.

"I like your shirt," I whispered, then cleared my throat.

He looked down at it. "Yeah . . . I . . . I don't remember where I got it. My mom, maybe. I didn't know there was a dress code." He blushed a little. Gah! He was *adorable*.

"There's not. You look fine."

Then he looked back at me. His eyes were dark and serious, but there was a little light in there, too, a candle on the darkest night. Suddenly, it felt like there was a bridge between us, linking us, and, Dad, I had the semi-coherent thought that if I could walk across that bridge, I'd be in the most beautiful, happiest, safest place in the world.

Then, alas, moment interruptus, courtesy of Elisabetta, one of the little cuties who is a regular here, tugging my hand. "Lauren, Lauren, Lauren, Lauren, come see what I just made! I worked the computer by myself, Lauren, and I made you a picture!"

"It's all right if you go," Josh said, and

those words hit me in the chest like a sledgehammer, because he sounded . . . he sounded so sad. So lonely. It wasn't all right.

"Do you want to have a glass of wine sometime?" I asked, ignoring Elisabetta, who was jumping up and down, practically tearing off my arm.

"I don't drink alcohol."

"Coffee milk, then? Dunkin'? Water? Tea? Del's lemonade?"

"Um . . . okay. Yes. I would like that." He blushed again but didn't look away.

"I'm asking you on a date. Just to be clear." Because this moment was infused with importance, with promise, I couldn't just drift off like a feather on the breeze hoping he got that.

Josh's face didn't change. "In that case, definitely yes."

Thank *God*. Fortune favors the bold and all that. "Okay. Um . . . Elisabetta, honey, one second." I pulled her hand free and took out my phone.

"She likes you," Elisabetta told him. (Awesome wingman, my Elisabetta.)

"I . . . I hope you're right," he said to the girl, and my heart, Dad! My heart!

Guess I wasn't just pretty and shallow anymore.

He was looking at me so . . . so thoroughly, like he could see that bridge, too, and he wanted to cross it, too.

"Your number, sir?" I asked, dousing any cool-girl vibe I might've had going.

He gave it, and my fingers shook as I typed it in. Then I held up the phone and took his picture. "So I can remember that shirt," I said.

He smiled, and a bolt of pure golden light flew across that bridge straight into my soul, and listen to me, Dad, I have never, ever, not even once, had thoughts like this. "Thank you for coming tonight," I said.

"I was just walking past."

"Don't ruin it. Let me think you were stalking me in a not-creepy way for the past few years."

"I wasn't."

"Hush. A girl can dream." And then . . . back to awkward. "I mean, not that I was dreaming you were . . . and also, obviously, I'm not a girl, I'm a woman. Never mind! Bye." Then I let Elisabetta pull me away, and I looked over my shoulder.

He was still looking. A very positive sign.

So, Dad, that brings me to the last thing on my list.

Meet the man you'll marry.

Consider it done, Daddy. Consider it done.

34

Joshua

Month fourteen
April

The letter sat on his bureau, where he'd put it since Sarah had dropped it off.

Josh, #12.

He still hadn't read it. Why would he? He could keep this thing going forever if he didn't open that envelope.

A month ago, Radley had moved into the house in Cranston and was stripping the wallpaper. He sent daily updates and photos, commenting on how the snowdrops had popped up on the lawn, how the daffodils would burst soon. It would be lovely. It already was.

But Josh didn't have plans to move just yet, because moving . . . that would be the end of the time he'd lived in this apartment with his wife. He suddenly understood why so many folks on the forum had left their houses shrines to their lost spouses. Because it was comforting. Because once he sold this place, he would never be able to come back.

But things were changing whether he wanted them to or not.

The apartment didn't smell the way it used to. Lauren's shower gel had turned rancid (damn that organic stuff), and he'd had to throw it away. Her pillow had lost its Lauren smell, no matter how deeply he inhaled. He'd started sleeping in the middle of the bed.

And he had the new job. He was getting acclimated to working with other people, daily updates, action points, Zoom meetings (God bless the mute and video cut buttons). Frank the Realtor had rented out a floor of office space for Josh's new team in the Hanley Building. He took his new engineer out for dinner; Erika had worked in Singapore but grew up on the East Coast, and she was thrilled to be back near her family. He hired a whiz kid—Mateo Cano—out of the same MIT program he'd been in, and he'd start in June. As for his administrative assistant, he offered the job to Cookie Goldberg.

"I live on Long Island," she said in her gravelly voice. "What do you think, I'm gonna move for you?"

"I was hoping," he said.

"I have nine grandchildren within two blocks."

"So you tell me."

"I guess this is the end of the road, then," she said, and for some reason, though he had only met her in person at Lauren's funeral, his throat tightened.

"Thank you for everything," he said, clearing his throat.

"You bet." And then she hung up, as unsentimental as ever. He sent her a severance check of $25,000 and the note *Take the grandkids to a national park on me.*

Cammie, his favorite working girl, recommended someone for the job, and so Josh was now in charge of three people—Erika, Mateo and Andrea, who was in her fifties and immediately became the mother of the group, reminding people to drink water and go home on time. She went on coffee runs and bought art and plants and miscellaneous stuff for the offices to "sex it up in here." Within weeks, Josh couldn't remember how he'd lived without her.

When their business cards came, he looked at his for a long while.

Lauren would've been so proud.

Joshua Park, BFA, ScM, PhD
*Vice President and Lead Designer,
Biomedical Engineering
Chiron Medical Enterprises*

He gave one to his mom, and she put it on the fridge, like it was a drawing he'd made in kindergarten. He also sent one to Christopher M.

541

Zane with a note—*Hope you're doing well. Best, Joshua.* Maybe, someday, he'd go to Chicago and meet his half siblings. Maybe.

Being on his own wasn't what he wanted anymore. It was too lonely. He didn't want to revert to that dorky, solitary workaholic Lauren had dated. He wanted to be more. Loving her, and losing her, had changed him, and he didn't want to go backward.

But still, the letter waited. He found ways to pretend it wasn't there.

He had a life these days, sort of, even if it had started as a substitute for Lauren. He was a regular at the Eddy, though their ever-changing staff never could remember his name. He and Jen met there every other Wednesday for lunch, and sometimes Darius would join them. Radley and he still went there often, and since it was close to the office, he started taking his staff there, too.

He was heading up the robotics team at the Hope Center, which meant they would crush all other teams. He got his purple belt and graduated to be with the nine-year-olds. He visited the house in Cranston, which Radley was itching to name, and ripped out the kitchen countertops and took a sledgehammer to the hideous lime-green master bathroom. Radley had already furnished the office above the garage in anticipation of having his practice there.

The cherry blossoms burst forth, thrilling old

gray Providence with color and beauty. Sarah went on a dating hiatus per Radley's suggestion.

The letter waited.

And then, on a night in mid-April, two months after he was supposed to open it, Josh poured himself a glass of wine, called Pebbles up next to him, and held the letter in his hands.

Josh, #12

The last one.

For a year, she had walked him through his grief. For a year, she'd loved him from the Great Beyond, guiding him, getting him out of his own way, making him feel her love, hear her voice. For a year, he had had her even after he'd lost her.

It was time to read the last thing she had to say to him.

"Do you agree?" he asked Pebbles. She wagged her tail. "Okay. So be it."

He opened the letter. It was longer than the others.

My darling, wonderful, kindhearted Joshua,

I love you.

Picturing this year for you has been heartbreaking. In so many ways, I think I had the easier end of this stick. I got to die, and I had to leave you behind to do the work of living. I know it's been hard

543

and lonely and horrible. I'm so, so sorry, honey. The absolute worst thing about this disease was not that I was going to die from it. It was that I broke your heart, the one thing I swore I'd never do.

I am so sorry I left you, honey. I'm so sorry I hurt you and caused you to be sad and angry and isolated. If I have any say about it, I'll always watch over you and love you and smile down at you. I believe in your goodness more than anything else in my entire life.

So this is the last thing on my list . . . and it's the hardest one.

Find someone to love.

Oh, Josh. You're alive and wonderful. Let someone love you. Someone great. I want you to open that amazing heart of yours again. I want you to *be* loved. I want you to have a fight with someone and have hot makeup sex. I want you to be a father. I want you to love your second wife just as much as you loved me.

Don't let me be your life's tragedy. Let me be one of the best things that ever happened. One of the *many* best things that ever happened to you. Let our time together be a beautiful, happy time in your life that came to an end, but led to more happiness, more love.

You've mourned me enough, and I'm sure part of you always will. But the facts won't change. My life ended. Yours has not. You deserve everything, especially love, Joshua Park. You are single-handedly the best person I've ever met.

It's time to put me aside and move on without me. You can do it, honey. You've *been* doing it, even if you think you haven't. Time keeps spooling out the days and weeks. You're better now. You've healed. I know it. It doesn't mean you'll forget me. It just means it's time to find someone else.

On that note . . . I would like to present Sarah as a candidate.

My guess is that you've become friends, and you've seen her the way she really is—so devoted and hardworking, funny and smart and kind. I bet she's been there for you. I bet she loves you already. And I know she has wretched judgment when it comes to guys. You already know her, so you can skip over that awkward "where did you go to school" crap.

Also, she thinks you're hot. Which you totally are.

Think of me as your matchmaker from the GB. If it doesn't work, well, you gotta start somewhere, right? (Unless you married that woman you kissed a few letters ago, which makes *this* letter irrelevant.)

I think I'm stalling, knowing this is the last time you'll ever hear from me this way. I'm crying a little, Josh. Actually, I'm sobbing. I don't know how to end this, but I know I have to.

Take good care of yourself, honey. Be happy. Be full of joy. That's all I ever wanted.

Thank you for our life together. I was so happy. I loved you with all my heart, Joshua Park.

I'll see you again someday, my darling, wonderful husband.

Lauren

He put the letter down, tears blurring his vision. This was it. She was gone. Again.

And suddenly it was there, right in front of him, the one memory of Lauren he'd been trying to bury. He couldn't turn away from it anymore, couldn't shove it down, couldn't avoid it.

Suddenly, he was right back there again.

The last day of Lauren's life . . .

The last hour . . .

It was time to remember that day. Then, maybe, he could let her go.

35

Lauren

No time left
February 16

T he pneumonia came fast and furious, a thief in the night, robbing her of air. She was dimly aware of feeling awful, her chest heavy. Two days ago, on their third anniversary, she'd been fine.

In a matter of hours, that changed. She'd been tired when she went to bed, sure, but somewhere in the night, true exhaustion set in. She pushed the covers back, too hot, then fell back asleep, the fatigue heavy and black. She coughed, her back spasming, but even that sharp, twisting pain wasn't enough to keep her awake. Her chest was working, trying to get enough air. She could hear the noise of her own breathing—gasping—but she was so, so tired.

"Honey? Lauren?"

With an effort, she opened her heavy eyes.

"I think you're sick," he said, and she nodded, her head like an anvil. A sharp pain stabbed her on each inhale. He clipped the O2 monitor to her forefinger and stared at it, then put on the stethoscope and listened to her lungs. "Shit," he said. "Can you cough, honey? Get some gunk up?"

This was not their first go-round with pneumonia, after all. He pulled her upright and she tried, coughing into a tissue. Gross. Nasty, thick mucus the color of moss. Not a great sign. More coughing, accompanied by a wrenching back spasm. Josh massaged the muscle and increased her oxygen flow.

After her first round of pneumonia, they'd bought a percussion vest, a heavy, battery-operated thing that looked like a life jacket. Josh clipped it onto her now, and the thudding began; it was designed to loosen phlegm and help her clear her lungs. It felt like she was being punched, and she nearly tipped over with exhaustion. She tried to breathe deeply but the stabbing pain cut her off.

"Try huffing, sweetheart," he said, phone to his ear. "Hey, Dr. Bennett, it's Joshua Park. Lauren's got pneumonia again, I think. O2 sat is seventy-nine, lungs have crackles and she's sweaty and feverish."

Lauren got some more crap out of her lungs, but it was scary, how much shit was in there.

Then she was asleep again, even with the vest pounding away. She was aware that Josh was carrying her, putting her in the car, since it would be faster than the ambulance. He held her hand as he drove; it was only a few minutes.

He pulled up in front of the ER doors, got out and carried her inside. "My wife has pulmonary fibrosis, and it looks like she has pneumonia. She's a patient of Dr. Bennett's, and she needs a bed. Now."

They listened to him. She was a frequent flier here, after all.

Then she was in a bed, and there were a lot of people around her, and they were saying the too-familiar words—sats down, temperature up, heart rate too fast.

"Lauren? We're going to intubate you, hon," said Carol, one of her favorite nurses.

Lauren looked at Josh, his face tight with fear, held up her hand with the thumb, forefinger and pinkie sticking up. *I love you* in sign language. Then she made the *L* sign and put it against her forehead. *Loser.* Their little joke. Her arm flopped back on the bed.

He managed a smile. "I love you, too, loser." One of the nurses gave him a sharp look, and Lauren smiled. There was the pinch of a needle, and then she was floating on the darkness.

Later, Jen was also there.

"Fight it, sis," she whispered, her eyes wet.

Lauren nodded, squeezed Jen's hand, fell back into the nothingness of sedation. Was she dying? The pneumonia was different this time, heavier, bigger.

The next time she woke up, there was her mom, white-faced, hair messy. Sarah, murmuring something, smelling nice. More sleeping. Stephanie, smiling encouragingly. "You're doing fine, sweetheart," she said. "Rest."

And always, Josh, calm, steady, there every time she opened her eyes. She knew time was passing because of the stubble on his face. *Oh, Josh.* She loved him so much. She wanted to know how sick she was, but she couldn't talk, so she just raised her eyebrows and looked at him.

He didn't move for a minute, then gave a small nod. "It's pretty bad, honey."

She pressed her hands together to make a heart, and he smiled, but tears were in his eyes. Then sleep pulled her again, down, down, into the soft, comforting blackness.

Later, she was asleep but not as much. Floating. Something large and heavy was on her chest, and even with the ventilator pushing air into her, she could tell it wasn't enough. She was so tired. Even though she'd been asleep, she was exhausted.

Was this it? Was she really dying this time? She wanted Pebbles, her sweet little companion through all this. She wanted to see the kids, but she didn't want them to be scared or . . . and then she was back in the nothingness.

Awake again. Josh in a different shirt. Time had passed, then. She just wanted to look at him, drink him in. Jen was crying, so unlike her. Lauren raised her middle finger, and smiled around the tube, and everyone laughed. Josh kissed her hand, and oh, that smile, those eyes, his beautiful face.

Yes. She was fairly sure she was dying. Panic flashed, but the nothingness sucked her down again.

Sleep, wake for a few minutes, sleep, smile, squeeze Josh's hand, sleep. She dreamed of Hawaii, swimming in the impossibly blue waters off the Nāpali Coast. She was in their honeymoon house and heard the roosters. She dreamed of holding Octavia as a newborn, and woke up to feel the baby snuggled against her, the smell of her head so welcome in the midst of the sharp and sour smells of the hospital. She stroked her niece's cheek and was asleep again, dreaming of Octavia as a teenager, her hair so dark and beautiful, and Octavia was talking about a dance and what to wear. Sebastian was kissing her cheek and playing with her hand, in real life or in the dream. She felt a tug. Real life, then. She opened her eyes to smile at him and touch his cheek. Her arm felt as heavy as lead.

She dreamed of him as an adult, driving her to the Cape house, which was different in the dream, but the same. Pebbles was in the back of the car, and Josh was waiting for her on the deck, smiling, wearing that awful Western shirt from the Hope Center reopening. Then she was at Sarah's wedding and forgot she was maid of honor and was trying to put on makeup as she stood on the altar. Josh washed her face with a warm cloth, and fixed things. These were all the things she'd miss, she realized. The washcloth felt so real.

She opened her eyes. Josh *was* washing her face. She smiled at him, oh, God, her chest hurt so much, everything hurt, her head, her skin, her bones, but seeing him felt so good. So . . . safe.

She smiled and then the darkness pulled her deeper, and it was good, it was easier there, the enveloping blackness.

She wasn't getting better. She was getting worse.

Death sat close by. *Dad? Are you here?* She fell asleep before she could wait for an answer.

Awake again. Josh. Jen. Mom. Ben and Sumi. Then sleep.

The next time she woke, Dr. Bennett was there on one side, Josh on the other, stroking her hand, a blue shirt this time. "Hi, honey," he said, and she loved his soft, deep voice so much. "We need to . . . talk." His face spasmed with grief.

Shit. Her heart thudded painfully. She tried to squeeze his hand, and he squeezed back. *Don't be scared. Don't be scared. Don't let him know you're scared.*

552

"Lauren? Lauren, hey." Dr. Bennett took her hand, too, which was totally not encouraging. "We lightened your sedation so we could talk. Can you hear me?"

Lauren nodded. Dr. Bennett pushed the button on the bed and raised her to more of a sitting position. God. Her chest burned and hurt, jerking with the effort to breathe, fighting the respirator. She tried to let it breathe for her, since she obviously was doing a crap job. She looked at the monitor. O2 sat 70 percent, heart rate 115, blood pressure 185/121. Her head was killing her. She looked at her hands, and the fingernails looked faintly . . . blue.

Not good. Not good at all.

Her whole body was so heavy, as if she'd been pumped full of iron.

Dr. Bennett—Kwana, she'd asked to be called way back when—sat next to her on the bed.

"Lauren," Dr. Bennett said, her eyes kind . . . and wet. She gripped Lauren's other hand. "The news is not good, honey. Your arterial blood gas is morbidly low. The X-rays show your lungs are filled with fluid, and your sats are way down, even with the ventilator." She waited a beat, making sure Lauren was hearing all this.

She was, unfortunately. Even though she'd known it was coming, the realization was a physical blow. She couldn't look at Joshua.

"You've been on antibiotics, but we're not

getting anywhere in clearing the pneumonia. Your lung function is . . . quite low."

She nodded. Squeezed Josh's hand. Her chest was working hard, even with the ventilator in, and it hurt.

"Your organs are shutting down," Dr. Bennett said, "and we can't . . . we're out of options."

Lauren closed her eyes. Out of options.

This was it. She was dying. Her beautiful, happy life was ending. She'd known it would, but now that it was here . . . shit.

She opened her eyes and looked at Josh. His mouth trembled. He tried to smile, but his eyes filled. "I . . . I'm so sorry, honey," he said, and his voice broke. He bent over and pressed his forehead to hers.

Not yet. Not yet. Oh, please, not yet. She didn't want to do this to her husband.

Be brave, honey. Her father's voice. Oh, thank God, he was here.

Josh. Oh, Josh. I'm so sorry.

Tears spilled out of her eyes, and he held the sides of her face, wiping her tears away even as he cried with her. Her heart swelled with sorrow and regret that she was leaving him. The love of her life. The love of her *life.* She lifted her hand to his hair, relishing the silkiness. Stroked his cheek before her heavy arm dropped back to her side.

I'm so sorry, honey. I'm so sorry.

"Are you in any pain?" Dr. Bennett asked.

Lauren nodded. Her chest ached, and a knifelike pain stabbed on every forced inflation. Flashes of light went off in her head like lightning strikes, searing and sharp. Her chest worked, and she could feel her breath crackling. Air hunger. Such an ugly, cruel thing.

"We'll get you some morphine. But, Lauren, if we extubate you, the end will come pretty fast," Dr. Bennett said, and Lauren had to give her credit, because though her eyes were shiny, she wasn't crying outright. "You'll have a few hours, maybe less. If we keep you on the ventilator, it'll be more like a day, maybe three. The choice is yours."

Well, shit. She'd give anything for another couple of days . . . but being on the ventilator also meant being unconscious. She could die that way, just slip away, pain-free.

Joshua deserved more.

"Your mom, Jen and Darius are in the waiting room," Josh said. "Sarah's on her way."

She pointed to the tube and mimicked pulling it out. "You want us to extubate you?" Dr. Bennett asked, and Lauren nodded, looking into Joshua's eyes.

I'm sorry.

After a long second, he nodded, too, and then put his hand up to his eyes.

She reached for him, her arm not quite making

it, and he caught it, took her hand, kissed it, his lips staying a long time. She felt his tears drop on her skin. She squeezed back, but she was so weak, she wasn't sure he felt it.

Though she tried not to, she fell asleep again, still holding Josh's hand. Distantly, she was aware of more people in the room, adjusting her, moving things. The tube was pulled from her throat, and she gagged a little, getting another stab with the effort. She could hear herself gasping, her chest working hard—oh, shit, it hurt. She heard a moaning sound. Hers, she assumed.

Someone was putting something in her hand. "Just press this button when you need more pain control," a female voice said. She pressed, and a warm wave enveloped her, making her float. Morphine. Ooh. That was nice. Her head pain went away, and her chest didn't hurt as much, wasn't jerking so much. Even her breathing was easier, thank God.

"Atta girl," the nurse said, and Lauren opened her eyes and smiled.

Josh was standing right next to her, his face ruined.

"Hi," she said, her voice a croak.

"Hi, honey."

"I love you." It was hard to get the words out.

"I love you, too. So much."

The nurse adjusted her and, with such kindness, brushed her hair and washed her face gently, gave her a sip of water. "Thank you," Lauren whispered.

"You're welcome, honey." The nurse dropped a hand on her shoulder. "I'll pray for you both." She was crying.

Nurses were the best. "Do I look . . . pretty?" Lauren asked her husband, and she managed a smile. Even her face was tired.

"Beautiful," he answered, trying to smile back despite the tears in his eyes. "You . . . do you want me to get everyone?"

She nodded. "Then get . . . rid of them. Just . . . us." They'd talked about this . . . Lauren didn't want her mom and sister to witness the moment of her death. She didn't want them to hear her last breath.

"Just us," he said, and kissed her, his lips so warm and wonderful, then left the room.

She didn't want Josh to suffer through this—her final minutes, maybe hours, but she knew he wouldn't leave her. She wouldn't leave him, if the case were reversed.

She took a hit of morphine and closed her eyes, and when she opened them, her family was there—Mom, Jen, Darius, Sarah, Stephanie, the Kims, all their faces a study of grief and fear and love.

Darius was holding Pebbles in his strong arms. He put the dog on the bed with her and put her hand on the dog's head. Poor Pebbles. *I'm sorry, honey,* Lauren thought. Her dog. Her friend through all this. Pebbles's tail wagged, but she stayed still, as if she knew her job.

"I love . . . you all," Lauren said, gasping a little, her voice weird from the days of intubation. "Be . . . happy . . ." She couldn't finish.

"She wants you to be happy when you remember her," Josh said, his voice low and calm, his words exactly right.

"Be at peace, darling girl," Ben said, leaning in to hug her. He was crying.

"Take care . . . of him."

"I will. I always have."

Lauren nodded and managed a smile. Sumi was next, crying too hard to speak, but she held Lauren's face in her hands and kissed her forehead.

"Goodbye, beautiful," Darius said, hugging her, and she managed to pat his cheek. "I'll take care of them, don't worry." He had such lovely eyes, even when they were streaming tears. He kissed her hand and moved aside for Stephanie.

"Thank . . . you for . . . raising him," Lauren said, her words barely a breath. Her mother-in-law kissed her on both cheeks and her forehead.

"I'm so glad you married my son," she said, and it was so generous, so *kind,* that tears spilled out of Lauren's eyes. "God bless you, angel."

Then it was Sarah, next in this awful, beautiful line of her people, her family, her best friend.

"You did so good," Sarah said. "I love you. I'll miss you so much." Her face was scrunched with crying.

"Love . . . you."

Sarah hugged her, jerking with sobs, then kissed her cheek, and then it was her mom's turn.

Oh, Mommy. Poor Mom.

Her mother bent over her and held Lauren's face in her hands. "I love you, baby. I love you. Daddy will be with you. Don't be scared." Her voice was surprisingly strong, and Lauren was so glad. She sounded like her old self, before Dad died, the impressive mother who always knew the answers.

Lauren tried to inhale her familiar mom smell. "Sorry," she whispered. *Sorry to make you lose a child. Sorry to give you more pain. Sorry if I ever disappointed you.*

Her mother's face contorted. "I'm sorry, too, honey. I'm so sorry."

"Love you . . . Mama. Be . . . brave."

"You're my best girl. So strong. I love you, honey."

Lauren tried to smile, but the fatigue and pain were pulling at her, even as tears slid down her cheeks. A low moan came out of her without her consent, and she gave herself another hit of morphine, barely able to press the button.

Then Jen. Oh, Jen. This was the hardest yet. "I love you so much, Lauren," her sister whispered fiercely, holding her close, and Lauren managed to turn her head and kissed her sister's cheek twice.

"Best . . . sister. Best . . . friend. Love you."

Jen clutched her hard and let out a horrible wail, and for a second, Lauren couldn't bear it, she couldn't stand the pain, and she felt herself slipping away from the unbearable grief.

Then Josh pulled Jen back. "Don't let that be the last thing she hears from you, Jen," he said firmly, and Lauren loved him so much in that moment. His kindness, his strength, his understanding.

"You're right," Jen hiccuped. "Shit! Fuck. Fuck, fuck, *fuck*." And Lauren couldn't help but let out a little laugh, no matter how it hurt her chest.

"Perfect," said Josh, and somehow, her family laughed.

"I love you, sissy," Jen said, her face crumbling. Then, because she was Super Jen, so amazing and strong, she pulled herself together and smiled, bright as the sun. "See you on the other side."

Lauren gave her a thumbs-up and smiled back.

Then Josh showed them to the door.

Lauren could hear them murmuring, the soft sobs. Her own eyes streamed with tears. She was so loved. She loved them all so much.

Pebbles was warm against her side, the sweet dog, her fur silky under Lauren's hand.

Then Josh was climbing into bed with them and wrapping his arms around her. "You did great, honey. My brave, brave wife." He felt so good. So much like himself.

"I . . . love you," she whispered.

"I love you, too. With all my heart. With my all lungs and liver and pancreas."

"Kidneys . . ."

"And kidneys. Both of them."

She felt him crying, felt his warm tears sliding against her temple. The breathing was harder now, and she tried to sneak the air in around the scars, the fibers, the fluid. *Don't pant. Don't fight. Don't scare him. Die gently.* Another hit of morphine so he wouldn't hear her gasping, feel her body struggling. *Help me, Daddy.* The urge to struggle passed.

"I'm so . . . lucky," she managed, and Josh sobbed then.

"I love you, Lauren. I love you so much. You're everything to me. I'm the lucky one."

"Beautiful . . . life." Her chest wasn't working anymore. "Love . . . you." One more breath. Just a little more air, please, Dad, for her last words.

Go for it, baby.

With what felt like a superhuman effort, Lauren pulled air into her poor battered, exhausted lungs, hearing the squeak and rasp, and willed those last remaining spaces in her lungs to open. She looked at her husband. "Thank . . . you."

Because what else was there to say?

And though his eyes were wet with tears, she saw that flame in the dark, saw all the feelings he had for her, and she truly *was* so lucky, the luckiest woman on earth, because she had been loved by Joshua Park.

"It's okay if you go," he whispered. "You've fought enough. I love you. I'll always love you, Lauren. Rest now, honey. I'm right here with you. I love you. I love you. I love you."

Though her eyes are closed, Lauren can see the strange, liquid golden light, so warm, so alive. She hears her father's voice, feels him close to her. She knew he would come. She knew it.

She can see herself, lying in the bed, Josh holding her close, Pebbles on her other side. Her husband looked so ruined, holding her against him. Her own face, Lauren notes, is white. But she isn't gasping. She isn't clawing and scared. She's . . . quiet. Not quite gone yet, though.

Her poor body. It had worked so hard. It had done so well. She's proud of it, grateful to it for putting up with all that it had. So many healthy years, so many happy times, walking, swimming, cuddling, holding, carrying. Images flash through her mind—jumping rope with Sarah as kids. Hiding in Jen's closet and scaring her. Pushing Sebastian on the swing. Holding Octavia. Swimming in the ocean with Josh. Hugging Josh.

Making love with Josh. Laughing with Josh.

That body deserves to rest now.

Her new self is strong and warm. There's no pain, no weight, no fatigue, no chest pain.

I've been so happy, she tells her father. He knows this.

Everyone should get to die like this, in the arms of the person they loved best. Josh's love shines out of him. Lauren watches as he pushes her hair back from her face and kisses her lips, and the light in her new self bursts out, filling her, filling the room.

I love you. I love you. I love you.

It's time for her to go now. Her father agrees.

One more second, one more for Josh. She wills her love into Josh with the last beat of her heart, and then she is ready.

She sees the knowledge hit Josh. He crumples, laying his head on her chest. Her old body is done, but she's more *here* than ever.

He'll be all right. She knows this.

The light grows even brighter, so bright she can't see Josh anymore, but she feels him inside every molecule of her, the pulse and thrum of his life.

She *is* the light now, and though her old body is done, and her old self is gone, her true self would never leave him.

He was, and is, and always would be, the love of her life.

36

Joshua

It had taken some time to get over that final letter. To remember her last day in all its excruciating, beautiful detail.

In some ways, it was like losing her all over again. But when he reread the letters, when he saw the scope of what she'd done, he was so, so grateful for her kindness, her forethought. She had spent her last months thinking about his life after hers, and how to help him.

And she had. Because of her, he had Radley as a friend. He had a new job because he'd gone to that conference. He was part of the community, more than he'd ever been. He owned a new house that, someday, would be his children's home. He knew karate.

He was so grateful that, for that first year without her, his wife's love had walked beside him.

And he *was* better. He was doing fine. He'd invited all of Lauren's family to have pizza at his offices one night, and pushed Octavia and Sebastian around in the comfy office chairs, making them shriek with glee. The next week, when Jen had her third baby, he'd visited her and his new baby niece in the hospital, and he didn't cry. They asked him to be godfather to Leah Grace, and of course he said yes.

A few weeks ago, he'd flown to Singapore and spent two weeks there, working with the team, attending meetings, going out for dinner. The company put him up in a swanky rental apartment with a balcony overlooking the sparkling city and told him it was his whenever he needed to come out. They showed him the design for an MRI-guided ultrasound device that would ablate tiny particles of brain matter for people with persistent tremors. It had the potential to treat epilepsy with some modifications, too. Within an hour, Josh had tweaked the design so it required two fewer parts and would cost significantly less to produce.

Back in Rhode Island, he packed up the apartment, putting all but two photos of him and Lauren in a box. He put her more valuable jewelry in a safe-deposit box to give to Sebastian, Octavia and Leah someday. He kept a few things from his married life to bring to his new house, then invited Lauren's friends to come and take whatever they wanted—a rug, a lamp, a painting.

And then, amid the boxes and paintings in the now-echoing apartment, he took off his wedding ring.

He moved into his new house, not a hundred percent sure it was the right time. It was right enough, he supposed. Every night, he lay awake for hours, a feeling of the surreal hovering over him in this new room with its different shadows and unfamiliar sounds. The wind shushed in the leaves, and he could hear the waves of Narragansett Bay sloshing at the edge of his property. His neighbors often hosted parties, and the sounds of music and laughter drifted on the air. They were good sounds. He'd get used to it.

He was grateful to have Radley on the third floor. They ate dinner a couple of times a week, sometimes watched TV together. He threw his friend the promised graduation party and met Radley's classmates and other friends, among them Cammie, who gave him a big hug and invited him to Shine's grand opening.

Josh had asked if he could invite Jen and Darius and the kids to the graduation party, and of course Radley had said yes. Sarah had been invited, too, and he watched her that day, her ease with Radley, the way she scooped up Octavia and pushed Sebastian on the swing.

It *would* be convenient, he admitted silently, to marry his wife's best friend. He definitely cared about her. Loved her, even. She was pretty in a way that was different from his sparkly wife, and Josh thought that was a good thing. Sarah would give him space for Lauren's memory. She could tell him stories of Lauren as a kid . . . and herself as a kid, too. She liked him. She was kind and hardworking. That could be enough.

Still, it took him another month to ask her out. He called rather than texted; it felt too momentous to do without hearing her voice.

"Hey, you," she said. "What's up?" He could hear the voices of her colleagues in the background, the shrill of a ringing phone.

"I was wondering if you wanted to have dinner with me," he said, and the words were not hard to say.

"Sure! When?"

"Uh . . . Saturday?"

"Okay. Where?"

"I don't know. I'll make a reservation." He hadn't thought where just yet. Somewhere romantic, he guessed.

"Great. Text me the details. I can meet you there."

"I'll pick you up." He paused. "Sarah?"

"Yes?"

"I'm asking you on a date." Once, Lauren had said almost the exact same words to him.

There was a long silence. "Oh."

"If it's a horrible idea, tell me now, okay?" It hadn't occurred to him that she wouldn't want to date him; he hadn't even thought to wonder. It was Lauren's idea, and Lauren had known them both so well.

Another pause. "Um . . . it's not a horrible idea. Not at all."

Nothing else. Another beat passed. Another. Another.

"Okay, I'll text you tomorrow," he said.

"Yeah. Great. Talk to you later, Josh."

He picked her up on Saturday night. She wore a flowered dress that caught the breeze, flashing a glimpse of her excellent legs. She had always been lean and athletic, and those were some great legs.

"Hi," she said, and he leaned in to kiss her cheek, the way he always did, as she leaned in to hug him. He ended up kissing her on the ear instead.

"Sorry," he said.

"No, no. This is a little weird, but . . . it's really nice, too." She got in his car, filling it with a spicy smell, deeper than Lauren's perfume. "Where are we going?"

"Mill's Tavern."

"Nice."

He pulled away from her curb and drove through Providence. After a minute or two, he realized he should speak. "How was your day?"

"Good! It was relaxing. I did some gardening. You?"

"Also good. I worked, but I also took Pebbles for a swim."

"Oh, does she love being near the water?" Sarah asked, her voice warming. She loved that dog. A good sign.

"She does. She swims around, barking like a maniac. I think she's trying to herd the fish."

She laughed.

This could be it, he thought. Josh and Sarah, Sarah and Josh. Why not?

They got to the restaurant and were seated at a nice table. Josh had worn a Radley-approved outfit from Banana Republic—chinos, a checked purple-and-blue shirt cuffed at the wrist, loafers with no socks (which felt weird and was something he would not do again).

"You look nice," he said to Sarah.

"Thank you. So do you."

Their server came over. "Hi! Welcome to Mill's Tavern! Are we ready to order our drinks?"

"I'm not. I don't know about you," Sarah answered.

Josh looked up. "I'll have a glass of sauvignon blanc—oh, hey."

It was the woman from the vet and the marathon. And the Eddy. Duffy the dog's owner.

"Hi! How are you?" She beamed, clearly recognizing him.

"Good," he said. "Very good. Um, Sarah?"

"I'll have a cosmo," she said. "Grey Goose, very faintly pink, squeeze the lime. Thank you."

Quite specific, and ordered firmly. Sarah would be good with kids, he thought.

"You got it! Nice to see you," the server said to Josh, going off to put in their drink order.

"You know her?" Sarah asked.

"I've run into her a couple times. We use the same vet. Also, Providence."

"Can't swing a cat without hitting someone you know." Sarah settled back. "Don't you hate when they say, 'Are *we* ready to order?' Like it's the three of us having dinner?"

"I never really noticed."

"Drives me crazy. 'How do we like our dinners?' 'Do we want dessert?' I feel like I'm three and my mother is saying, 'We love broccoli! It's our favorite veggie!' " She laughed and after a second, Josh smiled.

The waitress came back with their drinks on a tray, set Josh's wine before him, then slowly, slowly attempted to get Sarah's cosmo to her without spilling a drop. It was filled to the rim, and Josh stared, hypnotized as she lowered it closer and closer to the table. The pink liquid shook, but didn't spill. Would she be able to manage the surface tension of the liquid?

No. As she set it on the table, it sloshed just a bit.

"So close!" she said.

"Um, I hate to be a pain," Sarah said, "but I said very faintly pink. Do you mind taking this back

570

and getting me another one?" She was already handing the glass back to the waitress.

"No, no, not at all. I'm really sorry."

"No, it's not your fault. It's the bartender's." Sarah smiled, though Josh could tell it wasn't a real smile. Once, he wouldn't have been able to tell the difference. Lauren had taught him so much. The waitress went off to replace the drink.

"So," Josh said. "Any . . . summer plans?"

"Other than visiting your place? No." She flashed a smile. He hadn't planned on inviting her to stay just yet. The house was a mess at the moment. Would it be rude to tell her no?

It would be. He nodded, forced a smile and wished he'd brought some index cards.

"How was Singapore?" she asked. "You only said that it was a good trip. Tell me about it."

And so he did, and he tried to give details, the way Lauren had once instructed him. He told her about the beautiful city, the impressive Chiron headquarters, the orchids of the botanical gardens, the food.

"I would love to go there someday," she said. "I'm not really well traveled."

The server was back, and this time, the drink was neither spilled nor too pink. "Are we ready to order?" she asked, and Sarah gave him a wink.

"I'll have a Caesar salad, no anchovies," Sarah said.

"There are anchovies in the dressing," the server said.

"I know that. I just don't want little fishes lying across the lettuce."

"Got it."

"And I'll have the petite filet, medium, which means I want it pink and warm in the center." Yes, Sarah was a woman of firm opinions and clear instructions.

"And your sides?" the server asked.

"Instead of the crispy potatoes, I'd like the mashed, and a side of asparagus."

The server scribbled furiously, then turned to Josh. "And you, sir?"

"I'll have the grapefruit salad and the salmon," he said.

"Great choices. How are we doing on drinks? Oh, gosh, I just brought you yours. Sorry. Um, let me know if you want wine with dinner! Okay!" Off she went again, her long ponytail swinging.

"She's nice," Josh said.

"A little chirpy," Sarah said, rolling her eyes. She took a sip of her drink. "This is not Grey Goose," she sighed. "Is it really that hard?" But she smiled.

"Tell me about when you were a little kid. Did you always want to be a social worker?" It was a dumb question.

"How are our drinks?" said the waitress, there again.

"They're great," Sarah all but growled. To her credit, it hadn't been thirty seconds since the drink was delivered.

"Super!" The waitress was like Tigger, bouncing off. Josh and Octavia had watched a Winnie-the-Pooh movie last week when he babysat the older two kids. That had been a fun night.

"So you were asking if I always wanted to be a social worker." Right. He should be talking with Sarah. "Truth is, I didn't really know what that was when I was a kid. In high school, I wanted to be a psychologist, but the money for a PhD was too much, so I went for the master's of social work. Did an internship for social services. I loved it. I hated it and I loved it, you know? I mean, no one who works in our department totally loves their job, but—"

She kept talking, and Josh nodded in what he hoped were the right spots.

Lauren thought this would be a good idea, he reminded himself. First dates always sucked.

Well. His and Lauren's had not. But comparison was the thief of joy, as Teddy Roosevelt had once said (and Lauren had often quoted him). She'd loved that guy. Who didn't?

"What are you thinking about?" Sarah asked.

"Oh. Uh, Teddy Roosevelt."

"Am I boring you?"

"No! Sorry. Just . . . never mind."

Sarah seemed to be done talking about her job. Maybe she'd ask him about something. It was kind of her turn.

"Watched anything good on Netflix lately?" she asked. The waitress brought their salads, smiled and left.

"No. No, I don't watch much TV." He used to, when he was married. It had been cozy then, sitting on the couch together, making out, handing Lauren tissues when she cried, because she loved the sad, sappy movies. He opted not to mention his first two months as a widower, when he'd watched thousands of hours of television. Still, he should say something. "*The Great British Bake Off* and *Star Trek* reruns, mostly. The original TV show."

"Are you kidding?" Sarah asked. "Oh, Josh. They're so hokey! The new movies are so much better. That one with Benedict Cumberbatch? I loved that one."

The old series was *not* hokey, but he didn't want to get into an argument about it.

"How are our salads?" the waitress asked.

"Fine. Great," Josh said, though he hadn't had time to pick up his fork.

"Excellent." She beamed and left.

What had they been talking about? "Have *you* seen anything good lately?" Josh asked.

"Actually, I've been watching this documentary. Josh, you'd love it. It's about this plastic surgeon in India who does really extreme cases. Like, there was a little girl who had two noses, I shit you not."

"Wow," Josh said. It *was* right up his alley.

"And there was this other guy who had warts all over his body that made him look like his hands were the roots of trees."

"Tree Man! I saw that one," he said.

"Wasn't that incredible?"

"Here we go!" announced the chirpy server, and Sarah was right. She had a bright, birdlike quality about her, like a chickadee, interested and energetic and . . . fluttery, somehow. "Let me know if everything is to your satisfaction."

"Stay right there," Sarah ordered, cutting her filet in half. She inspected the middle, which was pink, then pressed her finger against it. "It's fine. Thank you."

"Enjoy!" She flitted off again. Yes. A chickadee. He always liked those birds, their bright black eyes and intelligence.

"How's your mom?" Sarah asked, and that was easy to talk about, because his mom had just been to Sedona with Sumi and had funny stories of the lady who did yoga buck naked. Well, it was funny when Steph told it. Not so much now, he guessed. He wasn't great at delivery. Or Sarah wasn't amused.

They talked about their families, Jen's new baby. "Where did she come up with the name

Leah? Is that a family name? I always think of Princess Leia."

"Well, what a great role model, right?" Josh said. "I don't know how she picked it." He took a bite of salmon, wishing he'd ordered something else, then remembered a random fact. "If you're Jewish, sometimes you give a baby a name that starts with the same letter as a person in your family who died." While Octavia's middle name was Lauren (and how Lauren had loved that), Josh now wondered if Jen had thought of that tradition when picking out her second daughter's name.

"They're not Jewish, though, right? Darius isn't, is he?"

"They go to Blessed Sacrament. I don't know if Darius was raised—"

"Miss?" called Sarah. "The asparagus? Thanks!" She lowered her voice. "I'm sorry. I wanted to catch her before we got too far into the meal. You were saying?"

"I think . . . it doesn't matter."

She was Lauren's friend. She was hardworking and loyal. She was funny (sometimes). She was very particular about food and treated the waitstaff poorly. She smelled nice. She was attractive and healthy.

But he wasn't feeling it. *Give it a chance,* he told himself. *Lauren wouldn't have suggested this if it was too far off.*

The asparagus came. "How are we liking everything?" the server asked.

"We don't know yet," Sarah said. "We haven't had a chance to eat the asparagus."

"Oh. Sorry. I'll . . . let me know if you need anything."

Sarah ate some, and offered some to Josh. He took a few spears. She asked if he'd bought any more furniture. He told her yes and detailed his new appliances.

But aside from medical shows about rare health conditions, the conversation didn't exactly flow.

The server wrapped up Sarah's leftovers, and they ordered coffee and a crème brûlée to share.

"Oof. This was a great meal," Sarah said a little while later. "I'm gonna have to run it off tomorrow. You want to go together?"

"No, I have something to do," he lied. "I'm, um, fixing something at Donna's." Now he would have to go to Donna's and find something to fix, because he hated lying.

"You know, that reminds me of something. When Lauren and I were little—"

"And how is the dessert?" asked the waitress with a big smile, sliding the check on the table. "Did we like the crème brûlée?"

"Jesus!" Sarah barked. "Can you leave us alone for, like, ten consecutive minutes? This is his first date since his wife died! Stop interrupting!"

Everyone went quiet, and the waitress looked stricken. Literally, as if Sarah had just punched her. "Oh, my God," she said. "I'm so sorry! Obviously, I didn't . . ." Her face crumpled, and she started to cry. "I'm so sorry," she whispered. She held her hand up to cover her mouth. "I'm sorry, I don't mean to cry. Or interrupt. We're supposed to check on you a lot. It's policy." Her voice shook. "I'm sorry for crying. It's just . . . I'm very emotional lately. My dog died two days ago."

"Jesus H. Christ," Sarah said, tossing down her spoon. "Are you comparing his wife dying to your *dog?*"

"No, no, I'm not, I just—"

"Duffy?" Josh asked.

The server looked up as if surprised he remembered, then nodded.

"I'm really sorry," he said.

"No, it's not . . . God, listen to me. Your *wife* died, and I'm telling you about a seventeen-year-old dog. I'm an idiot. Have a good night. I'm really sorry." The last few words just squeaked out of her.

She left, and Josh looked at Sarah.

"That was memorable," she said. Then she shook her head. "I'm sorry if I made a scene. I'm just . . . I don't know. Nervous."

"Why don't we get out of here?" Josh suggested. He paid the bill in cash, leaving a hefty tip for Duffy's grieving owner, who was being lectured by the manager.

They went outside. The sky was still light, and it was a perfect summer evening. "Let's go down to the river," Sarah suggested, and they did. She took his arm. It didn't feel bad.

There were plenty of people outside, enjoying the weather. A hint of red sunset lingered in the west. Josh and Sarah walked along Canal, into the greenway that ran along the river.

"Um, Josh," she said, "I've always thought you were really, um, good-looking. And of course, the world's best husband."

"Thank you."

"You're welcome." She waited, tilting her head expectantly.

"And you're, uh, pretty. Very pretty." She looked at him. He looked back. "I guess I'll kiss you?" he asked.

"Go for it."

He leaned in. Her lips were soft and firm. She tasted like steak. Otherwise . . . nothing.

Then she pulled back. "I'm sorry, that was like kissing my brother."

Oh, thank *God*. "Yeah," he admitted. "Definitely . . ."

"No sparks."

"Exactly."

"Shit," she said. "They don't make men like

you anymore, Josh. It would've been wicked convenient if this worked out."

"I thought you were rude to the waitress."

"I thought your conversation was flat and boring."

They looked at each other, then started laughing. "Failed experiment," she said, and gave him a hug. "I wonder if Lauren is disappointed. I think she kind of hoped we'd connect."

"Yeah."

"I don't know," Sarah said. "I can't say I'd want to be compared to her for the rest of my life, to be honest with you."

"No, I understand."

They sighed at the same time, then laughed.

"Sarah?" came a woman's voice. Two women dressed in athletic gear had stopped.

"Hey, Helen!" she answered. "Hi, Kelly!"

"I haven't seen you in ages," the first one said. "We're getting ice cream. You want to join us?"

"Um . . . this is my friend, Joshua Park. Josh, my coworkers, Helen and Kelly." Josh nodded at them. "Helen had a baby a couple months ago and I haven't seen her since. How is the little prince?"

"Really, really good," Helen said. "Did you hear I had an emergency C-section?"

"No! Are you okay?"

"It was very dramatic! I was . . ." She glanced

at Josh. "You know, it'll keep. You're with some-one."

Sarah glanced at Josh, and he got it. Their date was over, and he was fine with that. "If you want to hang out with them . . ." he suggested.

"Are you sure?"

"Yes."

She smiled, her first real smile of the night, maybe. "Still friends?" she asked.

"Absolutely." He hugged her, waved to the ladies, then turned and walked up the hill.

His wife had been wrong.

Interesting. A first. He hoped she was watching and got a kick out of that lackluster meat kiss.

Well, it was a beautiful night, and the city seemed happy. It didn't seem right to go home just yet. He walked up Elizabeth, turned on North Main, and there was the restaurant he'd just left.

The chirpy server was sitting at the bar, blotting her eyes on her napkin.

He went back in and slid onto the stool next to her. She glanced at him and did a double take.

"I am so, so sorry, sir," she said. "I ruined your date."

"Your dog, huh?"

"I know. It was the stupidest thing to say, and there's no comparison."

"It's okay," Josh said. "I'd be wrecked without my dog."

"Pebbles?"

"Yes."

"It's a really cute name." She smiled at him and wiped her eyes again.

"Did you get fired?" he asked.

"No. They're really nice here. Which is great, because I've been fired from three restaurants this year alone. They just took me off the floor for the rest of the night. Suggested I have a drink to buck up a little." She toasted him with her glass. "It's ginger ale with a teeny bit of rum, because I don't really drink." She looked around. "Where's your girlfriend?"

"Oh, she's not . . . that didn't work. She's a friend. My wife's best friend from childhood. We were trying to click, and we just . . . didn't."

"That sucks."

"It's a relief, actually."

"Again, I'm so sorry about your wife. I bet she was amazing."

"She was," he said. "She absolutely was."

"Can I buy you a drink?" she asked. "I owe you."

"No, I'm fine," he said. "I don't really drink, either." He looked at her a minute, studying her profile. She had very long eyelashes, and they looked real. Her nose had an appealing bump at the bridge, and her skin seemed very clean. "Would you ever want to go out with me?" he asked.

The question came out of nowhere. He didn't regret asking, though.

No. He didn't regret it at all.

She turned, her eyes wide, and blinked a couple of times. "Sure. Yes. Absolutely." Pink flushed to her cheeks. Pretty.

"You don't have to say yes," he added. "You know. Just because you ruined our dinner, or because I'm a tragic widower." He was flirting. Wow. He was *flirting*.

"No, no! You're wicked hot. Oh, God. I'm sorry. Should I have said that? Well, it's out there, isn't it? I mean, you have a mirror, you must know." She was blushing furiously now. "Yes, I would go out with you. I thought you were nice the first time I met you at the vet's."

He smiled, then extended his hand. "Joshua Park."

She took it, and he felt attraction flow up his arm like cool silk. "Rose Connelly," she said.

He froze, still gripping her hand. "Rose?"

"Yes. My mom was a huge *Titanic* fan." She pulled a face. "But I have to say, I love that movie, too."

He let go of her hand. "Rose was my wife's middle name."

Her mouth parted a little. "Really."

He nodded. They looked at each other a long minute. "Can I have your phone number?" he asked, and she patted her apron for a pen, found one and wrote it down on a napkin. Very old-fashioned of her.

"Okay, then," she said. "It was . . . yeah. It was very nice to see you, Joshua."

"It was very nice to see you, too, Rose."

He should go now. Another minute, and he'd lose the cool factor. But somehow, he suspected Rose Connelly wouldn't mind.

"I'll call you tomorrow," he said.

"I'll be glad when you do," she answered.

Get out before you ruin it, he told himself, so he left, feeling . . . well, feeling a little . . . elated. He forgot where he'd parked the car, and just walked for a while in the soft summer air, the sounds of music and people and sirens all blending together like a song.

Rose Connelly. Rose.

If a person believed in that kind of thing, a person might wonder at how many times Josh had run into Rose Connelly in the past year and a half. The vet's office that first time. The mall, the first night he'd met Radley when he'd punched the rude customer, unknowingly defending her honor. The marathon, where she'd helped him. Last Christmas, when she'd literally been right in front of him, stopping him in his tracks.

Gertie the psychic had mentioned roses, too.

Josh stopped walking.

Holy shit.

And now, the first time he'd ever considered

dating anyone other than Lauren, Rose was here again.

A person—a husband—might read into that. He might think his wife worked in mysterious ways to take care of the man she had loved so much.

"Thank you," he said, looking upward. Those had been her last words to him. "Thank you," he repeated. He knew, he *knew* tonight had made her happy.

Which was all he'd ever wanted.

EPILOGUE

Joshua

Fifty-four years left

Lauren's Garden at the Hope Center had become Josh's favorite place in Providence. He walked past it almost every day, in fact, and most days stopped in for at least a few minutes.

But today was special. On this sunny spring day, they were planting Lauren's tree, and the May weather couldn't have approved more. The carefully planned garden was bursting with color and life, from the pink crab apple blossoms to the pale purple of the lilacs.

Everyone who had loved Lauren was here. Jen stood next to him with her three children— Sebastian getting tall and gangly, little Octavia, pretty in her blue dress, a cloud of dark curls around her perfect face. Leah, now almost three, was trying to climb out of Darius's arms to get into mischief. Josh smiled at her; she reminded him of Lauren so much. Next to them, Donna and Bill, who had gotten married last year. His own mom and the Kims. Ben gave him a nod, ever reassuring.

Asmaa was talking about the garden, and how

families came together here to grow their own vegetables, to teach kids about botany, to have a beautiful oasis in the city. Josh was so grateful to her for still doing the good work that had given him a second chance to meet Lauren, and later, the chance to give back and get out of his shell when he was grieving. Mara from RISD was here, and Bruce the Mighty and Beneficent, who had donated ten grand in Lauren's name.

Radley, the world's best friend, stood with his fiancé, Frank the Realtor. They had their own place now, just down the road from the house in Cranston. Sarah was here, too, of course. Good old Sarah. She was dating Mateo, one of Josh's engineers, who was five years younger than she was and, from all appearances, smitten.

There was another person here. Someone Lauren had never met, someone standing at Joshua's side, her hand in his.

His wife.

Pretty Rose with the pink cheeks and dark hair, now even more beautiful. She was pregnant, though they were keeping that to themselves until the first trimester was past. Josh suspected his mom knew, though, because when they'd come here, she had handed Rose a bottle of water and asked if she wanted a chair.

His mom caught his eye and smiled. Yep. She knew. That was fine.

Josh looked at the dogwood tree, now nearly five feet tall. Its trunk was straight and strong, and the blossoms Lauren had so loved seemed to float on the air, perfect in their simplicity, their beauty.

It would grow well here.

"I'll turn it over to you, now, Josh," Asmaa said.

Rose squeezed his hand. "You've got this," she whispered. He kissed her temple and went to the microphone.

For more than three years now, he'd taken good care of Lauren's tree. It was time to give it a home. All these people would know this was Lauren's garden. They'd all come see her tree. Someday, Josh would bring his kids to this garden, and they would play here.

It was nice to think Lauren would see them.

His throat was tight, and everyone was looking at him. Right. He was supposed to talk now.

"Lauren was . . . remarkable," he said, and his voice was strong and full of emotion. "The best sister, daughter, aunt and friend anyone could have. I was so lucky to be her husband."

He glanced at Rose, who gave him a watery smile and a nod. The only thing she'd ever said about Lauren was how much she wished she could've met her. They had a lot in common, Josh thought. Kindness. A huge capacity for love.

"Lauren died too soon," he continued, "but

she lived with such love and happiness, such joy and purpose. In my eyes, she was perfect." He stopped, swallowing. "She taught me how to live, even when she was dying. Even after she died—especially after she died—she was my best teacher. It's my honor today to dedicate this tree to her memory. She loved this place, and she loved all of you."

Everyone clapped and sniffled and wiped their eyes. A gardener was waiting by the tree, and as Josh approached, he set it in the hole and gave a nod.

Everyone was quiet. With his back to the crowd, Josh reached into his jacket pocket, took something out and dropped it into the hole.

His wedding ring. The one Lauren had given him. It gleamed there, nestled against the dark earth. Maybe it would grow into the roots themselves and become part of the tree itself. Josh hoped so.

Then Josh covered it with a shovelful of dirt and handed the shovel to Donna, who did the same. Then it was Jen's turn, and Sebastian's and Octavia's. Darius helped Leah, who said, "I did it, Daddy!" and everyone laughed. The shovel was passed from person to person. His mom, Sarah, Asmaa, Ben.

"You too, Rosie," Jen said. "You're family. Don't be shy."

Rose looked over at him, and he nodded. Her

cheeks flushed, and he knew she was glad to be included.

A little while later, as everyone left through the garden gate, Josh stayed, holding back. They were all going out for lunch, the first time they'd all be together since his and Rose's wedding a few months ago.

When no one was left and Josh was alone in the garden, he turned back to look at the tree. It seemed as if it had always been there. He couldn't wait to see it grow.

A small breeze rustled through, ruffling his hair.

For a second, he felt his wife, felt her love wrap around him. She had promised to always be with him, and he believed her. *I love you,* he thought. *I always will.*

Rose was waiting for him just outside the garden walls. "You good, honey?" she asked.

"I am." He kissed her gently and, unable to resist no matter who might see, put his hand against her stomach. "I love you," he said, because it was true. Then he took her hand, and they caught up with the others, and the sun seemed to glow just a little bit brighter in the vast and brilliant sky.

Center Point Large Print
600 Brooks Road / PO Box 1
Thorndike, ME 04986-0001 USA

(207) 568-3717

US & Canada:
1 800 929-9108
www.centerpointlargeprint.com